ALSO BY ANDREW ELGIN

The Harmony Series

Finding Harmony, Novelette prequel

Seeds Of Harmony, Book 2

Ambassadors Of Harmony, Book 3

SONGS OF HARMONY

A HARMONY NOVEL

ANDREW ELGIN

ISBN: 978-0-9978816-7-7 (Ebook version)

ISBN: 978-0-692-70298-7 (Paperback version)

Cover Design by VisualArts on Fiverr.com

Sixth Sense Books

150 Buck Run E

Dahlonega, GA 30533

Email address: andrewelginauthor@gmail.com

CONTENTS

To Maggie, for finding me
To Judith, for helping me

ACKNOWLEDGMENTS

It's not easy, this acknowledgment thing. Unlike the Oscar winners who have their catalog of names ready to reel off, I have not got an easy list of people.

That said, however, I would like to acknowledge the numerous writers of science fiction I devoured early on. If I mention those influences, then I must also acknowledge my mother, who introduced me to the fascinations of libraries very early on. And, if my mother, then my grandparents who also loved to read, and were responsible for instilling that love into my mother who passed it on to me.

And so it grows and grows.

More specifically, I'd like to thank the early readers of this book who now wouldn't recognize what it became: Michelle Felicetta and Eric Hughes.

Of course, if it wasn't for Maggie, my wife, encouraging me, nothing would have been done. And if Judith Tarr hadn't got down and dirty with the first re-write, I probably would have thought I was OK, when I certainly wasn't!

Apart from these few, I'd like to also acknowledge all the writers I've read since my teen years, even the historians, because they all taught me something about writing.

A special thanks goes to the following people, who gave vital support during the first launch of this book: Cynthia Garbarsky, Susana Gama, Susan Orton, Linda Harrington, Cynthia Gillen, Peter McPherson, Julia Marks, Glenda Spiwak, Melanie Johnstone and Connie Baldwin.

PROLOGUE

Two Planets
Finding one planet able to support human life was quite rare. But in one system two such planets existed; Haven and Harmony, both circling the same sun. That sun was nowhere near any center of human civilization, even using astronomical measurements. Neither was it close to any trade route. The system was essentially unknown in an unexplored, minor part of the galaxy.

A colony class ship, immense in size and aspiration, carrying everything needed to jump-start life on a new planet, had malfunctioned. Navigation awry, its target planet long since lost, it tumbled out of the blackness into this isolated system and, following an old and, by now, useless schedule, woke the people it carried. Their observations and measurements at first confused them before they finally accepted that fate had decided they were to live when they could so easily have been corpses turning to dust, traveling without end. They blessed the luck which had brought them to this system and set about the slow task of maneuvering to rendezvous with their new home. But which one?

The choice seemed obvious. They chose the inner of the two available planets and named it Haven. Against all odds, with very few minor exceptions, it was rich with everything they would need from the very start. Fortune, or fate, was again on their side, it seemed. Why bother even looking at the outer planet? It had no easily accessible ores. In comparison, it had nothing to offer for quick and steady growth.

Seen from the edge of the system, Haven seemed to hurtle where her sister glided. Yet, to the grateful, lucky, new inhabitants, the seasons seemed normal. All that they missed was a moon to light their nights. But they could live, were living, without one.

It was only after they had begun to forge the beginnings of a fresh, world-spanning civilization that some, still amazed at the fate which had brought them, wondered whether they had made the right choice. They had left a planet scraped clean of all that it could offer them. It was the reason they had left. Did they have to repeat that here? Wasn't this a chance to be different? Think differently? Act differently? Instead of forcing their will upon the land, could they not, perhaps, be less voracious, less demanding? Perhaps the other planet would have been the right choice. No metal ores in easy reach would have meant a different start, a more cooperative beginning. It would have allowed the growth of a closer relationship with the planet. They argued that, if they had chosen the other planet, they would have had all the metal they needed in the ship itself anyway, so huge was it. Why be greedy from the very start?

And so some of the people, looking for a new way of living; a way, they felt, which should have been chosen, took a ship to the outer, slower planet with its beckoning moon and they named it what they dreamed of: Harmony.

But Harmony was not welcoming. There were trials which tested the resolve of them all. Severe weather and sickness took their toll. In the face of this seemingly unrelenting struggle, some of the colonists were found wanting. Sadly acknowledging their weakness, these few said farewell to their dream and left to travel back to Haven. They set off in the ship they had arrived in, but not one survived the return journey. The cause was never established. On board, apart from the bodies, there were some samples of plants and some recorded stories of strange things that had been witnessed or perhaps experienced back on Harmony; tales which made little sense. These tales became rumors. And the rumors grew and spread. Harmony became, not a dream, but a nightmare: a place where people lost their humanity, became like beasts living in a stone age. In the minds of those on Haven, Harmony was a warning not to try to change their nature. The stars would be theirs only if they took what they needed, not if they denied themselves.

On Harmony, the now isolated settlers continued the struggle to survive, as well as to understand the planet. They strove to listen to it, to become close to it. And, slowly they spread and they learned. They learned of the planet, but they also learned of themselves, and the knowledge they gained brought them new awareness and began to change them in subtle ways that, because they were gradual, became accepted as normal. In their stories and memories, Haven became a distant, unbalanced place of destruction and metal and blinkered ignorance where people confused progress with wisdom.

As they grew slowly in different but always human ways on Harmony, so those on Haven grew in the same way humanity always had. Industry and government, education and politics, exploration and invention became more intricate and less personal and always bigger. And all around them, in the moonless night sky, the unknown stars shone and teased them with the need to find their own kind; to reconnect with them. But to do that required combining driving leadership, innovation and the constant investment of energy and inspiration to reach toward a common goal. Whenever those elements existed at the same time, they were never harnessed effectively or for any useful length of time. And most of the time they did not coexist.

The original colony ship had long since been gutted and re-purposed as the basis of factories and mines and machinery, as it had been designed to do. Some small ships were necessary to dismantle and transfer the colony ship to the planet's surface, piece by piece. Those tiny offspring themselves broke down eventually. But, before the last of them failed, a new one was built. But there was nothing for it to do. It served only one purpose; to provide a tangible connection with the stars in the night sky. In due course, another was built. And later, another. But none of them could travel beyond the system of their birth. Their purpose was to provide a connection with the unspoken dream of Haven; to find the rest of humankind.

Despite having the ability to travel, there was hardly any contact made between Haven and Harmony, because Haven felt there was no need. No metals meant no progress to those on Haven. Harmony had been a failed experiment early in Haven's history. It was a planet for the curious only. Not for anyone who wished for the stars. Harmony was no place to find civilization. Once in every several generations a ship had been sent, but there was no real purpose to it beyond the technicality of the voyage itself. Harmony was a useful target. It was close enough to make a voyage there and back feasible, and far enough to make a voyage a useful test of equipment. After such fleeting visits, tales were told of a strange affliction, a curse whereby nobody could leave Harmony alive if they stayed too long on the surface or ate any of the food or drank the water. Those on Harmony came to resent such contacts, seeing them as unwanted invasions of their privacy and as intimidatory displays. Haven became an unspecified but potent threat to their way of life.

Haven's rulers infrequently combined political profit with scientific advance. They used Harmony to exile the very occasional high profile 'irritant', when a visible, but expensive, 'mercy' was politically valuable. Of course, there was no way of ensuring such a prisoner's safe arrival. But it was technically very useful for testing new ship designs.

So the two planets, carrying the same human seeds at different rates around the same sun, nurtured and grew them in different mediums to have different aspirations. Harmony and Haven passed through the same seasons at different times and at different rates.

And the sun remained in the center, pulling the planets along, like children.

1

By the time the shuttle door lifted, Lisick, Gerant and Bellis, the housekeeper, had been waiting for several minutes, intensely curious as to why it was here. Also more than a little alarmed by it, by the strangeness and angularity, the size and power of it. The harshness of its engines battering the day sounds away had warned them of its arrival. Plus, Pasker had been quick to summon them to witness the strange thing sounding as if it was tearing the sky apart. He had been sent back inside, much to his annoyance. To everyone outside of it, the craft was wrong. It was metal - so much metal! - and sharp angles and it smelt wrong and it was of nothing natural. It was an offense to the land it was resting on. The small group of silkies had scattered into the undergrowth at the first roaring sounds and were only now studying it cautiously from a safe distance, snickering quietly to reassure each other.

The quick descent had heated the craft and it gave off clicks and hisses as it cooled. A few moments passed before anyone was visible. Then a man wearing a full helmet attached to a suit of some sort of shiny material stepped off the ramp. He stopped a few paces from the three and thrust a document at them, waiting until Gerant had reached out slowly and taken it.

"Read it! Assuming you can read." the crewman said, his voice sounding both hollowed and distant by the helmet, before turning abruptly and disappearing back into the gloom of the craft.

He reappeared shortly dragging a large chest down the ramp. He opened it up to reveal that there were, in fact, two lids, two chests, one inside the other. Off he went again, watched curiously by four pairs of eyes (Pasker was not to be denied a view, albeit from just inside the doorway) and also with some trepidation as to what would happen next.

He returned, accompanied this time by another crew member, also wearing a suit and helmet. Between them they had a limp body. Without a pause, they marched down the ramp, dumped it just off the edge, by the side of the double crate, and returned again to the interior. By the time the three arrived at the body, the door was closing and the large and unnerving craft was virtually airtight again.

Lisick was first to react, moving swiftly in her jerky fashion to discover it was a young man, a teenager maybe, maybe older. The dirty pale face, sunken features and lank, dark hair made it hard to determine. The concern on her face was replaced by a venomous glare at the ship.

"What gives them the right to do this?"

By then, Gerant and Bellis were kneeling, touching the newcomer's cheek, feeling for a pulse, brushing the hair back, checking for wounds.

"Let's get him inside," said Gerant. He peered inside the crate to confirm it was empty. Then he paused a moment to close his eyes and appeared to be thinking, before shaking his head in irritation. He easily hauled the limp body up, draped it over one large shoulder and made for the wooden building about fifty paces away, seeming not to notice the extra weight.

Once inside, they made the new arrival as comfortable as they could and left Bellis with strict instructions to have food ready and to come and get them when he woke up.

"I could read nothing of use in either of them," Gerant said, tipping his head at the craft outside. "Not closed, but not knowing anything. Some fear, maybe. I didn't have much time. How about you?"

"Me? Nothing. Didn't even try. Well, never mind. We have to deal with it." Lisick was nervous and it showed in her clipped speech. "They scare me, though. I mean, I knew they came here. But seeing them? That's different. It's real. But why now? What do they want?" She hugged her thin body. "I don't like them, Gerant. Whatever it is they want, I don't like it." She nodded at Gerant's belt. "What's that they gave you? Hadn't we better see what it is?"

Gerant pulled it out, laid it on the table, holding it flat with one hand while Lisick paced nervously behind him. He finished and turned to her with a sour look on his face.

"They want plants. Certain plants. They've got drawings here of the ones they want. That must be what that box out there is for." He held it up for Lisick to see.

She squinted at the drawings, trying to recognize what they were of. "Plants?" She looked up at Gerant. "They came here for plants?"

"And to dump the boy, don't forget."

"But what do they want our plants for?" She gestured angrily at the drawings. "And I can't make out what those things are meant to be. They look dead to me. Do you know what they are? And when do they want them, anyway?"

"It says 'immediately' in the letter."

Lisick snorted her derision at that. "Oh, yes! Of course. We have been waiting for them to arrive with bunches of plants in our arms, so we could give them to them straight away. They're idiots!"

Gerant had been studying the drawings and now he looked up. "Maybe Bellis would recognize them. She's good with plants. I'll ask her."

"But why do they want them? And why now? And what if we didn't give them anything? What then?" Lisick demanded.

"There's another part of this thing I haven't told you about." Gerant's voice took on a heavy tone. "They threaten us. Or, actually, they threaten Harmony." Gerant acknowledged Lisick's shock with raised eyebrows and a curt nod at the document. "They threaten to spray poison on Harmony if we don't give them what they want. Apparently, that thing out there is equipped and ready to do it."

Lisick was aghast. "No, no, no. That can't happen! We must stop that. We must find those plants now. Show me again. We'll get them. We'll get them."

Before Gerant could reply, Bellis called them from the door. Pasker was beside her, eager to be part of this most strange and wonderful day.

"He's starting to wake up."

7

"Oh, great! Another problem to deal with," said Lisick. "Show Bellis those drawings and get started. I'll look after the boy. I'm not much use for anything else." To herself, she muttered, "Where is he going to go? And how long will he be around here? We've enough to do without him taking up our time."

She waved Bellis over. "Gerant has something to show you. You might recognize the drawings. Can you help?"

Bellis studied the drawings a moment or two before recognition dawned. "Oh I know these! They are good drawings, but they look like they are of old, dead ones. That's what made it confusing." She pointed as she spoke. "That one there, that's kefalos for certain. That one next to it, that looks like soldier grass gone to seed. The other two are brittlebane and scorry. Oh, and that small one down there, that is definitely minnit. See the leaves? Definitely."

Gerant was impressed. "And where can I get hold of these?"

Bellis laughed. "They are all growing outside of here." She looked at the surprise on their faces. "You two know everything there is to know about Harmony, except for what's right in front of you! I suppose you want me to get them for you?"

"Please, Bellis, if you could. Possibly the whole thing, roots and all if possible? The open box they brought out is for them." Gerant's politeness hid his embarrassment at his lack of awareness.

"Well, that was easier than I thought," said Lisick with relief after Bellis had left. "Still doesn't mean I like any of it, acting like we're their servants. Jumping when they say. And that threat! That's not something I'll ever forget. Nor forgive. Ever!"

"I agree, Lisick," said Gerant, shaking his head in disbelief. "It's sad to realize that's how they think."

"Sad and scary!"

Gerant nodded. "While we're waiting, shouldn't we be seeing about our guest? I dare say he's not happy."

"What are we going to do with him, Gerant? What can he do here? He's useless to anyone."

Gerant put a finger to his lips, thinking. "I'll find somewhere for him, Lisick. I'll ask around. There's always a need for extra hands."

"Yes. If they know what they are doing!"

"I'll go and help Bellis, hand over the plants and then get started on finding a place for him. You try to find out what you can. I'll be back later. Maybe tomorrow. Maybe later. You can handle things until then?"

"But I can't read him as well you can, Gerant. You know that."

Gerant paused at the door. "That's just extra. He needs help now. That's what I'm going to do."

Lisick found the patient sitting up, sipping at some soup Pasker had brought from the kitchen and looking pale still. Pasker himself was standing, watching, determined to stay, no matter what. "You were unconscious when you arrived. Do you know how long you had been like that?" she asked.

A shake of his head, his dark brown eyes wary and watchful.

"Do you know who you are? Your name?"

He started to speak but had to clear his throat, as if it was painful. "My name is Javin. Javin Sarnum."

"Do you know where you are?"

"No."

"We'll come to that later, " she said. "What's the last thing you remember?"

Javin screwed up his face as he tried to remember. "I think it was being arrested. But I don't know what for. I think I was getting something to eat. In a queue. And then they arrived." He shook his head. "I don't remember much after that. Do you know why I'm here?"

"We'll leave that to later as well, shall we? And what was it you did? Before you were arrested I mean. For a living? Did you live in a city?"

Again, some careful thought. "Yes. In a city. Definitely. In Westbay. I sold things. Electronics."

"So you were a trader then?"

"You could say that, I suppose. Yes. A trader." Javin replied.

"How much of it was illegal, Javin?"

Javin turned a startled face to her.

"Oh, come on! You were taken by them for something, and it wasn't for standing still, was it? You must have done something to upset them."

"I don't know why they came for me. But they did. And if they were going to arrest me for that, then they would have to arrest a whole lot more people. I wasn't the only one!"

"Calm down, boy," Lisick said. "You might be right and you might not be. I can't tell yet. The point is there are more important things to deal with."

"Like what?"

Lisick didn't answer at first. Just looked at the young man in front of her, as if assessing him. "Where do you think you are?"

Javin shrugged. "I don't know. Your clothes look, well, they look old and dirty. But that might be to hide something else about you. Maybe some police station? Some sort of holding area? With food? I don't think I was charged with anything. Maybe you're part of some sort of assessment team before I get charged. Is that a question you ask people to see if they are on drugs or something? I've been drugged, but I'm not on drugs."

"Wherever your home was, you're a long way from it, Javin."

"Was? What do you mean 'was'?"

"I mean," said Lisick, very slowly, "your home on Haven. You're not there now. You're not on Haven anymore. You're on a different planet. On Harmony. And you're not going back. Ever."

There was silence.

"Pasker. Take him outside and show him. It'll be quicker. Not where they landed. The other side."

A few minutes later, with Pasker acting as support, Javin was staring around him.

There were trees, or things like trees. Tall, spindly things with long, upward curving leaves, like spines. Some fat yellow and blue striped winged things as large as his hand floated off into the distance. At his feet, the ground was covered with a multitude of long intertwined strands of some sort of plant, vaguely green. It pulsed a little, or seemed to, whenever he moved his weight. The sun was low in the sky but looked smaller than he was used to.

"This is either really advanced gaming programming, or she was telling the truth," Javin said.

"That's Lisick. And she always tells the truth. Whether anyone wants to hear it or not. I don't know what you mean about gaming programming, though," replied Pasker. "Have you seen enough?"

He steadied him back inside, back to the couch again. Lisick was waiting, twisting one strand of hair in her long, bony fingers.

"Believe me now?"

"You live in a wooden house?"

"That's what got your attention, boy?" Lisick smiled and shook her head. "Yes. We live in a wooden house. Actually, it's a large house. We call it The Hall, because, well, that's what it was built as."

"More food?" asked Pasker, reaching for the now empty bowl, and left before Javin had a chance to reply. Lisick wasn't entirely sure that Pasker's intentions were pure. She thought he was probably thinking about getting a quick snack for himself.

"What are you thinking about now?" she asked.

Javin shook his head as if he didn't know where to start. "Why am I here? And what did you mean I can't leave? Why?" He looked at her with eyes full of puzzlement and fear combined. "I don't know what to think, what to ask. What's going to happen to me?"

Lisick pushed her hair back from her face again. "Look, boy, I know there's a lot of questions and there's a lot of things you need to know. There are two ways of doing this. The slow way and the quick way. Slow means you get to have all the answers over time and the quick way is you get them all at once. I don't have time for the slow way, so here's the quick one." She counted off the answers on her fingers.

"One, you're here because you upset some important people back on Haven. I don't know what you did, but you did something because that's the only reason to explain the very few people that we have ever heard of arriving from there in the past.

"Two, you can't leave because there's no way of leaving. That's a fact. Shh!" This was to quell the questions she saw coming. "And don't think that you can go back the same way you came. They didn't want you there, so they're not going to take you back. Simple, and obvious, I'd think.

"And three, I have no idea what's going to happen to you because that's going to depend on you. But one thing's for sure, nothing you learned to do so far in your life is going to be much use here. Now I've got to get on with my things and you can ask Pasker for anything. He's the one with the food. Bellis, when you meet her, she's the one who cooks it."

The look she gave Javin as she got up to leave quashed anything he might have wanted to say, and then she swept out.

Javin spent the next several days beginning to understand some of what Lisick had said.

Once, outside, trying to get used to all of it, he watched Bellis picking some plants for their meals. They were growing in an irregular-shaped bed. She didn't pick all of them, but moved amongst them in what seemed a haphazard way, leaving some and taking others.

"Why don't you just pick all of them?" he asked her.

"Because some of them need to be left to grow more."

"What's the difference? They all look the same to me."

Bellis smiled. "They might look the same, but they don't all feel the same." She saw the puzzled look on his face. "It's part of this link we all have? With Harmony? Never mind. It's just something you get to know. You'll get to know it well enough on your own." And that was the end of that conversation.

Then there was the time he became bored with looking at the new things around, knowing nothing about them, and wanting something that made connections inside his head. Something familiar. To block the boredom, he decided to find Bellis. The kitchen where she spent most of her time was very large. Even though he knew nothing about cooking, he could tell it was much larger than it needed to be. Where Bellis worked was but one small area. He felt awkward, standing in the doorway, watching her. Finally, he decided to ask Bellis what is was that Lisick actually did that kept her so busy.

"She listens to Harmony. Finds out what's going on."

"That doesn't make any sense, Bellis."

She stopped and dried her hands. "Look at me, Javin and tell me what I'm thinking."

"I don't know! How can I do that?"

"Make a guess, then."

"You're thinking about making a meal?"

"That's not really saying what I'm thinking. That's what I am thinking about, perhaps. But what am I thinking? There's a difference."

"Is there? Oh. So... you're thinking about... how long to cook everything?"

"That was a guess as well, wasn't it?" Bellis was smiling.

"What else could I do? I have no idea what you're thinking, do I?" Javin sounded frustrated.

"Actually, that's something you could end up being able to do; know what others are thinking." Bellis turned back to her task. "Really, it's more like what emotions people have. That can be done. Like now, Javin. What's the main emotion I have in my head, without being able to look at my face?"

Javin shook his head. "I don't know. Maybe you're happy. Happy at teaching me something I don't understand."

Bellis turned to face him again, her smile broader. "What I just asked you to do is what Lisick does, but in a much bigger way. You had a guess that I was happy. And, maybe you were right. But Lisick, and Gerant as well, they listen to Harmony. They get to feel what's going on with the planet. If a place reports an infestation of some animals, Lisick and Gerant will be able to tell them why and what to do about it. Or, they will hear that one area feels wrong and direct people to make it right: unblock a river, or clear some land or whatever else they feel is needed to make Harmony better."

"That doesn't make any sense at all. Listening to a planet? That's crazy!" Javin's expression mirrored his words.

"You did ask. And that's the answer." She returned again to her preparation. "Everyone here on Harmony has a connection. Everyone has a way of connecting. For Lisick and Gerant, it's what they do, why they're here. You'll find your connection, Javin." She stopped what she was doing. "In fact, let's do that right now."

"Do what?"

"Find your connection. Or a connection at least. Come on. Outside."

Bellis frowned for a moment as if concentrating, and then gestured at the land in front of them. "There's a special place for you somewhere here. Go find it."

"What does that mean? And how?"

"You wanted to understand about the connection with you and

Harmony. Well, this is it. Find the place that feels special, that feels it's just for you."

"And I do that... how?"

"The 'how' is part of the connection." She clapped her hands in dismissal. "Now, stop wasting time and get started." And she went back to her chores.

Javin sighed and, not thinking of anything better to do, began wandering aimlessly.

Some time later, Bellis strode off to collect something from the garden.

"Is this it?" Javin looked up at Bellis as she came back with her apron full.

"What are you asking me for?"

"Is this my place? You said to find my place. Is this it?" He was sitting on the ground near an old piece of wood or what passed for wood here.

Bellis sat and spilled the plants onto the ground and began pinching leaves off, shaking her head with a smile.

"What does it mean?" he asked. "This is as good a place as any, isn't it?"

"Does it feel right?"

"How do I know?"

"There's a place for you. You'll know it." She smiled again. "It's not there though. Move somewhere else."

Javin shook his head and sat down a few paces over. "Is this it?"

"Stop asking and start feeling. Move somewhere else."

Javin felt this was just a waste of time, but got up and wandered away a little bit. Again, he sat. He looked to Bellis.

She shrugged. "Does it feel like it?"

It was his turn to shrug. Again, he got up. A new place. Down he sat. He kept moving around, always checking with Bellis who was taking far more interest in her plants.

He didn't bother with sitting down after a few more changes, just stood still at each place. There was no difference that he could see.

Bellis stood up, gathered her plants again. "You're getting there." And then she left him alone.

He had nothing better to do, he thought, so why not keep doing this?

He continued to move from place to place. It all felt the same. Except... here. Just here. He felt lighter. More relaxed. Or something like that. He took a step to the side and the feeling went. Step back and the feeling came back. There was nothing visible. No marker he could see.

As he was experimenting moving back and forth, Bellis came back out.

"This is my place, isn't it?", he said. "It feels... better."

She smiled again. "That's Harmony. Harmony and you. Now go and find the place that is the opposite of what you feel there."

Javin looked at the ground spread out around him. It seemed huge. And he felt so small.

That was a long day.

Some time after, he was sitting outside trying to see if there was anything visible about 'his' spot when Lisick wandered out, stretching as if tired. She noticed him, shook herself, and said, "Nothing to do? We'll solve that!" She marched him into the kitchen, dragging him by the arm, where Bellis was working as usual.

"About time he learned something useful, Bellis. Teach him how to make a blade, will you?" And off she went before Bellis could remind her that she also had work to do.

That was the beginning of another long day. Instead of finding his own spot, he had to be able to cut a piece of leather into a square.

"And how do I do that?" he asked, holding up a fist-sized piece of black stone and a raggedy piece of leather.

Bellis smiled (she was always smiling, Javin realized) and said, "To cut, you need a sharp edge. To make a sharp edge, you must find it in the rock. And you find it by getting rid of what is blunt."

"And, but I'm getting tired of asking this, how do I do that?"

She pulled some slim, short wooden sticks out of her apron and another, lighter colored stone. "With these. You can make the blade stone really sharp. You'll find out how, I'm sure." And again, smiling, she left him to it.

At the end of the day, he was bleeding from several small cuts on his hands and legs. He had reduced the black stone to the size of his thumb, but one edge of it was very sharp and he was able to cut the leather.

Feeling inordinately pleased with himself, he found Bellis seated, eating at one of the large tables in the kitchen. Javin proudly showed the almost square piece of leather, together with his blade. Bellis took the blade from him and turned it in her hand to inspect it.

"Sit down and I'll get you some food."

"What do you think, Bellis?" He smiled, as the food was placed in front of him. He picked up a spoon and was about to eat as Bellis placed something beside his bowl. It was a blade. No doubt of it. And, if that was a blade, then his effort was a hammer.

It was about the length of his hand and about two fingers wide tapering to a sharp point. The other end was rounded and fit easily in his hand. It was, quite simply, beautiful. And effective, as the ease with which it sliced into the leather made clear. Javin held it admiringly. He looked up at Bellis. She simply arched her brows, as if to say, 'Well, that's what you're aiming at. Think you can do it?'

Suddenly, Javin didn't feel so smug and was a little less hungry as well.

The next day, he made one in half the time which was twice as good and which got a grudging nod of encouragement.

He was making progress.

When Gerant returned, however, five days after setting out, looking weary and dirty from travel, and said that he had found a place for Javin, it knocked back down what small confidence he had gained with Bellis' help.

2

The third day after Gerant's return, Javin and Bellis were sitting together on the ground, picking over some vegetables, throwing out the small and the bug-eaten ones. Three days and Javin was realizing that things did not happen quickly. Apparently he was waiting for someone to take him to his new home. Not that he wanted to think of that. This place, with Bellis, and Lisick and Gerant, this was home. At least, it felt more like it. It was becoming familiar. And now he was to leave.

He was used to sitting and feeling the silence around him. He was learning to live in that silence.

And then Bellis broke into it.

"Before I have to go back and finish the meal, tell me something about your life. Anything at all."

Javin, unprepared, thought for a moment. He still couldn't think clearly about the time when he was younger. "I don't know, Bellis. There's stuff that's missing in my head. It's all a bit jumbled up. I suppose it's the drug they used on me. And the things I do remember, they wouldn't make much sense to you. In fact, I don't think much of my life would make much sense here. There's nothing here to compare it with." He dismissed the idea with a shake of his head.

"Do you miss it? That life back then?"

Javin had never really thought about it in that way. He considered for a moment. 'Yes. Maybe. But not as much as I thought."

Bellis flashed one of her smiles at him. "Well, maybe you'll like Harmony better."

Lisick found him a little while later, sitting again, feeling the warmth and happiness of a full stomach. She folded herself down easily, as if her body was a collapsible, jointed thing, In her usual (or so it seemed to him) brisk fashion, she said, "It's about time you started finding out what your talent is, Javin."

Javin turned on his side, the better to look at her, not really looking forward to what was to come. He had no idea what it would be, but with Lisick, everything was urgent or needed doing now or was so complicated that he had no idea what she was talking about. If Lisick noticed his lack of enthusiasm, she ignored it and went straight to the issue. "Everybody has a talent, Javin. That's what we call it. A talent. It could be anything. You have to find out what yours is, that's all."

"I don't know what you mean." Javin was hesitant to speak, fearing Lisick would just shout and make it more confusing.

She had pushed back her hair, a habit of hers, and fixed him with her steady grey eyes. "You know what I do? What Gerant does?"

"Not really. Something to do with listening to the planet." He couldn't hide the nervous smile as he said it because it still didn't make any sense to him. Speaking it aloud had made it sound slightly ridiculous.

"Laugh if you like, boy. But it's the truth. I'm good at it. So's Gerant. But what are you good at? That's the point."

"I found my special place. Bellis helped me understand that was me and Harmony together."

Lisick sniffed dismissively. "Hmm. A start, I grant you. But there's much more than that. Did you ever get a feeling that something was wrong about a situation, or a person? You knew they were telling you something that was a lie, but you couldn't say why, you just knew it? That sort of thing. Has that happened to you?"

Javin thought a moment. "I'm not sure. Maybe. There was the time when Marrit had been trying to sell me a pile of... of stuff," he had said, catching himself before blurting the truth. "But I never could trust him or anything he said."

Lisick waved him quiet. "What about knowing what people were thinking? Did that happen to you?"

Javin shook his head.

"What about healing people? Or hearing someone speak inside your head?"

"No." His eyes widened at the thought. "Why?"

"Because you're now on a planet where everyone can do something like that. Those things I just mentioned? They're the common ones. Everyone can do something. Sometimes very well, like me and Gerant, or not so good, like many others. But we all can do something. And the one thing we can all do is hear Harmony."

"What, like a song, you mean?"

"Bug me, boy! No! Not like a real song!" She considered this a moment. "Although maybe some do hear it like that, I suppose." Her focus returned to him. "Here. Try this. Close your eyes and listen."

"Listen to what?"

"To Harmony, boy! Harmony! The planet you're sitting on. Now close your eyes."

Javin closed them.

"Now, what do you hear?"

"The wind... you... my breathing."

"Behind those things. What do you hear behind them? What's underneath them all?"

Javin squeezed his eyes tighter as if that would enhance his hearing. "I can't hear anything. Nothing."

He opened them to see Lisick staring at him, her head tilted to one side. "Everyone hears Harmony. Maybe it's too soon for you. Maybe She won't speak loudly to you." Javin fancied he could almost hear pity in her voice. "Maybe you'll never hear Her as She truly is." Then she straightened up again. "But that should never stop you from trying to hear Her. Always listen. Always." And with that, she had stood up easily and swiftly, unfolding upwards, and walked away a distance before stopping and turning to face him. She crooked her head to one side and narrowed her eyes. But whether she was looking at him or listening to something he couldn't hear, he did not know.

"There's something more to you, boy. Something more. But I can't tell what it might be." And then she turned and left for good.

Javin had presumed the lesson was over.

The next day, Gerant told him he was nearly ready.

"Ready for what?" was Javin's immediate question.

"Ready to live here. Not this place. But with a family. This family says they'll be happy to take you in and have you help them on their farm."

"A farm? But I know nothing about farming!"

"Well, I'm sorry that we don't have much in the way of anything else here. But farming's what we do have lots of and that's going to teach you a whole new set of skills. Besides, it'll be good for you."

"Really?" Javin was highly dubious. He didn't want to ask why, because he doubted he'd like the answer.

"Really. And we don't have the time to spend with you here. We've our own jobs to do. You need to see more of Harmony than this."

"I don't suppose there's much I can say about this, is there?" asked Javin.

"Not really. Torrint's going to be coming in a few days."

"Torrint?"

"The trader. He'll be taking you there. You'll see, it will be fine."

Javin wasn't so sure.

3

F ive days later, Javin found himself bundling his few possessions
together; a change of clothing, a fresh knife (courtesy of Bellis) and
very little else. Bellis stood beside him outside the Hall as he waited for
his ride to his new home. From his vantage point on the top of the hill,
he could see two wooden wagons; solid, rectangular things, slowly
rumbling up the curving trackway, still some distance away, being
pulled by two large beasts.

"Are they both really listening to Harmony?" he asked her, for neither
Lisick nor Gerant had been seen since he had woken.

"Yes. Really. That's what they do. I keep telling you, but it's true. They
are listening to Her. And they're telling others what they hear. I'm sure
they would come if they could." Bellis smiled encouragingly at him.

Javin wasn't as sure. Lisick, he felt, would be happy never to see him
again. And as for Gerant, well, he wasn't sure how much of the time he
had spent with Javin was out of duty or because he wanted to.

Javin realized that he felt nervous. "Where is it I'm going?" he asked.

Bellis shook her head, her face expressing her ignorance on this
subject. "I'm not sure. I only know it's over the mountains, that way,"
pointing to the distant hills away to her left. "Probably a few days away."

Javin nodded, feeling lonelier than he had ever felt before.

"And this trader...?"

"Torrint. His name's Torrint. He travels over a large area. Knows a lot of people. He's a good man. Oh! Here's Gerant come to see you off!" Bellis spoke brightly, but she looked relieved that she wasn't going to have to deal with all Javin's questions herself.

"Here, Javin, you're going to need this, more likely." And Gerant flung a large coat which Javin fought with to make it into something he could add to his bundle.

"Who are these people again I'm going to see?" Javin continued to wrestle with the coat.

"They are Hanlar and Paysa. They have a daughter. And they live in a place called Mark. And you're not going to see them. You're going to live with them. Help them."

"I can barely help myself, Gerant. What makes you think I can help them?"

"An extra pair of hands is always useful on a farm. You'll see."

Javin had finally made the coat small enough to wedge under the strap with his other pitifully few belongings. His legs felt weak and he sat on his bundle, not wanting to say anything for fear his voice would tremble.

Gerant didn't help by ruffling his hair and saying, "It will be alright, Javin. You'll come to love this place as much as we do."

"I don't have much choice, do I? After all, I can't ever leave it, you say."

There was an awkward silence for a while.

"Oh! I forgot! I have some food for you to take and share with Torrint. I'll fetch it!" And away Bellis went as the first of the two wagons breasted the rise. It slowly creaked and rolled to where Javin and Gerant waited.

The driver, Javin saw, was a tall, thin man. He had a long, glum-looking face, made thinner by his receding hairline, and a yellowish cast to his skin. The wagon came to a halt and the driver climbed down, pausing to spit out a wad of something by the wheel and wipe his mouth with his sleeve. His coat, which came to mid-thigh, ending in a ragged hem, was patched here and there and was a faded blue in color. Beneath it, he wore a loose shirt. There were short trousers or leggings which ended just below his knees. From there down, the skin was bare. He wore moccasins on his feet that at least looked sturdy if not matching in color.

By this time, Bellis had returned. "Here," she said, thrusting a bulging package into Javin's arms as he stood up. "There's dried fruit and meat and some bread in there. Oh! Hello, Torrint. Good to see you again. Are you well?" This all came out as one breathless sentence.

Torrint nodded slowly and smiled at her, showing teeth which were light blue. He pointed at Javin. "Is this the package to deliver?"

Javin felt annoyance at being labelled thus and was about to say something when Lisick's voice cut through.

"Ah! Not gone yet! Good! I need to say something to the boy before he goes off."

Javin didn't know whether to be more offended at being called 'boy' or 'a package'.

Lisick bustled towards them in her angular, awkwardly energetic way, hooking vainly at her hair to try to keep it behind her ears and away from her face. "So, did you hear Harmony yet?"

Javin shook his head.

Lisick pointed a bony finger at him. "Don't stop trying, boy. Never! There's something about you. I sense it. Don't stop trying. You'll hear Her one day. I know it."

Javin had no idea how to react to this.

"One day, boy. You hear me? But you have to find out what your talent is. You have one. Find it! And start remembering. There have to be things in your head you can't see now. But you will, boy. You will!" She looked around as if seeing the others for the first time, "Good day to you, Torrint." And with that, she walked off, elbows and knees and flying hair and awkwardness, back to her work, her mysterious connection with Harmony.

Another, shorter, awkward silence following her leaving was broken by Gerant thanking Torrint and making sure he knew where to take Javin, with unfathomable references to landmarks which obviously meant something to the trader. Quickly then, Javin found himself being helped up on the seat beside Torrint. There was a small doorway just behind it leading, Javin supposed, to the interior of the wagon. Torrint glanced at Javin and then the wagon was lurching into motion and Gerant and Bellis were waving him goodbye.

And that was it! Javin did feel rather too much like a package.

Torrint seemed content with silence, wedging a small bunch of leaves in his mouth and chewing on them. Every now and then, he would lean to the side and spit. Javin felt very much alone as they traveled, wordlessly, back down the hill and out across the land until the wooden hall was barely visible in the distance. Then, as the sun was approaching the horizon, Torrint eased the wagon to a halt. Climbing down, Torrint removed the harness from the huge beast which had hauled them this far and turned it loose after hobbling it. By that time, the second wagon had arrived and pulled up parallel, leaving a space of about five paces between the two. The other driver hopped down easily and dealt with his beast in the same way as Torrint. He looked younger than Torrint, slim but with broad shoulders, and his long, dark hair was tied back with a piece of cloth. His clothes were a similar mix of materials and patches. Javin stayed on his seat, not knowing what to do. That was quickly resolved by Torrint.

"Make yourself useful, lad. Get the fire going. There's plenty of kindling around and more than enough to make one. And the sparks you need are in the back of the wagon here. Banith and me'll get the food ready. We'll eat what Bellis gave tomorrow as a snack as we travel."

Collecting wood was easy enough. But lighting it was another thing. He looked in the back of the wagon where Torrint had indicated there were 'sparks' but couldn't see anything like that. In the fading light, he could make out some small barrels lashed to the inside. Around them were what looked like skins or maybe cloth. And there were tubes and boxes in abundance and some things which looked like feathers and other things which looked like dried meat hanging from the roof. There might have been a place for a bed in there, but he wasn't sure. It looked crowded and jumbled.

Torrint came to find him. "Not been introduced to sparks, have you?" It was more a statement than a question. "'Bout time to learn, then." So saying, he took a small clay pot from inside another, larger one, scooped up a small leather bag from beside the first pot and stalked back to the front of the wagon, holding it by the strap attached to it. Removing the top, and taking a few long, dried leaves from the bag, Torrint dipped them into the pot and gently breathed on them. Smoke began to curl upwards. He placed the smoking leaves at the base of the kindling and blew again. Soon, flames rose up and Torrint replaced the lid on the pot.

He handed it back to Javin by the strap. "Always put embers back in and seal it up. It'll keep well enough, because fires can be hard to start. You can do it, but it's easier to keep the embers glowing. I'll show you how to collect the warmings when we get to a pond. They keep the sparks safe." Then he motioned with his head and Javin took the pot back and nestled it back in its original place and replaced the bag. He then wandered over to the hobbled animals. They were called mandria apparently and he went to them just because he wanted to take a closer look and there was nothing else to do. Although they were tall and muscular, he felt safe being near them. He spent some time simply watching them and, occasionally, reaching out to give them a tentative stroke or two. Soon, he turned back to the wagons and the fire.

By this time, Banith had placed three packages made of large leaves on a round piece of clay resting on the fire. A clay bowl was placed carefully to one side to warm the contents. As Javin watched, Banith kept the packages moving and fed the fire with small pieces of wood to keep it hot. Using a stick with a charred end, he prodded the packets around, turned them over and also kept moving the bowl. It took time and careful attention. Torrint just sat, chewing his leaves and staring off into the distance.

"What's cooking?" Javin asked.

"Some meat, some leaves and some fruit. And that's simesh," Banith added, nodding at the bowl.

That appeared to be the end of that conversation. Neither trader was garrulous, to say the least, both seemingly quite content to be silent. Javin wondered if this was normal for them, and feared that it was.

Finally, Banith was satisfied everything was ready. He used another thick piece of wood and hooked one package at a time from the clay skillet and placed them each on a close woven platter, before handing them around. He sprinkled some ground herbs into the wooden bowl before pouring the contents, with the aid of some thick cloths, into three wooden mugs, which he also passed around. Javin unwrapped his meal, nodding his thanks to Banith. The whole process was unlike anything he had ever encountered. It took so much effort to make such a simple meal! But it tasted good, whatever it was. The meat was juicy and flavored with whatever Banith had wrapped up with it. It had definitely been worth the wait. He realized he was hungry.

After the meal both traders were content to sit and watch the fire. Javin drained his drink which had a surprisingly pleasant, minty tang to it and finally gained courage to break the silence.

"Where is it we're going?"

Torrint spat to one side before answering. He was back to chewing his leaves again, although still holding on to his now empty mug. "A place called Mark. Taking you to a family there."

"Do you do this sort of thing often?," asked Javin.

Torrint shook his head slowly. He did everything slowly, Javin had noticed. "No. People like you, from Haven? There aren't many of you here. One in the last twenty years?" Banith confirmed this with a nod of his head.

"Why did those others come here?"

Torrint shrugged as if it was none of his business. As if he didn't care. "Who knows? They upset someone and it was easiest to send them here? Although I can't think why." He was silent a moment as he moved the wad from one side of his mouth to the other. "Maybe it was a punishment."

"Do you know where any of them are now?" Javin was hopeful he could meet up with any of them.

Torrint shook his head. "I know where they were. But not now. They move on. Same as you will."

"What do you mean?"

"This family we're going to. They have enough to feed you and you'll get to work there. But, you won't stay. You'll move on. Because you'll want to do more than work on a farm. It will get to you, this place, and you'll want to do more. You'll move on." There was a smug certainty in his words.

Javin thought this over but couldn't feel how he felt about it. "Do you know this family well, then?"

"We trade. They buy. There's three of them. One girl. Plenty of work to do."

In the silence following, Banith asked Javin, "So what did you do that got you sent here? It must be difficult for you. I suppose this is nothing like you were used to?" The words came slowly, as if he were not used to talking freely. Or, maybe, Javin thought, he was not used to having a conversation.

Javin considered which question to respond to first. "Yes, it is different. Very. So different I can't even tell you. Everything is different." He plucked a small plant from beside him and held it up. "This is different. I don't even know if it's poisonous or good to eat. I don't know about plants. I lived in a city." The word obviously meant nothing. "It's big. Very big. Many thousands of people live there. Tall buildings and lots of metal." There was still no reaction. He pointed to the hobbled beasts. "I've never seen anything like them. They're huge. I've never seen anything, any animal as big as that, back on Haven. I didn't see many animals at all. Not that I can remember anyway." He paused a moment, thinking. "And the air. It smells completely different. But it's like I can see further. The sun. That's smaller, much smaller. But the moon? That's new to me, and I like it. There is no moon on Haven." He shrugged. "There's so much else. Too much different. Even the food." He shook his head to show his confusion.

"But what happened to get you here?," Banith repeated, adding to the fire.

Javin stared into the flames a moment, trying to remember. "I don't know. I can't remember. I keep trying, but I can't. I think it's the drug I was given when I was brought here."

There was another brief silence, and then Javin couldn't contain himself any longer. "And there's this thing about not being able to leave, and about hearing the planet and knowing what my talent is. I'm supposed to have one, but I don't even know what that is or what it means. It's like everyone's speaking a language that I can't understand. It doesn't make sense! None of it!"

Neither Torrint or Banith said anything, but Torrint nodded slowly, although whether in agreement with Javin or at some private thought was unclear. It was all the response Javin would get.

The following day they made slow progress up towards a pass in the mountains. It was a repeat of the previous day, except with increasing elevation. There was one exception; an unscheduled stop. An animal carcass lay not far from the track. Javin guessed it was about as long as his leg, maybe more, and it was covered, what he could see of it, in thin grey and brown horizontal stripes, extending all the way down the long, thin tail. Torrint, hauling on the reins, used his chin to point. "That's a pecorna. A cat killed it earlier, but it ate it's fill, left the rest and is sleeping now. Somewhere else. It's safe enough."

Safe enough for what, thought Javin. Instead, he said, "A cat? Really? The animal that's about this big?" And he held his hands shoulder width apart.

Torrint cocked his head to one side and moved one of Javin's hands further apart, to where they could have held one of the wagon wheels. He checked the width, nodded and jumped down. Javin hastily re-thought what a cat might mean here as he jumped down after him.

Javin squatted down by the carcass beside Banith, noticing the chunks of flesh missing. The size of the bites helped in his reassessment of what 'cat' meant. Banith had a wide-mouthed glazed clay pot with him and what looked like a set of slim sticks. Javin thought the back of his wagon must be full of sticks of different lengths. The reason for the interest in this carcass was, apparently, two large orange shapes resting on the body. They were about two hand spans in breadth and seemed to flex gently. He was about to prod at them but Torrint caught his hand.

"Don't! These are numbugs. Not good to touch. Watch."

He gently eased a stick underneath one of them and then quickly flicked it so that it tumbled and landed on its back. A set of thin legs waved feebly. He repeated the action on the second one.

Torrint waved Javin to him. "Go ahead and touch now if you want. The underside is safe. But the top side, the orange, that's where the juice is. And that's what we're going to collect." So saying, he took the pot from Banith and placed it beside one of the creatures and then held it up over it with what was a pair of simple wooden tongs. The creature wriggled slightly. Banith took the other two pieces of wood and placed one on each side of it near the top of one of the wings and then began to run them down, squeezing gently as he went.

As he did so, drops of a clear liquid began to ooze from the creature and dripped into the pot. He repeated the process several times to drain as much as he could before treating the other one in the same manner. At the end, Torrint placed the creatures back on the carcass and both he and Banith threw the sticks away.

"They feed on carrion," explained Torrint. "Another creature comes along and decides to eat them, they end up with no feeling at all in their mouths." He held up the pot. "We mix the juice with some clay and some water and sell it. It's called deadspread. Good for pain and aches. But raw like this, you won't feel your hand for a day or so if you touched it."

They returned to the wagons where the pot was carefully sealed with something like wax from another pot before being stowed away. Everything was done slowly here. Then the rumbling, jolting journey continued. There were so many pots, Javin thought. And none of them had labels! How did they know which was which? He briefly considered asking Torrint, but rejected the thought, knowing he would get an answer he would not understand.

Two days later, two days of creaking wagons, an aching backside, few conversations and quiet meals, they crested the pass and Torrint pointed out their destination. A wisp or two of smoke could be seen. There were what looked like a few houses visible, but not much beyond that. "That's Mark, down there. Two days away. That's your new home."

Javin peered ahead. He felt disappointed. "It's not very big. How many people live there?"

"Enough. Enough to make it a place worth living in."

"And that's where I'm going to live? With this family?" Javin felt depressed at the thought. "What are they called?"

"Farmers?"

"No, their name. Like mine is Sarnum, Javin Sarnum. What's theirs?"

Torrint chewed a moment before answering. "Sarnum? That was your father's name or your mother's?" Javin was about to explain but Torrint continued. "Anyway, it doesn't work like that here. It's not just one name. There's Hanlar and there's Paysa. They got together and had a girl. She takes half the last name of each parent. At least, until she wants to make her own name. Hanlar's last was Gorthen and Paysa's last was, let me think...oh, yes, Hommerit. So, I suppose you'd call them the Gommerits.

Maybe they call themselves the Gorthommerits." He shrugged. "You'd have to ask them."

Javin was amazed. "But that doesn't make sense! How does anyone know who anyone else is? Shouldn't they have huge long names by now? All their parents' and grandparents' names?"

Another shrug. "It works for us. People tend to choose how they are called. Keep the first name, but choose a last name. So, Hanlar, I happen to know, called himself Gorthen, because that was the name of his uncle." Then he added, "Not that he is called that by anyone else."

And on they rumbled and creaked.

Not only was this place strange, thought Javin, but the people in it were crazy.

4

"I think you should take a break, Javin." Hanlar handed over the leather water-bottle. Javin gulped greedily.

"I didn't know it would be this hard," he gasped. "I don't want to do this, Hanlar. I don't like it and I don't want to do it. Really."

Hanlar nodded sympathetically. "I can understand that it is different."

"No, you don't understand. I never even saw a farm before. I bought food. I ate it. I never grew it." Thinking back to his journey here, he added, "I never cooked it, either." He gestured at the field they had been working in, digging and weeding all day. Hard, physical work. He sunk, slowly, to the ground, flexing his hands to get some feeling back into them, staring at the blisters. It was his fourth day and he was by now fully aware of the truth of Gerant's words; that there was always something to do on a farm. He couldn't work out if the days were truly longer on Harmony, or whether his perception was skewed by his getting up early and working long hours. There were no clocks. Time was told by the pain in his body, the angle of the sun or the hunger in his belly. Mostly by the pain.

Hanlar squatted down next to Javin. "I can finish here, Javin. You go back and have a rest. Maybe some sleep?"

Javin shook his head. "No, Hanlar. I mean it. I can't do this. I don't want to do it. I hate it."

Hanlar sat opposite him and asked, "So what does that mean?"

"I don't know. It means I hate this."

"And then what?" There was only curiosity in the question.

"Like I said, I don't know." His voice was quieter now that he had said it, admitted it.

It had all seemed so different when he had arrived. Torrint and Banith had said their goodbyes, which consisted mainly of a quick bob of the head at him before clambering back on their respective wagons and lumbering off without looking back.

There had been the first meal together. The adults, Hanlar and his wife, Paysa. He, a man of middling height, serious eyes, a ready smile and a slow, almost languid way of talking. His wife was a short, round, jolly woman with a long braid and an easy laugh. Their daughter, Tarla, blonde hair already half way down her back, was usually quiet and had an air of reserve, almost of expectation about her, which his arrival disrupted. That first meal was a time for being polite and welcoming and gently enthusiastic while sizing each other up.

His first impressions had been that he was going to be in the way of the two adults. They were efficient and he was going to slow them down, hold them up, make life difficult. It would be an embarrassment, him being there. Even the basics of living there were unknowns. What he might take for granted, they might see as an impossibility, and vice versa.

Tarla, though, looked on him as a novelty. She was excited he had arrived. He was new. Someone else to look at. Someone to dream about. His arrival was like magic; promising so many wonderful things, stories, excitements, newness! Tarla kept smiling at him as if she couldn't believe he had actually arrived. Every now and then she asked him questions, most of which he couldn't answer; things like what he did on the other planet, how he got here, what was it he missed most? What was it like there? Were there wooden buildings or earthen? What was his favorite thing to do? Had he had any girlfriends? What about farms? Did they grow the same things? On and on, and he did the best he could. But mostly, he didn't have the words. And if he had the words, he lacked the knowledge.

The first day was about trying to fit in, even if he didn't really want to, or knew how. It was the time for looking around the farm, being surprised at the size of it, at how it seemed to straggle all over the place, of trying to remember so many new things, new words, new ideas.

And the day after had been the first long, long day of work with Hanlar. It was supposed to be a way of breaking him in to this life, this farm, these jobs. Digging in one field, herding strange, unhelpful, antagonistic animals in a different place, planting in a third. That night's meal was quieter.

The next day was like the day before, but more painful and just as understandable.

And this morning, up and again at work, digging and planting and just being physical. And the worst part of it all was that Javin knew he had seen what every day in the future would be like. How every day to come would feel like. How much he did not fit in.

He had tried to say it all, his disappointment, his sense of alienation, his lack of empathy with this type of life. But, saying he hated it, was too short, too swift, too shallow. But it had been said.

"Yes, but what now?" asked Hanlar.

Javin stared off into the distance, not really looking at anything, but only aware of the unknowing; the bleak future and his empty past. It all coalesced here and now. "I don't know. I mean that I really have no idea. Is this my future? Working on a farm? With you? I don't know what else there is. I don't know if there's anything else I can do." He spread his hands to show the emptiness he felt, the blisters adding their testimony. "I mean it, Hanlar. All I do know is that I can't do this. But other than this?" He shrugged and shook his head.

"Is it the pain? Have I been expecting too much, working you too hard?" Hanlar seemed genuinely concerned that he had contributed to Javin's despair.

Javin's gesture dismissed the question. "It's the fact that I don't fit in. I don't know anything here. Maybe I was looking for something here. A future? My past is missing and maybe it won't ever come back. If I was thinking of a future it wouldn't have been this, though." He looked at

Hanlar as if searching for an answer. "I may not know my past, but I know, bone deep I know, that this is not how I want to live. This is not how I want to be." He lowered his head. "I'm sorry."

Hanlar stretched out on his back, flexing his arms to relax them before using them as a pillow as he stared up into the sky. Eventually he spoke without looking at Javin. "You talk of what you want and don't want. But it's not just you here."

"I didn't mean --," began Javin, but Hanlar carried on as if he hadn't spoken.

"Everyone here has something else going on. You talk of your future, what you want, as if you are alone. Alone and with nothing and no-one. And it's not true. Everyone has Harmony. We are never on our own. But you sound as if you don't know that, don't understand that."

"I know about it. But I don't know it. Bellis helped me to find my place on the ground outside. And I know that Gerant and Lisick do something, but..." He trailed off.

Hanlar nodded and then turned on his side to face Javin. "You'll find it, Javin. Or it will find you. I can't do anything about your past. And, to be honest, I have no clue about your future either. One may be gone. The other is in your hands. Maybe it would be best if you left. Just walked away right now and found out for yourself about Harmony. You'd probably die of starvation or poison yourself though. And then we'd feel guilty. Or, maybe, the reason you're here is to listen to Harmony. To tune in to Her. Maybe the reason you're here is to end your loneliness. And that will tell you what is next in your life." He rolled back to gaze at the sky.

"And how do I do that?"

Hanlar made an 'I have no idea' face. "I don't have to have the answers. You have to have the willingness to listen, to learn."

There was silence between them.

Hanlar sat up, gazing at nothing in particular. "Well, are you going to leave?" He gestured at the country around them. "You are free to go and you're welcome to stay." He turned to look directly at Javin. "But be clear on one thing, Javin. I am not keeping you here. I am not making you stay. All I am doing is giving you some help, giving you some space to learn, to listen. Which means, if you have problems here, you deal with them. You do not affect this family. Agreed?"

Javin studied Hanlar for a moment, then he nodded. "That's fair." He sighed. "But, Hanlar, I have to tell you, I still will hate this."

Hanlar stood, brushed his hands clean and smiled. "How you think about it is up to you. That's your freedom. Now, I, at least, am going to get on. You're welcome to join me... if you want to earn your meal, that is."

Mention of food made Javin realize he was hungry. "And when will that be?"

Hanlar paused for a moment and half-closed his eyes. "Paysa says it'll be ready when we get there." He saw Javin's jaw drop and the confusion in his eyes and his smile turned into a hearty laugh. "You've never heard about this, have you?"

"What did you do?"

Hanlar's smile was still huge. "It's something many, many people can do. Or so I'm told. We can hear each other. In our heads. You've never done this, have you?"

Javin was still struggling with it. "Did you just talk to her?"

"I suppose you could call it talking. More like... ," here words failed Hanlar. He made vague stirring motions with his hands as if that would convey what had happened. "We can hear each other if we decide to listen. I heard her in my head and we spoke about the meal." Hanlar frowned and said, as if to himself, "Actually, it's not like talking at all. I've never really thought about it before. I just do it." He shook his head to clear it. "It works. It works for us."

"Is that going to happen to me, the longer I stay here?" Javin asked.

"I have no idea, Javin. None. Everyone here has a talent for something. Maybe it will be yours. Maybe it will be something different."

"So, what you're saying is --," began Javin.

"What I'm saying," Hanlar interrupted, "is that we have work to do, and then a meal to eat. Talking can wait."

By the time they had finished and were walking slowly back, Javin had resolved that he would take what he could learn from his time on the farm, before leaving to find out what other sort of life he could live. For he knew that this was not what he would be doing for long.

"Hanlar? Why are we working so far away from the house? There's all this empty, unused land here. Over there, there's a fence, and there's some animals further out. And no crops I can see. It's like a, a mess! Sorry. It is. It just doesn't make sense."

Hanlar nodded. "I can see you might look at it that way. The answer is that that's the way Harmony wants it."

Javin stopped trudging and put his hand up as if to pull Hanlar back. "Wait! Are you seriously telling me that a whole planet, this planet, the one I'm standing on right now, knows exactly where it wants a field or where it wants some animals to eat? Seriously? It tells you this? Really?"

Hanlar turned back to face him. "Whose land is this, Javin?" He gestured expansively around him. "Is it mine? No. I look after it, that's all. I don't own it. The land is Harmony's. It is Harmony. That means She has every right to say what happens to it, doesn't it?"

"But, how?"

"How does She tell us? Let us know?" Javin nodded. "Well, first we have to ask, and then we have to listen. Really, that's Paysa who does that. She's much better at hearing it. Or, maybe it's a feeling she gets. I don't know which it is. The end result is that if we get an idea about making a new field, for example, then Paysa, sort of... ," he smiled ruefully. "Actually, I don't really know what she does. You'd have to ask her. But she gets to know if it's a good idea or not, if Harmony is in agreement with it or not."

Javin chewed on his lip for a moment before shaking his head in disbelief. "What you just said, Hanlar? I have to say it was absolutely no help at all. I still can't believe it. I can't believe any of it."

Hanlar cocked his head and smiled gently. "Well, Javin. It's like this. You're on a different planet now. That's how it works here." His eyes closed briefly. He opened them and grinned again at Javin. "And Paysa says if we don't get home soon, she and Tarla will have eaten our share." He continued trudging. "I hear Paysa. She hears Harmony. You'll end up hearing somebody or something yourself, I would guess. Now, let's go eat, shall we?"

NOTES FROM HAVEN

Notes From The Lander

From: A Popular Rebellion? Published 1204

"...So it was that the anti-technology movement gained ground. The (unwritten) manifesto, evident in the speeches and communications, focused on the idea that Haven was the opportunity for a fresh start for humankind. Instead of devoting time and energy on disrupting the planet, forcing it to give up its metals and ores, it would be more proper, so the argument went, if humanity were to take a more respectful view of where they had fortuitously landed. There were hints that there was a strong belief in providence and that a higher power was to be thanked for the colony ship to have been guided here...

...The end result of this political maneuvering was that a ship was provided to transport all those who wished to leave and live on Harmony. The catch was that the ship would leave very soon after the announcement, giving little time for preparation by those who had asked for such help. The ship, Lander 1, would remain the property of Haven and would be returned, on autopilot if necessary, after a 'reasonable' period of time on Harmony. The protests at such a short time were large and loud, but quickly the various groups became organized and a remarkable collective scramble gathered implements and all the necessities of life which was to be restarted on another planet....

There was an almost palpable sense of relief when the ship had left orbit. It was felt that anyone who had raised a dissident voice had had their chance of leaving and now, Haven could get back to being an organized, industrial planetary civilization where opposition no longer existed...

The period known later as The Schism is difficult to date accurately. Some contend that it began in the years immediately following the first landing. Others will date it from the first extant recorded objection to mining which was in 173. Still others argue for a date nearer 250 as that was about the time an organized community opposed to increasing use of technology was recognizable as such. All are agreed, however, that it was considered to have ended with the launch of Lander 1 in 323. As we now know the post- Schism period was merely a hiatus in the rebellion against technology. A very long hiatus, it is true, but a hiatus nevertheless."

From: A Citizen's History of Haven (603)

The notes, from which a selection is taken below, appear to have been gathered together originally by Stella Langriss, a crew member of Lander 2, who had placed them all in a pouch, labeled with the date and time of discovery, under her name where they were automatically filed with the Central Library in Resolve, the then-capital city. How they were misfiled is unknown.

All that is known for sure is that the craft, Lander 1, arrived back at Haven with all 47 personnel on board dead. The craft, on autopilot, went into orbit and the deaths were only discovered after some period of time had elapsed. The colonists had decided that living on Harmony was preferable to living on Haven and had packed Lander 1 with everything they thought they would need. The idea was to send the craft back on autopilot. Therefore, there was little urgency to meet with Lander 1 when it was first detected. It was some time before Lander 2 was able to dock with her sister craft, but it would have made no difference as the small crew of Lander 1 had long since died. (The fact that there was anyone, dead or alive, on Lander 1 came as a complete surprise to everyone.)

These notes had obviously been collected by Stella Langriss as part of her duties as a result of dealing with the bodies. It was only when the library catalog was being upgraded and the collections digitized that a student at the university came across the collection of notes and recognized them for what they were: an invaluable insight into one of the most famous episodes in our history.

The names of the writers are now unknown, as is the original sequence. Some were voice tapes, some were electronic files, and some few were handwritten. Some were damaged in various ways so that only a very small number appear to be complete. But that is also conjecture.

The whole collection is now available to be viewed, but the following comprises a short selection of excerpts to provide an insight into the events following what has come to be known as The Schism. As ever, what is not said is just as tantalizing as the details which are supplied.

[Written on paper]"... It so nearly came to blows. We had all shared the same dreams, had been determined to live our beliefs. But, the [indecipherable].... The remainder were determined to send this ship back on autopilot. Their hatred of all technology was irrational. This ship could have provided them, with us! with so much useful technology. The original plan, agreed by all, was to send it back, but stripped of any useful tech, such as lab equipment, computers, any metal structures which could be utilized in various ways. In other words, anything which would have made life easier for us all at the start of the new colony. It was simply prudent to learn to survive at first with as much help as we could have. However, that changed not long after landing and, apart from the Direct Communication Devices which had been manufactured prior to departure, very little was removed from Lander 1. Those DCD's were harder to use than we thought. Only some few people were able to send or receive anything at all, and much of that was garbled. They were disappointing. Even when disease spread, the lab equipment was not used. It was said by some that it was wrong to have such equipment and that it should be destroyed..."

[Another recording, which has deteriorated over the years, speaks of the early days on Harmony] "... It was hard living. Much harder than any of us thought it would be. The weather felt malevolent. That's the only word I can use... [garbled section]... came back inside. Plagues of insects, or what looked like insects, ate everything. Earthquakes happened daily it seemed and there was... [garbled section]... beautiful. Truly beautiful. The sunsets, the silence. They were real. As real as the way Janickson sealed my slashed arm with just a touch..." [It ends here and is one of the more frustrating entries. It is unclear what is meant here.]

[Written on paper but in a different hand to the first record] "... After the first plague which killed about 20 or so, there was a decision to split into two. Those who wanted to could strike out and attempt to settle a community about a day or two away. I think the idea was that it might be the plants we were eating which were the problem and that different vegetation had been spotted further out. I don't know who was the first to show strange talents, but it soon spread...."

[Perhaps the same person who recorded the second excerpt?] "... none of us knew what we were capable of. I heard Estillena talking to me. Talking! Inside my head. She was inside my head.... And now that idiot man practiced throwing stones at a target. He just smiled at me, stood still and there was the sound of a stone hitting the target... I couldn't do anything. [Long, garbled section]...I think they are going mad. I have to believe that, because I know I am not mad. I know it, but I can't prove they are. What other explanation can there be?"

[The following is a transcription of a brief, damaged electronic recording. It is a male's voice.] "We gathered what specimens we could. I think we wanted to continue [garbled]... research into what we had witnessed amongst ourselves. I still don't believe what happened. Yes, I saw it, I witnessed it, but I can't explain it. There were some strange theories being suggested about the planet, about some strange change in our blood, but [garbled]... Perhaps we should never have gone there."

[This seems to have been amongst the last notes made by the crew. It is not possible to estimate when the deaths started, nor how long it took before all were dead.] "I think I am the last. I am finding it hard to write. I can't see to use the recorder anymore. Like the others, I am not in pain, just not healthy. I don't know how to say it. It is as if I am drifting away. No anchor. Nothing to hold me here. Nothing to hold on to anymore. There is something huge and nameless missing from my life. And that is what is taking my life away. I can't find the words. I don't care either."

After The Lander's Return

From 'The Public Recorder', Spring 1, 20, 325 (A printed publication):

"They have returned, the cowards. They have come begging for forgiveness and for restitution. They stole the ship. They stole equipment and food and medicine. And now they return begging for forgiveness.

And why would we forgive them? A young society has been torn apart by their selfishness and deceit. Their actions threatened the very stability of this, our home. And now they come back.

We had thought we had healed the wounds they tore in us, in our way of life. But the fact they were only scabbed over has been proven by the outcry, the whole planet's outcry, as the ship comes back to its rightful home.

The question yet to be answered is, 'Why should we allow them to come back?'. They turned their backs on this planet. What right, then, do they have to be readmitted?"

From 'The Public Recorder', Spring 2, 28, 325 (A printed publication):

"Now we know they are dead. They and the dreams they had, the selfish dreams they had, they are also dead. Now we cannot allow their remains to be on the surface, for who knows what plague they carry?

Why they died, we do not know. How they died is likewise a mystery. All that we do know is that some few botanical samples were reported as being found by the first, brave decontamination crews who went aboard. Why those plants were chosen we have no way of knowing. Perhaps they were to be used to invade Haven, to destroy our native species. Perhaps they were the source of powerful mind controlling drugs, to be used to enslave us to their desires. We do not know. All we can hope is that everything in that ship, everything which had been exposed to the evil influence of that planet, has been systematically destroyed by the authorities, and will never be able to threaten us in our homes."

From the notebooks of Serrin Olsen, clerk of the works (an honorary title, now defunct, for the person responsible for the contents of the governmental archives):

"Spring 2, 35, 325. Six sealed casks, lightweight, metal, handles on top, no markings on the sides, about one meter in height, accepted into high-security storage area 3. Papers did not accompany them, but the presidential seal was evident in the accompanying folder. It would appear that the contents were sealed in vacuum, hence the need for high security to ensure continued integrity. All calls to chase up paperwork ended in one or another nameless office with assurances that all would be made regular in due course, but that it was an emergency and some consideration should be given. ...

Spring 3, 16, 325. The casks remain in secure storage. No paperwork forthcoming. Area will be sealed permanently in due course to ensure that nothing will be done with them until proper procedure takes place."

From the memoirs of Hirren Fordun, a high-ranking Council member, "The Duty Inherent", privately printed in 361:

"It was only later, after the Lander 1 had been fumigated, that a carefully doctored version of the process was released to the public. This was to ensure that the horrors of the dead passengers was not to be transmitted, for fear that there would be some movement for their burial or some form of remembrance on Haven.

It is prudent to assume that the majority of the colonists remain on Harmony. In any venture such as this, there will always be those for whom the dream is better than the reality and they will always wish never to have started. And to assume that only these very few survivors were all that remained of such a well-equipped expedition is either naive or ignorantly hopeful. The mass media were carefully nurtured as to what to say and how to say it so that all sympathy for the dead and those who remained on Harmony would be snuffed out before it could take root. The greatest fear was that a similar dissident movement would arise and, this time, completely destroy the fabric of society.

It has to be said, however, that in the first day, even the first few hours, when the Lander 1 was first boarded, it was unclear how many bodies there were, or what, if anything, had been brought back from Harmony. There were rumors, unsubstantiated at the time, that certain items, even a survivor, had been smuggled out before any authority was in place. I have my own views on this but cannot prove anything.

Some used this whole episode, where lack of order was evident, as a sign that some form of military arm, military discipline, if you will, was lacking in government in such situations. Certainly, the prison population increased, and there were numerous groups all claiming to have special interests in maintaining the harmony of the planet, of 'looking after it', as they put it. Such dissidence did make it harder to ignore the call for military involvement.

The problem was, and remains, one of, where is the line drawn for military involvement in government?"

From 'The First Millennium: A Soldier's Perspective" by Colonel A. J. Aggar (ret.), published 1000

"At the time, there was widespread anger upon hearing of the Lander's arrival back at Haven. This was not tempered by the news of the deaths. Indeed, it could be said to have intensified as a result.

The reason for this hostility is made clear when one looks back through the media archives of the time. The press had been working hard to discredit the emigrants. It was the press who gave this period the label of 'The Schism' and generally made all of those who left into selfish, ignorant dissidents who would rather die on a foreign planet than work to try and accomplish useful goals on Haven.

They were called by various names at various times, but the result was that even the corpses which circled Haven were denied burial on their home planet and were, instead, ejected into space.

This entire episode illustrates the power of unchained opinion in the mass media. More importantly, the unrest caused by the initial departure as well as the possibility of further unrest with the arrival of Lander 1, proved the value of having a reliable, disciplined cadre on call to maintain order.

It was, in fact, the origin of the growth of the military arm in society."

5

It was the end of another long day outside. Javin hated to admit it, but he was aching less now. There was no enjoyment still, but there was a reduction in the pain he was feeling.

He pushed open the door and the small, sealed clay pot, which was hanging behind it, clacked against the wood as it always did at the end of its leather cord.

"Are you tired, Javin?" Paysa was preparing the meal, with Tarla's help.

"Mmmhmm."

"Good." Paysa swung round, her long braid nearly hitting Tarla, who moved her head just enough to avoid it. It looked like a well-practiced move. "We've decided, well Tarla suggested it, that we help you find... how did you put it, Tarla?"

"To help find your talent, how you can live better on Harmony," Tarla spoke without turning, intent on her task. Her voice was quiet compared to her mother's brisk, bright delivery.

"Yes. That's it. Talent and Harmony."

Javin still had no idea what she was talking about.

Paysa beckoned him over to the table. "We'll eat first and then we'll try something. Hanlar can eat later so we can be undisturbed. I've told him. Now sit and eat."

Javin sat, grateful to rest. Mother and daughter quickly laid out the dishes; some stew meat and vegetables, the hot, sweet drink called simesh Javin had come to think of Harmony's version of coffee and some sliced dark-green fruit in a bowl with a sweet sauce ready to pour over them. His stomach growled quietly in appreciation.

Tarla served him as Paysa explained. "Hanlar told me how you feel." She put her hand up to stop Javin. "We're married. We think to each other. We're close. We can't keep secrets, even if we wanted to. And if we did...," she shrugged and pointed to the door. "If we did, then that would get broken."

"That pot?"

"That pot is us, if you will. Inside is something we each hold precious, and no, Tarla, I'm never going to tell you what it is." She smiled briefly at her daughter. "We made it when we decided we were to be together and if we ever decide not to be together, then we'll break it and take back what we put there. It's there on the door so we see it every time we go out. So that's why he told me. And so we, Tarla and me, thought we could help in some way."

Tarla took over as Paysa spooned her food up. "I thought you should find out what your talent is, Javin." She blushed a little as she spoke in her quiet voice, looking more at the table than at Javin. "Everyone has a talent. That's what we call them, anyway. Something they're good at."

Paysa took over again. "We thought we could help you find what yours is, Javin." She licked a piece of meat from the edge of her lip. "So we set up some things we can try. Well, actually, what you can try." She took a sip of simesh. "What do you think?"

"Honestly? I have no idea what to think. I just assumed that I would be able to listen to Harmony, whatever that means. I've heard it said, but I've never really given it much thought. I don't know what it is, to tell the truth. I thought doing things like you and Hanlar do was for people born here."

"I don't think so,"said Paysa. She put her hands together in front of her, fingers interlinked. "This is how I always see us and Harmony.

Together. Inseparable. I think the longer you're here, the closer you'll get to Her. And that means finding your talent."

While Paysa spoke, Javin had been rapidly spooning up the fruit after drizzling the sweet, sticky sauce over it. He licked the spoon and then his lips clean and looked regretfully at the now empty bowl.

"The only talents that I've heard of so far are things like you and Hanlar do; talking to each other somehow. Lisick and Gerant did that, or something like it, back where I arrived. Are you saying there are other things, talents, I mean?"

Tarla was clearing the table. "There are all sorts of things people do. Some of us are better at some things than others. That's why we call them talents."

Paysa had left the table only to return with three bowls in her hand which she placed on the table between herself and Javin. They were covered with a piece of cloth. Tarla rejoined them.

"What talents are there, then?" Javin asked. "Tarla, what's your talent? What is it you do?"

Tarla blushed again, looking at the table. Paysa answered. "Actually, we don't normally ask people what their talents are. It's thought of as being a little rude. It's like asking something very personal, like, I don't know, like... asking if they've hurt someone, for instance. You let people tell you, if they want to, when they trust you. But you're new and we're trying to help so, in this case, it's fair to ask. I don't want you getting into trouble later, that's all.

"Tarla does have a talent, don't you? It's still growing, but it's hers. Why don't you tell him yourself? After all, this was your idea."

Tarla took a deep breath and seems to be plucking up courage. After a moment, she managed to look at Javin. The earlier excitement at his arrival and the rain of questions had slowly changed into a quieter phase. She rarely asked questions now but spent a lot of time staring at him. He had caught her sometimes with a look of yearning, sometimes with a sadness he did not understand. She was rarely at ease near him but liked being near him. Where her voice had, at first, been bright and eager and her smile open and ready always on her face, now her voice was smaller and had a nervous edge to it, as if she could not trust it. "I can... understand people." She shook her head, correcting herself. "No, not understand. That's not quite right. I can hear how people feel. I can sense them, like I can hear how they feel." She looked to her mother for support. Paysa nodded encouragingly. "It's like a sound I hear. I'm not really good at it yet, though"

Paysa put her hand on Tarla to stop her. "Tarla cannot see what you think. Can you, love?" Tarla was back to staring at the table again. She briefly shook her head. "Nobody can do that, as far as I know," she said with conviction.

"But Bellis said that it was possible. When I was at Landing. She was trying to teach me." Javin was confused.

"I have no idea what they can do at Landing, but I can tell that here, where we are, nobody I know can do that." Paysa frowned. "I think you think Tarla here can read your mind, don't you?" She gave Javin no opportunity to affirm or deny that. "Nobody can read your mind. Certainly not Tarla. All she said was about hearing people and how they felt." She reached for Tarla who looked even more uncomfortable. "This was her idea, so don't try and think anything bad of it." She patted Tarla reassuringly, never taking her eyes off Javin who had been completely surprised by what he'd heard.

In truth, Javin really hadn't got to thinking what Paysa had accused him of. Faced with her second-guessing his thoughts, he was astute enough to apologize. At the back of his mind was his promise to Hanlar about not involving the family. The situation seemed to come under that promise in some fashion. "I had no idea... I mean, I didn't think..." Javin gestured placatingly as he tried to speak. "I'm sorry! Tarla? I'm sorry." Another brief bob of her head. "And Paysa? I'm sorry." A slight inclination of her head showed her acknowledgment. "I never meant... Ah! This is impossible!" What had started as a way of keeping a promise to Hanlar had suddenly become something larger, something which served to show, again, how little he knew of anything here. He cradled his forehead in his hands. "I am sorry. I am also, part of me, not sorry. And that's because you're asking me to know things no-one has ever told me. And that's not fair." He looked up at them, feeling defiant but trying not show it. He needed to learn. He needed them to teach him. "But I am sorry for breaking the rules and for not understanding. I promised Hanlar I would not let my feelings interfere with the family. I apologize if I have broken that promise." He looked directly at Paysa now and took a deep breath. "I am grateful to you, and to Tarla, for this help."

Paysa had softened as he had been speaking. "You may be right, Javin. Maybe it was too much to take in straight away. There's so much we take for granted. It is my turn to apologize to you for forgetting that you are still very new here." She flashed a smile. "Like a newborn."

"Sometimes, it does feel that way," Javin agreed with a wry smile. "And I do need to learn. Like a child, I suppose. I'm not sure if this is going to be breaking any rules, and, I'm sorry if it is, but, Tarla, can you please tell me what I am feeling?" He looked to Paysa for her reaction. She nodded acceptance.

"You have to know something else, Javin," Paysa said. "Doing something like this, like Tarla can do, it can seem to be very, very much like spying. Like looking at things you're not meant to look at. So, when you asked if she could do it, that's being respectful of her and giving her permission. It's a good way of going about it."

"But what if I didn't give permission? What if Tarla, or someone like her, just wanted to look in my head just to see how I felt about something?"

Tarla looked to her mother. Paysa nodded her to speak. "It's not like I do this all the time. I know I'm only beginning to do this, but, I can't do it all the time, even if I wanted to. It's like mother and father always listening and talking to each other. Nothing would get done. Same for me. I have to live my life in my head. So I don't go around poking into others. I mean, it's simply not polite!" She looked shyly at Javin. "It's best if someone invites me to listen to them. Easiest, in fact." She paused slightly and her eyes lost focus. "As for what you are feeling now," she said, "it's like a mix. Nothing steady." She moved her hand round and round. "Everything is moving. I don't know how to describe it because I've not heard it before." Her mouth tightened as she sought the right words. Then a smile. "Confusion! That's what it feels like. Confusion." She brought her focus back to Javin and raised her eyebrows in a question.

Javin smiled in turn. "I would have to say that sounds pretty much perfectly like what's going on. Confused. I am most definitely feeling confused. Thank you."

She shrugged to indicate she was finished.

Paysa beamed a congratulatory smile at her daughter, and rubbed her hands together briskly, a signal to move on. "Now. Let's get you started, shall we, Javin? Let's see what your talent might be. Hanlar won't be back bothering us until I tell him." And she lifted the covers from two of the bowls. "In this one," she said as she pointed, "there are some small seeds. And in this one, I have got a little water."

"What's in the that bowl?"

"Let's leave that for a moment." Paysa tipped the tiny red seeds out and spread them out a little with a finger. They were small enough that, by pressing a fingertip into the pile, ten or twenty would stick to the skin.

Javin looked expectantly at her. "What is this?"

Still prodding at the seeds, Paysa said, "Some people can move things without touching them. These seeds are small. Maybe you can move them. Or just some of them."

"And I would do that... how?"

"I don't know. How do you do anything? How do I talk to Hanlar? I just decide and then it gets done." She smiled encouragingly as she motioned at Javin. "Just try. See if you can move even one small seed. Like this one, here." And she prodded out one from the rest with the blunt tip of a fingernail.

Javin stared at it, not knowing what to do. It was nothing like finding 'his' spot on the ground with Bellis. That was a feeling he was looking for. Here, he had no idea what he was meant to feel or do. Paysa and Tarla were both looking at him with eagerness, to see what he could do. He didn't want to let them down. Plus, he wanted some sign he was able to do something on his own; make his mark in some fashion. Even if it was moving a tiny red, shiny seed.

So he stared at it and dared it to move. Nothing. He imagined blowing on it and seeing if that would work. Still nothing. He shut his eyes tight and frowned and thought hard about what he wanted, and still nothing. Then he began to wonder what plant it was from. And how was it gathered. And then he knew that he had completely lost any focus he might have had.

He sat up with a sigh. "It's no good. I don't know what I'm doing

49

here. I can't think of a way of doing this."

"Well, perhaps you need to stop thinking and let it happen instead," Paysa replied.

"How do I stop thinking about it? It's there in front of me! You've asked me to do something and then said, don't think about it. That makes no sense."

"Tarla, do you think about what you're doing when you hear people?" Paysa turned to bring her daughter into the conversation.

Tarla shook her head. "I started out that way, but I soon found out that I can just... I don't know... switch it on." She shook her head again. "I just do it, I suppose."

Paysa turned back to Javin, a triumphant smile on her face. "There you are! You see? You just do it. Like Tarla said."

Javin did not feel at all confident that Paysa's advice was particularly easy to follow. Instead, he pointed at the bowl with the water. "And what talent would involve this, then?"

Paysa sat back in her chair, folding her arms across her stomach. "Some people can make things hot or cold, or they can see if something's hot or cold. I'm not quite sure what it is, but I know Hanlar knew someone who could make water hot by holding it in his hands. You could try some of those things with this."

Javin was definitely unsure about this experiment. "I'm not even going to ask what I should do, or how I should do it. But, if you say it can be done... ," And he leaned closer. At first, he tried looking at it hard to see if he could see anything new about it. Then he tried holding the bowl in his hands. He put it down and place his hands over it for a while. In fact, he tried anything which came to mind, including stirring the water with a finger. But nothing happened.

He sat back in his chair. "Sorry. I don't seem to have any talent for that. Maybe I just don't have a talent."

"Nonsense," said Paysa, pushing the last bowl, still covered, in front of Javin. "Try this one."

"What is in the bowl?"

Tarla smiled. She was not at all disappointed that Javin had not succeeded at the earlier tasks. It seemed she was looking forward to this one. "Mother put something in there. But you might be able to see it."

"See it? How?"

Paysa sat back again. "There are people we call 'eyes'. They can see things which are not in front of them. They can see things in other rooms, for example." She frowned. "Truth is, Javin, 'eyes' are not always liked. Some people really do not like them. They can hate them, in fact." She looked up at him. "It's not fair, I know. Tarla here can hear how people feel and that's fine. But, if you knew that she could see what you were doing in another place, it would be like there would be no privacy. Tarla has to be near the person. An eye can be nowhere near. Hanlar and I can be a long, long away from each other and our speaking still works. But, people often don't think of it in the same way. An eye can be a very lonely person if they let others know that's their talent. It's not fair, but it's how it is here."

"And you want me to see if I'm an 'eye'?"

"Of course! If we know that, we can help you. Plus, it's not that common."

"You wouldn't know it if it was, though. Would you? Not if people won't admit to being one."

"True. But here it's safe to find out. Safe to practice." And she motioned at the bowl. "See if you can see inside. It's near and you can even hold the bowl if that will help. Might be you need that if you're starting out. You're a newborn, remember?" Her grin was infectious.

Javin did everything he could think of; closing his eyes, holding his breath, holding the bowl up to his head. Finally, he put the bowl down and shook his head sadly. "Maybe there's nothing in it, and that's why I get nothing?"

"Mother?" Tarla asked.

Paysa reached out and gently removed the cloth to reveal another helping of the fruit drenched with the sauce. She pushed the bowl toward him. "Sorry, Javin. You're obviously not an eye. But maybe that's for the good. Even if you're not an eye, you can still eat that up." She handed him a spoon and smiled and patted his arm as he took it. "Don't worry, Javin. Everyone has a talent. It will just take time. That's all."

Tarla's face also dimpled into a quiet smile as Javin happily took up his spoon again.

6

Tarla, perhaps emboldened by spending time with Javin and being able to talk with him, went back to asking Javin questions about his previous life on Haven. Instead of a stream of questions, now it was just one or two at a time. She was interested in his kidnapping and journey through space. And another question, slipped in, about a girlfriend. How was he captured? Did he fight? What was it like in space? He could provide few details. He had been rounded up by police and taken away in a vehicle. But he had been drugged with a spray and had virtually no memories of anything until his arrival.

The lack of details was not such a let down for her, but it did serve to remind Javin how ragged his memory really was.

One day, after a particularly hard morning, trying to move a herd of belligerent animals into a new pasture, Javin and Hanlar were taking a break in the shade of a bush.

"What are those things we were just wrestling with called?" asked Javin.

"Gomars."

"I think I have another name for them."

Hanlar smiled in sympathy. "Probably better you keep it out here. I heard a few words you were using and, although I am not really sure what they meant, I got the idea of what you were saying."

"Hmmmph." Javin was on his back staring up through the fronds above him. "They have the attention span of a child and the strength of... of something much bigger." He winced as he rubbed gently at his side. "Those things, the gomars, they really like head butting, don't they? What do you do with them? It'd better be worth it, whatever it is."

"We pluck the hair once a year when it gets long. When treated with the right plants, which we don't have here, it apparently changes color. The color depends on the weather. I haven't seen it, but Torrint told me about it. We sell to him and he sells to the ones who can make it change color." Hanlar shrugged. "I suppose it would be pretty."

"You haven't seen it, then?"

Hanlar shook his head. "Probably couldn't afford it, either. Apparently it's quite popular in other places, but what would we do with it here?"

Javin did not know how to answer that. "Wouldn't it be easier," he said, "to ride them instead of trying to poke them in the direction you want to go?" He stretched to try to ease the muscles in his side.

"See those big, round dark leaves? Just to your left? Pick one of them, crush it and rub it on the bruise."

Javin did so. "Oooooh! That feels good." He grabbed another leaf. "What's this stuff called?"

"It's minnit," said Hanlar. "And that herding we just did? That was the easiest it's ever been. Thanks to you."

"You mean you do that on your own?" said Javin, amazed at the thought and impressed at Hanlar at the same time.

Hanlar nodded. "Here, let's have our lunch now before getting on."

"Not more gomars, please!"

"No," Hanlar smiled as he broke some dried meat off and handed it over. They both chewed in silence for a moment.

"Do you still hate it here as much?"

"I'm not sure. Swearing at those animals helped a little." Javin smiled a little. "Let off steam, I think." He thought little more. "Maybe I don't hate it as much. But that might be because I'm a little more used to it. One thing I am sure of is that this is not the life for me. I know that much." He shrugged. "I'm sorry. I know I need to learn, and I will. And I'm grateful for you teaching me. But..."

Hanlar nodded his understanding. He chewed a little more before changing the subject. "Is Tarla bothering you? She seems to be always asking questions."

"No. It's only a problem if I can't answer." Javin shook his head. "That's the real problem, Hanlar. Not her. There's too much I don't know. And there's a whole lot more I can't remember."

"Still no more memories?"

"No. It's like there's a wall in my head." Javin built an imaginary wall in front of him with both hands. "On this side," he motioned with his right hand, "there's everything I've done for, I think, maybe three to four years. Maybe more, maybe less. The journey is still a blank, but I know I was drugged for that. And on the other side," using his left hand, "there's a whole empty space. I don't know anything about that. I don't know my parents. I can't remember anything about my childhood. Nothing. It's a blank!

"The one thing I am sure of is the memories I have since I arrived here. Those I know are real. I think all the other memories are real. But I don't know."

"That must be hard for you, the not knowing. And I hear that finding your talent hasn't exactly been easy, either."

Javin smiled ruefully. "I don't seem to be able to do anything."

Hanlar took a round piece of fruit and expertly twisted the top of it off. Then he peeled the rest of the skin away with his thumbnail, eating half of it and offering the rest to Javin. Javin found it to be delightfully juicy and refreshing and nodded his appreciation.

Hanlar wiped his mouth with the back of his hand and let out a contented sigh. "So I suppose that you haven't had much luck with hearing Harmony, either?"

"I would think I'd know it if I did, so, no." Javin wiped his hands on the ground to get rid of the stickiness. "To be honest, I have no idea what any of that means, Hanlar. Not one small clue."

Hanlar pursed his lips as he thought about how to explain it. "I'm not sure how to tell it right, or even if it is the same for everyone. But as far as I know, to me, anyway, it's a bit like hearing a song, or sometimes it's like something that you just feel is right and everything sort of fits together. Like, you have a connection with what's happening around you." He paused and Javin could see him scouring his memory for better ways of saying what he instinctively felt and knew. "It's like the difference between looking at, say, that piece of land over there," and he pointed as he spoke, "and really knowing what the land was growing now and what it was capable of growing."

Javin had turned to look at where Hanlar had pointed and sat for a moment, gazing. "I did spend a little time with Bellis, back where I landed --"

"It's called Landing. That place is called Landing," Hanlar said.

Javin nodded. "Well, at Landing, Bellis told me to find my spot there. I had to find a spot which felt right for me. And also a place which didn't feel right. It took a long time. But I don't think I felt anything like you said. One bit felt good and the other didn't. And the rest of it, I didn't feel anything at all. I could have just fooled myself into thinking they were different."

"Well, maybe it will take its own time, but I'm sure Harmony will get to you as well."

"Yes. But what if it doesn't? I'd be like someone who's blind while everyone else can see. A blind man, with no memories. Or deaf to whatever it is that everyone else hears."

Hanlar had no answer to that.

"I can't go home. I know that because I'm pretty sure if there was a spaceship available someone would have mentioned it. I'm cut off in more ways than one." Javin began plucking at the leaves on the minnit plant. "I'm stranded here. I can't seem to remember very much. I don't understand what I'm doing here, the things I do here with you. And I am also, apparently, unable to hear or connect or whatever it is that everyone else here can do. Plus I have no talent" He threw the leaves away. "What would you do if you were me?"

"I don't know. I'm sure it's hard for you. Maybe the only true connection you can have is with yourself, your memories. Perhaps we need to forget about everything else and help you that way. There are healers. They can do many things. Perhaps one of the things they can do is heal your mind."

Javin chewed on his lip as he thought. "How would I find one?"

Hanlar sighed. "It's not going to be easy. We could send word out to Torrint maybe? He might know of someone and be willing to take you. There's not a lot of traveling done. People stay where they are. They don't go very far, generally."

"There's no healer here, then?"

"Mostly we look after ourselves. Herbs and such. Some of us have a little talent for easing pain and helping healing. But nobody here has a real healing talent."

Javin stood up. "So what you're saying is that there might be healer somewhere who could bring back my memories, but we have no idea where he or she is or even how long it might take to get there, assuming Torrint wants to take me, and we can get in touch with him... or her." He took a deep breath. "And then, of course, there's the assumption that I'm going to be happy getting those memories back again. Doesn't sound that hopeful, does it?" And he walked off.

Hanlar sat and watched him, unable to offer any comfort.

For the next few days, nothing more was said, in Javin's hearing anyway, about talents or hearing Harmony or his memories. Javin had the distinct impression that Paysa and Hanlar had had another talk about him in their silent fashion. His mood had become more one of quiet depression, of unwilling resignation. The talk with Hanlar had made him realize just how cut off he was here. This way of life was not going to change. He was going to be doing this, living like this, for the foreseeable future. All he knew was that this was not what he would have chosen for himself. But, and here was the problem, he had no idea what alternatives there were. He felt trapped, and not just through his lack of knowledge. There was no easy transportation, nor an easy way to send a message or talk to anyone, not even the neighbors, who were a long walk away; a day there and back, according to Hanlar. The sense of his isolation was becoming stronger. And he did not know of anything he could do to alter that.

One morning, as he and Hanlar were about to head off to the fields, Paysa called out. "This has gone on long enough, Hanlar. I think we need to do something." She glared at her partner and brushed at her head as if she were brushing away a strand of hair. "And you can stop that right now. You know I'm right."

Paysa hauled on Javin's arm and told him to sit down.

"I think we need to sort some things out. And I think we should do that now."

"We should be going out to that far field --," Hanlar began.

"You can get on with that by yourself." Paysa seemed all bristle and sharp-edges. "You were capable before Javin arrived. You can do it again now. I am going to have a word with Javin here." And she waved Hanlar off as if she were shooing a child.

She looked down at Javin who had sat himself down on the edge of the porch and was looking confused. Had he done anything wrong? He had kept his promise, as far as he was able to. He couldn't think of anything which might have caused her reaction.

Paysa sat down next to Javin. A determined look on her face as she took in the land around them. She finally faced Javin and reassured him. "There's nothing wrong. Well... not in the way you might be thinking. You've done nothing wrong. Apart from being like a small thundercloud around the place." She forestalled anything Javin might have said by resting her hand lightly on his arm. "And you have a perfect right to be like that. I have absolutely no idea what I would be feeling if I was in your position. And that's what I want to talk about with you.

"I know what you promised Hanlar, and what you both have been talking about." She let a small smile slide across her face. "No secrets remember? But I think it's time, it's way past time, in fact, to face up to what is going on here. And what is going on with you. And, more importantly, what can be done about it.

"You can't spend the rest of your life hating what you do. Nobody should. And I don't believe that you do not have a talent." She shook her head vigorously to underscore her words. "It's just not possible. Everybody has some talent. And as for not hearing Harmony, being apart from Her, that's not possible either. And I don't care what you think about that, I know that it's not possible. What it means is that we; Hanlar, me, Tarla, we have to find out what it is that can be done to make this happen. If we can't get your memories back, then we can help you find your connection, your talent."

She patted Javin's hand. "There's no reason why you should remain feeling so lost. Now, I can't stop you hating this life, although I can't understand it. I love it. It's perfect. It's where I know, really know, I belong." She threw her hands out wide as if trying to encompass everything around her. "But you got thrown into it. I understand that. But...," she shrugged her reluctant acceptance of Javin's obvious idiocy.

"Hanlar thought he was doing right by letting you get on and maybe find your own way to liking this life. But, even after this short time, I know that's not going to happen, is it?"

Javin, who had been wondering where this was all going, shook his head slowly. "I just can't see this as being what I do. Not forever. I'm sorry."

"Sorry isn't necessary. You are who you are." Paysa was all business now that she was approaching the real reason for talking to Javin. "I have been doing some thinking. And I, that is Hanlar and I, even if he hasn't thought of it yet, we think that what you really need is less work and more time to get to know Harmony. You can do it working away with plants and animals. But maybe it's time to try something new. Instead of working on Harmony, you should try resting on Her, let Her get to know you in a different way. Let each of you find each other. I think that you need to stop working so hard and that it would be better to just let yourself find out about Harmony yourself."

"Just wander around? Is that what you're saying? Doing nothing?" Tempting though that might have been in the first few days, Javin realized how much the discipline and routine of work was helping him get through the days.

"Sort of. I'm far too busy at this time of year. Helping harvest seeds, spin, preserve food... ," she dismissed all these tasks with a wave of her hand. "So that leaves Tarla for most of it. I'll help where I can, and so will Hanlar." She turned to peer closely at Javin. "I am trusting you, Javin. You've made one promise to Hanlar. Now you make one to me."

Javin sensed her seriousness and, nodding, said, "What is the promise?"

"That you do nothing to hurt Tarla. Nothing. She is young. You are a stranger, new here. Do not hurt her."

Javin tapped himself on the chest with his hand. "I will make that promise, Paysa. I will do nothing to hurt Tarla in any way. Promise."

Paysa continued looking at him for a moment longer before finally nodding, as if she had found something she was looking for. "Then it is done." She patted him on the back. "Also, we will send a message to Torrint to come and get you." She noticed Javin's eagerness. "It will take time, I've no doubt. Perhaps he will know where a healer is who will help you. Even if he doesn't, you will meet others who might know. All we do know is that there is no one here to help you. So, between now and then, you will have plenty of time to be with Harmony and to find your talent. Now, run after Hanlar and tell him that tomorrow, he's working alone. And don't forget your promise."

Javin got up. "I won't. And that's a promise, too. Thanks, Paysa. Thanks for trying to help. I do appreciate it. Really. I just hope it works out."

"So do I, Javin. So do I. Oh, and there's no need to tell Hanlar." She tapped her head and smiled. "I just let him know."

Javin smiled back and set off. He had made a promise to Paysa and he was sure he could easily keep it. He would do nothing to hurt Tarla, but could he stop Tarla from being hurt anyway? He had doubts about that.

The next day was the beginning of the new regime. Javin sat on the porch, in the same place as the day before, not knowing what else to do. Breakfast was never a family affair. Normally, he had eaten with Hanlar before they left together. Usually, they were on their own. Sometimes Paysa was there. Often Tarla would drift in and eat with them. Today had been different. He had taken some fruit and some water with Hanlar as usual, but had not rushed. When Hanlar had stuffed some dried meat and a small round of something which Javin thought might be cheese into a small leather bag, he had felt a small pang of guilt, knowing how hard Hanlar already worked. Hanlar, however, stopped and smiled at Javin.

"Don't you go feeling bad about this, Javin." He wagged his finger at him for emphasis. "What I do is the same as always. With you or without you, it is always there. And Harmony will always help. You need to find your place here with Her. And Paysa is right. You won't find it with me. But I hope you will find it soon. For your sake." And he was on his way.

Javin had moved to the porch, chewing on the fruit, an oblong, tart-tasting item, wondering what to do and how to make sure he kept his promise to Paysa. Tarla was just in that transition between girl and woman. A long, golden braid and an open, smiling face and with a talent which, apparently, meant she could hear how he felt. A mix of innocence and expertise which was a little unsettling.

He tried to recall anyone like Tarla from before his arrival on Harmony and only ran into the same blankness as always. As he tried, yet again, to find some details of his past, Tarla sat down beside him.

"Hello," she said shyly.

"Good morning, and thank you for being willing to help me with all this." And he spread his hands to encompass the view in front of them.

Tarla bobbed her head. There was an awkward silence for a moment.

"Perhaps you can tell me one thing I've been wondering about?" asked Javin. "How exactly will Torrint get a message asking him to come here? I don't understand that at all. How does anyone get messages here?"

A look of relief flashed across Tarla's face. "Actually, there's no sure way of doing it." She tilted her head. "Over there are our neighbors, Sallnat and Fellisin. We will try to find Sallnat and tell him. He has a cart which can take him to the road. And there he can put up a notice for Torrint. If Torrint sees it, and it suits him, he will come. If someone else sees it and knows where Torrint is and is likely to meet up with him, then he will take it to him. If not... ," she shrugged.

"So it could take a very long time, then? I hadn't realized." Then, "Why does the neighbor go and not one of you, of us?"

"We don't have a cart. We did have one, but we traded the dog, Kellar, we traded Kellar, for some other animals. We traded with Sallnat, actually. It's a long way to the road. It would take far too long to walk. I haven't been there myself."

"A dog cart?"

"They're big. The dogs are big." Tarla held her hand at about head height, as she was sitting on the ground. "They're very strong."

"I never knew. Is Torrint the only trader, the only one who could take me?"

"Mmmhmm."

There was another silence. Then Tarla, visibly plucking up courage, said, "Perhaps we should start and see what we can do to help you?"

Javin inclined his head in appreciation. "That would be wonderful. Thank you very much." Out of the corner of his eye he was very aware of Paysa's presence just inside the doorway. "So... how do we do that?"

Tarla's face took on a serious look. She rested her hands on her knees and looked at her feet. "Harmony is sort of always in my head. In our heads. It's like a sound, or not a sound, but like just knowing there's something else inside, but not scary. She is always there, but in the background. You can choose to hear Her more loudly. Often, in the day, what I'm doing drowns Her out. But I know, always I know, that She is there and I can stop and She comes back again." She frowned a little as she concentrated on getting the words right. "If you stop thinking, just relax, you can hear Her." She smiled briefly. "At least, that's the way it works for me. Maybe for you it would be a feeling more than a sound. Or maybe it might be something else." Still not looking at him, Tarla asked, "Have you felt anything like that since you've been here? Something new, some new feeling in your head?"

"Just that time at Landing when I felt one patch of ground felt different to the rest."

"You're not going to learn anything staying here and talking. You should go somewhere new and try to learn what Tarla's telling you." Paysa had been watching them and had decided it was time to intervene if anything was to get done. "Start off near some water. By the pond or by the stream. See what happens." Tarla and Javin got up. "And don't be late for lunch. I want you back here to help me with it, Tarla." Paysa caught Javin's eye and glared meaningfully at him.

On the gentle slope at the back of the small house, there was an equally small pond fed by a narrow, lively stream. The water spilled from the pond into a channel and ran down into the house, filling the large bowl there and flowing away through another channel towards the stables. Javin had never been here before, always working in the other direction with Hanlar. It was peaceful. The sun, smaller than he was used to, was warm and it was a pleasant spot to be.

Tarla motioned him to sit where the stream entered the pond. "Perhaps listening and watching the sky will stop you thinking. Perhaps Harmony will come to you when you are still."

It was the first of many attempts to 'hear' Harmony. It was very pleasant, and Tarla was good company, but, after a while, both of them knew it was not happening.

After a last attempt, which consisted of lying under a large bush and watching the sunlight flickering through the fronds, Tarla judged the height of the sun. "It's time we were going back now."

"I'm sorry I'm such a poor student. I feel I've wasted your time today."

Tarla shrugged. "It's nice to have a break from chores. I don't mind." And she blushed.

She paused, just enough to allow Javin to walk beside her. She had been quiet all through the attempts, allowing him the best opportunity possible, although he could see that she really wanted to talk. He had looked up several times to find her staring at him with an expression he felt sure he knew but didn't want to admit to himself. Briefly he wondered if that was his talent; being able to understand what she wanted. But he dismissed it with a wry grin. It was too easy to see what Tarla was really interested in.

After eating a simple lunch, where the rich-tasting bread complemented the tart berries and there was the inevitable cup of simesh, Paysa cleared the table and sat back down again.

"No luck, then?" she asked.

Javin shook his head. "I don't seem to be able to get what's going on with Harmony. It's not for the want of trying or lack of help." Here he smiled at Tarla who flashed a beaming, bright-eyed smile back at him.

"Maybe it's all locked up with the memory problem. Maybe, if you get them back, everything else will follow."

Javin shrugged. "Maybe."

"What about talents? What shall we try, do you think?" Paysa turned to her daughter. "Any ideas? I have some time now."

Tarla looked unsure.

"Well, what do we know about talents?" Paysa used her fingers as she spoke. "There's empaths, like you, Tarla. Then there's eyes. And healers. And touchers, movers and finders, speakers and... who have I missed out?"

"What are all those you just said? Touchers? Finders?"

"They're the words I use for them. Others might call them different names. A toucher can touch something and know what happened to it, where it's been, who's handled it and so on. My father was one. Not great, but good enough. Came in handy when trading. And finders are the ones who can find things. Like springs of water. That stream you were sitting by today? A finder found that one. A speaker can be one of several types--"

"Stop, stop! This is too much at once."

Paysa grinned a little sheepishly. "You're right. We should talk less and do more." She looked around and then pointed. "Tarla can you get that for me, please?"

'That' was a carved piece of wood. Javin wasn't sure what it was meant to be, but it looked old and smoothed by much handling. Paysa turned it over in her hands, her eyes softening before she placed it in Javin's.

"There. Just get the feel of it and see if you can get anything from holding it." In answer to the query in Javin's eyes she added. "Could be anything. A picture. A sound or even a smell. Maybe just a feeling."

Javin tried his best to have some sort of impression. But nothing happened. After what he hoped was a decent period of time, he carefully put it down with a sigh. "Sorry. I seem to be saying that a lot."

Paysa stroked the wood gently with one finger. "This was my mother's. My father made it for her. His first gift. She always cherished it." She looked up, her eyes bright with memories. "Ah well. Never mind." She glanced around for another idea. "Perhaps we can try something else."

"Maybe," said Javin, "it's better if I try to find all this out on my own? You keep telling me that it's natural, that I should feel it. So it would be best if I wasn't pushing after it so much, perhaps? Just letting it happen. I know you want me to fit in. I know you want to help me. But I feel guilty enough for not working with Hanlar. And I'm stopping you and I'm taking Tarla away from her chores as well. It doesn't seem fair.

"Perhaps I should do what you suggested at first; take a little time on my own just to see if anything happens. But I'm not going to keep doing it. If I can have one more day? That should be long enough, shouldn't it? Whatever happens, in two days, I'll be back helping as much as I can. At least until Torrint shows up."

Javin noticed Tarla's crestfallen look which she tried to hide. He knew he was depriving her of something she had longed for, but he saw the understanding and appreciation on Paysa's face.

"You may be right, Javin. And it may also be that you are the clever one here." She patted Tarla on the shoulder as if to offer some brief consolation. "Don't be late for the meal. Nobody can speak you, so don't wander too far. I dare say your appetite will guide you back in time, won't it?"

Javin nodded and smiled. He leaned over the table towards Tarla. "Thank you again for your time and your thoughtfulness today. I will always remember it." She nodded mutely in return, not daring to look up.

As he left, Paysa mouthed 'Thank you' at him. He couldn't help but feel that Tarla would only remember the disappointment he had given her. But at least, it was a memory.

7

Being on his own outside, with no idea of what to do or how to do it, convinced Javin that it was a pointless waste of time. It also made him aware that he had been keeping promises to others but had nothing similar to offer himself. Being alone on the farm with nothing to do only served to emphasize his feeling of isolation which verged, at times, on desperation.

He had wandered away from the house, not knowing where to go. Aimless meandering had led him to the hill behind the house again. This time, he had gone a little further, up to the top, from where he could see over the roof and some way into the distance. Beyond were the stables, currently empty most days except for the large beasts, the mandrias, the same type that hauled Torrint's wagons. The strange patchwork of fields, some dotted with animals which he guessed were gomars, was more visible from here. He couldn't see Hanlar, but there were many tall growths blocking his view. There were no obvious boundaries. Nothing to say where this farm might end and the neighbor's began.

This was the first time he had truly been on his own. The times at Landing, he had been separate from the others, but someone, usually Bellis, had been nearby to check in on him. Today he had nobody nearby. Nobody to look in on him. Nobody to see if he needed a question answered. It was strange, and he wasn't sure how to adjust to it. Above, the sky was clear of machines. Only clouds and natural flying things, birds or something like them. No machines anywhere. No sounds of them humming quietly, making machine noises, providing the background to the few memories he had. No metals and the echoes of hard surfaces. The alien nature of this world was unsettling, not because of the massive differences, but because of the minor ones: the smells, the noises, the sounds. He couldn't be sure, but he felt slightly heavier, but maybe that was simply due to eating well. And the food was certainly different. He was on a truly different world, so different that it had taken him until now to begin to appreciate how strange it was.

Just below the crown, on the side opposite to the house, was a place where bushes and shrubs were interspersed with larger tree-like growths. It seemed as good a place as any to rest. Sitting beneath a shading tree (or whatever it's called, he thought), he realized that he didn't care at all about getting a talent, about hearing Harmony. It was what everyone else wanted for him. What difference could it possibly make if he 'heard' Harmony, or if he could move things with his mind? It would not change his situation. He would still be here.

It was not what he wanted. And what he did want he could not have, apparently. There was nothing he could do about any of it; not about reaching Torrint, not about finding a healer, not about getting his memories back, not about his life. Nothing. And, although he could think that, and had been thinking it since arriving at the farm, this day it began to settle inside him, become a burr in his head. And, as he sat and stared and felt his aloneness, his powerlessness, so it began to rub at him.

Despite not wanting to have it intrude, he was aware that there was also guilt nibbling at him. Guilt at taking the time off to relax, knowing that the other three people were busily working. He wondered if this feeling was truly his, a part of his real being, who he really was. Was he actually someone who truly cared about others, or was this a change which had happened since his memory loss? Was it normal for him to make promises to others and feel the need to keep them? It felt natural, but what did he know? Wasn't there the possibility that he was a heartless sociopath who lived only for himself?

There was the inner confusion and then there was the outer world, where nothing happened. Nothing except sunlight fading into the strange new moonlight and unending work. But if there was nothing inside him that was truly himself, then nothing outside mattered. So where did guilt come from? Why keep promises?

Unable to resolve anything, he decided that he would find Hanlar and go back to working. It was, he thought, the only thing he could do and have some measure of control over. He could work until he ached, until his body begged him to stop. And that would be his choice. He could then, he realized, know himself through the pain he gave himself. It was the only way to prove to himself that he was someone; a separate being, an individual. No past and no future. Only the present ache, where the body was central and the mind had only a minor supporting role.

With that resolution made, he set about finding Hanlar. He didn't feel like having to explain his decision to Paysa, so chose not to ask her to ask Hanlar where he was. Instead, he decided to keep going in the general direction he had seen him take in the morning and look and listen really hard.

It took some time, but he eventually caught up with Hanlar as he had put a shovel down and was kneeling by a bag, tugging it open.

Hanlar looked up and noticed the change straight away. "Are you sure you don't need more time? I don't mind. I'm quite used to working out here--".

Javin cut him off. "I'm ready to work. That's what I want to do."

Hanlar thought about saying something else but then thought better of it. Instead, he gestured at a bag on the ground. "This needs planting in that area I just finished digging."

"No. I want to do the digging. You plant. I'll dig." And with that, Javin picked up the shovel and began turning over the soil in a way which, as Hanlar would later describe it to Paysa, was as if he wanted to kill something, but didn't know what it was he was looking for.

That evening, the meal was conducted mostly in silence. Javin felt a small and brief twinge of guilt when Tarla sat down. She looked as if she had been crying and was not capable of meeting his eyes. Hanlar and Paysa chose to say nothing, hoping to let emotions drain themselves with time. Javin had no wish to talk to anyone, especially about his decision to ignore the whole 'connect with Harmony' thing.

As the table was being cleared and Tarla headed out for her evening chores, Hanlar called her back. "Why don't you have an evening off? I'm sure that Javin wouldn't mind taking care of the mandria for a change, would you?"

Javin had been going to sit outside until it got dark. He shrugged as if it would not be a bother to him.

"They just need a brushing and make sure the water is flowing to them. Check the feed and collect any hairs around. They like the stables for some reason although they'd be fine outside. But, it's where they like to go at night, so that's how it is." Hanlar spoke without emotion, but Javin knew that he was anxious to get him out and allow him time to let off any coiled up energy he had left after the afternoon's labor. Hanlar was helping Javin keep his promise to the family by getting him outside and away.

He walked down the slight slope to the stables. They were really not much more than high walls made of wood and clay, covered with a sloped roof of more timber and tightly woven or plaited fronds tied to it. He was aware that his body certainly knew of his efforts today, just as he had promised himself.

Entering the stables, he saw there were three large mandria already there who turned their heads to look at him. They were larger than the ones that had hauled Torrint's wagons, standing taller at the shoulder than Javin by a good two handspans. Large eyes of a startlingly bright yellow gazed at him with quiet interest. They were massive creatures but incredibly gentle, as Javin had learned. They looked quite capable of destroying the stables simply by leaning on the wall, but instead stood in a little group in the middle of the space as if they were nothing more than a few friends waiting for the last one of their group to arrive. And here he was.

Javin, despite never having had anything to do with animals before (as far as he knew, he always added in his mind), had never felt the least bit concerned at being near them. He had watched Hanlar and Tarla brush and feed them several times.

The mandria ambled a little nearer on wide, flat feet with three broad toes splayed out; real toes, which curled and gripped and were equipped with blunt black nails or claws. They wanted to inspect him better, nostrils wide as they took in his scent. The spiral-shaped horns were flat against their huge heads, forming coils out of which stuck large, shaggy ears. One poked a very long, very slim tongue, split near the end so that there were two independent tips, and rested it gently on his arm, as if tasting him, the tips dancing delicately across his skin, before withdrawing.

Javin didn't know why, but he felt safe with them. First, he picked up the wooden rake and dragged out the manure and dirty straw, piling it up outside to be collected later for fertilizing. He leaned and pushed and cajoled his way through the mandria to find the water trough. He made sure that the flow was unobstructed. He plucked out some stray debris and made sure that the overflow was able to drain freely before picking up a large stiff brush from its place near the door.

Dragging the brush across their hides seemed to be a soothing experience for them. A deep out-breath, like a sigh, escaped, stirring the dust on the floor, and the mandria lowered his head, closing his eyes as Javin brushed the loose hair out. He grabbed it with his free hand, depositing the pile in the wide clay bowl next to the brush's place. He would take it with him when he left. The fibers were thick and rough but they could be washed and made into pads and cloths which were heat resistant and highly durable. Paysa showed him the end result, but it was Tarla who actually made them.

If the brushing seemed to relax the mandria, it definitely relaxed Javin. Being with these beasts, brushing them, feeling more than hearing the reverberations they made deep inside their deep chests, was more calming than anything else he had done since his arrival. He enjoyed the rhythm of the brush and feeling the warm breath of one of them on his neck. The tiredness of his body, as much as the quiet companionship he felt, allowed his mind to drift. After a while, he began to hear a sound, almost a tune, in his head. It drifted in and out of his awareness. When he tried to listen to it, it lessened, became almost silent. When he went back to brushing and mindless drifting, so it became more evident, but always only in the periphery of his hearing. It deepened his relaxation, seemed to ease the aches and pains of the day. As he finished with the last beast and put away

ANDREW ELGIN

the brush, so the music drifted into silence, completely vanishing as he left the stable with his handfuls of hair from the mandria. Because it felt like a real tune, it didn't seem to be anything like Tarla had tried to explain. He thought it might be some old song from his past trying to break through. Which made him happy at first, but then he swiftly returned to his earlier mood. If that was all he got from his past life, was it really worth it? A snatch of a song. No. It was not worth getting his hopes up for.

Back in the house, Paysa was finishing up some chores in the kitchen area, while Hanlar was working some leather on the table. Tarla looked up briefly with still sad eyes as he shut the door and placed the hair in the larger receptacle there before turning her attention back to the mending in her hand.

Javin cleaned his hands off, poured himself a drink of water, still slightly cool from the spring behind the house, and leaned against the wall as he drank it in one long series of swallows.

"How did it go?" Hanlar asked.

"Good. They seem to enjoy it, don't they?"

Hanlar nodded. "They're gentle. It's good to be around them." It was Javin's turn to nod agreement. "Why don't you take that job over for the time being? There's plenty of other things Tarla can do and you don't seem to mind."

Javin thought for a moment. "Yes. I can do that."

And so it was that each day ended with Javin tending to the beasts, arriving with a tired body and leaving with a relaxed mind. The anger was muted somehow by the beasts. They accepted him as he was and did not care whether he had any talent or any memories. He looked forward to their company. And, every now and then, sometimes stronger, sometimes weaker but always present, was the 'almost music', the 'nearly song', in the background, the sounds which seemed to accompany his time with the mandria.

The days passed and the idea of reclaiming his memories became more remote. Javin worked his body hard to burn the rough edges from his anger to where it might be able to slide more silently down into his life, leave the surface, become less. His body became tougher, and as a result, his strength and stamina grew. The tasks were the same but becoming easier. But that did not mean that they had any deeper interest for him. Life on the farm was not becoming more attractive. It was still just work and nothing else. It seemed that Hanlar and Paysa had given up on him discovering his talent, and Tarla had come to accept that there would be no possibility of bridging the gap between herself and Javin. But he could still see the disappointment in her eyes. Javin had decided that he would leave as soon as possible. Torrint or some other person with transport would be available. And whenever that was, he would go with them. Where would not matter. But leaving would be his choice and no-one else's.

It was in that frame of mind, of thinking about leaving, that Javin was with the mandria again one evening. The sun was low and the air warm with just a gently erratic breeze stirring the topmost strands of a mound of straw, about hip height, just inside the stables. As usual, the mandria were waiting for him and, as usual, took turns to smell and taste him. It had been a hard day for Javin. The morning had consisted of digging a long trench to take water to another field. That had been followed by wrestling the striped pecornas, their usual humming sounds making a softly complaining choir, into a different field where the grazing was more lush. Then there had been the backbreaking task of harvesting weaver's weed which grew in clumps where water was close to the surface. The reed-like plants had roughened edges which would rub his arms raw if he wasn't careful. Cutting, carrying and stacking them for later soaking and beating into threads which could be woven (hence the name) had taken the rest of the day. And here he was now with this last chore.

The water trough needed cleaning out as usual and a fresh pile of feed needed to be brought in and placed where the mandria could nibble on it during the night. Javin finished cleaning out the trough and making sure the water supply was not obstructed outside as it trickled in under the wall of the stables. Then he raked the floor clean. Satisfied with that, he decided to take a rest for a moment and eased himself down to sit against the wall from where he could look out the door and watch the play of light and shade. The mandria ambled over to him, huffing and making those deep thrummings which rumbled over and through him. It was almost like being massaged by the sound and he automatically relaxed even more.

As he did so, the music, the tune he could almost make out, began to increase in volume. He had never heard it in the fields with Hanlar, so he assumed it was something to do with the sounds of the big beasts affecting his hearing. A part of him wondered again if it was a tune from his earlier life and that his memory was coming back to him. He didn't recognize it, but, then again, without any memory, that wasn't surprising. Before, it had been much quieter. This time, however, the sound was stronger, more nearly a tune he could hum himself. It was somehow simpler to listen to or perhaps the familiarity of it made is easier to follow. Whatever it was, he allowed himself to let it into his head. He reached up idly to scratch the large head of the nearest mandria under the chin; an act which caused the thrumming to increase markedly. Javin smiled to himself. The music in his head, the contentment of the beasts and his own physical release made for a dreamlike state.

Scratching and listening, he could almost see how the music might go. Not listening so much, as understanding the tune and what it was going to do. He gradually felt more comfortable with this understanding. Still scratching, his glance fell on the pile of straw by the door and he thought about how that task was still waiting. At the same time, he felt like there was something missing in the music, just a short series of notes, a cadence or two, which would complement it, give it something new. He heard the music and he heard the sounds he thought would enhance it. Suddenly, the mandria jerked its head away and huffed twice in what felt like a warning. Javin was jerked into full awareness himself and saw, without believing, the pile of straw in mid-air falling to the ground beside the beast as if it had been thrown by invisible hands.

Javin was astonished. There was no sudden wind. That was obvious from the stillness of the plants outside. And yet, it had happened. He was too amazed to realize that the music was no longer audible. All he could see was a thrown pile of straw and no explanation for it happening.

The mandria soon got over its nervousness and began to pick at the straw and chew. Javin, however, was not so sanguine and looked for any explanation, but found none. He got up to see if there could have been any more straw stored out of sight and which might have fallen. But it was obvious that it had been the pile by the door which had been thrown. There was no other straw.

Mystified but without answers, Javin turned to completing his task; the spreading of the straw and the brushing. As he worked, he wondered if he should say anything. Perhaps something like this was normal, although he very much doubted it. But during the course of finishing brushing the mandria, he had decided to keep it to himself. If it happened again, then he would say something. For now, though, it was simply a strange incident, which, the more he thought about it became a little less strange. Just something which had happened.

He was not to find out if it would be repeated, because, on the following day, just after midday, Torrint's wagons were seen creaking along the pathway to the house.

8

Torrint had arrived. Javin was told by Hanlar, who had been informed by Paysa.

"Let's go back and meet them. We'll be in time for some lunch." Hanlar brushed the dirt from his hands.

Now the moment had arrived, Javin felt a little sad. A part of him regretted leaving Hanlar with so much work to do. It didn't matter that Hanlar enjoyed it or that he didn't seem to think of it as work; the feeling persisted. Javin wiped his hands on the front of his tunic and held out his hand to Hanlar, who looked at it as if he didn't know what to do. Javin leaned forward and grabbed Hanlar's rough hand and shook it. The puzzlement was still evident.

"It's something we do where I grew up. A way of saying hello, or goodbye, or thank you. That's all." He shrugged. "I just wanted to say thank you and also goodbye."

Hanlar was still mystified but smiled anyway. "So there are things you do remember?"

"Things like that, they're sort of buried in me somewhere deep enough that they stayed, I suppose," Javin said. "I only just realized that I knew it." He smiled slightly. "I really do want to thank you for helping me, Hanlar. I mean it. I don't know what I would have done otherwise."

Hanlar brushed that aside with a motion of his hands. "No need to thank me. You helped me, remember?"

"Anyway, I'm sorry I've been in a bad mood for most of the time."

"But the mandrias help, don't they?"

"About that --."

Hanlar stopped him. "Tarla will be all right about looking after them again. She had a rest as well. And I do know that she will miss you. A lot." Hanlar shrugged. "But she will get over it. Now, let's get back. As you know, we don't often have visitors, so it's important we spend as much time as possible with them. Much to be talked about. Fresh news! And I will have to buy Tarla something to cheer her up, I suppose." He smiled a genuine smile which reached his eyes, and they began the walk back to the house.

"Why didn't you trade with Torrint when I arrived?" Javin asked.

"He was doing a favor. He didn't arrive to trade, but to bring you," Hanlar explained. "He could have tried to sell something, but he didn't. But now he's back again, he'll want to take advantage of it. That's why I like him."

When they arrived, Torrint was sitting on the porch, long legs stretched in front of him, sipping on the inevitable beaker of simesh, and Banith was leading the mandria down to the stables. Paysa and Tarla were investigating the back of Torrint's wagon and inspecting various items.

As Javin and Hanlar walked up, Torrint acknowledged them both with that slow nod of his head, his face showing no particular emotion.

Tarla had spotted her father and rushed up to him with several long, bright feathers in her hand. They seemed to glow and reflect light in a shimmering kaleidoscope of color.

"Oh, please may we get these? They are so beautiful! I've never seen anything like them before." She stroked them gently against her cheek, eyes closed, savoring the feel of them. Hanlar grinned knowingly at Javin and cleared his throat.

"Well, we'll have to see if we can afford them. There's all sorts of things we need."

"Oh, but these are so beautiful! Just think how they would look inside! They would make anything better!" Her tone was pleading, her face imploring her father to see what she saw in them. Paysa watched her with a smile on her face.

"What exactly are they anyway?" asked Hanlar. "I don't recall seeing such things before."

Torrint wiped his mouth on his sleeve and put the beaker down beside him carefully. "Those are the feathers of a gorry. Good ones, like those, are rare."

Paysa sniffed. "Bound to be, aren't they? I don't suppose you have any that aren't so good?"

Torrint just cocked his head to one side and a wry grin spread slowly across his face.

"No. I thought not. Silly of me to ask, wasn't it?" Paysa harumphed and turned back to her investigation of the wagon, but there was a smile on her face as well. Tarla meanwhile kept pressing Hanlar to feel the feathers for himself.

"All right, Tarla. I make no promises. We'll see if we can afford them." This was met with a squeal of delight. "I can't promise, Tarla! Oh, why do I bother even trying?" Hanlar grinned hugely at his daughter. "Go on. Take them inside. I'll sort something out with Torrint."

Watching them, Javin realized that having the trader arrive like this was a big event. It was like seeing into another part of the world. He hadn't understood that when he had arrived, but watching it now, he felt, once again, how isolated everyone was, how apart they were. The banter, the haggling and the wonder at seeing new things made such visits hugely important, he realized. He now understood better what Hanlar had said, that Torrint had not offered any trading opportunities when he had brought Javin because he knew that being taken in by the family was far bigger than anything he could do. But today was obviously different.

Later that day, as they sat finishing a meal of meat, spiced (free of charge) from one of Torrint's pots, some vegetables and hunks of bread to mop everything up, Hanlar and Torrint disappeared outside to settle up. Paysa and Tarla looked over their purchases approvingly, pointing out the finer details to each other. Banith had gone to check on the mandria and brought back some hair he had brushed out. Paysa pushed some more bread and a beaker of simesh at him as thanks.

Soon enough, the other two men returned. Torrint eased himself onto a stool, declining the offer of a chair, saying that they never made them in a way which was comfortable for him. He accepted another beaker of simesh and turned his attention to Javin.

"I got the message and I'm here. But what is it you actually need?" His clear eyes fixed themselves on Javin over the rim of the beaker.

"I want to find a healer who can help me get my memories back."

"Memories? You can't remember anything?"

"I can only remember some things. And nothing from early in my life. I'd like to get them back."

Torrint nodded. "That would be... annoying, I suppose." He paused. "I know a few healers. And maybe one of them could help you."

"But you're not sure." It was a statement, not a question.

"Obviously not, since nobody I know has lost their memory before. But," and he spread his hands, "since some healers are better than none, it's worth going to see them, don't you think?"

Javin nodded. "How long will it take, do you think?"

Torrint smiled, showing his blue teeth. "As long as it takes. Maybe the first healer will be fine. Maybe none will be able to heal you." He stood and bowed at Hanlar and Paysa, a smaller bow to Tarla, touching his brow as he did so. "Thank you for the trading and the food. Banith and I will leave in the morning." He turned to Javin. "Early." And with that, the two traders left, to sleep with their wagons, Javin supposed.

9

S itting next to Torrint, Javin watched the countryside ease past them. Leaving the farm, he took a far keener interest in looking at it than he had when he had arrived.

As promised, they had set out very early, the sun barely above the horizon. Javin had bundled his few possessions together and hoisted himself up beside Torrint. With a last courteous bow to the family, Torrint had eased the wagon into motion. Javin had said his goodbyes the previous evening. Despite his eagerness to leave, he had found it difficult to find the right words. It wouldn't have mattered what he had said to Tarla. She had not been able to hide her disappointment, her sadness, and had clung to him for a brief moment as her parents stood close by with a sad, knowing look on their faces. She had not come to the door to wave him off. But, when he looked back one last time, he saw her being hugged by her mother as Hanlar raised his hand in farewell.

It was not long before all the familiar landmarks were behind and what lay ahead was new and unknown. Torrint was still not much interested in conversation, so there were long periods of silence as before. Occasionally, Javin would ask about some part of the landscape and Torrint would tell him about it briefly before lapsing again into silence.

Javin realized with something of a shock that he was actually missing the hard work, the laboring in the fields. It had been a routine he had known and come to accept without wanting to acknowledge it.

"When we stop," he said, "I can look after the mandria for you. I used to do that every evening back on the farm."

Torrint continued his chewing and nodded toward the beast. "This un's Kesit." Using his thumb to point behind he added, "The one pulling Banith's wagon is Kasser. Make sure they have no sore spots from harness rubbing them. Hobble them, brush them and in the morning check them over again for bites or anything else. They'll feed themselves, plus they like a little bit of water."

"I can do that. Is there anything else I can do to help?"

Torrint scratched behind his ear with one long finger as he thought. "Maybe. It's going to be a while before the healer. We'll see what else you're good at."

"How long do you think it will take to get there? Is it very far?" Javin was eager to know.

Torrint jutted his lower lip out and wrinkled his nose. "Depends."

"On what?"

"Trading, the weather, if Kesit stays healthy, lots of things."

"Well, how far is the nearest healer?"

"There's one in Red River, and another in Sweetwater. Either might work. We'll see."

Javin felt himself becoming annoyed. "And how far away are they?"

Torrint frowned at him. "How far? How do you measure? I measure in days, or trades, or sometimes the weather at the turn of seasons. And one affects the other. A big trade adds days. Many small trades add days. No trades, fewer days." He spat out the leaves and wiped his mouth. "How far they are is how long it will take to get there. If you get your memories back before then, that's fine. If not, you won't have lost any more, will you?"

Javin didn't know how to respond. Yet again he was faced with another huge gap, impossible to bridge, between what he knew and how the people on Harmony thought. How could he explain highways or speed or distances so that it would mean the same to them as to him? Defeated, it was his turn to lapse into silence.

That night, Javin took over the care of Kesit and Kasser from Banith, after being shown how to hobble them with two lengths of braided leather passed around and between their front legs and tied loosely.

Brushing them, he felt himself begin to relax again as he had with the ones back in the stable. He even heard a snatch of that music again. It sounded familiar. If only he could recall where he had heard it before. It was frustrating. If it was his memory coming back, then maybe just allowing it to happen would be the best thing he could do. Maybe the healer would be a waste of time.

Until he was more certain, he decided to say nothing.

The days passed slowly, allowing Javin to find a new rhythm. Sometimes he walked beside the wagon or sat with Banith. There was the faint track which they followed, undulating across the ground, two half-covered wheel ruts, vague depressions, barely visible. Each evening and morning he tended to the mandrias and listened to the music which came through when the wagons stopped creaking.

One evening, sitting up against one of the solid wheels, staring into the red embers of the fire, Javin asked, "What's the strangest thing you've seen in your travels?"

Torrint sucked on a tooth for a moment, pondering. Before he could speak, however, Banith said, "For me, that would be the fire on the ground, moving slowly along. That was very strange to see."

"Fire? Moving along the ground?" Javin pointed. "Like our fire here?"

Banith shook his head. "This was much, much bigger. There was a huge fire, much smoke. It looked like a mountain was on fire. It was a long way away, but the ground was on fire, or it seemed to be. It seemed to be coming from the burning mountain. It burned everything it touched. I couldn't get near to it. It was like it was tumbling very slowly." Banith's hands moved to show what he meant.

Javin puzzled over this for a moment. Then he said, "Was this mountain, the one in the distance, did it have rumblings and loud noises as well as a lot of smoke?"

"Yes."

"I know what that's called! That's a volcano! And the fire on the ground, that's lava." He gave a short laugh, shaking his head in surprise. "Now how did I know that, if I can't remember anything else?"

"Lava. Volcano." Banith spoke the words slowly as if to memorize them.

"Maybe you're getting your memory back a bit at a time." That was from Torrint.

"Have you ever seen a volcano yourself, Javin?" Banith asked.

Javin smiled ruefully. "That's the problem. I know the word, what it means, but I don't recall having seen one. Maybe I did and that's how I know the word. I just know that's what they're called and what they do." He gave a small sigh, as if of regret. "What about you, Torrint? What's the strangest thing you've seen?"

"That would be the first time I saw the sea." He smiled at the recollection. "All that water in one place, not going anywhere else."

"You've seen it more than once, then? Is it far from here?" Javin put his hand up to stop any answer. "I'm sorry. You can't tell me. It depends on how long it takes to get there, right?"

"All I can tell you is that it would take a long journey to get there." Torrint considered this a moment, then added, "Very long."

Javin wondered what that might translate as. "So the next place is Red River?"

Both Torrint and Banith nodded.

"And that's much closer, I hope? And with a healer?"

"There was a healer there. Maybe still is. We'll see." That from Torrint.

"How long ago were you there last?" asked Javin.

Torrint thought for a moment. "Last time we were there was... beginning of the summer?" He looked to Banith for confirmation, who nodded his agreement.

"So not that long ago, then?" Javin was eager to find out as much as he could. "We're still in summer now, aren't we?"

Again, Torrint nodded. "Yes. You arrived at Landing maybe around the middle of summer. Maybe later." He dug a finger into his ear as he thought more. "Probably about then."

Javin thought back and realized how much time he had already spent here. Back on Haven, he felt sure, summer would be nearly over in the same span of time. "So this is late summer, is it?"

"No. Late summer happens when the mandria stop shedding and the coat grows thicker. Still a long time for that to happen."

Without a calendar, without clocks, Javin realized, he had no way of knowing just how much time was passing. Here, you told the time by what happened to animals' coats! The beginning of summer suddenly seemed a long way off. In all that time perhaps the healer had left or died or given up healing. His hopes, which had begun to rise, fell swiftly.

Torrint, oblivious to Javin's hopes, said, "We should be seeing the red hill soon, and after that, it's a day or three to Red River. Then we trade."

10

Torrint was right. The next day, an abrupt hill with sheer red cliffs, deep red in the sun, was duly passed, and two days after that, they pulled up on a slope leading down to a cluster of buildings. Red River. So called because it ran through the same red rocks the hill had been made of.

They made camp, even though it was the afternoon. "We trade tomorrow," Torrint explained as they went through the familiar routine. "They will know we're here. We don't start late in the day. Trading should be relaxed. Allow people time. There is never a rush, or there are regrets. And regrets are not good for business." He suddenly seemed loquacious, albeit with spaces between sentences. But Javin realized he was explaining for his sake, to help him understand the proper way of things here.

"Imagine if someone traded with us in haste and went away with something they did not want. There would be a very long time before they saw us again. A long time to build up distrust. And, we must have trust, Javin. No trust, no trade."

The next morning, they set off directly after breakfast. Torrint normally leaned against the wagon as he ate. This morning , however, he had closed himself off in the rear of the wagon, reappearing after a short while with a brief nod to Banith. As they drew nearer, the scattered woodlands gave way to occasional fields and hedges in the now familiar scattered, seemingly random, arrangement. Some few houses with their tell-tale thin flag of smoke from the chimneys were to be seen some distance from the path which was becoming more defined. It was impossible to know by looking where one family's fields began and a neighbor's left off. There was an informal blending of human effort and natural growth which could only happen over time and with continual care. Fences disappeared into stands of trees, became trees (or what passed for trees in Javin's mind), or ended in carefully tended patches of some plant or other. The effect was undeniably intriguing to the eye, which sought for, but failed to find, obvious patterns in the landscape.

"I can't think that anyone here has much to trade with, have they?" asked Javin as they rumbled slowly along.

Torrint flashed his blue-stained teeth at Javin briefly. "Every place has something to trade. Always something. Here we are going to buy good plait which can be made up into bags or hats or belts by those who've a mind to do it." He pointed across Javin at a tall crop of red and yellow flowers growing a pace or two back from the track. "Those? They are a type of flake. Good for nice smells if you burn the dry leaves. They are not the best quality this year, but good enough. There'll be some hides as well." He shrugged. "Depends. But there's always something. Even if it's just information."

"Information? What sort of information can you buy or sell?"

Torrint tilted his head and smiled. "Whatever is valuable, obviously. News from one place to another. Between people. Good crops in one place, or bigger numbers of pests. Whatever is valuable. You, for example. You are information. New information."

"How am I information?" Javin wasn't sure whether to be interested or offended.

"You have stories to tell." Torrint shrugged. "So, you have only some memories, but they are new here. That's information. Whether you want to tell them to others is up to you. And if you want to trade them, that's for you to decide."

Javin couldn't help but be intrigued. "How can I trade my memories, even if I had any worth trading, that is?"

"Trade is exchanging things, yes?"

Javin nodded.

"You have memories, which are really just new stories for people here. And people here have food and shelter. Which is not what you have." Torrint looked him squarely in the eye. "You have a ride. But that's all. You help with the mandria and that's payment at the moment." Torrint pointed back and forth between the two of them. "We are trading. But perhaps you didn't know that?" Then he lapsed back into silence and left Javin to mull over the idea that, perhaps, he could end up as a story teller. After all, people here never went anywhere (apart from Torrint and Banith, of course). He remembered the eagerness with which Tarla had questioned him. Would it really be possible for him to make a living off his past? No matter what, Javin had to regain his memories.

The distance between the homes lessened as they went on. In the place of fields of crops or small herds of animals, there were gardens with brightly colored plants and what passed for trees growing in them as well as some smaller animals moving around. The occasional dog cart was also seen moving along paths off in the distance. The dogs, Javin noticed, even from that far away, really were as big as Tarla had intimated. They pulled small carts at a steady pace with one or sometimes two people in them, much faster than Kesit's steady plod. Eventually, some time before midday by Javin's estimate, Torrint led the wagons a couple of paces from the center of the path and brought them to a halt. There was nothing to suggest any heavy regular traffic. It was a quiet place. But then, Javin reminded himself, the whole planet was quiet.

He had not really known what to expect about actually trading. Javin thought that there would be a lot of people and there would be some pushing and shoving, loud voices and generally a crush of people.

The reality was entirely different. Torrint and Banith eased the wagons so that they were back to back, about five paces apart. The mandria had been led off and hobbled in an area where they could graze and then some boards were laid across two trestles and Torrint placed what seemed to be an arbitrary selection of goods on them. That done, he and Banith sat on small stools and put their feet up. Javin was relegated to either the ground or anywhere on the wagons he wanted.

While they waited for anyone to show some interest in their arrival, Torrint offered some unexpected insights into his life.

"You might as well know, probably guessed, that Banith and me have talents?"

Javin nodded.

"Guess mine."

"I don't know." He was genuinely puzzled. "Able to guess the right price of something?"

Torrint smiled, showing those unsettling teeth. "Try again."

Javin shrugged. "I have only heard of some talents. I can't guess." In the face of Torrint's amusement, he blurted out, "You can see the future?"

To his amazement, Torrint nodded. "More or less. Yes. And Banith? What do you reckon his talent is then?"

"Look, that was a lucky guess. I have no idea what talents there are. So, if you really want me to guess... ," Torrint nodded, "then I'd say Banith can move things with his mind."

It was Banith's turn to grin. "That would be fun, I think. But, no, that's not me. I can pick up something and get a glimpse of its past." He shrugged as if there was nothing else to add.

"I look forward. He looks back, said Torrint. "I look for trade and he looks to see if the trade is a good one, if what is offered is really as it is said. So you can see how such things can be helpful in what we do?"

"I suppose so. But what's more puzzling is why are you telling me?"

It was Torrint's turn to shrug. "Could be useful. If you end up trading. Could be something you do. And, we're together now. It's right that you should know how we work."

Javin didn't know how to respond. Here was Torrint, the taciturn trader, sharing secrets with him. Almost as if he were expecting Javin to be a trader. With Torrint and Banith. It was acceptance. It was a gesture which meant much more than what was said.

"Thank you! I am very grateful for you telling me."

Torrint pointed one long finger at him. "And if you tell anyone else... ." His voice tailed off into an implied threat. Javin raised his hands to show his agreement to secrecy.

And as suddenly as that conversation had started, so it stopped, leaving Javin to consider how much two such talents could be useful when trading, and wondering when, if ever, he would develop a talent and what it would be.

Shortly after, a couple of women ambled towards them, chatting and carrying a large, shapeless leather bag between them. One was tall and rangy with a permanent frown on her tanned face whilst the other was only a little less tall but sturdy, with strong, stubby hands and eyes that looked like they had laughed a lot. They both had long, loose hair tumbling down their backs. The taller of the two had kept her brown hair from her face with a strip of cloth tied at the back of her neck. The other woman had plaited her hair in a complex style so that three separate braids; one on each side and one down the middle of her head, met at the back where they were tied off with a piece of leather, allowing the rest of it to swing free. They arrived seemingly by accident at the improvised table where Torrint nodded affably at them. They seemed not very interested in what they saw and neither Torrint nor Banith seemed anxious to speak with them. It was not at all what Javin expected.

Finally, the sturdy one heaved the bag onto the table and asked, "What will you give us for this?"

Torrint leaned forward without getting up and opened the bag with one finger, inclining his head and squinting to see inside. "Is that all, Elissa?"

"Of course it is," she smiled. "And you won't find better while you're here." Jerking a thumb at her companion, she continued, "Serrine and me, you know our work. We make the best plait and have done for years. In fact, with all those years of experience, our plait's not just the best here, but probably there's none better. That'd be my guess. Well?" And she folded her arms, her whole body challenging Torrint to disagree with her assessment.

Javin now watched with interest, wanting to see how this would play out. Torrint made a begrudging nod with his head, but his face made it abundantly clear that he was still not totally convinced of the truth of Elissa's argument. He peered once more into the bag. "Is this the same amount as last time?" Elissa and Serrine both nodded. "Hmmmm. Credit or trade?"

"Bit of both would be fine."

Torrint paused, more for effect than anything else was Javin's opinion. Finally, he placed his hands flat on the table and peered up at Elissa. "Start with the trade and we'll see about the credit." And Torrint nodded at Banith who stood up, took the bag inside his wagon and returned with it empty a moment later, handing it back to Elissa.

Then the real haggling began. So much of this spice, or that dye or some fresh deadspread. 'And what about these herbs? Or that cloth? And that's a ridiculous amount for all that work we've done and why are you being so mean? And as for those feathers, they're damaged surely?'

And from Torrint it was all, 'But I have costs as well, you can't get better than those, this is the freshest you'll ever find, here, if you don't believe me, taste it yourself'.

On and on and to and fro, and a pile grew slowly in front of the women until they were satisfied. The finale came in the shape of a transfer of some carved wooden pieces, each with a splash of blue on them. The women appeared to want to haggle further, but under Torrint's steady stare, they backed down and scooped the pieces up with a quick flick of fingers to forehead. Torrint responded by tapping twice on his chest and extended the hand palm up to them.

Elissa and Serrine bagged their goods and wandered away again, deep in conversation, passing the next people arriving to trade.

"What are the wooden things they took? I've not seen them before," asked Javin when they were out of earshot.

"Credit."

Javin gestured him to explain further.

"My credit. The blue is me," he said pointing to his distinctive teeth. "Next time we come through here, they'll bring them out and we'll disagree on how much we agreed they were worth, and then we'll end up agreeing and I'll get them back until next time."

"What about other traders? Would they take them?"

Banith grinned. "There are no other traders. Only us. Worked metal is rare. Very rare. Credit is easy. As long as everyone agrees what it is. It could be worked stone. That's valuable because it's rare to have good crafting in stone small enough to trade. Anything that can't be eaten or planted or which will rot or dissolve. We made our own from a wood that we got from the south a long time ago. Doesn't grow here, so it's what we use."

Javin could see how simple and sensible the process was. It worked. That was the main thing.

As time passed and Javin had nothing to do, he decided to look around. As he was about to go, Torrint called out to him, "Here. Buy some fresh bread for us," and he tossed a small bag which rattled as Javin caught it. He made a 'what now?' face at Torrint who merely smiled and said, "Go and look around. You'll find it," before turning back to his latest customer.

Javin wandered aimlessly for a while. He opened the leather bag Torrint had given him and saw a strange collection of several tiny pieces of gold, half the size of a fingernail, a few equally small circular pieces of metal he thought were probably coins of some kind, and a variety of other objects: a large black pebble, or maybe it was a seed, something that looked like a bright red shell and two or three of the credit tokens, but smaller than the ones he had seen earlier. He had no idea what any of it was worth.

Red River looked and felt like a small place. The center of it, where he had left Torrint and Banith, had patches of green and the tracks leading into and out of it were wider, but they were still tracks. There were few people around. The whole place seemed... so small, so quiet, so strange. The few people he did see were off in the distance. Everyone else seemed to be either inside or perhaps were now trading with Torrint.

Javin began to feel hungry and turned a corner only to nearly bump into a woman. She avoided him neatly by stepping smartly to one side, her lined face further creased in a wide smile, blue eyes sparkling with good humor.

"I knew it! There you are! Right on time!" she chortled.

Javin, having regained his balance from nearly colliding with her, just stared at her in confusion.

"Right where I saw it. Never fails." She peered more closely at Javin and became a little more serious. "I saw you," she explained, speaking more slowly now. "I knew you'd be there. I was ready." Another pause, then a sense of confusion. "Are you ill? Why are you looking that way at me? You don't look ill." She sized him up before continuing a little more gently. "Do you mind?" She reached out to rest her hand on Javin's arm. He was still unsure how to react to this woman and her initially cheerful foreknowledge of his being there. She closed her eyes for a moment and then frowned before opening them again and taking her hand away.

"I don't mean to pry, but there's something missing, something not quite right." She wrinkled her nose as she tried to find the right words. "It's like there's something, some connection, missing. It's like, and I don't mean anything bad by it, but it's like you can't hear Harmony." A nervously apologetic smile flashed across her face.

Javin had begun to relax his body, but he opened his eyes wide at the diagnosis he had just received. "You're right. Absolutely right. I'm not from here, from Harmony." He pointed up to the sky and felt vaguely foolish as he did so. "I'm from Haven. The other planet? I got kidnapped and dumped here. And everyone tells me I should be hearing Harmony. But..., " he shrugged, "I can't seem to. So you're exactly right."

"Haven? Hmmm. Not heard of that place. But it's good to know," said the woman, before hurrying to correct herself. "I meant, it's good to know I was right, not that it was good you can't hear Harmony, or not knowing of Haven." She reddened in embarrassment but found a way out of it by introducing herself. "Sharna. Sharna Messilna." And she made the same gesture he had seen before of touching her forehead with her fingers and turning them out towards him. "Everyone here knows I'm an eye, that I see things. It doesn't bother them. I'm respectful. They all know that. I saw us, just before it happened, nearly walking into each other and I thought this one was close. I didn't really take the time to look at you properly." Her gaze swept over Javin a little more carefully this time. "I am so sorry." Her voice took on a sweetly sad tone as if sorrowing gently for his lack of understanding.

Javin remembered something that Paysa said about one of the talents being called an 'eye'. "Are you saying that you saw us meeting like this? You can see things that are going to happen?"

The woman nodded and smiled at Javin as if he was a very young child who had just discovered something so obvious as to be not worth mentioning.

"So you saw us talking like this as well, then?" Javin asked.

The woman shook her head. "I shut it off after seeing the near miss. If I kept looking all day, I'd never get anything done, would I?"

"But how do you know when to look or when to stop looking?"

She made a puzzled face. "I just know. That's all there is to it. It's as if I'm nudged to look." And she made small movements with her hands to emphasize her words. "And your name?" she prodded.

"I'm Javin. Javin Sarnum." he said, nodding gravely in return, unsure now what to do with his hands.

She held his gaze for a moment before shaking her head. "You don't really know very much about us, do you?" She hurried on before he could say anything. "Where are you heading after here?"

"I don't think Torrint said. We were hoping there's a healer here."

"For you?"

"Yes, I... would like some help. Nothing serious. It's about me being able to be more comfortable here, that's all."

"We did have one. But Harmony took her back a while ago now." In response to Javin's obvious confusion, she clarified by adding, "She's not here. Dead? Back with Harmony." She stamped one foot. "On our legs on the surface, we're here like this. In the ground, we're with Her." She changed topic abruptly. "Maybe the next place will have one. A healer." She pointed over Javin's shoulder. "That way is going to Blackeye and Sweetwater, I think. Maybe five, six days' walk? Could be more. I've never been there. Maybe Torrint is heading there. Blackeye's small, I think but Sweetwater is bigger, so I've heard. Maybe you'll be lucky there."

Javin's head dropped as he heard her speak. He hadn't realized until now how much he had hoped he would find help here. And now, nothing. Only maybe's.

Sharna reached out and patted him gently on the arm. "I'm sorry for you. I'm sure it will work out in the end." She cocked her head as she looked at him. "You don't look ill, if that's any help. So maybe it will be something that will heal itself?" She smiled hopefully.

Javin sighed and grinned mirthlessly back. "Maybe. I can hope so. You've been kind." He turned to go and remembered the mission he was on. "I forgot to ask. Where can I buy some bread?"

Sharna pointed back the way she had come. "Down there. There's a turn to the right and a small home facing you. He often has extra. Just tap on the door if it's shut. And, Javin...?"

"Yes?"

91

"Harmony will help you. You will hear Her. I know it." She flashed one last smile at him and carried on her way.

Javin didn't really know how to make anything of what she had said, so he just watched her walk away. It was only as she was turning another corner that he realized she had no shoes on. But then, he recalled, neither had Elissa and Serrine. He shook his head at the strangeness of it all and tried to shrug off his disappointment and focused, instead, on buying bread.

He had no idea what to pay with and simply tipped the contents out into his palm and offered it up to the baker to pick what he wanted. "I'm buying this for Torrint, who sent me, if that's any help."

At this, the baker drew his hand back and then looked more carefully at what was being offered. "Torrint, you say? In that case, I'll take this here," picking one of the small blue credit tokens, "and I'll add another loaf in to make it up." Returning with the extra loaf, he added, "Tell Torrint I will not be wanting anything this time, but to make sure he has some of that blane brandy next time. Keeps the chill out in winter."

Javin assured him that he would. By the time he returned, Torrint and Banith were re-packing the wagons and generally tidying up. He passed on the baker's message and Torrint raised his eyebrows in surprise at the mention of the brandy, but then nodded to show he'd remember. Banith smiled and sniffed the bread appreciatively. "That's going to be very good to eat." He tucked it away and carried on packing.

Javin handed the bag back to Torrint who didn't bother to check the contents. "There's no healer here."

Torrint nodded. "I know. Apparently she died not too long ago, and they haven't a good healer to replace her. Haven't anyone to replace her, actually."

"I met someone who said that there's a place not too far away where we might find one," Javin said.

"Sweetwater. Yes, there'll be one there. For certain." Torrint gazed down at Javin. "This was always going to be uncertain. Too small for a good healer to stay at. But it was on the way to Sweetwater." He turned back to the wagon. "A few days yet, but we'll be there soon enough. Now, if you'll get Kesit and Kasser, we'll get ourselves going."

"We're leaving now?"

Torrint nodded but continued packing. "Start clean and clear and leave in the same way. We stay overnight in a place this small, we look desperate and they look to take advantage. So we leave and anyone who missed us won't miss us next time through here." He turned finally and leaned on the wagon. "We did well enough. And so did they. So it's time to go." And he nodded Javin towards the mandria.

Much later, under a sky full of stars and the bright moon, the three of them ate a third of the fresh bread and some dried meat and fruit. Apparently, cooking every night was just too much trouble. Even though Javin knew where Red River was, he could not spot it now. There were no lights shining, no sounds of machinery, no hustle of people. There was only the silence. It was beginning to sound normal.

The next morning neither Torrint nor Banith were in the mood to rush, so Javin found himself the only one awake and alert. He hadn't slept well, being bothered with too many thoughts about what life would be like without memories.

As it was, the sun was bright and warmth was creeping into the air as Javin found himself a stub of bread and some fruit, the latter edging towards staleness now. He gazed off into the distance where the vague marks of passage indicated a track, but could see nothing. Giving up, he wandered off a few paces to a rounded rock, just the right height and size for lying back on and watching clouds, which is what he did as he chewed his breakfast.

He wondered, again, what Sharna could have meant by Harmony helping him. However he mulled it over in his mind, it made little to no sense. Giving up, he let himself gaze into the sky, eyes half-closed, enjoying doing nothing. His mind, however, kept wanting to do something. And so he found himself wondering about the mandria and what they thought of it all, assuming they had thoughts. He supposed it was a good life for them. They weren't rushed, always had good grazing and were looked after. He thought back to tending the ones at Hanlar's and how much he had looked forward to that at the end of the day.

He thought about grooming them now and lifted his head to locate them. They were idly munching on some sort of shrub a short distance away. Stretching out again, he let his mind see them close up, see the lighter markings on Kesit's hide; a small pattern of paler stripes. He wondered if Kasser noticed them in the same way, and, as he thought that, so his vision blurred and then he was looking at Kesit, close up. Right there, in front of his eyes, the stripes stood out sharp and clear. Much clearer than he had thought. But it was too close. And a part of him knew he wasn't seeing this. He was looking up at the sky and seeing Kesit as if he was right beside him at the same time. A small, amazed part of Javin told himself that the two things could not be happening together. Yet they were.

The surprise made him choke on a piece of bread and he sat up abruptly. As he did so, Kesit's hide vanished, to be replaced by the wagons. But seen from a distance.

Javin's lungs didn't seem to know which was more surprising; the intrusion of the bread, or what he was seeing. He shook his head as he tried to breathe and looked to find the mandria again. As he did so, the distant view of the wagons vanished and he found himself looking at the mandria who had turned their heads to him, obviously attracted by the sound of his choking.

Javin blinked and rubbed his eyes. He held them shut for a moment, but when he opened them again, the world was as it should be, the mandria were back to grazing again, and the last crumb was coughed up. Torrint looked over at him quizzically from the back of the wagon.

"If you think you'll survive the day, we'd best make a start."

11

The three of them, with the mandria grumbling their bass notes as an accompaniment, rumbled and creaked their way across the countryside. Javin had not said anything to the other two about the strange thing with his vision, and they had apparently not noticed anything to remark upon. So the first day was silent as usual. The wagon was never comfortable. There was no suspension, nothing to ease the bumps and roughness of the tracks they followed. Torrint had apparently become used to it, but, by the afternoon, Javin had had enough of an aching backside and sore lower back and got down to stretch his legs, Torrint nodding amiably at him as he jumped to the ground. As the mandria were steady but slow in their progress, it was very easy to keep pace with them, even to move ahead of them without too much effort. This Javin did.

The act of walking somehow seemed to make it easier to think about his future, about the straw moving, the vision of the wagons through the eyes of the mandria, about his life in general and what was happening to him. All he knew for certain was that he was uncertain about virtually everything. He had no clear recollection of his early life, he had unexplained things happening around or to him, and it wasn't even clear if he could or would stay with Torrint. There was not even any certainty about being healed enough to have his memory back.

And would he want them? This was not something he felt like talking about, assuming he could have a talk, that is. It was almost too personal for a conversation. He had to come to terms with it himself, in his own way. Nothing anyone on this planet could say to him would be of any use. Even the few others from Haven, if he met them, would not be able to help him understand his predicament any better. After all, he had been exiled in the most definite way possible. There must have been a very good reason for it. Perhaps he had been someone wholly unable to fit into society on Haven through anti-social tendencies. Had he been a murderer? But why exile a murderer? Perhaps he had been a holy man, made miracles happen (which would be ironic, given my present situation, he thought) and 'they' couldn't kill him because of their beliefs? Or had he been a terrorist, attacking the government? But, again, why not simply have him killed? There seemed to be no easy answer. But, even if the memories were bad, if he got them back, they would be his. His life would at least have a depth to it, even if it was not something he wanted to dive into.

In the late afternoon, having walked out the aches but resolving nothing else, he waited for the wagon to catch up to him and clambered aboard. Torrint spat a stream of juice over the side to talk better. "Did it help any? The walking?"

Javin smiled and shrugged. "I don't know. Maybe."

"Decide anything?"

"Only that I have no idea what my life was and what my life will be. I'm pretty much stuck here with no direction, nothing I can think of doing. I have to tell you, Torrint, it's a strange feeling."

Torrint nodded and then hooked the wad of leaves out, throwing them away. He ran his tongue around his teeth searching for any stray fragments and spat again. "Sweetwater's big enough for you to have options. Even if there's no healer there or none that can help, you'll see what's possible. Might give you some ideas, at least."

"So when do we get there?"

Torrint pointed with his chin at the rough track they were following. "This will take us to Blackeye first. Smaller place on the way. People there came from Sweetwater originally. I suppose they didn't like to have too many people around. Anyway, we can trade there a little and then carry news to Sweetwater and then find your healer." He glanced across at Javin. "It will be two, three days after tomorrow to Blackeye. Then maybe two or three more to Sweetwater. That good enough for you?"

Javin smiled back ruefully. "Would it make any difference if it wasn't?"

It was Torrint's turn to smile, a rare occurrence. "No."

"How small is this Blackeye place? Compared to, say, Red River?"

"You could fit Blackeye in Red River and lose it, I reckon."

"And it's called Blackeye because...?"

Torrint obviously felt in an expansive, communicative mood. "You'll see for yourself. There's tall plants there. High as this wagon. Pretty, too." He motioned with his hand, drawing as he spoke. "Lots of gold and white petals and in the middle, a black patch. That's where the seeds are. That's why they are called blackeyes and that's why the place is called Blackeye." Torrint was silent for a while. "Useful plant, the blackeye. Not many places where it grows well. This is one of them."

Javin knew he was going to have to ask. It was Torrint's way. He never gave out a lot of information at once. But he was happy to play along. He waited for a few more turns of the wheels. "Useful in what way?"

"As a glue. Powerful stuff. You need a lot of seeds and you soak 'em and pound on 'em, and what's left you mix with ash and then store it under water. We're out of it, and this is a good place to buy it."

"Store it under water?"

"Because as soon as the stuff dries, it sets. Hard. And I haven't heard of anything to loosen it when it does. Always get a good price for it. Always running out of it. People always want to stick things together."

Javin pondered this for a moment. "How did anybody find out how to do that; the pounding and the ash and the water? And that would make the glue? How does that happen?"

Torrint pushed out his lower lip. "Some things just happen, I guess."

The next morning Javin tried again to repeat the vision with the mandria, but without success. As before, once they had set off, he had another walk after sitting in silence for a while. It allowed him to think as well as avoid the discomfort of the wagon seat. With neither Torrint nor Banith being great talkers, the silence was the same walking as riding for most of the day.

He had taken to walking ahead of the wagons, following the slight indentations of the track with the occasional bare patches. For a lot of the time, he simply let his mind hop and skip, settle and stray wherever it wanted. Thus it was that he dipped into how he felt as he regained consciousness after his arrival, the look of disappointment on Tarla's face, how good Paysa's meals smelled, how the soil felt on his hands as he worked with Hanlar, the colors of the city he had last lived in, the smells, the sounds of it. A string of things. And, intertwined, the snatch of that annoyingly familiar tune. It arrived when he wasn't thinking about anything, but as soon as he tried to remember where it was from, it vanished quickly into silence. He sometimes found himself humming it before realizing he was hearing it in his head. He always seemed to come into the middle of it and leave before the end arrived.

That night, after a cooked meal and with the moon looking down, the three of them sat gazing into the remains of the fire.

"Do you really not remember anything before you came here?" Banith looked up from the leather strips he was braiding into a new bridle.

"Oh, I can remember a great deal of what it was like. I can see the city and even recall the names of people I knew there. But," and he made a fist with his right hand and banged it into the palm of his left, "I keep hitting this wall. I can go back only so far. I'm not sure, but maybe two or three years and then no more. There's nothing there."

"What's that like, having no memory? Is it like a blackness in your head, a blank, or what?"

Javin considered for a moment how to explain it. "I'm not sure I can tell you. You have memories of your past, right?"

Banith nodded, his hands continuing to work.

"How do you know they are memories? Your memories?"

Banith paused as he thought, his head cocked and eyes half-closed. "They have a feel to them. I know them because they feel right."

Javin nodded. "Exactly. I can make things up, I can imagine things about my past, but none of them feel right. None of them are mine." He gestured out into the night. "When I'm walking, I try to remember my life. A lot of the time, I hope for things. I recall some things which happened to me, that I know happened to me, and then I add something else. My mother looked like someone I knew in the city. Or, I lived in a place I'd seen on a screen sometime." He dismissed Banith's quizzical look. "A screen? I can't explain it here. Something you can look at, see things in, but it's not a mirror. But the point is I know when I'm making things up, when I'm hoping, because none of them feel right.

"It's the same problem you have explaining to me about how you and Harmony know each other. You can tell me things, but none of them make any sense to me. None of them feel right." He shifted his body slightly to a more comfortable position. "You and Harmony is like me and my lack of memory. I can't explain it to you and you can't explain it to me." He turned his gaze back to the fire and gave a slight sigh. "Maybe, one day, when I get my memory back, if I get it back, I'll finally get connected to Harmony." He looked up and smiled ruefully. "Maybe that's what the problem is. You can't connect with Harmony if you can't remember who you are."

"Might be that it's the other way round." Torrint leaned forward a little, also gazing into the fire. "Might be that once you get to hear Harmony, you get your life back as well."

"Maybe," Javin acknowledged. "Maybe."

"One thing's for sure," Torrint continued. "It can't stay like this. Something will change. Either you and your memory, or you and Harmony. Nothing stays the same." He stood and stretched. "And I think something is going to happen soon." He turned to his wagon and clambered in.

"Does he know something I don't?" asked Javin after a moment.

Banish shrugged. "Maybe. Prediction isn't his talent. He can see ahead a little, but he's talking about a feeling.Call it a sense, a premonition." He grinned. "You don't have to have a talent for that. Everyone can have a premonition. You just have to let them come to you. Anyway, if he's right or if he's wrong, we'll know soon enough."

"How soon is soon?"

Banith thought for a moment, his eyelids drooping, an inner silence. Then he looked across at Javin. "I'd say by the time we hit Sweetwater. If not before." He stood up. "And you have been here more than long enough without things happening, haven't you?" He looked up at the moon as if an answer were there. "Yes. I think he's probably right. Something's going to happen. A change is coming." He looked down at Javin still seated on the ground. "We just don't know what it is. That's all."

The next two days, before they arrived at Blackeye, Javin spent most of the time walking, letting his mind drift, hearing snatches of music and feeling frustrated. If this connection with Harmony was going to happen, he still had no idea how that would change anything. So he could 'hear' a planet? What good would that do? As far as he could tell, from everyone he had met so far, people were still people, just a little more weird. But was that due only to this strange connection? Or were they normally strange? Would he, then, in turn, become strange as well? And how would he tell? A labyrinth of thinking, except that his labyrinth only came to a dead end. There was no way out it, no conclusion.

He had no new visions about the mandria, not even when he was grooming them. Nothing unusual happened, despite what Torrint might have felt. He was still without a past and without an idea about the future. Maybe Sweetwater would have an answer for him. Maybe. Everything was a 'maybe'.

They had traveled through some low-lying hills with boulders of a dark grey color with whiter streaks in it, forming irregular mounds as if they were bursting from the ground, reaching upwards from beneath the earth. As they progressed, the space between these mounds lessened. Torrint called Javin back to the wagon around midday.

"Best sit up here for a while. These rocks, they can have cats in them."

"Cats?"

Torrint raised a cautionary eyebrow. "Numbugs on the carcass that time?"

"Oh! Cats! Right. Thanks."

"I don't look ahead all the time. Just know when to be safe." He paused, as usual. "We go round these hills and then we'll camp tonight. It'll take a time, but the rocks end soon enough. Not that cats are going to bother the beasts. Tomorrow, we'll be in Blackeye. Not long. A morning going between two hills where it opens into a small valley. That's Blackeye. A day there, then two days and Sweetwater after that."

"Do you remember all the countryside you pass through?"

Torrint shook his head. "I remember what I need to. I know when I'm going the right way. Plus, there's usually a track." He pointed ahead of them. "This one's faint, but easy enough to follow. When there's been a rain that can wash it away, that's when memory helps."

"But it's just countryside," Javin protested. "Hills and plants and things. It all looks the same to me."

Torrint wrinkled his nose. "Seems that you don't see things I see." He stuffed a new leaf into his mouth, a sure sign of an end to a conversation. Javin resigned himself to trying to see what it was Torrint saw. But, no matter how long he stared, it was just a jumble of hills and vegetation and rocks and nothing else. There was also that annoying tune, fading in and out.

That night, after their cold meal of stale bread, dried meat washed down with water, Torrint appeared to be lost in thought. At least, more than usual. He frowned and shifted uncomfortably for a while before shaking his head as if in disbelief.

Banish, still working on the bridle, noticed. "What is it?"

"Something's wrong ahead. Beasts not cared for. Fruit rotting on trees. Sheds needing repair. Doesn't look good. Doesn't feel good." Seeing Javin's expression Torrint said, "I'm an eye remember? And I can see less than a day ahead. And I don't like what I see here." He shook his head again. "This does not feel good. Not at all. And any questions you might have right now, Javin, they can wait."

Torrint's unease spread and even the mandria kept up an unusual and steady deep rumbling undercurrent of sound through the night. To Javin, it felt like his whole body and mind were on edge, but with no obvious reason. He wanted to ask questions, but Torrint looked in no mood. He had already made that quite clear. Banith obviously trusted what Torrint had said. He tried, at first, to carry on with the bridle, but finally put it down and stood by the wagon, staring out ahead, wanting to see Blackeye and the cause for Torrint's unease. Nobody slept well or long and the wagons were ready to roll at first light.

If there was tension the previous night, it ratcheted higher as they passed between the low hills and entered into the small valley. The blackeye plants, many twice as tall as Javin, swayed slowly in the breeze ahead of them. But the visually striking picture they posed did nothing to diminish the growing nervousness which gradually gave way to something like irritation and frustration; unease.

They had to pass through a veritable forest of the tall plants, the view ahead blocked by the thick stems and large, yellow-tinged leaves. Finally, rounding a bend, they saw the first of the buildings which made up the tiny village.

At first, they looked just the same as buildings he had seen in other places; hardly a straight wall, roofs at various angles and a blending between the earth and the house which made it hard to know where one ended and the other began.

But then he noticed that there was no smell or sign of smoke. Not one house had a fire going as far as he could tell. And by now, Javin knew how much a part of life here a fire was. A fire was needed not just to cook a meal, but to smoke meat, to keep water warm, for all the small jobs needing doing in and around the house. And letting one go out was a sign you were lazy or incompetent. Starting a fire, he knew from experience, was harder than keeping one smoldering. If there was an obvious sign of something wrong, this was it.

All three were on edge, and becoming more so, the closer they got to the heart of Blackeye. Finally, Torrint hauled them to a stop by the side of one house where the door hung raggedly and weeds were beginning to gain a foothold inside. Kesit and Kasser made their unease known by stamping and by tossing their heads, although whether they were only reflecting back to the people what they were radiating, or it was their own sensibilities they were voicing, was hard to tell.

Torrint lips were thin lines, tension showing in his jaw, as he looked around.

"Can you see what is wrong here?" Javin asked.

Torrint snapped his head round to look at Javin, something like fear in his eyes. "I do not want to look. Not like that. I'd rather see with my own eyes than try 'seeing' that way."

Javin jumped down and turned to find Banith walking up to the wagon, shaking his head.

"This is all wrong. All wrong." Looking up to Torrint he added, "I'll go that way," pointing ahead. "Why don't you and Javin take a path each and we meet back here as soon as possible?"

Torrint nodded and climbed down. "Keep the beasts harnessed. Let 'em drink if they want, but I want to be ready to go." He stalked off to the right in his long, loose-limbed style.

Javin nodded after him and put a bucket beneath each beast before setting off down a path to his left. He didn't know what to expect or what to think. He could see that there had been no obvious activity for a while, but for how long, he could not tell. Plants were growing into windows, doors were moving slackly in what small breeze there was, the one house he went into, the hearth was cold. There didn't seem to be any obvious disturbance. No furniture overturned, nothing to show any violence.

Past the last house, the view opened up a little and there was nothing else that he could see to investigate. He turned to retrace his steps and heard Banith calling. There was something in his voice which made Javin run as fast as he could, at the same time as being aware that he didn't want to arrive.

At the wagons, he turned to follow the route Banith had taken and met with Torrint at the same time. His face reflected Javin's fears and they both hurried on.

Rounding the last wall of the last house, they found themselves facing a slightly larger building, possibly a barn or a workspace. Banith was sitting slumped on the ground to the side of the large open door. At first, Javin wondered if he was injured. But when Banith looked up, his face told him that it was not so.

"In there," Banith motioned with his head, his voice empty. "They are in there. All of them."

Javin and Torrint exchanged looks. Taking a deep breath, Javin entered, aware of Torrint close behind. It took a moment for his eyes to adjust to the dimmer light inside. He didn't know what he was looking for until he felt Torrint nudge him hard and point near his feet.

Javin gasped as he understood what Torrint had indicated. There, strewn across the floor as if they were old toys, lay the bodies of the villagers. They had been there long enough to have become dried husks in clothing which was falling apart. They were seemingly tumbled together, a random collection of arms and legs. Hair moved gently in the light breeze. Javin saw, just before he catapulted backwards through the door, that some of the hands and feet lacked fingers and toes. The bodies had been gnawed on, even those of the children.

He gasped for air at the same time as trying to retch. Tears poured down his face, but he wasn't aware he was crying. He did not know how to think, let alone what to think. To come upon such a scene with no warning, nothing, made it harder somehow.

Torrint came out a moment later, his eyes wet, his mouth a thin, tight line. He stood and took several slow deep breaths, looking up at the sky as if for some understanding.

"We should go," he said.

Javin didn't believe his ears. "Go? How can we go? We don't know what happened here! We can't leave them!"

Torrint turned his fear and anger on Javin. "Yes? So we should bury them? Dig their graves? What can we do here? Nothing!" He made slashing motions with his hands. "It has happened. It is ended. We can do nothing for them. Don't you understand that?" He leaned in at Javin, breathing hard as if he wanted to strike him down, do something to vent the pressure in him.

Javin did not back away. "I understand they are dead. Every single one of them! Even the children. And you want to run? How do we know that it wasn't some disease which killed them? Maybe we're already infected. Maybe we're going to die like them. We run away, we maybe take it with us." Javin was trying to get his head working again. "I don't know what to do, but we need to find out, don't we? We can't just run and leave them. I can't do that. I can't."

"Harmony would not do that." Torrint sounded so certain. "She would not kill them with a disease. And if it was a disease, She would make sure that it killed only these. She would not let it spread. That is not Her way."

Javin threw his hands up in despair. "Not Her way? You don't know that! You're trying to make yourself feel better about leaving! Harmony? The damned planet? She is responsible? Is that what you're saying? That the planet," here he stamped his foot, "this planet actually killed them and that's just fine by you? Are you seriously saying that is how it is?"

Torrint made as if to brush Javin's words out of the air. "You are new here. You don't know Harmony. You cannot even hear Her. You have no connection with Her. You have no right to speak, because you don't know anything."

"I know what is right and I know that leaving here without doing something is wrong. Banith? You agree with me, don't you? We have to do something."

Banish was still seated on the floor. He shook his head slowly, his voice low and desolate. "I don't know. Whatever it was happened some time ago. It affected the whole village." He sighed heavily. "But I don't know what there is that we can do. We cannot bury them. There are too many. And, in time, this whole village will be overgrown. They will get a burial, a slow one, a proper one, from Harmony." He looked up beseechingly at Javin. "What can we do?"

"I don't know, except that there has to be something." Javin was desperate. "We're human. It's what humans do for other humans. I just don't know what." Suddenly he jabbed his finger at Banith. "You just said it was in the past, yes?"

Banith nodded.

"Then you can find out what happened, can't you? You can tell us. It's your talent, isn't it? Holding something and seeing its history? That's what you do. You can find out what happened to them."

Banith stood up and backed away from Javin. "Oh no, no, no. No, don't ask me to do that. You're asking me to look at them as they died! You can't ask me to do that. No!"

Javin would not be denied though. "There is no other option. None!" He turned to Torrint. "You said we were going to Sweetwater after this, yes?" Torrint nodded. "How is it possible that nobody in Sweetwater has nothing to do with these people here?" Torrint frowned. Javin knew he was not saying it well enough. His mind was still swirling. "Those dead people in this building? Some of them must have had relatives or friends in Sweetwater. You said they came from Sweetwater. They can't be close to each other and have nothing to do with each other." Torrint looked thoughtful. Javin glared at both of the traders, trying to find the right words to act as levers. "You said trading is about information, about using it, right? Well, if this isn't information I don't know what is. And, if we go into Sweetwater with just this, not knowing what happened, what will they think of you, of us? Don't you see? We have to find out! And that means Banith has to look at what happened. He has to."

There was silence for a while, nobody looking at anyone else. Finally Torrint nodded at Javin, his face taut, his voice flat. "Yes. We cannot face friends and relatives without information. You were right. I was wrong. We must find out." He turned to his partner. "Banith, you have to do it."

Banith looked as if he wanted be anywhere other than there. "I don't know if I can." He put his hand up to stop Javin from speaking. "It doesn't mean I won't. But I have to have something I can touch which will show me what I need to see. Clothing won't do. It's too vague, too much history. There has to be something else. Something recent, close to the time they died. Something I can hold." He looked from Torrint to Javin and back again. "You're going to have to help me find it, whatever it is." He pointed to the building. "And it's going to be in there."

Torrint took a deep breath and rubbed at his eyes as he tried to get ready to go back in. He let out his breath in one explosive sound and then waved his hands in dismissal. "I cannot simply go in there again. I need a little time. I will go and I will help you, but... ." He walked away a short distance, lost in his emotions.

Banith looked to Javin who said, "I don't know what I'm looking for, but I'll go in with you."

Banith stopped at the door, his face pale. "I need something that looks newer than most other things. It could be anything; a fresh piece of unworn pottery perhaps. Maybe a new bag. I don't know what it will be, but the closer it was made to the time, the clearer it will be."

The two of them entered reluctantly and tried to see if whatever would work was visible from the door. This second time of looking, knowing what was there, Javin noticed something else.

He tugged at Banith's sleeve. "These people, it's like they were together and, I don't know, but I'd guess that they were in a circle. See? There's a gap in the middle and most of them, their heads are toward the middle as well. Have you heard of anything like that? Some sort of religion?"

Banith looked, a puzzled frown on his face.

"I know what it is." Torrint had come in and was standing behind them, tears edging down his face. "They had gone deaf."

"Could be," said Banith, nodding, still trying to regulate his breathing.

"Deaf? How would that kill them?" asked Javin.

"Deaf to the song. Deaf to Harmony. They couldn't hear Her anymore. They lost their connection."

"Song? What song?"

Torrint dismissed that question. "Later. Now we help Banith to find out more." And he gestured at the bodies.

The next few moments were ones which Javin would never be able to erase from his memory, no matter how fervently he wanted to. Crouching, not touching, trying not to see what he was looking at, wanting to get out, wanting to find the object so he could leave with a good reason. None of them said a word. The only sound was the catch of breath in a throat, the rustle of their clothing as they stood, stepped and knelt again.

Finally, interminably, Banith spoke. "This will work. This will be enough." And he headed for the exit. All three of them were blinking in the sunlight, drawing in the air which suddenly felt cleaner.

Linked together by the invisible chain of shared experience, all three turned and walked back to the wagons, the silence hanging over them like a shroud.

Banith went to his wagon, motioning to Torrint and Javin to remain with theirs. "I need to be alone. I'll be as quick as I can."

Torrint stood and rubbed his arms and then his legs, as if they had gone numb, as if to reassure himself that he was still alive. He stomped his feet and then disappeared inside his wagon. He re-appeared moments later clutching a small clay flask.

Jumping down beside Javin, he pulled the stopper out and offered it with a nod of his head. "I think this will help."

Javin took it and gave a cautious sniff. In answer to his inquiring glance, Torrint added, "Blane brandy."

Javin took a sip and felt the warmth flow down into him. He hadn't realized how chilled he had become, despite the warmth of the day. His mouth filled with the taste of something sweet and his nose filled with what he could only later describe as the scent of summer, its warmth flooding his body.

Gratefully, he handed the flask back, and Torrint took a much longer gulp before replacing the stopper.

There was an awkward silence. Neither wanted to speak about it, but it was too big to ignore. So they said nothing, for nothing else could be spoken of yet. And they waited for Banith.

Finally, he re-appeared. Wordlessly, Torrint held out the flask. Banith flashed a tight smile of appreciation and took a quick, small sip and handed it back.

He slowly lowered himself to the ground, resting against the wheel as he collected his thoughts. The other two crouched to face him.

He held out his hand. "This is what I used," he said, as they peered at it. Torrint's eyes widened in surprise. It was shiny and seemed to have an edge to it, and maybe a handle. It had been battered out of shape. "Yes. It's metal. I found it near this recently carved wooden belt cinch." He held out his other hand. Javin looked at it, seeing how similar it was to what held his leggings up: two holes at angles where he threaded the ties through and knotted them. It kept them from tangling and was easy to adjust.

"But this metal. It's definitely recent and it couldn't have come from here. So I thought it would be better to try with it first." Banith paused as he re-ran what he had seen, taking a shuddering breath as he tried to control his voice. "You were right, Torrint. They had gone deaf. And this metal thing, this did not come from Harmony. It came from up there." He gazed upwards. "Not from Harmony. From some place else." He held out the metal object to them. "This... thing, whatever it was, was worn by someone who came to Blackeye from beyond Harmony. This is not anything to do with Harmony. There is no history of it here. It feels wrong. And it was left here. I think it was a gift, maybe. And I think, from what I could gather, I think that Harmony knew it was wrong. I don't know how it was wrong, but I saw how this metal was the reason they went deaf. I don't think any of them, any of the people here, knew it was wrong at first. But, then they did and that's when this got beaten as if they wanted to destroy it." Banith's voice lowered. "And that's when they went deaf. And that's why they were all together." His voice broke as he re-lived the last moments he had seen. "They were all together in that place because they were trying to apologize, trying to hear Harmony again." He looked up, tears streaming down his face. "Oh, Torrint! They were trying so hard. Some of them were even eating the soil. They were so lonely! It was awful... ." He sobbed, great shuddering gusts of breath. He flung the metal away. "I hate my talent. I hate it! I don't want to feel this. I don't want to feel what they felt! I hate it."

Torrint offered the brandy again; the only thing he felt he could do. Javin picked up the metal and placed it in the back of the wagon, without Banith noticing. Torrint saw him, however, and he dipped his head and closed his eyes in a quiet 'Thank you' at him.

NOTES FROM HAVEN

The Rise Of The Military

Taken from "Yearly Report Of The Office Of Unity, 1025":

"... And so, the figures show very clearly just how vital the use of armed forces are in maintaining a peaceful and manageable population. Strikes were fewer, protests smaller and production improved overall. The suggestion that a military commander of appropriate rank should be on the board of most governmental offices should be taken under serious consideration. Likewise, the training and supply of the armed forces should also be increased to a level commensurate with their extra activities."

From "The Minutes of the House of Representatives, Lander 12, 1053":

"Motion: That the Commander in Chief and his Executive Officer shall be considered de facto members of the House by virtue of their positions and shall be liable for nomination for Privy Council positions as well as for positions on the Governing Body itself. Passed, 130 - 16."

Source: "Internal eyes-only memorandum, C-in-C Army HQ, to Staff Officers, Solstice 5, 1090":

"Note: All Staff Officers of Grade 4 and above will make it their duty to, first gain seats on all local governmental bodies and, second, to work towards controlling said body. This can be done through direct elections, or through acquiring posts of sufficient weight to allow control of the work of the body.

This has become necessary as, in recent years, there is a general slackness in government, particularly with regard to the venality and general lack of personal discipline shown by a majority of elected officials.

It is not the intention at this time to overthrow the government in any fashion. However, it is the intention that the discipline of a military commander is present at all times, in all levels of government so that the other elected officials can be guided by example, or by gentle coercion when necessary, to have the proper regard for Haven and its populace at all times. There has long been too much personal aggrandizement in office, the taking of bribes and so on, which serves only to weaken the regard the population has for its rulers. It is, therefore, the intention of this memo that steps are taken to reverse this situation and that within a short space of time government may once again be seen as a privilege burdened with responsibility.

It is the firm conviction of this office that only the military can provide a sufficiently powerful example to the civilian wing of government.

This order to be in effect immediately. Further communications will give blueprints and suggestions as to how to achieve this goal as quickly as possible."

The Coup

Internal Broadcast, House of Council. 08:38 Aggar 7, 1095 :

"To all Councillors in the buildings. It appears that troops are massing outside the city limits, but there has been no order given. The apparent reason is to prevent possible riots on the anniversary of the curfew for all students. The President, Marak Sarnum, has declared a state of emergency and has issued a decree ordering the troops to disperse and return to their barracks. He has taken his family into the Presidential quarters inside the Council building as a precaution. It is the advice of this Council and of President Sarnum that its members remain in session.

Those who have left are being sent for to return immediately. This session will remain in existence until such time as the state of emergency is considered to be over. Please return to the Chamber where an emergency debate is in progress."

Extracts from live news feed, date as above:

"... [Timestamp 08:56:34] The images you see now are of troops blocking the road. We have heard that the same thing is happening on all major roads into the city. No-one is being allowed to enter or leave. As you can see, there is no violence. All guns are either holstered or shouldered and the atmosphere of the troops seems to be quite genial....

... [Timestamp 10:21:06] We have just heard that the Commander in Chief of all armed forces, General Mikkan, has been seen entering the city with a small entourage. Reports say that he had an armed escort of somewhere around twenty men...

...[Timestamp 10:44:18] Shots have been fired! Shots have been fired! I repeat, there has been shooting. I am told that it sounds like heavy machine guns, and possibly a grenade was heard. Certainly an explosion of some kind. We cannot get any closer. All troops are now on alert, guns at the ready. We have been turned back twice now. We will attempt again to find a way through this cordon and see what is happening inside. All we know so far is that, inside the cordon, all electronic media, servers, cameras and anything which can transmit, have been offline for several minutes. No news is coming out. We shall try again to get closer..."

[This was the last intelligible report sent from outside the city for two days.]

Presidential Office, Aggar 10, 1095:

"It is with deep regret that this office announces that the President, Marak Sarnum, together with his wife, Sallinam, have been found dead inside the Presidential residence. There had been long, detailed and constructive negotiations between the President and General Mikkan on the role of the military and how the rebel troops could be most easily disbanded with minimum loss of life.

It was during a mutually agreed brief suspension in these discussions, when General Mikkan and his staff had left for a short break, that an intruder, obviously sympathetic to the rebels, apparently entered the residence and shot the President and his wife.

Since then, there has been an exhaustive search for the perpetrator or perpetrators and, obviously, a great deal of constitutional debate at the same time.

As a result, General Mikkan has reluctantly agreed to become President by acclaim of the Council members in session. The vice-president could not be reached at his country estate in time for any swift resolution.

Javin, the son of the president and his wife, has not yet been found. It is assumed that he was upset or startled by events and has run away and hidden. There are many places a young boy could find to hide. So far, he has not been found, but the search is widening for him and all are confident that he will be discovered shortly. As yet, the killer or killers have not been found, but there are several leads which are being followed."

Extracts from the dissident underground newspaper "Resist!" widely circulated after the coup. It is not now known who wrote, printed or distributed it:

"...We must never forget that Haven is not just a toy for whoever wants to control it. This military usurpation of power will not last. It is up to all free-thinking peoples to oppose this illegal rule in every way possible. Oppose it in silence by rejecting its illegal legislation. Oppose it loudly by joining together in the legal demonstrations. Oppose it in any way you can, but oppose it you must!"

"...If the military continues their harassment, then make their lives difficult in return. Abandon the cities and take to the fields and forests. Learn again that we can provide for ourselves, grow what we need. Retreat from the technology which tracks us and controls us. Rediscover the strength of those who rejected the original tyranny here and left to form their own colony on Harmony! We can learn from them, follow them, have their ideals be ours!"

The Plan

Private journal entry of Councillor Herban Low - handwritten, no date, but assumed to be sometime after 1097. He maintained the journal after he resigned up until his death in 1101:

"Mikkan surprised us all today! How he maintained the presidency [words crossed out and illegible]. But, considering the turnover of members in the past years, it is clear that he is sure to have supporters.

He actually wants to go to war with Harmony! The exact words he used: 'go to war'. For all I know this is the only recording of the event as it was in a closed meeting of the Security Council. I will be glad to vacate my seat soon and take up fruit growing!

But go to war? Really? We now have more armed people than ever before in our history. And a planet we have not even had contact with for hundreds of years is now, apparently, a threat to us.

A part of me wants to admire him for saying it to us with a straight face! But I cannot condone this. I cannot vote for it. The reasons he gave were so vague, so obviously ridiculous, so based on a desire to act powerfully, to be a bully, that they are beyond belief! Really? There is really a race of super beings, of some sort of genetically mutated humans on Harmony? And they want to conquer us? [Words crossed out and illegible]

I pointed out that everything about Harmony points to them having no obvious industry, no means of traveling through space, and no reason to do so. These were brushed aside and ignored and instead a promise to show us secret research undertaken by Mikkan at his own expense would persuade us of the validity of the threat.

My doubt is infinite and my disgust with this mockery of a presidency just as large."

Private journal entry of Councillor Herban Low - handwritten, no date, but is after the previous one:

"I am resigning with immediate effect. I have no choice. After today's vote to approve funds for building a fleet of ships to attack Harmony, it is clear that there is nobody, no group left capable of standing against Mikkan's authority. It must now be only a matter of time before the presidency is abandoned and we are all placed under martial law. Civil rights will no longer exist. I have done what I can. I can do no more. And yet I feel I have failed. I saw retirement as being a time of reward for years of service. Now I see it only as a way of passing time in sadness at the spectacle of this planet's sinking into hopelessness and despair."

Private electronic recording of a meeting, presumably having taken place in Mikkan's office. No date and no means of identifying the speakers.

... Speaker #1: "We have found some definitely interesting aspects of the samples you provided.

Speaker #2 [Mikkan?]: Define 'interesting' for me.

#1: Well, without getting too technical, it seems that there are certainly some compounds, proteins if you like, which could certainly affect neuronal transmitters, maybe even create new, linked proteins which would alter synaptic processes, create new genes, maybe even new types of brain cells. However, we can't be sure of the purity of the samples due to degradation over time in transit --

#2: Assume that what you just said was too technical and start again.

#1: Um, yes. Er... Perhaps...

Speaker #3: Well, it seems that the plants have a definite effect on brain chemistry, on how the brain works. What those changes might be is impossible to say because all we're doing is looking at the chemistry, if you like, not at how the chemistry affects the biology.

#2: What would you need in order to find out how this chemistry you have discovered would affect the brain?

#1: Well, obviously, a brain. A human brain.

#2: But not a brain in a jar, is what you actually mean, isn't it?

[Several seconds silence]

#3: We have no way of knowing what effects there could be. And, for all we know, there may be something vital in how the chemicals, the proteins, the controlling mechanism, how that is delivered. It might be that it has to be consumed directly, or in water, or... . We must even consider the possibility that the composition of the plants has changed since they were harvested.

Speaker #4: We can provide you with the people if you can provide us with results.

#1: It could take a very long time indeed to even discover how to administer--

#2: As he said, we are interested in results. We will provide facilities, funds, samples and everything else you need. Think of the possibilities. You will be engaged in cutting edge research. No results will be wasted because everything you will be doing will be new. You will be making huge strides in new and fascinating areas. Rewards, honors, recognition: all these will be yours without a doubt. And, beyond that, whatever you uncover will be of use to this, your home. And the more we find out about Harmony, the better position we will be in to determine our own future in that regard. Tell me one thing.

#3: Yes?

#2: Do you believe, from what you have seen so far in these samples, that this is an area previously untouched or unconsidered in your area of work and that there is much to be discovered?

#1: Oh, yes. Certainly. That is certainly the case.

#2: Then we are agreed. Thank you, gentlemen. We will be in touch with you shortly with details of the facility we will prepare for you.

[Sound of door shutting]

#2: Make sure their families are with them when we relocate them. It makes for a more amenable working environment.

#4: And the test subjects? Who do you suggest?

#2: That's the easy part of all this. And as for how those plants really affect people? That should be easy, as well. Where there's no metal to be had, think how much a simple thing like a knife will get you? Trade some metal items for a voyage on a ship. What could be easier?

#4: Is that recorder still on?

#2: Ah, yes. Thank you."

From the unpublished memoirs of Colonel Mikkan:

"I did not want the boy killed. The death of his parents was unavoidable, given the circumstances. But I had come to know the son. I became fond of him. His intelligence and energy were what I fancy I would have seen in my own son if I had married. But, more than that, I believed I saw something in him which I felt would be of value to this nation, something which, if nurtured properly, could be immensely useful in uniting all factors. After all, he was his father's son. There was a legacy there.

But, it could not be done immediately. There had to be some time gone by, a time when he was nearing adulthood when he would be old enough to be presented as a figure to respect. And, with my weight and influence behind him, it would have been inevitable.

However, the progress we had looked for in society was slower than we had hoped for. It became obvious that something stronger than a figurehead was required to drag these people into a more forward-thinking, optimistic and energetic direction. We had, for too long, assumed that we would be forever alone in the universe. We no longer had great dreams. We were, so to speak, sleeping. I always believed, and still believe, that we have a duty to ourselves, our heritage, and to our fellow human beings elsewhere in the universe, to seek each other out, and to reunite. We need, we must, return to the stars and join with our brothers and sisters again. It is where we came from. It is where we must return to.

That is why I wanted to have Harmony as a target. It didn't matter what the target was, as long as it was not of this world, and Harmony was easiest. I needed something to drag us out of lethargy into growth and aspiration; something we had lost gradually over the years.

And that meant that the son, Javin, was no longer needed. I still did not want him killed. It seemed cruel enough to deprive him of his memories. The technique used was rough and ready, but effective. I did have reports on him and his progress over the years. As I had seen in him, he had a natural talent for leadership, for attracting followers, for doing more than surviving. That is when I considered moving him to Harmony. The idea grew and it did seem to present us with an excuse to perform another run to Harmony, to try out new equipment and to collect samples, even to collect some people for observation. Plus, I felt better knowing that, at least he would be living somewhere where nobody knew him and where he could live out his life in peace. Amkar (Mikkan's second in command) never did feel the same as I did about this, but he did see the potential for increased efficiency of the overall project.

I admit to wondering every now and then what became of Javin."

12

It took two days to reach Sweetwater. Actually, they saw it after a day and half of pushing the mandria hard. Banith, Torrint and Javin were all silent as usual but for a different reason. Each one was filled with the weight of what they had seen. Javin felt there was nothing he could have said which would not have sounded trivial or demeaning to the memory of the people who had died.

He kept running through what they could possibly say to the people of Sweetwater. How would they react? The relatives in Sweetwater, perhaps they had already 'seen' or somehow known about the disaster. If what he had learned so far was true, it was unlikely they were bringing fresh news. But he didn't know what to do if they were. The plain fact of it was that he felt helpless.

They came to a rise of hills, slowly sloping up from the relatively flat, wide valley they had entered upon leaving Blackeye. They labored to the top of the rise, the mandria breathing heavily and making their displeasure known by the tossing of their huge heads and the incessant flicking of their tails.

From the top they could see the town in the distance, with a silvery sparkle of the stream, which gave the town its name, running down from the opposite hills. Javin could see that it was certainly much bigger than Red Rock. Like that place, Sweetwater was not so much a close collection of buildings, but a sprawl. Isolated buildings dotted the landscape, the distance between them shortening as his eye found the center. He knew it was the center because he could see two tracks meeting there. The one they were on continued ahead into the hills on the very far side of the wide valley. It met the other one which, following the path of the stream, headed down the valley, away into the distance where he thought he could see some higher hills or rocky formations.

Torrint hauled the mandria around to a small outcrop of rock topped by some low bushes. "We can't get there today," he explained. "Kesit and Kasser are too tired. If we keep pushing them, they'll be of no use at all. They'll drop. They're strong, but they do not have speed. They cannot keep going. They reach their limit and then," he grimaced, "they are finished, ill. Very ill. You look after them carefully. Check everything about them. Look for sores and muscle strain. We need them well. Not just tomorrow, but for the days after that."

Despite the emotions from Blackeye still gnawing at him, Javin welcomed the time with the mandria. It allowed him to focus on something else. He took his time checking each of the mandria in turn. He found a raw spot on Kesit's shoulder and rubbed some liniment in it. Then he checked the harness and spent time softening the leather and binding a patch of folded cloth to it to lessen the chance of making it worse.

Running his hands down their legs, he felt heat in a couple of places on Kasser's front legs and Torrint, taking a break from applying some thick grease to the axles, gave him some ointment he could apply. As he worked, so the rumbling of the two beasts began to tail off into shorter, more breathy sounds, more reminiscent of how they usually sounded. He made sure they had water, giving them most of what was left in the barrels, and he also gave them some of the feed which Torrint reserved as a treat. He finished by brushing them down and collecting the wiry hairs.

During this, Javin found himself feeling lighter than before, the tension leaving him, and he realized that he too was able to breathe more deeply.

By the time he had finished, the light was failing and the moon was rising up the sky. It was still a new enough sight for him. It drew his eye even as he was sitting on the ground, chewing on some dried meat. Looking up at it, suddenly he felt a deep yearning to be back on Haven, memories or no memories. To be amongst the bright lights and the familiar smells, the hard, flat roads and solid buildings with tall, straight walls. Few stars were visible in the night sky of a city. Few reasons for looking up. For a moment the need to be back there was so pure that it stabbed his chest and his breath caught in his throat. There was a desperate craving to be in a place where he felt he could at least understand how everything worked, where he could feel that he fitted in. Instead, he chewed on the tough meat which now had no taste, the darkness now feeling like it was a threat. And Haven was where that piece of metal had come from. That had also been a threat, apparently. Both Torrint and Banith had known that the metal had come from there. Haven was responsible for creating that scene, those deaths. In the midst of Javin's longing there was also a sense of guilt. Guilt because of being associated with that metal, as if he were, in some indirect way, also responsible for all those deaths.

Neither Banith nor Torrint could be bothered with a fire, so Javin sat in silence in the dark feeling more alone, more separate than ever.

That night was long for everyone. They were tired from the journey and from dealing with their memories and reactions but were unable to rest. The news they carried, the sights they still held, would not let them alone.

It was no surprise that all three were up early, each snatching a wordless breakfast of stale tasting water and the remains of the smoked meat of the night before. The sunrise was blocked by thickening clouds, and a breeze sprang up, strengthening into a steady wind as they prepared to leave. Torrint inspected the mandria with Javin and nodded his approval of what he saw. Despite the grumbling of the beasts, they were quickly harnessed and hitched and moving off.

Torrint was tight-lipped as usual, but Javin could no longer keep silent as they approached the town. There was a question he had been wanting to ask since the previous evening. "Do you think they know already; the people in Sweetwater, I mean?" If they did know, it would mean they weren't going to be the ones who carried the bad news first. It would mean he wouldn't feel quite so guilty, for some reason.

Torrint shook his head. "I don't know. I can see people. But I can't see what they know, what's in their heads. And, if they have known for a long time, then how would I tell anyway? There was no sign that anyone else had been there since... ." His voice tailed off.

"What if they have people like you, Torrint? Eyes who can see what's going to happen? Wouldn't they have told people we were coming? Told them what we know?"

"It's possible. There are bound to be some eyes there. But whether they want to be known as eyes is another thing. Plus, I have met only a few who have owned to it and none of them, like me, can do more than see. We don't hear anything."

"But they'd see what happened when we tell people about what we saw, wouldn't they?" Javin persisted, wanting to understand what was ahead of them. "They'd see some sort of disturbance, surely?"

Torrint nodded.

"So we're going to be telling them something they already know, aren't we? Someone will know what's going to happen?" Javin continued the line of thought. "That means that everyone knows the future. There can be no surprises then, can there? So are we really going to be telling them something new, some new information?"

Torrint was silent for a moment, staring ahead, then he gave a heavy sigh, as if reluctant at being forced to speak. "It's not that simple. If I look ahead, it's because I choose to look. I don't get to see everything that's going to happen all the time. I have to want to look ahead and know where I want to look. And that means that, unless someone in Sweetwater actually chose to look, then they won't know. And, yes, it's possible that someone was actually looking out for us, for when we would arrive to trade. But, they wouldn't bother to watch us all the way into town, would they? They'd watch just long enough to know it was us." He stopped to rub his forehead in a tired fashion. "Being an eye is just that. It's seeing something. But if I look in one place, I only see that place for a short time. It's like you turning your head. You don't see what's behind you, do you? You have to choose where to look." He shrugged. "It's the same for me, for other eyes as well, I'm sure." He was silent a moment. "Whether or not anyone knows about Blackeye, we're going to tell them because it's our responsibility. A duty. And it's not one I really want, if you want to know."

There was the hint of rain in the cool wind as they entered the town. Consequently there was hardly anyone about. The damp seeped into their clothing and drew warmth from them.

They hauled to a stop in the center of the town, close by a strange building. A central pole held up a roof which covered a roughly circular area of beaten earth. A low wall of brick and stone and clay ran around the circumference with a few breaks in it to allow entry. A small boy was huddled up against the pole, wrapped against the cold and damp in a bundle of clothes, so that he looked like a collection of rags with a head. As Torrint stopped, the boy looked up and nodded. "Torrint. Good to see you."

Torrint nodded gravely in acknowledgment and clambered down slowly. He gathered his coat around him as he walked back to Banith. They conferred a moment before Banith nodded once in agreement. Torrint fished around in the back of his wagon, hauling out a short leather waistcoat which he put on under his coat before coming back to Javin. He had slipped the metal object into one pocket.

He inclined his head towards the circular building next to them. "We decided we should tell the Group what happened first. Most of the people here will know it then as well." He turned to speak to the boy, still huddled. "Can you get the speaker for us? We've news we need to pass on. Quicker is better."

The boy unravelled himself and bobbed his head before scampering away in a tangle of flapping cloth.

"What do you mean about telling the Group? Who and what are they?" Javin had many questions. "What will they do? And how are we going to tell them anyway?"

Torrint and Banith were already under the roof. "The Group's the same people as you met back at Landing. Gerant? Lisick? Remember? They are the ones who can understand what is happening on Harmony, not just in this place, but all over. Telling them, they might know something we don't. And even if they don't know, it might help them understand something else happening." Banith paused and pointed up at the pole. "And this is how we will tell them." Then Javin saw what he was indicating. At the top of the pole, right under the roof, were two large circular discs. What really caught his attention was how out of place they looked. They appeared to be machined or pressed in some fashion. They were each the width of perhaps two hand spans. Looking more closely at them, he was convinced they were made of some sort of plastic. That had to mean they had not been made here. He was amazed and confused in equal measure.

"What are these things?"

It was Torrint who answered. "We call them deecees. They probably had a longer name once. But that would have been long ago. They come from your planet originally. The ones who came here first, the first settlers? They brought them. They connect us, the people here, with the Group back at Landing. And don't ask me how they work. I don't know." And with that, he eased himself to the ground, resting against the pole, wrapping his coat tight against the cold wind.

"But that would mean they are... ," Javin was trying to work it out in his head, but gave up. "They're really, really old! And they still work?" He peered more closely, trying to see wiring or anything else he could recognize. It was frustrating, not being able to see more. Yet, at the same time, he was excited at the existence of something which had come from his home, even if it was hundreds of years ago. He felt strangely proud of the fact that they still worked after all this time. Strangely proud in the same way he had felt strangely guilty about the metal. Haven was a source of conflict in his head.

Before he could ask more questions, the boy returned with a thickset man with heavy jowls and thinning hair who was hurrying along on slightly bandy legs and obviously not enjoying the exercise. He entered the space and took a few moments to catch his breath. His eyes were deep set and dark, with a piercing gaze which he turned on Torrint who was standing again, his height making the trader seem to loom over him.

"I'm Bendiss, the speaker here." His voice was surprisingly high-pitched and had a querulous tone to it as if he didn't like being summoned thus. "Why the hurry? There's always time. But the boy was very insistent and mentioned your name, so I'm supposing that you know what you're asking?"

"This is something the Group needs to know. And, after that, everyone here needs to know it as well. We've carried this for longer than we want, so the sooner we can let it go, the better." Torrint spoke softly. "If we could have the people here...?"

Bendiss looked at the three men as if weighing the truth of Torrint's words. "We'll see if you're right soon enough." Without taking his eyes from them, he called over his shoulder to the boy. "Lannis! Call them in. Tell them it's urgent and we need them now."

The boy, Lannis, bobbed his head in acknowledgement and ran off again, but this time calling out as he did so. "Sending! Sending now! We need you now! Sending! Urgent sending! Sending! We need you now! Urgent sending!" He headed towards the nearest large buildings, still crying out.

Bendiss folded his arms and had a skeptical tilt to his head. "What is this about? If I find that it has anything to do with your trading, you will be in much trouble here."

Banith stood forward. "I'll do the telling. I know the details. It's about Blackeye."

At the mention of the name, Bendiss became more attentive. "What of it? What is the message you want to send?"

"I have never done this before, so I do not know how it works. But, I have information that the Group must know about. My talent is to see the past when I touch an object. I have been called an eye to the past. I do not see ahead, only back. And that means I have images in my head, but I don't know if I need to use words with you?"

Bendiss rubbed at the stubble on his cheeks. "You're a new mind to me, so I think it best to try with the images first. If I have questions, I'll ask. Does that suit?"

Banith nodded. "But how-- ?" he began.

"By holding the pictures you want me to see in your head. Choose the first one, or the most important one and keep it clear. You can do that? When I have that one, I'll let you know and you go to the next one until finished." When Banith nodded, Bendiss continued. "It's easier if I hold you, touch you. Shoulders work well. Closer is better." He placed his hands on Banith's shoulders and leaned his head forward until their foreheads were touching. "When you're ready, let me know. Just see something and I'll try to see as well." He frowned in concentration.

Banith took a deep breath.

After a moment, Bendiss's face took on a grim expression. At one point, he opened his eyes in shock. As they were engaged in this, so people began to enter under the roof. They were silent, but looked with interest at Torrint and Javin and also at the two others engaged in silent communication. Javin watched as the arrivals sat on the floor seemingly anywhere. A few of them exchanged knowing glances, as if this was confirmation of something they had seen in some fashion. The boy, Lannis, had also returned and was sitting on the wall, counting the people, by taking pebbles from a pocket and placing them on the wall one at time as the people entered.

As the floor filled in, Bendiss asked a few quiet questions of Banith and, at one point, asked to see and hold the metal he had taken from Blackeye, nodding as he put the images and words together. Finally, he was satisfied that he had everything he needed. Banith sat himself down and Bendiss turned to the people. First, he gestured to Torrint and Javin to sit. Javin had no idea what was happening and Torrint put his finger to his lips, blocking the questions Javin had.

"I thank you all for coming so swiftly," Bendiss began. "It is as Lannis said, an urgent sending." He glanced questioningly over to Lannis who counted the pebbles and nodded his head. Javin assumed it meant there were enough people. Certainly, there seemed a good number of them there, and all surprisingly quite still, apart from the usual few coughs and slight fidgeting.

"Although all of you know what to do, it is my duty to remind you," Bendiss continued. "Take the time now to relax your bodies fully. Breathe deeply and evenly. Stretch if needed. Clear your minds. Be calm and relax. When I take my place against this pole, underneath the discs, that will be the signal for all here to gather your attention fully upon the sending." He pointed to the discs above him. "Then, let your imagination and certainty know that you are allowing yourself to give power to these and allow the sending to take place."

The rhythm of the words suggested a well-worn formula, but one which was still adhered to; the people stretching limbs and rolling shoulders, breathing in and out heavily. It certainly wasn't anything like Javin had expected and filled his mind with more questions. A deeper silence now settled on the crowd.

"All of you here will know of the message and you will be responsible for spreading exactly and only what that message is." Bendiss glared at the people. "You have no right to change it to something else. You have no right to alter it to fit your life. You have only the right, the duty, the responsibility, to make sure that those not here understand the message. If you cannot do that, you may leave now with no loss of character or respect." He let the silence stretch as he waited for anyone to stand up. Nobody did. Satisfied, he nodded and turned abruptly to point at Banith. "This man has provided me with a heavy message, a clear message, a vital message. Neither he nor his companions are in any way implicated in what you are about to witness. They are blameless. Because they bear bad news, they are not themselves part of it. I hope that is clear to all?" A final glare. He then took up his position with his back to the pole.

"Now, begin to focus your attention. Send the call out that we might be heard in Landing." He then closed his eyes as the crowd obeyed his request.

Javin had been looking around, trying to understand what was going on. When Bendiss asked for their attention, Javin was caught unawares. It was as though there was a wave of something which washed over him. He could not describe it, only feel it as it passed through and over him. It made him feel lighter and he was aware, in a way he could never describe, that he was just one small part of a larger thing. The crowd had an identity, a power, a presence of its own. And he, Javin, was swept up in it and, for a moment, he lost touch with the ground he knew he was sitting on. Or, rather, he lost the sensation of sitting on the ground. His attention was elsewhere, not centered in himself. It was, instead, on the two flat panels at the top of the pole. All his attention was being drawn there, gently but implacably. He became aware of his membership of, and his place in, this assembly of people.

It was easier for him to close his eyes against the dizzying sensation. At first, as he did so, there was no sound. Just a potent silence. Then, in the midst of this crowded silence, there was something, a voice or something like a voice. It sought attention. It sought an answer. It sought to be heard. It sought a response of some kind. And, for a time which could have lasted a second or an hour, no response came. Then, suddenly, there it was. It was different, and that made it the response.

And then, as if floating into his mind from unseen corners, Javin slowly became aware of sounds, of a voice, of small, shifting pictures, of an awareness which was not his. And all of this carried in it the tale of Blackeye. The count of the bodies, the metal, the overgrown trackways, the crumbling buildings, the deaths, the means of death and the other people, the strangers who brought the metal. It was all conveyed in one seamless tapestry of sensations, words and pictures, and it contained within it everything that Javin, Torrint and Banith had experienced, but as a whole, not in fragments or even sequentially. Somehow, it all made sense and was perfectly clear in his mind. Behind that flow of information, Javin could sense the crowd acting as witness to it all as well as maintaining the channel. There was shock and there was horror, but these were muffled and suppressed.

Then there was a time of silence and of cessation. And the other voice or non-voice made a reply of some kind. And then there was further silence which slowly degraded into the common, everyday near quiet of a group of people trying to be still. The connection had ended and Javin became aware of his body again. He couldn't see the sun behind the clouds to make an judgement on how much time had passed. All he knew was that he felt cold and stiff and needed to stretch. It was apparent that it was true for many others around him.

As the sending had seemingly come to an end, he wanted to know what had happened and how. There was no formal end as there had been a beginning. The crowd began to disperse in the still damp air. Their concerns were more about what they had learned. From what Javin could understand, they had experienced it as if they themselves had been to Blackeye and seen it all there. Somehow, what Banith had passed on to Bendiss had been shared with each person in the hut. It had also been passed on to Landing in some strange fashion. Hushed whispers began as the people shared what they had each felt and seen and heard in the exchange. The larger group of senders (as Javin now thought of them), broke up into smaller groups as they left the hut. Some were silent and thoughtful, others sought to confirm with others what they had experienced. Still others were crying openly and being comforted by those around.

It was as if he was the center of a storm about to sweep through the town. It brought back the earlier feelings of guilt at bearing the news, of feeling responsible. Despite the strangeness of it all, Javin felt an emptiness. It felt unfinished somehow. Just letting all the people go without some sort of ending seemed wrong. Javin didn't know how to phrase it. He turned in response to a gentle tug on his arm and found Banith looking at him. Behind him, Bendiss was now seated with his back against the pole, his knees up and his arms draped across them, hands dangling. Torrint, off to one side, was standing looking out, seemingly lost in thought. Lannis was still seated on the wall.

"It was the first time for me as well," said Banith. A smile briefly showed itself. "Strange, wasn't it?" Javin could only nod. Then his stomach gave a deep growl. He grimaced apologetically. Banith smiled again, this time for longer. "Me too. A small amount of that dried meat only goes so far. What do you think, Torrint, shall we go eat?"

Turning, the tall trader's eyes re-focused. He rubbed his hands together briskly. "I think so. A good meal that someone else cooked will help greatly. If you need us...?" This last was said to Bendiss who shook his head without looking up.

"I doubt more details will be needed. Go eat. Lannis here will fetch me something as needed."

As the three of them left the hut, Javin asked, "What happened and why is Bendiss still sitting there? And what's going to happen next?"

"Let's get some food first. Then we can think how to answer those questions." Torrint stopped so suddenly that Javin nearly bounced off him. "And remember. We were the ones with the news. We're the ones who saw it. There will be people here who will know we saw their dead loved ones." He jerked his head at the hut. "Doesn't matter what he said in there, we're still the ones who told them of the dead and why they died. If it were me, I don't know which would be harder: knowing they were dead or knowing how they died. Nothing's going to happen. I've seen that. But you might pick up a lot of things you don't need and that aren't yours." In answer to Javin's unspoken question, he added, "Things like anger and other emotions. You might feel them. But they're not you." He pursed his lips as if deciding whether to add anything, but, deciding against it, he turned and marched on to a large building ahead of them.

Javin found the meal strange, but not because of the food. It was good and fresh and spicy and accompanied by a semi-alcoholic drink whose name he failed to catch. It was strange because this was the first meal he had not felt he had earned or had a part in preparing. The first meals at Landing didn't count.

They were seated in what looked like a large room in a larger-than-normal home. It was not what Javin would have thought of as a restaurant. There was no menu. You got what was available. It was simply a place for people to come and sit and eat and drink.

What should have been a relaxing experience was marred by the effects of the recent news. People whispering and looking shocked. Some braver ones coming to Torrint and asking for details, which he or Banith carefully repeated. Javin never got answers to his questions about sending the message.

Being amongst this number of people was now, Javin realized, unusual. It was the biggest group of people he had seen since his arrival. That newness meant that it was unnerving. He became aware of feelings, of emotions around him and was thankful for Torrint's words. Not having been amongst people for so long, he hadn't realized just how much he used to absorb from them. He flashed back to Haven, or what he could recall of it, and understood far more precisely just how little of his emotions and reactions were purely of his own making. It was a sobering realization. It was with some relief to him when they were able to leave and return to the hut and their nearby wagons.

There were a few people waiting quietly inside the hut, sitting with their backs against the low wall. Bendiss, now wrapped up in several blankets against the pervasive chill, was finishing some bread and drained the last of some juice as they arrived. He shook his head at them.

"Nothing yet. Maybe they'll be sending soon." He gestured at the people there. "You're welcome to stay and wait with the others."

Javin didn't know if he really wanted to be with more people and was about to go to the wagon and wait there when he felt a strange tingling in his head, as if someone was trying to scratch his skull from the inside. Startled, he turned to find Bendiss sitting up straight, eyes closed and a look of concentration on his face. That something was happening was apparent from the attentive attitude of the onlookers. The itching became almost unbearable before quickly fading away. Soon after, Bendiss opened his eyes and stood up. He seemed more relaxed now and gathered his thoughts for a moment. Finally, he spoke directly to Torrint and Banith. "As you can tell, we have the Group's answer. It is as follows. First, they thank us for the information. Second, they will investigate this further and see if anything like it has happened elsewhere. Third, they suggest that Harmony be left to deal with Blackeye as it was She who brought this about. Last, they ask us to inform them of anything else which seems even slightly unusual, or not as it should be." He reviewed his thoughts and nodded as he found them to agree with his words.

Torrint stood for a moment mulling over the message. Finally, he touched his fingers to his brow and formally thanked Bendiss, bowed once to the onlookers and then headed to his wagon. Within a few moments they were all three heading off. The clouds were breaking up and the occasional sunshine warmed them on the outside, but Javin nevertheless felt a chill inside.

It wasn't until much later, when they had left the town behind and the sun had dropped, that Torrint came to a halt. His bleak demeanor had forestalled any possible conversation Javin might have wished to start. It was only after having settled the beasts and they were seated around a small fire, picking at some dried fruit, that Javin felt he could at last ask all the questions which had been piling up. Torrint appeared lost in thought still, so he turned to Banith.

"What happened back there?"

"Which part, Javin?" Banith asked.

"I don't know where to start. How did it work? The messages thing? Did they really send a message to Landing? And Landing sent one back? How?"

Banith shook his head. "I don't know. All I know is that those deecees in the hut were responsible. That and the people there. You have to have enough people to make it work, that I do know. That's why small places, like the farm you were on, don't have them. But how it works? I have no idea. They're old. Very old. Apparently they came with, or were made by, the first settlers here. That's maybe a story. They are certainly old. But beyond that? I don't know. I just know it works. We've been there when they've sent messages, but never been part of it. That was the first time for me, for us."

"What are they called again? It's strange to see something here made of what looks like plastic."

Banith looked puzzled momentarily. "Plastic? I don't know what that is. We call them deecees, but I don't know what that word means. It's what they've always been called. They are old and they are strange, but they work and always have worked."

"So where do you get them from, these deecees?"

"Landing. They have them, I think. The tales are that they are supposed to have lots of them there. If you live somewhere that has enough people, you can ask Landing for one and they'll send it."

Javin thought for a moment. "But that would take ages! Is that really how it works?"

Banith nodded. "Yes. It would take a long while. But, here, that is not so important, maybe."

Javin gazed into the fire, still aware that there was still so much he did not understand about this planet. He finished off his fruit and tossed the dark seeds into the fire where they cracked and spat blue sparks.

"Why are we here, then? Not back in Sweetwater?" And suddenly he remembered. "Hey! We were going to find a healer for me there! What happened to that idea?" This last was addressed to Torrint, who finally stirred. Unusually, he didn't stop to spit or jam a leaf into his mouth. Javin could not recall him not chewing for so long. He took it as a sign of deep disturbance.

When Torrint spoke, his voice was heavy and his words slow, slower than usual. "We are here so people can stop looking at us and thinking of their dead relatives. We are here because nobody would want to trade with us. We'll spend a day or so and then see about going back. I made a promise to you about the healer and I intend to see it through. But another day or so will not add hurt to you or make it worse for you. But it might make it easier for everyone. So we stay here." He looked back along the path they had taken but there was no evidence of any buildings in the gathering gloom. No lights showed, no sounds could be heard. Javin thought they could be miles and miles away, or just around a hill. "If people really want to find us, they can. We're close enough to be found. Far enough to be hidden."

Javin felt angry with himself for having forgotten about the healer until just now. He understood Torrint's reasoning, but it did not help to think that just back a few hours there could be someone who could help him remember who he was. He could walk back, but not in the dark. He couldn't do anything right now, and he didn't like it.

He went over the day again in his mind. Replay after replay. He still did not know how it had worked, but apparently someone from Landing had somehow heard them and answered. Lisick or Gerant. He knew them both. And thinking of them made him realize that, apart from Torrint and Banith here, probably nobody in Sweetwater knew them, knew what they looked like. There were so few people here on this planet and everyone knew only a few others. It was a strange thought; the separation, the isolation, the distances.

"What do you think of the answer Lisick and Gerant sent back?" He couldn't find the healer, but he could talk about people he knew. "Did it make sense to you? 'Leave it to Harmony'? Shouldn't they have a proper burial?"

"A burial is putting people in the ground, isn't it?" Torrint drawled. "They will end up in Harmony, one way or another, won't they? So what's better about digging holes for them?"

"But it shows respect! It shows someone cares."

"Seems to me that plenty of people back there cared. Digging holes isn't going to add to that."

The anger at the missed opportunity to find the healer, the evidence of advanced technology, the metal which came from Haven, the ability to speak across distances but not know how it was done, all of it came to a sudden point in Javin's mind. "So, whatever Harmony does is right? Can't be argued with? Even though young children died, were killed, in

Blackeye? That's fine! Because it was Harmony that did it. Harmony that killed them. They deserved it. All of them. Especially the kids, eh?" Javin's fists were balled in anger as he spat his words out. "They made a mistake and they were killed for it. That's not justice, that's... that's--"

"That's what happens here." Torrint's voice cut across Javin. "This is not your planet. This is not your place to judge us. You don't even have a talent, just potential. You have no right to judge us. No right. Harmony keeps us safe and we respect Her and what She wants. She lets us live here--"

"Lets you live? Lets you?" Javin could not contain himself. "Is that what you believe? That you have no rights? None? That She can kill you whenever She wants? Like squashing a bug? Is that how you see it?"

"It's not that simple--," Banith began.

Javi rounded on him. "It's exactly that simple! Harmony controls life and death here and nobody has any say in the matter? You were born here, Banith? Did you ask to be?" Banith shook his head. "So even though you didn't ask to be here, Harmony could kill you simply because She didn't like you. Maybe, with the very first settlers, the ones who weren't invited, that would be fair. But now? After all this time? Everyone here was born because She let the first ones live. That's not right. It's just not!"

Banith tried again. "We, all of us, have a responsibility here. A responsibility to Harmony. To live together--"

"I don't want to hear it." Javin was on his feet staring across the flames at the other two. "And you want to know why? It's because neither of you saw anything wrong in what was said. Neither of you, and nobody in Sweetwater come to that, thought that they should go and bury the bodies and show some respect. Nobody felt it was the right thing to do." He suddenly felt drained, empty. "And that's just wrong. It's wrong." Tears were in his eyes. "I don't want to be here, but I can't leave and there's nothing I can do to change this. And to think I could be killed any day by a planet... a planet! Just because it feels like it! People kill other people. Planets don't!

"I don't want to end up not caring about the dead. Maybe, when I get my memories back, I'll find out I was a murderer. But, until then, I want to think that I could at least care about others. And, yes, I should have done something. I'm just as much to blame. But so is Harmony, if you're right." With a final shuddering sigh, he turned away and found a place between the wheels where he could see the stars but hide his face.

He felt a greater distance between himself and anyone or anything now. It was, he realized, what being completely alone really meant. That feeling settled deeper into him as, little by little, he drifted reluctantly into sleep.

13

Javin was in a place he thought he almost recognized. He was walking down a lane, narrow and with high earthen banks on each side. It looked old, felt old. Ancient. The age of it was strangely comforting, as if the previous travelers, however few over the years, had known where they were going and had left that certainty and sureness of step buried in the ground itself, ready to leach into his footsteps and give him that self-same comfort. The banks either side of the lane curved away upwards. Perhaps the age-long use had worn the depth down. Or, maybe the banks had somehow grown to nurture and protect the way. On the top of the banks, which were just a little taller than his head, hedges of some sort grew in such a way as to block out any distant views. But the sunlight could still percolate through to where he was. The whole feeling was of seclusion, security, acceptance and an underlying purpose; even if he did not yet understand what that was.

He was walking. He did not know from where or for how long or to what destination. But he was walking with a purpose. As he walked, so the banks lowered a little until they were at head height. But, as they lowered, so the hedges thickened and grew taller, interweaving above him to maintain the secretive gloom. As he walked, he became aware that he could see what looked like a gap in the bank ahead. At least, it seemed it might be. There appeared to be a slight brightening emanating from there. It felt as if he was being beckoned in some fashion by the glow, as if it was his destination. He reached that point and saw the earthen bank still directly in front of him, but there was a hollow in the bank and the path curved to it. The slight glow he had seen was indeed coming from this entrance, this doorway. For that is what he saw it was, a doorway, and he felt the invitation to go through it.

He walked through, without stooping, although he was sure that it had looked smaller at first glance. The glow increased slightly inside. As he walked, downhill it seemed, he noticed the roots of the hedge protruding from the earth. He was aware that the earthen walls felt warm and dry, solid and secure.

As he went deeper, so there began to grow in him a sense of something important, an impending event to which he was, somehow, privy. He could not bring to mind what exactly he was there for, but he knew it to be of huge importance. And as that awareness grew in him, so did his excitement. But he was also aware that this was to be a solemn occasion, no room for levity in any way. Therefore, he kept his excitement in check, knowing he would remember the reasons for all this in due course.

Finally, after following a slow bend in the tunnel, he found himself before a wooden door. It opened into a room. The walls were of wood panels, plain worked, and the room was well lit by a source of light he was not quite able to discern. His sense of anticipation was now intense. He knew it was close, whatever it was. He knew he had to wait here until the next step in this journey was revealed to him. He was not nervous; there was just a deep-rooted sense of well-being, of something about to happen which would, in some fashion, change his life. It was a good feeling.

Something prompted him to turn around. He found that a man had entered the room from some unseen doorway and was waiting for him. The man was dressed in clothes which were beautifully cut and fashioned and scrupulously clean, with sharp creases and polished buttons. The whole effect was of crisp cleanliness combined with stately grandeur, for the man's appearance matched that of the clothes he wore. He was old yet with a keen eye and filled with vigor, slim but not thin, deferential but not servile, helpful yet in command. His whole attitude spoke of service and high office combined.

Without knowing how, Javin realized that there had been a courteous inquiry as to his readiness for the meeting. She was ready to receive him now, if he would come this way. At this, Javin knew with utter and complete certainty that She was the source of the light in this room. It emanated from Her. In Her presence, it would be dazzling! Unbearable! And he wanted so much to be in it, be in Her presence.

He followed the man around a corner of the room he had not been aware of and there, before him, were the doors to Her chamber, open for him, Her light flooding out, filling everything. But there was more than just light. Being this close, he could also make out sounds; a rich complexity of sounds, harmonics, melodies, symphonies and single, achingly pure notes. The sound and the light wove into each other, forming something almost tangible.

The man, the chamberlain or whatever his role was, stopped, bowed to Javin and indicated with the slightest of gestures that he should go on.

Javin could not see anything except the light ahead of him. It became brighter, richer. Somehow it seemed that it wrapped around him, enfolding him in its magnificence. It was light, for it filled his eyes and his brain. It was of Her. It emanated from Her and enfolded him. Then the clear, sweet-sounding blending of notes, of complex songs, also became part of it. They too wrapped themselves around him, dove into him, filled him, every part of him. She was pouring into him as much of Herself as he could stand. She wanted to fill him, to let Herself be known by him. She trusted him to accept Her and to know Her. And still the light poured in and still the sounds enveloped him, filled him and echoed within him. He was embraced and enfolded within it all.

It was sublime and humbling at the same time. If he could have moved voluntarily, he would have thrown himself on the ground in obeisance. He felt charged. He was graced by Her presence and blessed by Her light, fed by Her music.

Standing there, he could not utter a sound of his own. He was not sure if he could look upon Her directly. Was it even allowed? And then he knew that he dare not look at Her, only glance at Her from the corner of his eyes. Grace, beauty, vast intelligence and, most humbling of all, the gentlest and deepest and kindest humor he had ever felt. It was as if She knew him from his birth and yet She found him of worth and of delight to Her.

For the merest second, the slightest moment, he was aware of the side of Her face. The slightest hint of a profile and it was forever in his memory. That flash of a face was burned in him. The chin, the angle of the cheekbone, red hair tumbling, and, oh most glorious! Her eye! He could not ever describe it to anyone else. She was not looking at him. How could She, if he were to survive? She knew the weakness of him and forbore to look directly upon him. She saved him with Her grace, by looking just far enough away from him to allow him to see. With a direct gaze, She would not turn him to stone, but to pure light, where he might be part of Her light. She forbore from adding his sounds to Her.

The breath was sucked from him. He was weak with exaltation and joy. He became dimly aware that the chamberlain had appeared by his side, had guided him by his arm back to the room from which he had come. The light dimmed, the music softened. Was it because She had withdrawn, or had the doors been closed? He did not know. All he knew was that he was trembling with fatigue and excitement. Yet, She remained in him, in some fashion. In his mind? In his spirit? It was more than memory. It was as though he had been immersed in something wonderful and joyous and it had permeated throughout him, penetrating every aspect of him, impossible to remove. And he would never want to remove it. He knew that. He was utterly changed by Her. He had been blessed by Her.

He sat, unaware that he had been seated, trembling with the after-effects of the audience. He became aware of a responsibility he had had placed on him. A responsibility: a deep and abiding duty that he was eager to take up even if he could not articulate it. The awareness of it merely added another layer of wonder and gratitude and certainty.

He was exhausted and found that the seat he was in was immensely comfortable. He managed one more look around, knowing that this would be the last time he would be here. He felt vast regret. He wanted to be able to stay close to Her, never to leave. Yet he knew he could not. It was not possible. Feeling blessed, triumphant and exhausted, he struggled to stay aware, to remain present as long as he could. But even as his desire formed, he felt a wonderful lethargy begin to wash gently through him. He fell gently asleep into the calling blackness.

When he awoke, he opened his eyes to see the wagon's timbers overhead and was confused momentarily as to where he was. He was instantly flooded with sadness, knowing he was no longer there, near Her. For a moment, he did not move, fearful of losing the memories. He wanted to go back again!

As he lay there, the knowledge of the meeting, of what had happened, forced sadness away, leaving him with the need to share what he had witnessed, what had happened to him. It was so vitally important, so wonderful, that he knew he had spent a whole day there. Despite waking in the same place, he knew he had been with Her for at least one day. One whole day! How else could he account for the time spent walking there and then being before Her?

Torrint and Banith must obviously have missed him and wondered about him. He was curious as to the questions they would ask of him. The problem would be how much of it he could share. So much of it was what he felt and that was so difficult to express. She could not be described. Not by him, anyway. He was suddenly bursting with the news of his meeting with Her. The joy of that meeting, the expanse of it within him, felt as though it would erupt from him and he would only be able to smile and laugh when they questioned him. He had seen Her! He had been in Her presence! How could he not erupt with the immensity of it all?

So, as the rising sun lit his face, he lay there for a while longer, letting the feelings course through him again. He felt amazing! He was determined not to be the one who spoke about it first. It was for them to ask. It was his role not to boast. He would show Her he was worthy of Her trust through his silence.

The sun rose and the laughter inside abated a little, but not the sense of wonder and of grace and of joy. With great difficulty, he got up and performed his normal duties. Behind every action lay the awareness that he now had a vital role to play; something he did not fully know in his conscious mind. But, deep down, where the true mark of Her presence lay upon him, where Her sounds, Her songs, Her light, still remained, Javin knew that the knowledge was there, to be revealed to him. Hard as it was, he made every effort to act as he had been before meeting Her.

Torrint and Banith were already both up and about as usual. Javin could simply not understand why they did not say anything? Surely they had been aware that he had been absent from them for most of the previous day? Surely they had questions? Did they not want to know about Her? He had been absent for at least a day. It was inconceivable that they remain quiet, but that is exactly what they did.

Javin recalled that he had been angry the last time they had spoken. But he could not remember why. Perhaps they were still angry at him? He could not tell. All he knew was that he was determined to keep his secret until such time as they asked, but he could not believe they had such willpower to remain silent as they washed, ate, checked and re-arranged the stock in the wagons.

Javin played his part as always, but with a growing sense of bewilderment. He had to concentrate on what he was doing more than usual because the experience of Her infiltrated everything, every action.

Javin was sitting, re-living, again, the audience with Her, when Torrint finally came and sat beside him.

"Seems to me that things have changed here." He leaned back slightly as if to view Javin from a new angle. "This morning I look ahead and I see us heading away from Sweetwater. Not what I was expecting. But then again..." He spread his hands to indicate the inevitability of what he had seen.

Javin said nothing, waiting for the inevitable question. But it did not come. What did come was a surprise.

Torrint looked off into the distance. "You've seen Her, haven't you? Met Harmony." A slow shake of his head. "Never happened to me. But," he turned and pointed at Javin with one long finger, "with you, it's like a big sign on you. You're different. Act different. Act happy. Somehow seem more, what's a good word for it, solid. Yes, solid. Real. She must have come to you in your dream last night.

"People don't change the way you've changed since last night. Not without something to change them. All anger and blame one minute, all gentleness and 'life's wonderful' the next." He gazed off into the distance again and a certain wistfulness entered his voice. "Don't need a talent to see this. We both saw it straight away, Banith and me. Just need to look at you." His voice sank lower. There was a yearning in it. "I wish I could feel what you feel. I can see it in you, but..." He fell silent.

All Javin could think of at first was that Torrint had to be wrong about the time. It had surely been a day at least. It made no sense, but Torrint was sure. It would become clear later on. Then he suddenly felt sorry for the tall man sitting beside him. "I didn't know what it was. Was it really Harmony? Is that how She is? She was... magnificent!" His eyes filled with tears of sheer joy. "There are no words, Torrint. She is the most incredible, the most wonderful... I don't think there are the right words, ever. I did not ever think I could ever feel anything like this." He touched Torrint lightly on the arm as a sort of apology. "I did not ask for this, Torrint. She simply called me, took me. I am sorry."

Torrint, still looking into the distance, nodded his appreciation, but Javin could see that he also had tears in his eyes, tears of sadness. The two of them sat together silently.

Finally, it was Torrint who coughed and cleared his throat, rubbing roughly at his face, still not able to look at Javin. "We need to take you to where you can be with Her. That will be my service to Her. That's why we are not going to Sweetwater." He pushed himself up, paying close attention to a blemish on his leggings. "We will take you to be with Her, to know Her reasons." And he stalked off, leaving Javin still wondering, still amazed at it all.

By the time they moved off, Torrint was more or less his old self again. More or less.

Now that both the traders knew, Javin felt a sense of relief, but also, somewhere, an emptiness. He realized that beyond sharing the knowledge of the audience, he had no clear conception of what to do next. As if sensing that in him, Torrint pointed ahead.

"That line of hills? That's the beginnings of High Stones. In there's a place for you. Don't know how, just know that's the way to go. Do you feel it? Like being pulled there? All I know is that when something like this happens, Harmony's calling to you. And you have to go to Her, to where She wants you to go. And if you don't, it will end badly, if the tales are true." He flashed a full, warm smile at Javin. "And I get to tell the next tale! Being this close, that's worth everything." He turned his attention back to the hills. He was unusually talkative, giving information without being asked. "Be two days maybe. Maybe less. Nothing's going to be for certain now. Not now we're listening to Her needs, now that She's spoken to you. The land we're heading for rises and splits up and canyons are all over. It's a strange place. But no good for trading. No people and nothing there people need."

"But why am I going there? What for?"

"Maybe to find out what you're doing here," Torrint suggested. "You can't be as close as you need to be with anyone else around. It has to be you and Her. Alone. And don't ask me how I know that. I just do. Everything we do and touch and breathe is Harmony. That anger you had with Her last night?" He shook his head. "Means nothing to Her. But you do. You mean something, apparently. Living with just Her to listen to? That's important. That's why you have to be alone." He saw the look on Javin's face. "And don't worry! We'll leave you enough food. Banith'll make sure you're going to be safe." He paused and smiled again, this time to himself. "And so will Harmony. Do you really think that She is going to let you die? After calling you?" He chuckled. Then he became suddenly serious. "And I have been called as well, to be part of it. Banith and me. We are also called by Her." He touched his fingers to his forehead, then towards Javin. "Thank you. Thank you for this."

Javin bobbed his head, embarrassed, unable to think of a reply.

14

I took two whole days.

The wagons had followed the barely visible track into a land where gullies became canyons and rocks pushed higher and became cliffs. The going slowed as the way became narrower, and the track became more uneven, with the occasional larger stone or boulder needing to be moved aside.

As the walls grew higher around them and the plants became smaller and spikier, Javin felt less and less comfortable with the idea of being left here, no matter how often Torrint told him that they would leave him food, make sure he would be safe and that Harmony Herself would look after him.

Taking his seat again after he and Banith had levered another large rock to the side, Javin asked Torrint, "Are you even sure you and Banith will be able to get out of here? There's no way you can turn round and go back."

Torrint thumped his chest with a fist. "I feel it here. I feel it as if I am being pulled. And, if Banith and me, the both of us, are part of this, then She will take care of us." He grinned. Javin doubted Torrint had ever been this happy for this long.

"And that's what this is all about, isn't it? You trusting this planet?

Trusting Her? That she won't let you down? But she has let people down. She killed them in Blackeye."

"That is not the same. And you. You've met Her. You know. Yes, the trust is everything. But so is listening to Her. Hearing Her. This is not the same as Blackeye, Javin. Listen to what's inside you and you know that's true."

Creaking and rolling, the wagon turned a final bend. There, ahead of them, the track opened up into a wide bowl of rock. The cliffs, streaked with red and grey and yellow, their tops glowing in the late day's sun, seemed less imposing. Some few huge boulders were scattered and a small stream, issuing from one of the walls, curled around them before disappearing again further down the canyon. To Javin's mind, there was a sense of peace, of stillness, here which he had not been fully aware of since the dream.

Torrint hauled them to a stop and, standing on the narrow footrest, looked around, smiling hugely.

He jumped down and, turning to Javin, thumped his chest again. "Don't tell me you don't feel it. This is the place. This is where you get to know Her. You know this is the place!"

Banith had already left his wagon and was crouching by the stream, sipping from his cupped hands. "This water is very good. Very good indeed." He took a handful of earth and closed his eyes and turned in a slow circle, arms outstretched. Opening his eyes, he dropped the earth and looked at Torrint. "I can sense no danger in the past here. No hunting kills."

"So where does he live?" Torrint was as excited and animated as Javin had ever seen him. Both he and Banith were inspecting the ground, looking up at the walls, scrambling over rocks.

Javin, still seated on the wagon, looked on, but all he could feel was loneliness and uncertainty. Since that night, the euphoria had lessened. The experience had become a dream, and dreams were normal. A part of him wanted only to reclaim that night's feeling and share it with the two traders. Another part of him knew Torrint was right about everything but didn't want to agree, didn't want them to leave.

And if Torrint was right, then what would that mean? Would he get his memories back? Would he even want them back? There were so many questions. How would he live? What would he do here? What would he do afterward? Having that dream was one thing; and it had been a wonderful, powerful dream. But living here, because of that dream? That made no sense. But, then again, very little of anything had made sense since he had arrived.

Once again, he felt trapped by circumstance, left with no choice because he did not know enough to choose. It was unfair, just as his arrival had been unfair, as wiping his memories was unfair. He bowed his head, closed his eyes and hugged himself in consolation. And as he did so, he felt a warmth on him, spreading through his body, filling him with a sense of peace.

Opening his eyes, he saw that he was in the light of the setting sun as it slipped briefly between the walls, the rays reaching down along the canyon, falling on him as he sat on the wagon. Bathed in the unexpected warmth, he found a reserve of strength inside that allowed him to accept that, unfair or not, he would finally be in charge of his life, at least for a while. And that was something worth having.

"I think I've found the place," Banith called. He was standing on a ledge about twice Torrint's height above the floor of the canyon. Behind him was a large hole into which he vanished. A moment later he reappeared, beaming happily. "This is definitely the place. Come and see!" He beckoned at Javin, but Torrint was not going to miss out, and he was scrambling up before Javin left his seat.

A few moments later, all three were standing on the ledge admiring the view. Banith waved them inside, eager to share his discovery. "See? This has a nice bend to it. Stops the wind but allows some light." He scurried ahead. "And it gets bigger. You can easily stand up and stretch. Well, you can almost, Torrint. And a raised area for sleeping." He pointed as he spoke. "A place for a fire, because there's a crack which will take the smoke out. It's perfect."

Torrint made appreciative noises. "It could have almost been made for you, Javin." He frowned. "Maybe it was."

Banith shrugged happily. "Let's get you moved in, Javin." He headed off to the wagons.

"Well? What do you think? Can you live here?" Torrint asked.

"Do you think it was made for me?"

"I think it's possible. I believe if Harmony wants things to happen, She can make them happen. Maybe She made this years ago and only allowed us to find it. Or maybe She made it just now. Or, it's just a natural thing and we were lucky to find it." Torrint looked over at Javin. "But it doesn't really matter what I think or believe. This is yours if you want it. Do you?"

Javin looked around the cave, running his hands over the walls, trying to imagine himself alone here. "I think I do. I just don't know what's going to happen. That scares me a little."

"What I'd do? I'd find out what I can do. Try anything and everything." Torrint cast a sly glance at Javin. "You don't admit to a talent, so why not see what talent or talents you might have?" He brushed some dust from his sleeve. "It's you and Her here. But mainly it's you. I have no idea what will happen, or even what could happen. My sight gives me nothing. But my mind says that you have to learn something about yourself. Beyond that...?" He shrugged. "Now let's help Banith, shall we?"

But Javin did not move. "How long do I stay? And where do I go after? Torrint? What am I really doing here?"

Torrint turned back and sat cross-legged on the floor, gesturing for Javin to do the same. The trader waited for him to settle. "You're looking for answers and there aren't any which make sense." He waved his hand at the cave. "This? It might have only been here since just before we stopped the wagons. It might have been here since Harmony was born. As for how long you stay, there is no answer. You will leave when it is right. And you will know when that is. And where you go, you will know at the time. And what you will do here is whatever you will do." He saw the look on Javin's face and stopped. "Yes, I can see that's not very helpful, so let me try to put it another way then.

"I did not have the dream, did not meet Her. Yet both Banith and I have felt the same urge to come here. It was not just trusting, it was being led. For all I know, the mandria felt the same as well. You, on the other hand, have had no opportunity or reason to trust Her fully, only the dream. And yet, you must trust. Because I know, I know, that She will not speak with you and then leave you to die." He held out his cupped hands to Javin, his voice becoming more earnest. "You are held by Her, protected by Her. You are special to Her for reasons I do not know and cannot guess. This is where She wants you to be, so this is the place where She will take care of you. You can believe that or not, but I feel it is the truth. Whether you feel it or not, whether you want it or not, you are blessed by Her. Above all, Javin, you are safe. Know that, if nothing else."

Javin tried to accept and understand what Torrint had said. He rubbed his fingertips along the rough floor, and, nodding, took a deep breath. "I will try to believe that, Torrint. Truly, I will. It's just such a big step."

Torrint smiled and nodded. "Yes, it is! This is your first home on Harmony." He stood up. "So let us make it ready to live in, yes?"

15

As Javin was contemplating his immediate future, Lisick was pulling at her shawl against the stiff breeze as she walked, trying to clear her mind. The roof of The Hall was still visible behind her. She hadn't had any clear destination in mind when she had set out, but now she realized where she was headed. Ahead were The Caverns, where the original settlers, so many, many years before, had stored so much. Most of what was in there was a mystery now. A lot of it appeared broken or decayed. Crates of some once-shiny material were in tumbled heaps. Some had lost their tops and spilled their contents. Others were intact. It mattered little, because what was revealed was generally unintelligible, unfathomable or just strange. Objects with no discernible use now remained as witnesses to the passage of time and changing knowledge of the people who lived here. Any useable metal they might have had had long been stripped and re-used.

The only usable things remaining were the deecees. There was still a large number of these grey disks, with no apparent workings in them, made of a material which did not scratch or bend, piled in a rough heap. It was as if at some time in the past, they had been poured here and left. It was from this pile that one was taken when a village requested it. A dog cart, a backpack, a canoe; old means of travel for these older pieces of equipment which no-one knew anything about anymore. Nothing other than the fact that, somehow, if people were able to focus their thoughts at them, they were able to send messages back to Landing, to The Hall, to the Group, or what remained of it.

And that was what was troubling Lisick. That and the events at Blackeye.

Something was wrong and she could not define it or understand it. And both of those things made her more unsettled. If something was happening with Harmony, then she wanted to know about it. It was her job to know about it.

She kept walking, hoping that it would clear her mind, give her new insights perhaps.

She found herself at the entrance to The Caverns and stopped. Gerant was poking around in there. He was trying to find the oldest records, the ones on the strange, thin, strong sheets, to see if he could get any clues to what was happening now. He was determined to find something, anything, which would help them. Although she envied his energy, she was doubtful that he would find anything of use. She recalled the few times she had gone in there, early on in her time at Landing. A few containers with sheets and sheets of writing. It had seemed then, and still seemed now, that it was the wrong way to learn about Harmony, by poking around in the past. Still, she was willing to leave Gerant to his task, however hopeless she privately thought it was.

Peering in at the entrance, she knew that ahead, around a couple of bends, she would find the deecees in the dim light. And beyond them, in another, smaller rock room, the old records, and Gerant poring over them by the light of a lantern. But there was nothing here for her that made sense. She could feel nothing here. It was all too alien. She was descended from the ones who had made the equipment, but she doubted she shared anything with them. It was too different. Her ancestors, so long in the past, were strangers to her and to everyone else on Harmony, despite these caves and their contents.

A sudden shiver brought her focus back to the present and she turned to retrace her steps back to The Hall with nothing having been settled or revealed to her. Briefly, she thought about finding Gerant, asking how he was faring. But she had already felt the answer. It was his task to do, no matter that it was pointless. She sighed and set off back.

She thought to sit a while in the kitchen and let the usual warmth there soak away the chill. When she arrived, the boy, Pasker, was eating some fresh bread on a stool, just inside the door.

She smiled at him. "You're always eating, Pasker."

"I'm always hungry, Lisick."

"Anything new?"

He shook his head as he chewed. "I would have fetched you. You know that."

Lisick dragged another stool over and sat beside the boy. Bellis was busy at the hearth and acknowledged her with a quick bob of her head. "Tell me, Pasker, how long do you have left with us?"

"I came when the sun rose directly over that mountain behind us."

"That mountain being....?" prompted Lisick.

"Sentinel, Lisick," he sighed exaggeratedly in response to her insistence on his being accurate, correct, against all his adolescent tendencies. "I came when the sun appeared above it."

"So how much longer, do you think?"

Pasker screwed his face up in thought and held up one hand. "Well, the sun this morning was about five palms from Sentinel. So I would guess maybe another..." he looked at his fingers and moved his lips as he counted to himself before flashing both hands at her.

"And what is that number, Pasker?"

He screwed his face up, moving his lips as he flashed his hands again, but this time at himself. "Fifty?"

Lisick nodded. "What you showed me was fifty, but I think it's actually going to be a little more than that. Remember, it depends on the size of your palm and whether you were holding your arm straight out. But, actually, we agreed with your parents that you would be back to help them at the start of the winter. It's a while yet before then, lad. I'm sorry. But have you thought about staying on after that time? Not going back to the farm?"

Pasker shook his head. "I don't think I will, thank you, Lisick. I don't think I have the talent to do it."

"How do you know?"

Pasker picked crumbs from the bread, rolling them in his fingers. "I've watched you. You and Gerant. You seem to be able to just hear Harmony and know what is going on. I've tried, when I can, when I've been asked, to listen in, but..." He shrugged.

"We could help you get better at it."

He shook his head.

"Why not? You could be very good. You just don't know."

Another shake.

"What's stopping you then?"

He focused on the remains of the bread, picking at it. "Truth?" he mumbled.

"Of course. Always."

He took a deep breath. "I don't want to live like you and Gerant. I don't want to farm either. I want to travel and maybe be a trapper or fish. Perhaps, later on, I'll meet a girl and..." His voice tailed off.

Lisick smiled ruefully and tried another approach. "But what we do here is so important, Pasker."

"Maybe so. But it's not the sort of importance I want. Here, you are trapped. You can't go anywhere. Not for long, anyway." His voice gathered strength. "What you do is good, I suppose." Lisick winced inwardly at that. "But I like to see things for myself. Take that message you had recently. About a village somewhere and people dead. Yes, I was able to sense of some of what happened, but I also listen to you and Gerant."

Lisick ignored that last sentence. "What about the village?"

"You don't know what happened and even if you did, you wouldn't see any changes you said to make." He spread his hands. "I want to see things change. I don't want to stay here and not see anything. There's so much to see."

"But I feel Her, feel Harmony, here, inside." Lisick pressed her palm to her heart. "It's like nothing else. It's special."

"Yes, but it's special to you, it's what you feel. It's not what I want to feel. I want to feel with my body, my hands. See with my eyes. I know Harmony is always with me, and I can always feel... something. But it's not special for me the way it is for you. I don't mean to offend." He searched her face for any possible recriminations.

Lisick patted his arm reassuringly. "You told me the truth. That is important. That is what I try to hear in Harmony, always. The truth is all there is for me, Pasker. So, no, I am not offended." She smiled warmly at him. "You know, it just occurred to me? You're a lot like I was at your age." She laughed at the puzzled look on the boy's face. "I knew exactly what I wanted. I wanted to be with Harmony. Be as close as I could be. And that meant being here at Landing. I didn't know that part of it then, of course. But that's how I ended up here. And you, my lad, know exactly what you want. And just like me, you have no idea where you'll find it. But you'll know it when you meet it." She leaned over and plucked the crust from him, smiling mischievously. "I am a little jealous, but only of your youth. But not too much. Not too much." She popped the crust into her mouth and chewed happily as she waved him away.

He ducked out thankfully.

Lisick's good mood slowly drained from her. She watched Bellis long enough for Bellis to realize she was being watched. Wiping her hands dry, Bellis grabbed a handful of nuts from a bowl and came and sat on the seat next to Lisick. She offered some but Lisick shook her head.

"You're worried, aren't you?" asked Bellis.

Lisick just nodded.

"I may not have the answer, but I have good ears and I can sense things when needed." Bellis slid a nut into her mouth and crunched down on it, content to wait, and also grateful for an excuse to stop for a while.

Lisick pulled at her hair as it fell over her shoulder. "I wonder if Gerant and me will be the last Group ever. And, if that's the case, what does that say about us, and what we do? Or try to do." She sighed. "I know there have been two person Groups before. But... this feels different. This feels like the end." She tilted her head at the door where Pasker had gone. "That lad there, Pasker, he's as good as anyone who could do what we do. Some training needed, sure. But good enough. And he hates the idea. Nobody we've heard of wants to do this anymore."

Bellis eased the tiredness in her shoulders. "And don't look at me," she said. "We've been over this too many times before. I cook and I love the garden, and all the other things I've said time and again." A small smile and a nod of the head from Lisick. "So you think you've failed? Is that why you're like this?"

"More like I think I've failed Harmony. I've let Her down somehow. Not been able to understand Her better." Lisick rubbed her eyes, trying to feel fresher in her mind. "Take this latest thing, for instance. Somebody found a village and all the people were dead. All of them. No disease. It looked and felt like She had made all of them deaf." A look of exasperation crossed her face. "And I can't find out anything to explain it. Nothing! And I keep coming back to the idea that either I'm not good enough anymore to hear Her when She speaks, or..." and she trailed off.

"Or She doesn't want to speak to you anymore," Bellis finished for her.

Lisick nodded, close to tears.

"So what did you tell them, the ones who passed the message on about the village?"

"Gerant and I decided that if Harmony wanted them dead, then there was no need to go poking around there any more. We told them to let Harmony finish what she had started and not to go to the village." She sighed deeply. "I don't know if it was the right decision or not. Neither of us could sense anything. Anything! What I do know is that I am feeling old, Bellis. Old and weary. And the worst of it is that I am no longer sure I am doing any good. I want to help Harmony, understand Her, help everyone living on Her to be closer to Her. And I am not sure I'm doing any good."

"And what Pasker said just now didn't help at all, did it?"

Lisick shook her head, glumly.

"What's Gerant doing?"

Lisick leaned back, arching her neck to rest the back of her head on the wall, gazing sightlessly upwards. "He's searching the records. Trying to see if anything like this has happened before. It's a good job he kept up on his reading better than I have. I don't think it will help, though."

"So what do you think your options are? Surely you're not going to give up?"

"I did think of that, for just a moment, believe it or not. But, seriously, the only option I can see is to keep trying to hear Harmony better. Keep doing what I'm doing, but see if I can do it better."

Bellis dumped the remaining nuts in her skirts and folded her arms as she also leaned against the wall, her head tilted toward Lisick beside her. "What if you're doing everything right? What if you're doing everything exactly as Harmony wants? What if this whole thing, the village, your lack of closeness with Her, what if all that is exactly what is meant to happen? What if this is how Harmony wants things? So, if you are the last Group on Harmony, what does that matter? If Harmony hasn't sent you anyone, and you can't find anyone, does that mean you're a bad or weak person? Of course not! How many times have I heard you say that Harmony is bigger and more intelligent than anyone or anything else? If you are honestly doing everything you can, and I know you are, then you have nothing to be depressed about.

"Yes, the Group has been part of Harmony since Landing became Landing. But being that old doesn't mean that it has a right to continue being. Most of the time, you and Gerant work to help other people live closer to Harmony, to understand her. You spend your time teaching others, giving them information they need. Maybe it's time to stop that and to start helping Harmony. See what you can do to help Her. If this is a big time of change, then you should be trying to help Her, not help the other people.

"If you really are going to be the last Group on Harmony, then end it by devoting yourself to finding out how you can help Her, help Her understand us better, perhaps. If nothing else, then just spend the rest of your time being as close to Her as possible. After all, that's what I heard you telling Pasker you wanted when you were his age. Why not do just that?"

Lisick had turned to Bellis as she had been speaking and was tugging at a few strands of her hair. "Maybe you're right. Maybe I'm taking this too personally. But it is hard not to. It feels selfish, thinking of doing what you said. But maybe I need to think in different ways." She smiled fondly at Bellis. "Thank you. You do really have a sense of things, don't you?"

Bellis put up a warning finger. "Oh, no you don't! Don't even start trying to persuade me. You do your thinking and I'll do my cooking." She stood up, and the nuts tumbled to the floor. "Wonderful! More work for me," she said, stooping to collect them, smiling to herself, keeping her head down, allowing Lisick to leave more easily.

Lisick wandered out with no direction in mind. She was thinking about what Bellis had said, trying to feel if she was correct. As she did so, she became aware of another reason for her unease and uncertainty of late. She retraced her steps. Bellis truly did have a sense for things, so, maybe speaking to her about it would help.

And so she found herself back at the large, old kitchen, leaning on the door jamb and chewing at her lower lip. Working contentedly, Bellis did not at first notice that Lisick had returned. When she did notice her there, Bellis tapped the table, "Come and sit and get a drink while I finish off here." Lisick sat and poured some juice out for herself. Bellis stirred one three-legged clay pot resting on hot coals, sniffed the steam, added a pinch of something from a small pot, poked at the contents of another, larger pot and seemed satisfied.

She wiped her hands and came to sit in a chair opposite Lisick, poured herself some juice from the clay pitcher.

Lisick traced swirls on the tabletop with her fingers, head bowed, letting her hair hide her face. Bellis waited.

"There's something else. You know that spaceship from Haven?" Bellis nodded even though Lisick hadn't looked up.

"Of course! I'm not blind. Or deaf, come to that. Oh! That noise! But why did we give them those plants, Lisick? I mean, they're just plants. Harmony has plenty more to spare. But why? And, more to the point, why are we having this conversation?"

Lisick did look up at that, pushing her hair back. "You're sharp, aren't you? We're having this conversation because I think I might need someone else to think about it. That someone is you. And as to the why, that's for a very simple reason. We didn't have a choice. They threatened to attack Harmony if we didn't provide them. And, by attack, I mean kill off plants and trees and animals by spraying poison. That's why we did it."

"I guessed it was something like that, but hoped I was wrong. It's just... wrong." Bellis shook her head at her inability to find the words for how badly she felt, how it went against everything she knew.

"They came out of nowhere. Haven't been here for ages. Years and years and years!" said Lisick. "And why now? And that boy? Why him? Shouldn't we be able to know these things?" She spread her hands in defeat. "Gerant and me, we can't find anything wrong. Nothing. So, there's the problem that I can't hear Harmony any more, that I don't understand why a village died, that I'm probably a member of the last Group after generations of Groups, that suddenly Haven wants our plants for what cannot be good reasons, and there's a threat, which we cannot hope to possibly stop, to harm Harmony if we don't give them what they want. And who knows when they'll be back?" She shook her head ruefully. "Those are enough reasons to worry, don't you think?"

"And you're telling me because..?" asked Bellis.

Lisick smacked her hand down on the table. "Because I want some help, you idiot! Why else?" Immediately she was full of contrition, reaching to Bellis across the table. "I'm sorry. That was wrong. Please forgive me. I'm worried and I can't see what to do. I am sorry."

Bellis smiled reassuringly at her. "I can understand you being upset. Forgiven, Lisick. You are forgiven. But I do not know what I can do."

"I'm too close to this," Lisick complained. "I was hoping that a fresh outlook... I'm too wrapped in it and can't stop thinking when maybe I need to stop thinking and just feel the way out."

Bellis frowned in thought for a moment. "What if there isn't a way out? Not in the way you want? What if nothing is going to be as you want it? No plants taken, no unexpected visits, Haven happy, you hearing Harmony, nobody else dies? What if that's never going to happen?" She looked around for inspiration. "For example, in this huge kitchen, too big by far for our needs now, I prepare and cook food. That's what you see me do. But, sometimes, I want to make a particular meal, use some of what's growing in the garden. I have everything planned in my head, but I find that what I wanted to use is rotten or something's eaten them, or something else has gone wrong. Maybe I can't get the fire hot enough or a pot cracks. Whatever it is, it ruins my plans. You don't know that, neither does Gerant. All you see is the food I made instead arriving for you to eat. You don't see the changes I had to make. Well, maybe that's the same thing as with you and Harmony. You want something to happen, but it's not going to. So you have to change what you do. Make different plans, do different things.

"With me and the kitchen, the end result is feeding you. Well, with you and Harmony, what's the end result?"

"To help Harmony, I suppose. Help us, everybody, and Harmony live together. That's why we're here."

Bellis nodded. "And you are stuck thinking there's only your way of helping. What if there's another way? Other things you can do instead?"

Lisick considered this a moment. "Other things? Like what?"

Bellis smiled and put her hands up, palms facing Lisick, making the boundary plain. "I cook. That's what I'm good at. You look after Harmony. That's what you're good at. You don't tell me how to cook and I won't tell you how to do what it is you do." She leaned forward. "I'm certain that what you have to do is think differently. Stop trying to make everything under your control. After all, Harmony is a very large lady! I am quite sure She is capable of a great deal more than we think She is. Let Her do the things She does. You have to find a new way of being with Her. I'm convinced of it." She stopped just short of patting Lisick's arm.

Lisick returned to making swirls on the table again as she considered what Bellis had said. There was, she was sure, a basic truth in there. She just couldn't see how to apply it.

She looked up through her tangle of hair. "Bellis, my dear, I am grateful for your time, your words of wisdom, as well as your delicious food. I apologize again for my earlier outburst. You've given me much to think about. So, doubtless you will be relieved to hear, I need to go away and think about what you said, and leave you to your kitchen."

She drained the last of the juice and was about to leave when Bellis asked, "And when exactly is Gerant going to be back? This is my kitchen, but it would be nice if I knew what I was doing in it."

"Those old records are a mess... . If he finds something he might well lose track of time. I don't know."

"I know he took some food with him," said Bellis. "I should have asked him, shouldn't I? I can't complain and then do nothing." She gave a small shrug of resignation and looked at the food she had been preparing. "Hmmm. In that case, if you would care to eat with me here, it will be hot and clearing up will be easier, plus I won't have to waste any. Not that Pasker would let too much pass him by."

"I would be delighted, Bellis. Thank you." The prospect of company for a meal lifted Lisick's spirits so that a genuine smile came to her face.

16

J avin had begun by marking the days on the walls. But, gradually, he had abandoned this practice, not because of an unwillingness to record the passing of time, but because of a growing understanding that doing so was without meaning. He would not be showing the scratches to anyone else, and as a method of recording time, it seemed ridiculous the more he thought of it. The passing of days, at first irritating and endless, consumed with small concerns about food and water, heat and comfort, slowly became smoother as they flowed through him. They did not become a blur of sameness nor of boredom. Indeed, he found that each day was a separate and distinct event which disclosed itself more easily to him as he was willing to let it be disclosed on its own terms. That could not be shown in a scratch mark on a wall. Besides, such marks were either counting up from something or down to something. Counting up made no sense as he had no idea how many days were in a week or month or if they even had such things. And counting down was equally without point, for he had no idea what, or when, such an event would be.

He had begun by wondering what it was that Harmony was going to make happen around him and by looking for such events every day. Sometimes, he thought he saw meaning in some small occurrence, such as the shapes of shadows on the cliff walls. Sometimes, perhaps for days at a time, he felt or saw no such indicators in the world around him.

Gradually, however, he found himself beginning to see the world as it chose to represent itself to him, without his attempts to add layers of meaning to it. By no longer seeking for messages, hidden or overt, he discovered that the world, at least as far as he could travel in a day, was full of interest. He found that he could discover the interactions between water flowing and the patterns of grasses growing further downstream; how the wind and the rocks combined to carve shapes and to channel breezes and carry scents of distant places; the rhythms of the creatures, large and small, by day and by night, who shared his small empire.

He had also begun by sleeping badly, with much tossing and turning, of staring emptily either at the stone ceiling above him, or, wrapped in a blanket, at the few stars and an occasional glimpse of the moon he could see from his doorway. And when he slept, he dipped in and out of dreams of dead people, of sudden unsettling sights of Haven, and of times of unease, of a sense almost of imbalance. He awoke frequently feeling an itch in his mind he could neither identify nor scratch. He yearned to dream his dream again, the dream, the dream of Her. But it eluded him, which fed his sense of irritation on awakening.

As time passed, however, he found that he could sleep more easily. There was greater depth to it, a comfort not evident earlier. Now and then, with no obvious rhythm or cycle, nothing appearing to be the trigger, he caught glimpses of Her again. The length and curve of the eyelash, seen from the side. That slant of cheekbone, almost lyrical in the way it felt to him as it caught just enough light to be evident. The hair, a wonderful richness, of a color which teased the light and was never only one shade. It tumbled and caressed, moved and shone, covered and revealed. Another night the dominant memory would be of the chin and the hint of a smile on the full lips which eased so simply into the beginnings of a laugh, never fully seen, only imagined.

One night, one vision or part-vision, the next, another. Never two the same. Always some new aspect to be seen, cherished, stored in memory and reflected on in the daylight.

At first, he spent a lot of time trying to know what his talent was. He tried to convince himself that there had to be something he was able to do that was 'different'. Recalling Paysa, he tried moving pebbles with his mind. He tried moving water, flowers, anything. But nothing happened. He tried seeing what Torrint was doing, but fell asleep instead. He even tried calling animals, any animals at all, to him. Nothing.

Every day he hoped that something would happen to convince him that he was able to do something. The teasing memories of the hay and the strange vision with the mandria remained just that: memories.

Sometimes he would hear that music again and became more and more convinced that it was something he knew as a child and it was part of his memories, that they were returning to him. But no other memories came, no other sounds, no recall of his early years.

Occasionally, the music was louder, more insistent, but he could never quite 'get' it. It always remained elusive. He couldn't find what it was associated with. It simply 'was'. Just when he thought he knew how it went, the music took a different turn, leaving him frustrated.

Javin came to enjoy the solitude. This was despite the lack of anything significant happening, and despite the fact that he felt he was essentially doing nothing of tangible worth each day. He was, he came to realize, doing something. He was coming to terms with being on Harmony. The silence when the music wasn't in his head, the stillness, the aloneness, were dragging him closer to the planet in ways he could not really explain. The urge to leave and get back to Haven expired silently at some point and he didn't really know when. The realization grew that here he was free to do whatever he wanted, even if that included doing absolutely nothing at all. It wasn't that he lacked ambition, for he still wanted to know what talent he might have, but that the ultimate aim of each day was to be content. Simply that.

Some days he sat on the step of his cave. Others he took to the cliff tops, following a scrambling path he had found and spent the day exploring, seeing distant vistas, watching the clouds. Sometimes, he just walked the canyons to see what was there.

He realized, as he traveled more, that where he lived was almost directly in the center of the canyons. One path led in, the one he had arrived in, and one path led out. But in between, there were so many winding routes, looping back on themselves, dead ends, paths which brought him up to the tops of the rocks but with no way down again that he could find. It was a place which rewarded exploration.

Without noticing it, without actually acknowledging it, he was feeling his way into being a part of Harmony. He became quieter inside, calmer and less concerned that he had to achieve anything.

One day, sitting in the sunlight at the entrance, he realized that there was a freshness to the air. Summer was dragging herself away and autumn was on the horizon, waiting to make a proper entrance. Now, she was just sending out early messengers in the shape of cool mornings, sharper, clearer air, subtle new shades of color, creating a resonance deep within him that told of a change coming.

On this morning, as he sat, so he soaked in the sounds around, noting them unconsciously, labelling them. Water entering the pond nearby, the rubbing of a tree against a rock as it responded to the breeze, a small animal hunting, the almost silent hiss of the breeze passing over and between the tall, thin strands of plants decorating the top of the canyon walls. These were the normal sounds of his life here. But then, a new sound. A strange, distant bleating almost and in the background, a creak and a rumble. The latter sounding just like a mandria would when pulling a cart.

He became alert and focused more closely. Yes, there was definitely something coming toward him. It was coming from the opposite direction from where he, Torrint and Banith had come. It would inevitably bring them here, to him, at the heart of the place.

He was unsure of how he felt about it. After being on his own, suddenly it was not his choice to remain that way. He had always assumed that, at some point, he would leave of his own accord and be with others again. But now, that was no longer a choice.

In part, he felt irritated, but another, deeper part of him was eagerly anticipating whoever or whatever was arriving. There was a sense of foreknowing, of an importance as yet unclear attached to this imminent arrival, which held him still and passive, unable to move, unable to meet or to hide from whatever was coming. He sat and he waited as the sounds grew and the hairs on the back of his neck and along his arms flexed and sent shivers through him. And he had no idea why.

Finally, a movement below and to his left. Around one of the larger of the boulders jumbled on the floor, where the stream collected in a small pool before wandering away, a head appeared. It was not anything he expected. It was the head of a large dog. Brown and black and shaggy-coated. Chest high, Javin thought, as it paced slowly into the clearing below. Not just tall, but powerful with deep set eyes in the head. Tasting the air, its black muzzle swinging from side to side, the head turned to point at Javin. Their eyes held each other's gaze for a long, silent moment. The dog ended it with a huffing sound, and made one low, rumbling sound, half-breath, half-bark and looked back over its shoulder.

As it did so, another dog appeared, grey overall, but just as massive. Its ears were pricked and it looked to its companion, seemingly listening to something beyond Javin's ability to hear before turning to face him, tilting its head first one way, then another; judging, deciding, evaluating. Another huffing cough and they both sat keeping him in view but also able to look back the way they had come.

At that point, Javin forced his attention from the two beasts below and became aware that the strange noise he had heard was growing in intensity. It was similar to small stones or rocks grinding against each other, but with overtones of many small voices babbling away. Not a sound he had ever heard before. And then the creators of that noise wandered into sight. Without a doubt, they were the strangest looking animals Javin had yet seen. They seemed to be birds of some kind, for they had long, flowing feathers, or what appeared to be feathers, drooping from their wings and tails. These were mainly a beautiful misty blue but he could see variations shading into pink and yellow, even green, and each with something like an iridescence which made them seem to shimmer. He realized that he had seen something similar to these. Tarla had wanted one from Torrint's wagon, he recalled. And here was a flock of the creatures. Their name eluded him, however.

Apart from the feathers, the legs were bright yellow, the same color as the yellow dot on the side of each wide beak. They walked, or waddled rather, with a rolling gait, heads nodding from side to side as if in acknowledgement and continual recognition of their companions.

Seeing the pool, they made slight honking sounds and stretched their necks to sip and drink before spreading out and settling down, the sounds dying down to a background mumbling and grumbling.

Finally, a wagon, hauled by a mandria, came into sight. Leading it was a figure in a long cloak with the hood up against the breeze. Finding a suitably level place, they came to a halt. The dogs had not moved and the person turned to them momentarily before swinging around to search out Javin. He could not see the features, hidden in the shadows of the hood, but he was aware that he was being stared at. Finally, the hood was thrown back and the face of a young woman was made clear, the distance making any detailed observation impossible.

She called up to him, "I won't be here but for a day or so. Let them get some rest before I move on again, if that's acceptable to you? Do you mind having company?" Her clear voice carried easily. It took Javin a moment to find his own voice. "Of course not. That will be fine." He had to clear his throat a time or two before the words would carry to her.

"Good! Give me a few moments to get settled and then, maybe we can say hello properly?" And with that, she busied herself with the harness.

Javin felt the prickling and shivers intensify as he watched her. He decided that he ought not to sit and watch but help in some fashion, so he began the descent to the floor of the canyon. By the time he arrived, she had unhitched the mandria and was almost finished tidying something away in the wagon. The mandria rumbled once at Javin before turning to drink.

Now he was at the bottom, Javin realized that the two large dogs, appearing even larger now, had not moved and were still staring at him, mouths agape, tongues lolling. They weren't directly in front of him, being more to one side, but he was aware that he would have to pass uncomfortably close to them. Uncertain what to do, how to act, he remained still and hoped that the woman would provide some assistance at most, or reassurance at least. The prickling grew as he stood there trying to observe her more closely.

At the moment, she was busily engaged in doing something in the rear of the wagon, so her head and face were hidden. Finally satisfied, she drew back and turned to toss her long, red hair away from her face.

At which point Javin felt as though he had been punched in the stomach. He felt as if he couldn't breathe nor believe his eyes.

For, as she stood there, half turned away, the profile she showed, the cheekbones in the light, the eyelashes, the lips, the hair: everything was exactly as in his dreams. This was the woman. And she was standing, careless of his amazement and wonder, in front of him.

17

The woman paused as she saw Javin's reaction. Her eyes narrowed slightly and a frown of concentration passed briefly before she spoke.

"Why the look? Is something wrong?"

Javin shook his head, trying to shake away how he felt. "No. I'm fine. I - I just haven't had much to eat today and I was a bit too quick coming down here." The part about not eating was true. He had planned to eat later on, but the sounds of her arrival had distracted him. Then he gave a nervous smile, pointing at the impassive dogs. "And then there's these. I'm not quite sure about them, and whether it's safe..."

She flicked a gesture at the dogs at the same time as making a short hissing sound. Immediately, they turned their attention away from Javin and stretched. One of them, the grey one, took to furiously scratching behind one ear. Quickly, they were both sprawled on their sides and appeared to have given themselves up to dozing.

"There," she said. "Better? They are very possessive. But they know when I say things are all right." She peered a little more closely at Javin. "And they are all right, aren't they?"

Javin nodded.

"So that's the dogs dealt with. Now what's the rest of it about?" she prodded.

"I'm fine. Really. I just need to sit for a moment." So saying, Javin slumped down as his knees seemed to be made of water, managing to keep himself sitting upright with one hand behind him. "I'm not used to visitors." He waved his other hand at the animals, at her. "It's - it's a bit of a shock seeing you here. That's all it is."

"A shock. Yes. I can see it is. I apologize. However, if you don't mind, I'd like to have something to eat. You are quite welcome...?"

"Oh! I'm sorry. I'm Javin," he said from his place on the ground, putting out his hand to her

Instead of shaking it (Javin recalled, too late, that Hanlar also had no idea what he was doing), she grabbed it with both of hers and hauled him up to his feet. She was strong, Javin realized. He found himself being regarded quizzically by two serious blue eyes, startling against the slightly tanned complexion which was almost hiding the freckles, and which was framed by her dark red hair.

She dropped his hand and took a half-step back, as if to get a better view. "Javin? Unusual name." After another short, expectant pause, she gave an almost imperceptible shrug and then touched her forehead with the first two fingers of her right hand then turned the hand so that her palm faced Javin, just as he had seen Torrint do. "Meldren Harnatta." She looked to Javin for his response. As ever, unsure of how to respond, he simply bowed his head. "Pleased to meet you, Meldren." He had no idea what to do with his hands.

It was obvious that Meldren found his response lacking in something, for she pursed her lips in brief disapproval. "Where are you from, Javin of no name?"

"Oh! It's Javin Sarnum. That's my full name. At least, that's what I think I remember it is. I'm sorry, I don't know the greeting you use," and he made a half-hearted attempt at the gesture she had made.

That obviously intrigued Meldren. "You're not sure of your own name, or how to greet someone? Is that true? Of course it is," she answered herself quickly, and added, almost as an aside, "Hmmm. That might explain things."

Javin decided to tell the truth about himself, as far as he could. But he was reluctant to tell her that he had seen her so many times before. He was sure it would not be a good thing to do on first acquaintance. "I'm not from here. From Harmony, I mean. I was brought here, kidnapped actually, on Haven. You know? The other planet? And I don't have my memories. Well, not of much before I was kidnapped, that is. So, I'm not really sure of very much, and that includes this thing with touching the forehead. We, that is, I, used to shake hands, like this," and he stuck out his hand again. He realized he sounded as if he was babbling. And, he had to admit, he was. Meldren looked at his hand, then back at him. "You hold my hand and we shake. Like this." Taking her hand, he placed it in his and he gently moved them both up and down, Meldren watching his face all the while. He let go and shrugged. "That's what I do."

"Another planet? Strange indeed." She raised her eyebrows and gave a grudging nod. "Well, now we've welcomed each other, I would like to eat and drink. We started very early. Well before dawn, and I'm hungry."

"Why so early?"

Meldren wrinkled her brow. "The truth? I'm not really sure. For the past two days, I've had this urge to keep moving, more than most days. and this morning, I just could not keep asleep. Felt irritable almost. Irritable, that is, until we got started and then it was just a matter of keeping going until we got here. I was headed here anyway, but it seemed, or felt, more urgent this time. No idea why, though." She looked around as if the answer was just out of sight. "And now we are here, it feels... comfortable. Peaceful, I suppose." She smiled, dismissing her thoughtful mood. "And now, some food and drink. You're welcome to share and then you can tell me why you are here." She smiled and went to her wagon.

She shared some cold meat, still juicy, fruit and bread with Javin. He was grateful for the variety, having long since finished the dried meats that Torrint and Banith had left him. The fruits and berries he had found had been surprisingly filling. Nevertheless, the change was most welcome and the bread, in particular, tasted wonderful.

"Have you been here before?" asked Javin.

"Mmmhmm," Meldren nodded, her mouth full. She swallowed. "It's the only good place in here to rest and camp that I've found."

Pointing to his cave, Javin asked, "Have you noticed that cave before?"

Meldren studied it for a moment. The mouth was just in shadow, meaning, Javin knew, that it was past midday now. "I don't think so. But it's been a while since I was here. I'm not sure. Why do you ask?"

"It's where I've been living. Traders brought me here."

"You mean Torrint and Banith?"

"You know them?"

"I know of them. They're pretty much the only ones in this area. So why did they bring you here?"

Javin was unsure how much to say. "I had a dream. A really clear dream. It seemed very real at the time but I didn't know what it was about. Torrint said that it was about me meeting with Harmony and that I needed to be here. At least, he said that he felt he was drawn to this place and that meant that was where I should stay until..."

"Until what?"

"That's the thing. I don't really know. It was about me getting closer to Harmony, but I don't know what that is or what it means really. I don't know how long I've been here. I do know that it's relaxing and I've mostly enjoyed it in a strange way. But as for the real reason, or what's meant to happen..." He shrugged.

Meldren considered this for a moment, stifling a yawn. "So you don't know much about Harmony and us and everything? About talents and so on?" Javin shook his head. "How long have you been here? On Harmony, that is."

"I don't know. I don't know how to tell the time here. It's seemed long. But how long? I don't know that."

Meldren yawned again. "I'm sorry, but that food after the walk here... I'm tired. I need to sleep. Can we talk later? I promise I'll listen better then. I want to hear about you and Harmony and Haven, and about your dream." She ran her fingers through her hair and smiled drowsily at Javin. "Once I get some sleep, I'll be fine. Until this evening?" And she got up and clambered up into her wagon. Javin could hear some rearranging going on and then silence.

He sat for a while trying to come to terms with the fact that the person he had seen in his dreams was here. But, unless she knew it, or was somehow in on the secret, he could not see what difference it was making. It seemed more like something was teasing him. If he told her, and she rejected the idea, the fact that she had been in his dreams, then what? Exactly the same if she accepted it. What happens next? He could not see anything which made sense in either response.

As he climbed, quietly, back up to his cave, he vowed that he would simply wait and see what happened. Either he would feel it was the right thing to tell her or he wouldn't. It was going to be up to her and how she reacted to him that would matter. That, at least, is what he told himself.

He found himself feeling sleepy and settled down to make himself comfortable.

He woke up, confused as to the time of day, to the sound of water splashing in the space below. Peering out, he saw by the shadows that it was early evening or late afternoon and the reason for the splashing sounds was that Meldren was washing her hair in the pool. The suds came from her applying some sort of mixture from a small pot.

He watched her for a moment, his body unwilling to move into action. She was industriously rinsing the last of the suds when he decided he really ought to be down there. He couldn't put it off. Not fully awake, he was clambering down when he slipped and slid the last section, grazing his elbows as he did so. Wincing, he made his way to the pool, intending to rinse out any dirt and inspect the damage. Instead, Meldren, who by then had rubbed and squeezed most of the water out of her hair which fell past her shoulders, stopped him to take a look. Holding up first one elbow and then the other to her, her eyes took on a distant look as she placed a hand over each injury. Javin felt a warmth as she did so. She smiled at him and indicated he could put his arms down. Straining to examine them, he was amazed to see nothing more than a few pinkish-red dots and some clean skin. And there was no pain at all, not even an itch!

"How did you...? I mean, what did you do?"

Her smile widened. "I forget. You're not from here." She gestured at his arms. "That? That's something everyone can do, more or less. You could, I'm quite sure, if you tried. It's nothing. That's about all I can do, though. Small cuts and scrapes; they are the things I can heal. It's good you didn't break a leg!" She went back to vigorously rubbing her hair. "I feel so much better for that sleep. And being able to wash my hair? Wonderful! How about you?"

She was definitely more lively now than when she had arrived, and Javin realized that he was feeling better as well. Perhaps sleeping in the day was the trick!

"I'm going to make a fire," she declared. "It's perfect in here, plus it'll help dry my hair quicker. And you can tell me about your dream."

She was quickly efficient at creating a warm fire, more glowing than leaping flames. Her two dogs were drawn to it and lay down opposite Javin, their eyes on him reflecting the glow. She sat next to Javin but with her back to the fire to help dry her hair. "So you met Harmony? What was it like? What did you see? What happened in it?"

Javin was not completely at ease. Sitting by a female near his age was new. And, he had to admit, it made him feel good in a way he hadn't experienced since his arrival. It was, he also admitted, tempered somewhat by the steady attentions of the dogs. And then there was the problem of how to tell it. "I really didn't know it was a dream. I thought I'd been away for a day and couldn't understand why nobody had missed me." He smiled ruefully. "It was... I don't really know how to describe it. I never actually met Her, met Harmony, only had this sensation that She was close. Like really close. It was Torrint who said that's who it was and that I should come here. If he hadn't said anything..." He shrugged. "I've had a sort of dream about Her since then, but nothing like that first one." He gazed into the fire, as if searching for the right words in its glow. "I feel out of place. I mean, it's peaceful here and as long as I can find some food and keep warm, it's fine. But the winter is going to arrive at some point and then what? I suppose I'll leave and go somewhere warmer. But where that is, I don't know."

Meldren tested her hair with one hand and then scooted around to face the fire. She bowed her head and brushed her hair forward to expose more to it. From beneath it, she said, "I've never met anyone who had Harmony come to them in dreams. Only heard stories. And, yes, I believe Torrint. He knows the truth of things. I'm just surprised you haven't got a talent. I mean, dreaming with Harmony and everything. Ooph!" She sat up, her hair falling behind her. "I can't stay like that for long. Besides, it's dry enough. It'll do." She started combing it through with her fingers as she talked. "You say you don't know where you're going or what you're going to do, but I think you won't have to worry about that. I think Harmony is going to look after you. I think She always will. Me? I go where I want. Sometimes I feel drawn to one place more than another. I look after myself and there's always Skort and Fallack to look out for me as well." She indicated the dogs, now dozing opposite.

"That reminds me," said Javin. "Why are you on your own with those... bird things over there." He felt relief at having the conversation not be about him.

"Gorries. They're gorries." He could see her teeth in the firelight as she grinned. "You are most definitely not from here. Gorries are useful for the price their feathers bring. But, you can't keep many of them in one place for long, because, quite frankly, they stink the place out. Their droppings will kill off plants if there's too much of it. So, I got myself a small flock and I take them around and sell the feathers and the meat."

"But why. That is," he added hurriedly, " if you don't mind me asking?"

"No." She was silent a moment. "It's because I have a talent, but it's one I can't switch off very easily. It's always 'there'," she said, emphasizing its presence with her hands. "And it's not easy being amongst people. Because what I see are the colors people are. In fact, I see the colors of everything, all the time." She sensed Javin's question. "Everything, every living thing, at least for me, is surrounded by colors, by a shifting cloak of colors. Sometimes, those colors are more real than the things they surround. And, with people, if there are three or four of them together, it gets really hard for me to make them out. All I see is this rippling of colors. But it's not just that. Those colors, they tell me what's happening with people: how they feel, that sort of thing. It just gets too confusing, so I decided to be on my own, moving around, not being overloaded." She shrugged a little. "I actually quite like it. I can go where I want, when I want. Stay or not stay. It can get a little lonely at times, but..."

She brightened a little. "Anyway, as I was saying, sometimes, I can tell if there is an injury from the way the colors move, or don't move, as the case may be. Old injuries show up like scars a lot of the time. And, I'm not really sure, but I think that I see something like that on your head." She pointed to the left of his head. "There looks like something old, or maybe not old, but an injury, I think. Have you hit your head recently? That might be it." When Javin shook his head, she shrugged. "Sometimes it's hard to tell for sure, especially with someone new. It's like I have to learn the colors they have. That's another reason I don't like having too many people around at once. It's too confusing.

"One of the ways I've found to learn a person is to ask them something. Do you mind?" She flashed a smile when he nodded. "Telling a lie and telling a truth, when they are told together, one after the other, makes it easier for me to, how do I explain it? understand a person better. So," and here she shifted to face Javin. "I want you to tell me two things about yourself. One of them should be true and one of them should be a lie. And I'll tell you which is which just by looking at the colors as they change around you."

Javin thought about this for a moment. "So you can tell if I'm lying? If anyone is lying to you? Even when there's not much daylight?"

"It's not quite that simple. I can see colors changing, but what those changes are about, that's not so easy. Things like anger and joy, the strong emotions, they're quite easy. But the other emotions, the things that people are feeling, well, they are harder. I have to be with someone for a while before I can understand their colors. That's why I asked you to deliberately tell me a lie as well as a truth. And daylight doesn't matter. You don't have to if you don't want to."

"You said everything has these colors? Does that mean that each of the gorries has them?"

"Of course. They are alive."

"And does each gorry have different colors?"

"They are the same in lots of ways. People have big differences in colors. Skort and Fallack, they are different also."

"What about trees and plants? Do they have them? Can you see your own colors?"

"Trees and plants; yes. But they're smaller, fainter." A slight impatience entered her voice. "And no. I don't know if I can see my own. Like I said, you don't have to if you don't want to."

Javin stopped himself from asking the next question he had. "I'm sorry. I've never heard of this, so... yes, of course, I will do that. Let me think... Two things... I'm ready." He turned to face her more squarely. "If I sit like this, is it better or not?"

"Makes no difference to me."

"First thing then is that I was born on Haven, not Harmony." He paused. "Do I wait, or what?"

"Go on."

"Right. So the second thing is that I have a powerful talent, but not like any of the people have who were born here." He waited.

Her voice, when she answered, was hesitant. "One was the truth and one was a lie? I didn't see any difference. At least, not enough to matter. Was the second one meant to be a lie?"

He nodded, and then realized the shadows made that redundant, so he added, "Yes. The second one is a lie. I've no talent that I know of, despite people trying to teach me."

She considered this. "So, if you think you have no talent, but you haven't yet found what it is, I suppose that could account for it. Do you mind trying again? After all, it could be my talent is no good for some reason. Perhaps it's deserted me." She gave a short, nervous laugh

"Give me a moment to think. It's harder than I thought it would be, making up deliberate lies to tell you." He thought for a moment. "Ready? Try these two instead and see what you get. First one. I have no memories of my early life at all. Can't remember a thing about it and don't know why. Second one. After I arrived here, I was with a family of farmers and I managed, on my own, to move a whole herd of gomars to new pasture. It was much easier than I thought it would be."

He could hear her draw breath and felt her eyes on him. "The second one... Or maybe the first...? What is going on? Both of those look the same to me. You either have memories and you moved the gomars by yourself, which I doubt, or you have no memories and you didn't move them." A note of exasperation entered her voice. "I can't believe I am losing my talent. That just doesn't feel right. I can still see the colors around the dogs and I know where the gorries are because I can see their colors. But you? I can see the colors around you, but I can't tell which is the truth and which is a lie." Her hand smacked on the ground beside her in frustration. "This is just plain silly. Can I ask you one favor, please? Just for me, to help me, can you please tell me your name and then tell me you are someone else?" There was a note of pleading entering her voice.

Javin was just as confused as Meldren. "Of course, if it will help. Ready? Fine. My name is Javin. Javin Sarnum. And now, my name is Torrint. Torrint the trader. How was that?"

"Now, those I could tell apart." Relief was evident in her reply. "There's a sort of flicker and spout of a different color, blue-ish, by the side of your head, when you lied about being Torrint. It's really plain for me to see. And I didn't see it the other two times. Maybe just a tiny, tiny difference. But not like it should be."

Javin was even more perplexed now. "What does that mean? That I am lying about lying? That I really do have a talent or that I have my memories? But that's crazy! I really don't have any memories. Does it mean I do have memories, but I can't remember them? But that doesn't make any sense either."

When Meldren broke the silence, her voice was lower and somehow more musical. It was as if she was humming beneath her breath as she spoke. "I saw a herb growing by the pool. It's really good for making a drink. I'm going to make us some. If you can get some of those hot stones?"

While Javin was prodding out two small stones from beside the fire, she returned with a handful of leaves in one hand and a large wooden bowl half-full of water in the other. Placing it on the ground, she dropped the leaves in and picked up the stones, blew the ash from them and plopped them in as well. It was done so quickly, that Javin could not be sure whether she actually handled them or protected her hands with the cloth of her sleeve. Leaving Javin to stir, she went to her wagon, returning with two wooden mugs and a ladle.

She offered one to Javin saying, in that still fluid voice which sounded different, more musical somehow, "I think you'll like what this does. I've always liked it myself."

"What's it called?"

She shrugged, her face hidden in the shadows, the fire slowly dying away into embers. "Just drink it. You'll see," and she lifted her mug to drink.

As he did so, he heard, very faintly, the strains of the music that had teased him in the past. It almost seemed to match how Meldren had been speaking. The taste of the drink was very satisfying and he made noises of enjoyment to let Meldren know. There was an earthen taste in there, but also something richer, greener almost. Something very complex, evoking ideas of both vitality as well as calmness. Drinking it, he felt it spread through his body, leaving him feeling charged, yet at the same time aware of a lethargy holding him, making him think of himself as an observer in his own body, watching with interest what was happening. The mug slipped from his hands and it meant nothing. His vision sharpened as he took in each separate glowing ember, each leaf left in the wooden bowl, the individual fibers of his clothes, everything.

Without fear, without concern of any kind, he took it all in. As he looked at Meldren, he suddenly realized in a visceral way which brooked no doubt, that she was something far greater than she appeared. Different. Majestic, even. As he gazed at her, unable to move his focus, so he knew that she was more than just her body, she, no, She, was electrifying. Her presence, just Her simply being there, was enough to almost overwhelm him. It was magnificent. But he was not frightened. He did not worry. This was as it should be. He closed his eyes to keep that feeling inside.

As he did so, the music he had heard earlier seeped again into his awareness, stronger, richer this time. He realized that it was far more complex than he had first imagined. What he had heard before as a simple tune was now being played by a full-scale orchestra with so many other harmonies and subtle chords. It filled him, filled his head until he could think of nothing else. He was not just listening to it anymore, there was no room for anything else. There was so much of that he was the music now.

Now, he dare not open his eyes, for fear that the music inside him would be lessened. The music broadened his awareness, made him sensitive to the rock beneath the ground he was sitting on. And because he had turned his attention to that, so he was able to know it in a way he could never have described before. He sank into it. Felt the textures vary as he moved through it. Was tickled by the thin, dark streams of water flowing deep within it. Moving deeper, he brushed through different types of rocks, different textures, colors, sounds, sliding by him as he moved deeper and deeper. Now there was heat in his awareness, lava moving in strange, slow tides around him. There was a world of sensation and glacial movement and he was part of it.

With that realization, that acceptance, he began to move swiftly upwards to the surface again. Seamlessly, effortlessly, he saw or felt himself moving upwards. His body, he knew, was on the ground, but he was moving up and away, towards the night sky, feeling the cross-currents of air as they stroked at him. And always the music, lifting him. Higher he flew and higher still until he could see the curve of the planet beneath him. But he was not just seeing the planet. He could feel it, understand it, sense how it was alive, pulsing, singing to him, with him. The mountains and the oceans were in the music. Rivers added to the songs just as much as the trees and the plants. Just as every single person added to it.

Everything was there, beneath him, and everything was joined and enmeshed and perfect. And he was perfect and he had a place and his song was there and he surrendered his name, his being, to be part of it. He stretched from horizon to horizon, limitless, and knew everything on and in Harmony, for he was part of everything.

At some point, some moment, for some reason, he became himself, became something separate, knew that he had a body, that he was a thing called a person and that he must go back and inhabit that body, care for it. Spiraling, narrowing, lessening, he drew back down and the music moved from inside to outside, from being him to accompanying him. His vision blurred, became darker and darker as he drew near to himself again until, at the last, he saw nothing except blackness and heard nothing but his breathing and even that grew silent as he slipped into sleep.

18

Javin was woken the next day by Skort licking his face and adding variety by occasionally shoving at him with his muzzle. He stopped only when Javin waved him off feebly and managed to sit up, grunting and squinting as he adjusted to the light. The fire was dead and some cold ashes stirred gently in the breeze. The clicking and murmurings of the gorries were a background of now familiar sound. Beside him lay the mug he had drunk from last night. He picked it up and sniffed the dregs suspiciously before emptying it on the ground. A little further away Meldren was also stirring. Fallack was ministering to her in much the same way Skort had, and with the same effect.

She propped herself up, pushing her hair back to take in the world around her. Evidently she felt much the same as Javin, She looked around, eyes narrowed against the light, obviously trying to understand what had happened. Finally, she saw Javin.

"What happened? What's going on?"

He didn't feel much like standing up, so he just waved the empty mug at her. "I was about to ask you that. What did you put in that drink last night? More to the point, why did you make that drink last night? You could have poisoned me, or done... something," he ended lamely.

"Do you do this a lot, with everyone you meet, or just a few 'special' friends?"

While he was speaking, she was examining her mug, sniffing cautiously at what remained in it. Seemingly ignoring him, she moved carefully to the wooden bowl and lifted out a few of the leaves still immersed. Again, she sniffed at them, studying them carefully.

Javin continued. "This stuff, whatever it is, is dangerous! I saw things after drinking it that I have no words for. It's not safe and you should not have given it to me without some warning at the very least. No wonder you see colors around things. That stuff would make anyone see them--"

"Shut up!" Her voice cut across him. "You idiot! You really think I did this?" She held up the leaves. "I don't know what this is. I've never seen it before. I don't remember anything. So don't go accusing me of poisoning you." She glared at him. "For all I know, you did this. You poisoned me! It's what you do when you get lonely! What is this stuff you put in my drink? And what happened?" She became much more suspicious, inspecting her clothes. "What did you do to me? What sick little thing did you get up to?"

That was enough for Javin. "No, you listen! I have just this minute woken up, like you, after what is probably the strangest thing I have ever experienced. And, the way my life has gone recently, that's saying something! I did nothing to you. Nothing! So don't go accusing me of anything."

"So you're saying that someone else did this? Someone came here last night and made us this drink and we drank it down because we liked them so much and then we forgot our wonderful friend this morning?" She was scathing.

"No! I don't know anything like that." He felt he should be standing up for this, so he managed to scramble upright. The height somehow made his words more true. "I was sitting there, and you were over there. We, we, talked about you seeing colors. Do you remember that? And I tried telling you a lie and a truth. But that somehow was confusing. Do you remember that?"

Meldren gave a cautious nod, not willing yet to concede ground to Javin.

"Then...then you said you were going to make a drink. You'd seen a plant you knew about over by the pool. Do you remember that?"

Meldren was still suspicious, saying nothing.

Javin was talking as much to himself as he pieced his memories together, walking and pointing out what happened, reliving it as best he could. "I got stones out of the fire, you brought the wooden bowl. We put the stones in. Actually, you did. You were really quick doing it. I was impressed. Then the plant. Then I stirred it and then you filled each mug and we drank it." He stopped, looking at Meldren, imploring her to believe him. "That's what happened. That's what I can remember anyway. What about you? Do you remember that happening?"

"What I remember is that we talked about my seeing colors. After that...?" She shrugged, her mouth tight with unspoken accusations.

Javin tried to think of another way of convincing her of his innocence and of her role in the previous night. "There is an explanation. I know it. I just don't know what it is or how to convince you."

"Convince me of what? That you drugged me?"

Javin chose to ignore her anger as he tried to understand what had happened. "We both woke up from whatever it was in that drink. In other words, if anything happened, then it was that we somehow drugged each other." He batted away her response, rushing to speak first. "I don't know how and I don't know why. But that's the only thing I can think of. It makes no sense. But we both woke up together." A sudden memory caused him to rush on again. "Your dogs. They look after you, don't they? They woke me up, well, that one did," pointing at Skort. "If I'm so bad, then why didn't they protect you? Why did they wake me up and not try to eat me or something? If I'm so bad, did something so bad to you, why are they not bothered?"

For the first time, he could see his words having a positive effect. He pushed on. "Last night, you were seeing my colors when I lied. Look at me now when I'm telling you this and tell me what you see, what my colors tell you. I'm not lying! I did nothing wrong to you. I drank the drink and had the strangest experience of my life, then I woke up. That's the bare bones of it. And, as far as I can tell, that's the truth of everything that happened. Look at me and tell me I'm lying. Or look at me and believe me."

As he was speaking, Meldren took on that distant, unfocused look which meant that she was looking at his colors. After he had finished, she sat so that her chin was on her knees, her hair falling to hide her face as she hugged her skirts to her legs.

"What you said about the dogs? That's true. They would have defended me. And," a reluctant sigh, " I think you are telling the truth." Javin gave a sigh of relief. "As far as you know what that is, anyway." She looked up at him. "I'm not saying I believe everything you said, but I can't think why it happened. Or how it happened, come to that. You say you had a strange experience. At least you had an experience. I can't recall anything until I woke up." She scrunched her face up, thinking. "There's maybe a small 'something' that I can recall." She held her finger and thumb close together. "This small. Something. But I don't know what. Maybe if you tell me what happened to you, it might help?"

"I'll tell what I can, but maybe with some food? Now I'm awake and upright, I feel a little shaky. Ravenous but shaky."

Meldren felt the same. She checked briefly on her animals to reassure herself all was well there. After freshening up in the pond and eating some fruit and dried meat there was a noticeable easing of tension between them. They sat, each against a wagon wheel, out of the direct morning sunlight.

"What do you really think happened, Javin?"

He shook his head. "I really don't know. At least, I don't know what happened to you and I'm not clear about me, either. But something did." He paused for a moment, deciding how to say what he wanted to say. "I should have told you something earlier. But if I had, I would have sounded crazy. Or crazier, at least. And you might have left straight away." He put a reassuring hand out to Meldren. "Don't worry. It's nothing nasty. Just... well... weird is the best word." He took a deep breath and plunged on, looking straight ahead so that he wouldn't have to see her face, her reaction. He wanted to get it over with as quickly as possible now he had started.

"I've seen you before. Many, many times. I don't mean I've been spying on you. Nothing like that. But that dream I had that I mentioned? The one Torrint said was of Harmony? What I didn't tell him was that I saw a face in that dream. Only from the side. And I've seen it many more times in my dreams since then." He gulped a breath before hurrying on while his courage was still with him. "Meldren, it's your face. The side of your face. I'd know it anywhere. I've seen it so often. I don't know what it means, or whether it means anything to you, but I recognized you the first time I saw you. But what was I going to say? Oh, hello! You're the girl from my dreams?" He allowed himself a wry smile at the thought. "I don't think that would have been a good start. Not that this has been so great, either. But the point is, if I can see your face in my dreams, and you then arrived here, why can't what happened last night have something to do with it all? After all, you did say that you felt you had to rush here without really knowing why." He studied his hands closely. "That's what I wanted to say."

Meldren stared at him, wide-eyed. "Oh you are full of surprises, aren't you? I don't know what to think. I've been in your dreams?"

"Yes, but not in any, you know, strange way. Nothing like that. I've only ever seen your face. Or, rather, the side of your face." He shook his head, remembering. "You have no idea how powerful it was, that first dream. Amazing. Just amazing. I thought that that face, your face, was somehow the face of Harmony. But then I met you and you are a real person and I don't really know what to think about it now. The dreams were so real, so true."

Meldren stared off into the distance, obviously trying to make sense of Javin's story. "I believe in dreams," she said, "and the power of them. I believe you are telling the truth. I can see it around you. And you are right about the dogs. But that doesn't make any of this easier. What I still don't understand is what happened and why it happened."

"You can't remember anything from last night?"

She shook her head. "Maybe something. Maybe nothing. But you can remember things? What were they?"

Javin tried to explain what he had seen, what he had experienced. He stumbled over the words, paused several times to try and recapture the feelings, before excusing himself with, "...and that's about the best way I can tell it."

Meldren sat in silence for some moments, still looking puzzled. "Your colors, when you were talking about it, they were the brightest I've ever seen. On anyone! It was like you were surrounded by flames. I have no option but to believe everything you said. But that doesn't help me. Why did you see and experience all of that and I didn't? What was I doing? Why was I even there?"

"You said you could remember something small. What was it?"

"It was like I was being taken away, led away, into a room and the door was shut on me. But, just before it all went dark, before I blacked out or whatever I did, I heard something. Hearing you talking, it must have been something like the music you heard. It was nothing like as strong as yours, but it was there, in the background. And then it went and I woke up." She chewed on her lip as she thought. "Hardly seems fair, does it?"

"I agree."

"No, I mean that you aren't even from here and you get all this happening to you, get Harmony coming to you. And me? I get nothing. I get to go to sleep."

Javin hadn't considered that before. "But I still think you had an important part to play in it all. You had to be here. You were drawn here. You were in my dreams. You're part of it somehow."

"Yes, but how?" Her frustration was evident.

Javin closed his eyes, thinking and feeling his way to capturing an idea swimming around his mind. "What about this? What about if Harmony didn't just come to me, but She came to you as well? What if, without you, Harmony couldn't connect with me, couldn't make me listen? What if She made me see you in my dreams; made me ready, if you like?" He turned to face Meldren, his words becoming more urgent. "What if She really was here, with us both, last night? She used you to make the drink and that made me drink it and that made the connection?" He became more excited as the idea became clearer. "You said you didn't know the plant. I'm pretty sure I've never seen it here before. But there it was, growing. And you, or rather, Harmony inside you somehow, made the drink out of it. And, after you made it, She sent you to sleep? That would all make sense, wouldn't it?"

"I don't know. I suppose so." Meldren was tentative.

"Don't you see?" Javin was animated now, fully taken with this interpretation. "That would explain you not remembering anything after our talk of my colors. It would explain you, or Her-in-you, making the drink and you not remembering that. Then you, the real you, drank it and that would explain the music you heard before you went to sleep." He nodded to himself enthusiastically. "That makes sense of why you are here. It explains it all!" He smiled hugely at Meldren who was still trying to take it all in. "That makes you really important. Do you realize? I just got to listen and see things. You, you, on the other hand, actually met with Harmony, really had Her inside you, as part of you. How many people can say that, can say they were chosen by a planet, a whole planet?" He laughed out loud at the concept and at himself for saying it. It seemed only yesterday that he could not conceive of how people on Harmony thought about their home and here he was trying to persuade one of them that her home had chosen her! It was fabulous and ridiculous and hilarious at the same time.

His laughter slowly affected Meldren, bringing a cautious smile at first, before finally grinning at him as she began to see what had happened in a new light. His words were still not embedded as a truth inside her, but she was feeling her way to accepting what he said. And she liked the feeling it gave her.

The rest of the morning was spent tending to the animals, with Meldren berating herself for being careless of them. The look on Javin's face, whenever she spoke of her supposed failings, the quizzically comic upraised eyebrows and look of surprise, was always sufficient to make her stop and smile. The gorries were found roosting in various parts of the canyon. Their feet, supposedly the most prone to problems, were checked, accompanied by a great deal of noise and fuss and half-hearted lunges. After the farm work he had done, Javin felt more than comfortable dealing with these ungainly, slightly idiotic-looking creatures.

Skort and Fallack accompanied them both, yawning or panting, preferring to doze when opportunity allowed. At first somewhat intimidated by their size, Javin came to appreciate their gentleness and dedication to Meldren. Their eyes never left her, and when they closed their eyes, their ears swiveled to find her. Their heads were at the level of his chest, making the size and strength of their jaws more obvious. He was unsure about how to respond to them, or whether he should even try to approach them by himself, when the brown and black one, Fallack, decided for him. Javin was standing watching Meldren tie her hair out of the way before dealing with the next gorry when the dog moved over to him and swung his head into Javin's chest and made a low huffing sound, before sitting directly in front of Javin and looking at him.

"Looks like he's decided you can be trusted," Meldren smiled. "I'd suggest you let him smell your hands. Sort of your idea of holding hands to say hello, but in dog language." Javin did so and Fallack graciously sniffed and then tasted with the tip of his tongue. "Don't get too excited," she added. "Better to let him always make the first move. At least until he knows you better. And that doesn't mean that Skort agrees with Fallack. Yet." Javin was grateful for that advice.

The mandria, who's name he discovered was Sarlin, was brushed and talked to and patted and stroked and generally fussed over. It had managed to eat everything it could reach, so they took it down the canyon a ways, towards the gorries, and hobbled it there, where it made appreciative rumblings.

They stopped to freshen up at a little past midday and have some food. Javin felt more comfortable being with Meldren than he had felt with anyone else. Spending time together, looking after the animals, had been... companionable, better than companionable. Being close, concentrating on a task in front of them meant that he could let her presence seep into him. He liked it. He liked her. He liked being with her. After being alone, this was a new experience, one he liked very much. There was a sense of something having been shared and the beginning of something else.

The last of the dried meat was welcome, as were some berries Javin had stored in his cave. With his stomach feeling satisfied, Javin was sipping at some water. "I don't know about you, how you feel, but I've been getting this feeling. An irritation almost. You talked about being irritated before arriving here. I suppose that's the same thing for me. It's been growing as we've been busy." He puzzled at how to say it. "I think it's like a feeling to do something else. Maybe, leave here? It's like I feel I'm being pulled, or is it pushed, to go... somewhere. Does any of that make sense?" He was, he suddenly realized, not trying to work out what was going on around him. Instead, he was completely at ease. It was a very pleasant realization. And it was centered on Meldren.

Meldren became still and closed her eyes as she listened to herself. "I've been feeling it too. Again. It's like the other morning when I got up early to come here. I can't really put words to it. It's more a feeling. And, yes, I agree with you. I think it's time to go." She opened her eyes. "But where?"

Javin thought for a moment with his eyes shut, like Meldren, but this time sensing something outside himself. It was as if he was sensing the wind, or something more subtle. He opened them. "I think that it's the way I came. Back out. Maybe back to Sweetwater. Maybe not. But I'm sure that's the way to start. Do you think this has anything to do with what happened last night?" he asked. "Are we being, I don't know, influenced again? And did that really happen last night? In the daylight, it seems unreal. Or, at least, less real."

"I know what you mean," Meldren said. "I haven't been able to stop thinking about it either. Maybe this feeling about leaving is because of that in some way. I don't know." She shrugged. "But, if it is, then we have to go. Because it's what Harmony wants us to do. But does what happened mean we are... that we have no choice? We both have the same feeling about leaving, but where will it end?" Her voice quietened. "What does Harmony want of us?" She looked away for a moment. "I also don't know about us, Javin. What do we do? I've just met you for the first time. You say you have had dreams about me for much longer. Then this thing last night." She shook her head again, trying to rearrange how she saw the world to take into account this new information. "Obviously there is something special, something different going on here. But what it is, who knows?" She turned to look now at Javin, her blue eyes searching his face. "I've really enjoyed being here. Being with you, looking after the gorries and everything. And I'm getting used to accepting last night's strangeness. It's been... I mean, it's something new. Different? Special?" She was obviously trying to find the right words for how she felt. "It's not just about last night, though. That's not what I mean. Or maybe it is. Today has been..." She gave him a small, nervous smile. "I mean, I like you. I do. Very much. I just wish I knew how to say what I want to say."

Javin also spoke quietly. "I like you too. I really do. You're the first person I've met here that I feel I can talk to and even be understood. And I want to be with you. I do. I'm like you, though. I have to believe that this is no accident, us being together. And, maybe you're right that it's what Harmony wants. But what about us? Where do we fit into it all? Do we have a choice about it? When you said that, it really made me think." He returned her nervous smile. "I want to be with you. But I also want something else as well. The point is, I want a choice in what I do."

"Exactly!"

"No. I probably mean it differently from you. Ever since I came here, in fact most of what I can remember, I had no choice in what has happened to me. I was kidnapped and brought here. Then I was sent to a farm to live. I was going to find a healer to help with my memories, but that didn't happen, because of the dream, and that meant I was taken here. Again, no choice. And now this feeling that I have to go 'somewhere'. That's not my choice, either. The only choice I really made that I can recall is wanting to find a healer to get my memories back. And then there's you. You arrived and I have to choose." He held Meldren's gaze for a moment, wanting and not wanting to speak. He spoke in a rush. "I'm going back to Sweetwater, to see if there's a healer there who can help me. I don't know if that's where you are going, but it would be wonderful to travel with you. And, if that's where Harmony wants me to be, then I'll be there, but for my own reasons. And, if it's not where She wants me, then that's too bad. Because I'm choosing this, for me. But I'm also choosing this for us. I need to know my past. I need to find out who I am, why I'm here at all. Harmony can't tell me that, only my memories can. And you need to know as well." His voice dropped. "I would so like us to be together for this."

Meldren had listened to him carefully, her unfocused gaze showing that she had been watching the colors change around him as he spoke. Then she seemed to take great interest in her thumbnail. When she spoke, her voice had a catch. "It feels right. What you said feels right. It does." She paused, weighing her words. "Before Harmony has anything more to do with you, with us, maybe, you have to find out who you are. You have to know that first. Then you can tell me. I can't explain it well to you, but the colors around you, even in the daylight, are bright and pure. Don't ask me what that means, but I've not seen them that way before around anyone. My guess? You're doing the right thing, for the right reasons." She grinned at him, but could only hold it briefly. "Of course, I could be fooling myself, and you." Another close examination of the nail and a pause, "But I can't go with you." She hurried on. "The one thing I know about myself is that I hate having too many people around me. Small places and few people for a short time are fine. But if there are too many people for too long they all push into my head. I can't stop the noise, the colors. I end up feeling sick. Once in a town, I was sick. It takes days for me to feel like I have got rid of all that noise. It's like it builds up in my head, everybody's in there, and I have to get rid of them. Clean them out, by being alone with my dogs and my gorries." She shook her head. "Your colors don't make me ill. But you have to trust me. That place is not for me, and you wouldn't like me if I was there. Besides," she hurried on to stop his protest, "I don't want you to have me to worry about when you should be getting healed. I've been traveling for a long time now without you. I'm sure I can last a few more days."

Javin's nodded a few times as if in response to an inner voice before he could look at Meldren. "I understand. Really, I do. I would hate to have you hurting because of me. I wish I could help you. But," a tilt of his head and it was his turn at a sudden attempt at a smile, "thanks for being honest with me. I am going to miss you." He frowned at her, still with her head down. "Very, very much. I am going to be so fast at getting healed, you won't have time to miss me." He took a deep, swift breath and gestured at the campsite. "We should get packing. I have some time left yet to persuade you to change your mind." He gave a brittle smile. "No harm in trying is there?"

She shook her head, although whether in agreement or not was not clear.

Neither could think of anything else to say as they set about packing up, hitching Sarlin and setting off. They agreed they were heading, at least to begin with, back to Sweetwater. The dogs didn't seem to mind, as they herded the reluctant gorries along. It was only the humans who had difficulty in being normal.

At one point, beyond the canyons around midday, they came to where a faded track curved away from the one to Sweetwater.

"Well, that's where I'm going to go," Meldren said, her voice a little too bright. "It leads on to a place called Luck. I have no idea why it's called that. Maybe it's got another name, but that's how I know it. And it's small. I like that. Sweetwater is too big for me. And down that way there's really nowhere else to go. At least," she smiled, "I haven't found any other tracks along there. It's about four days, I think. I might be remembering wrong. Beyond Luck, there are other places. But I'll be traveling slow. You'll find me easily enough. There's not many girls driving a herd of gorries, are there?"

Javin gazed off into the distance, as if the right words were out there somewhere. "I know how I feel about you. And you've said much the same things about me." He looked now at her, trying to be precise, careful. "But, is this really us? Or is it Harmony playing with us, making us have these feelings?" He reached for her hand. "I need to know this. I think I do know, but I need to be sure."

Meldren held his gaze as firmly as he held her hand. "I am certain. I know the things I feel which are mine and those which aren't. I've been on my own long enough to know what I feel and what is true for me. And this is true. And if it is Harmony playing with us, as you said, then I am so very grateful to Her for this. And if She put this feeling in me Herself, it's only because I was ready for it... ready for you." She laughed softly. "I've been thinking about us. It sounds like a story. Two strangers meet and they realize it's something... different. Special, in a way. And it happens quickly. Just like a story." She patted his hand. "I don't mind being in a story with you. Especially not this one."

Javin held her gaze. "It is sudden." He gestured back to the canyon. "I've spent days and days back there being on my own, nothing really happening. And then you arrive and, well, all of a sudden, here we are hurrying and we don't know why or what for. Is it all too quick? Or are we doing the right thing? I wish I knew, for certain. Not about us. I know how I feel about you. After all," he flashed a smile, "I've been dreaming about you a lot. How could I not like you? Not want to be with you?" He was serious again. "You and me sounds fine. Boy and girl together. But you, me and Harmony? Boy, girl and planet? That sounds a little strange, doesn't it?" He sighed heavily. "I'm not sure what I'm really saying--"

Meldren put her free hand to his lips to silence him. "Shhh! Thank you for wanting to be sure. I can't worry about Harmony. It's us that counts. And, as I said, I'm sure about what I'm feeling, even if it is the result of something strange, very strange, going on. I'm happy with what is happening. Is that good enough for you?"

Javin breathed a small sigh. "Thank you."

"Perhaps we should thank Harmony instead."

Javin shook his head. "Let's just keep it about the two of us, like you said. For as long as we can, anyway." He tipped his head questioningly. "You're sure you can't come with me?"

Meldren eyes shone as she shook her head. "Don't ask."

He took a deep breath. "I'll find you. I promise. I just hope I will be the same as now and that I'll like myself. That you'll like me."

Meldren put her hand on his arm. "Don't worry about that. Worry about getting lost. You're new here, remember? For all I know, you're going to be useless looking after yourself." Her eyes sparkled as she teased him. "Torrint brought you here, you walked out with me and now, for the first time, you're going to be on your own." She shook her head. "How will you ever cope?"

"Well, I guess I'll just have to try, won't I?" He turned his head slowly, scanning the land. "So, over there is where I should head, is it?" he asked, pointing in the direction they had come from.

Meldren just shook her head again. "Oh, you'll be fine, I'm sure." Suddenly, she wrapped her arms tightly around Javin, burying her head in his chest. "Just promise me you'll come after me quickly? Please?"

He bent to kiss the top of her head and wriggled his arms free to hug her back. She clung to him and tilted her head back, her eyes searching his face for reassurance. "I promise I will find you again." He smiled and touched her nose with his. "I'm crazy and you're strange. We're perfect for each other."

However long the kiss was, it was not long enough for Javin. And, from the look on Meldren's face and how her eyes brimmed, she felt the same.

She gave a watery little smile as she rubbed her nose. "Go! Get going! You have a good stretch yet. Stop wasting time here." She shooed him off, biting at her lip as she did so.

"I still don't see why you can't come with me." Javin made one last plea. "We wouldn't have to do this."

Meldren wiped her eyes with the heel of her hand. This time, the smile was firmer, more certain. "Now, go. The sooner you start, the sooner we'll be together again."

Javin could not argue with that logic, so he turned slowly and began to walk away. Every now and then, he would turn back to look and there was Meldren, standing and waving to him. Finally, he breasted a rise and waved at the now tiny figure, flanked by her two dogs, for a last time before reluctantly heading down the hill to where his memories might be found.

19

Javin, once he had started out, didn't want to stop: there was so much to return to. So it was that he arrived tired, footsore and hungry in Sweetwater when it was almost completely dark, the moon not yet up and only the fading afterglow on the horizon and some stars providing any relief from the blackness.

His eyes had become used to the decreasing light, so he was able to follow the track with relative ease. Arriving in the town, however, the darkness seemed more intense. The buildings were black shapes in the gloom, all details lost. He recalled the lights burning in Hanlar and Paysa's home and how bright it had appeared to be then. But on the outside, there was very little beyond some lighter blemishes on the darkness, soft glows with no distance to them. He could make out no details in the windows. They were for letting light in and for keeping the wind out. Their construction gave them a haze which made them useless for gazing through.

He wondered, for the first time, what exactly he was going to do. In his rush to be here, he realized he was without a plan. He had nowhere to spend the night and no idea what to do about food. He rued the urgency of his journey now. This would have been so much easier in daylight. He walked slowly along the main street, wary of the uneven surface with the occasional large stone waiting to trip him. Worse were the gaps where such a stone had been removed, but the hole remained.

The barely discernible outline of the place where the strange, ancient technology was housed; the device which had spread the news about Blackeye, was just ahead of him. He rested his hand on the low wall as he tried to recall the layout of the buildings. He recalled they had eaten at a place nearby and kept his ears sharp for any sounds which might help him, for he was not sure, in this darkness, where it was in relation to the communication hut. Finally, he heard what sounded like two or three people talking more loudly than anywhere else he'd passed. It was better than nothing, so he decided to try his luck.

Pausing on the street, he felt certain he was the only person outside. He wondered briefly if he was breaking any laws by being out at night. He had no idea what to do or if there was any sort of protocol to follow, so he decided to simply announce himself by knocking on the door and going in. He took a deep breath and was about to step forward and knock when the door flew open, a bearded, beaming head with twinkling eyes beneath large bushy eyebrows peered round it and boomed at him, "Come in, then! Don't just stand there! We're expecting you!" There was a fire burning low in the fireplace in the far wall, a table and stools were close by the door and the stranger gestured towards them. There was also the enticing smell of food which called to his stomach. Although there were only some candles and small wicks in holders, it was dazzling to his night-adjusted vision. He took a step, expecting a step up, but there was a slight hollow just in front of the door which he failed to see. He tried to catch his balance but instead caught his foot on the threshold and fell headlong into the room, desperately trying, and failing, to stay upright.

He crashed his head onto a stool and he felt himself bouncing off that onto the floor. His face felt numb. The last thing he heard was the voice saying, "Ow! I forgot to see beyond the arrival. Do you think he's all right?" And then he blacked out.

Some time later, Javin felt too sleepy to open his eyes. He didn't want to move or do anything. He wasn't in pain, but he wasn't comfortable, either. He felt like he was drifting along somewhere, perhaps the border between dreams and sleep, between the real and the imagined.

"I tell you, I don't know!" The voice, female, sounded tired and irritated. "If you'd listen, Fortin, I've told you I have no idea. All I can do is wait with the rest of you. Now get out and let me and him be." Javin liked the idea of being left alone. He sought the soft darkness again where there was nothing to bother him. But, as he sank, he felt a snag in his mind, a reminder that he had something important to do, if only he could recall what it was. But the thought of trying to remember was too big and clumsy for him to deal with, so he sank beneath it, gratefully.

Later, he was aware he was thirsty and that swallowing was unpleasant. He tried to move his arm to find out what was happening. He felt, instead, a touch on his arm and a voice, the same female one from before, saying, "You'll be fine. But you must rest and drink your medicine. I'll help you." A hand, cool against his skin, supported him, making him aware of how weak he felt. He didn't want to open his eyes. A cold, bitter liquid entered his mouth. He wanted to spit it out. Instead, he spluttered and coughed droplets of it as most of it went down his throat. He felt his face being gently wiped clean as his head was lowered back. His face remained puckered at the bitterness.

"It will help you mend quicker. Help you sleep through the mending." Her voice was soft, near his ear. He remembered that he had to remember something. He wanted to ask how long he had been like this, but the sweet blackness rose up to meet him before he could begin to shape the words.

He drifted up and down in that blackness, sometimes breaking free of it just enough so that he could hear sounds around him. Sometimes he heard her voice again, little snippets which meant very little, obviously talking to someone else. "He looked half-starved to me... It's a mess in there. Blows to the head are never easy... The herbs will stop the pain, but how he'll mend, if he'll mend right, that's not easy to say." Sometimes she spoke just to him. He knew those times because her voice was closer to his ear and softer. Sometimes, he felt sure he felt her breath on his face. "Don't worry. You'll be fine. You hit your head and you need to rest... It was an accident... My name is Della... I'm a healer... When you can, wiggle your toes or move your feet." He didn't feel like doing that just yet. Maybe later.

Sometimes, on the edge of the blackness, he glimpsed faces. Faces he thought he might know if only he could think. And then, sometimes, there were views of places, of a city. A skyline. Tall buildings. And then some sounds which almost seemed familiar at times. They were confusing. And in and around these confusions a buzzing sound, like music but at a vast distance.

Later, through gaps in the blackness, he opened his eyes to see a blurred face looking down at him, and sometimes just the ceiling with shadows on it above him. Then, he blinked hard to try to clear the blurriness. He tried to speak, but there was no sound. He swallowed hard to try and find his voice. He was rewarded with a sweet-tasting juice. He found that he could move an arm to his face. He was rewarded with her voice saying, "Well done! That's the way. You can do it fine." The bones of his cheeks and jaws were sharp under the questioning fingers and even the gentle touch made him wince.

Probably a little later, her voice asked, "Would you like to try some broth?" Javin tried to open his eyes to see the owner. He blinked hard several times, rolling his head gently to try and see better. The cool hand rested on his brow to stop him. "Don't do that! That blow to your head near killed you. Just missed taking an eye out, and then you smacked your head on the floor as you bounced off the stool, as best as I can tell. Front and back got it. You might have blurry vision for a while, but I can't see any permanent damage there. Just bruising is left, as far as I can tell. I think it's about time you started getting some strength back."

Javin licked his lips, trying to get some moisture to speak with. A cloth wiped his mouth and was squeezed gently to release a few drops on his tongue. "I'll get some water for you in a beaker when you can sit up a little more. Let's see if we can't get you started." And two arms came to lift him forward and up and place a pillow behind him.

"Keep your eyes shut for now. It'll help."

Javin nodded to show he had heard, but he also tried to see where he was. The two actions combined caused everything to swirl around and he vomited suddenly.

"So much for doing as you're told," said the voice in exasperation, accompanied by the sounds of a cloth being used on the bedding. "Could have been worse. It's not like you've got much in you. Now, don't nod, but listen. Shut your eyes or I'll have to bind them shut for you. Just let yourself settle to sitting first. One thing at a time." More sounds of movement, but he had no idea what they represented and he had no wish to vomit again. He smelt something. Something which made his stomach yearn.

"Now, I've got some broth here. Let me feed you, but keep your eyes shut!"

Javin let himself be fed. It felt wonderful! Full of flavor and sensation. He was still enjoying it when, abruptly, he realized he was full and could not have any more. His stomach protested. Instead of shaking his head, with all the attendant problems that might bring, he lifted his hand up.

"Ah! No more? I understand. You'll sleep well now. I'll leave you sitting. Less problem next time." He felt covers being drawn up to his chin and he let his head turn carefully to one side. He realized he was tired. Very tired. He slept.

When he woke again, he drank a little water with some help. He cleared his throat a couple of times and was finally able to speak. "How long have I been here?" His voice, he was surprised to hear, was little more than a croak, a rasp. He coughed again.

Della was sitting on the edge of the bed when he asked her. Her slightly lidded, light-grey eyes, with tired circles beneath them, scanned his face in a professional manner, looking for problems, for signs of healing. Satisfied with what she saw, she relaxed a little. "Before I answer that, can you please tell me your name? I have no idea who you are or where you came from. And you can tell me that later, or not, as you please. But it would be nicer if I could call you by your name."

Javin introduced himself, his voice hoarse through disuse. He even made a vague attempt at touching his forehead with his fingers as he had seen other do it. "Well, Javin, you've been here, in this bed for ten days. And you'll need at least that much again before you're able to be of much use to anyone."

As soon as she spoke, thoughts of Meldren flooded him and his eyes teared up. Della, misinterpreting, said, "But you'll be perfectly fine, I'm sure. The time will go quickly."

But Javin waved away her words. "Meldren!" His voice was not much above a whisper. "I promised her I would find her. She'll think I've abandoned her. I have to find her. I have to!" He made feeble attempts to move the bedding aside, wincing at the dizziness as he did so before he was easily stopped by Della.

Her long, strong fingers digging into his arm, she told him, "You are in no fit state to go anywhere. Not yet. You can't even get out of this bed. This Meldren person? She'll have to wait. You will have to wait as well." Her voice gentled a little, became more soothing, more tender. "It must be very difficult to be apart. But, if I know anything, then it's that if two people are really meant to be together, they will be. And if that's how you feel about you and her, then you will be together again. But not just yet. You must heal first. Get your strength back. I am sure she will wait and she will understand." She cocked her head to look more closely at him. "Now, I will do my very best to help you get strong enough to find her. But, if I am to do that, you must help me. And that means doing as you are told. You must rest and get your strength back and let your head heal. Is that clear?" She waited for Javin. "Is that clear, Javin?"

Eventually, he gave a slow, grudging sweep of his hand in response. "Yes. I will help you heal me."

In her turn, Della nodded acknowledgment of the agreement. She had a wide, clear forehead, a narrow, long nose leading to a wide-lipped mouth which creased easily into a smile and a narrow chin which matched and balanced her nose. She looked tired. At first, Javin thought that was because of looking after him. He came to learn that she always looked tired, but hardly ever acted it. She was perhaps the same age as Paysa. But there the similarity ended. Where Paysa had been a ball of bustling energy, Della was more... quiet? He wasn't sure how to word it. If Paysa had been of the earth, then Della was more of the water; flowing, gliding, smooth but always with a goal, an end in sight.

Her fingers, surprisingly strong and sharp, as he came to learn, were always moving over his face and head, checking and adjusting, her head held to one side and her eyes half-focused. At such times, he felt a strange heat coming from her hands and a feeling of ease from his body where they rested. Although he saw her eat, admittedly hurriedly at times, she remained thin. Her brown hair streaked with occasional lighter strands, was piled on top of her head and held in place, precariously, by a varying number of long pins of some kind of wood. Sometimes, the pins failed and strands of dark brown hair tumbled haphazardly around her head and shoulders until she remembered to pile them back up again. Occasionally, she braided the more intrusive tresses and tied those back separately so that he never saw her with the same hairstyle twice.

At first, after becoming aware of the length of time he had lost, he sank into a morose state from which it was difficult to move him. Della managed to brighten him somewhat by letting him sit in a chair by his bed. Progress, visible progress, helped him out of his depression. But it was never quick enough. The buzzing that he had heard in his sleep slowly changed into something else, something with more nuance; as if it was the same music, still distant but a little clearer. Slowly, he began to sleep well again. The faces he had glimpsed earlier no longer bothered him. Instead. he found that he was able to sleep peacefully and awaken tired but feeling rested. There was a clear distinction between sleep and wakefulness now. But he could not forget the faces and the vague emotions about them. They bothered him, but at a level he couldn't really connect with. Whatever it was, it was some place he couldn't find with his eyes open and his mind working. The thought of Meldren believing him to have abandoned her was a constant sharpness as well.

It surprised and disconcerted him to discover just how vulnerable and weak he felt. He found it difficult to concentrate on anything for very long. Even keeping a thought was tiring. But he could eat a little more and was able to move his head slowly without severe problems. One thing was always floating around in his head, beyond the pain and dizziness and the tiredness, and that was he was determined to leave as quickly as possible.

As he progressed he was able to slowly explore his surroundings. Della, he found, lived alone. His bed, or presumably it had been her bed, was off to one side of the larger of two rooms. She apparently was sleeping on a sort of couch on the opposite wall. He felt guilty at taking her bed. The other room he only glimpsed through the doorway. But what he could see from the bed was that her entire place was filled with plants hanging from the beams in the ceiling, growing in pots on the floor and by windows, dried in pots, seeds in cloth packets, something that looked like clay in heaps on a plate, and other things he couldn't give names to in piles, poking from clay pots, or simply resting on a handy surface. He found out that Della had collected most of this herself over time. Some had been brought to her, some she had bought, from Torrint he discovered, and it all made up her dispensary, her collection of medicaments. Speaking of Torrint gave him the opportunity to tell her of his arrival on Harmony; a story she quite obviously enjoyed for its newness, its strangeness. He had meant to add about his memory loss, but Della was called out by someone who wanted her skills for an accident elsewhere. By the time she had returned, he was asleep.

The next day, after he had eaten some stew, he was determined to stay in his chair longer and not give in and go to sleep in the bed. So, he asked how she knew what to use and when. She cocked her head and raised her eyebrows.

"I assume you do have a talent? If so, can you explain to me how it works, so that you can do whatever it is that you do? I doubt it. And yet you ask me how I know?" She puffed her cheeks in exasperation.

Javin thought carefully, ignoring the sarcasm. "I'm not sure how long I've been here, but I suppose I've been on this planet about... I don't know how long it is because I don't even know if your year is the same as the year of my home. I don't think I've lived through a winter yet. That's why I was coming to find you. I wanted your help. Before I hit my head. I was coming here with Torrint to find a healer. I didn't know it was you. And then we left quickly after telling about Blackeye and," he shrugged. "I ended up doing other things. But I did mean to find you." He yawned.

Della's gaze sharpened. "Why? Why did you want to find me? I can't see anything wrong with you. Not since you've been here. Just the blow to the head."

"I can't remember."

Della's surprise was obvious. "What? You can't remember why you wanted to find me?"

Javin suddenly felt more tired bringing this back to the surface. It felt as though it was another barrier to his return to Meldren. "No. Not that. I can remember arriving here, on Harmony. But not my childhood. Not my parents."

"When did you realize this?" Della was suddenly urgent, probing. "Why didn't you tell me this before?"

He smiled weakly, pointing at his head. "Other things happened." He yawned again, massively this time, his eyes watering.

Della asked again, "When did this happen? When did you know?"

Javin tried to think when he really wanted to slip into sleep. "I don't know. Back near where I first learned about this planet. Tarla. I was talking with Tarla."

"Tarla?"

"Mmm." It was hard just keeping his eyes open. Thinking was even harder.

Della shook his leg a little. "You remember arriving here on Harmony, but later on, you found out that your early memories were gone? Is that right, Javin? Is it?" She placed her hand on his head. "I need to know if I'm to help you. Javin?"

He was asleep.

Della lifted him to the bed with ease and laid him out, gently stroking the hair from his face. "I think I need to look a little deeper, Javin," she murmured, before hooking the chair with her leg and sitting down close to the bed. "I should have seen this. I should have looked better," her voice reflecting her irritation at herself. She breathed deeply once or twice to calm herself and then reached out gently with her hands to rest the fingertips on his temple. "Let's see what we can see, if I really try looking this time."

There was a pause for a while, not a sound in the room, as she bowed her head in concentration. After a while she sat up straight, flexed her fingers and rolled her head around, easing any tension in her shoulders. She muttered softly to herself. "Della, it's time you actually tried to be what you set out to be. So why not shut up and look? Forget what you were told about how things are supposed to be and just look!"

She made herself comfortable, sat back in the chair, folded her arms, bowed her head, closed her eyes and slowed her breathing. She remained like that for a long time.

20

When Javin woke next, he found his vision had cleared up greatly. But, better than that, his mind felt clear: the first time for a long time. Thoughts were no longer those blurry things which swam just out of reach. He could, he realized, pick and choose what to focus on. He lay there, gazing at the ceiling, still weak and empty, but able to think back to Meldren. The memories were sharp and painful, but he held on to them this time. Tears trickled down and formed small, cold pools in his ears as he sought to control his breathing. Sharp regret, aching guilt, gripping fear: he forced himself to feel each of them, and with each he promised himself to find her, to be with her.

As he lay there, the buzzing music formed a backdrop, a soundscape, swelling and dipping with his emotions. As he let himself feel again, he also realized that the tapestry of music sounded familiar. With a sudden intake of breath, he was back in the canyon, being taken away by the music. And what he was hearing right now was a part of it, sister to it in a way he knew but could never explain. Hearing it now, even dimmed as it was, lifted his spirits, made him feel that, again, there was more to him than just this weak body. There was hope in the music. And there was help, if only he could understand how to accept it.

Held in this realization, he was not aware that Della was watching him from the chair, a strange look on her face; part question, part wonderment, part tenderness. "Are you ready to eat, yet?"

Her question surprised him and dragged him back to the present. He turned his head and smiled at her. "I am hungry. But what did you do?"

Della rose quickly. "Food first. Feed the body and then the mind." She returned with a tray bearing some juice and some fruit already cut up. There was also a sliver of plain bread. She placed the tray where he could reach it easily and then took her place on the chair by the bed, plucking a piece of fruit as she did so.

Javin had carefully hoisted himself up a little and thanked her with a slow, very careful bow of his head. She moved to help him, but he motioned her back gently, before applying himself to the contents of the tray, surprising himself at the amount he was able to eat. As he ate, so Della sat watching him intently, nibbling on the fruit slice.

When he slowed, Della popped the last of the fruit into her mouth, wiped her fingers on her skirts and rubbed them together to check for any sticky residue before answering. She scratched her head with one long finger and a tumble of hair fell which she ignored. Finally, she sighed loudly. "I would like to be able to say that I know exactly what I did. Truth is, I don't fully know." Having started, she felt more able to relax and let her body slump into the chair more comfortably. Her gaze was up and off to the side, into the past, not at Javin. "I spent a long time, a looooong time, learning about people and what would help them heal." She waved vaguely around at the contents of her home. "All these here were part of what I learned. How much of this plant to give when you have an ache in your shoulder, or what to avoid if you have stomach cramps. Or where to place my hands to help heal wounds inside, or how to see what's the real problem with a twisted knee." She smiled and closed her eyes to hold the memories closer. Opening them reluctantly, the smile remained. "I should be able to tell you exactly what I did. Or, better yet, because I know you are going to ask this, I should be able to show you what was wrong with you. Healer's pride!" The smile became wry. "But I can't. And, do you know something else? I want to thank you."

"Thank me? What for? For being sick?"

"No! Well, in a way, yes. If it hadn't been for you, and you telling me that you had no memory, I probably would never have done what I did, whatever it was. You see, I tried to go inside your head and see what was wrong, or where it was wrong." She made a small, dismissive gesture at the look on Javin's face. "I mean that I am able to look inside people and see what is the problem. Same as some people can see things far away, but I see inside of the person in front of me, that's all. Anyway, what I did with you was different. Never did that before." Her smile returned to her eyes. "What I did was the purest thing I could do. It was what I have always wanted to do; really let the healing take place without thought, without plants or medicines of any kind. It's what I always dreamed I would do when I became a healer, when I first started out. I would just somehow...," she waved her hands vaguely as she searched for the words. "I don't know what it was. I just know that I actually did something right, just by letting it happen."

"But what was wrong with me?"

"Remember, I just said I can't tell you? Not in any way that makes sense, anyway. I was in there and I saw things and I felt things but they were what I saw and felt and not you." Seeing his frustration she scratched at her temple with that same delicate, long finger before continuing. "I've been trying to put it into words while you slept. The best I can do is tell you that there was a part of you, not a part of your brain, but a part of you, hidden away somehow." She grasped two folds of her skirt to illustrate what she was trying to say. She folded one over the other, bunching the cloth up. "It was like this in a way. It was folded in on itself, tiny on the outside but big on the inside." She drew back the top hand and stretched the material out. "I wouldn't even have seen it before if you hadn't said about your memory. But I... I sort of... it...." She puffed her cheeks in frustration and let her hands fall, releasing her skirt. "I think that somehow, it unfolded itself and that act of unfolding balanced your brain. Made it even again? Smooth? I don't know the words, just that I know you felt different before it and that you didn't feel the same afterward."

"Are you saying you found my memories?"

Della threw back her head and laughed hard and loud, startling him.

"What? Why are you laughing at me?"

The energy of her laughing had tumbled the rest of her hair down, but she was in no mood to deal with it, sweeping it grandly to one side as she grinned at Javin. "How like a man to ask that question! Only you can tell if you've got your memories back. How on Harmony would I know? You've got the answer in your own head and you go and ask me!" She shook her head again, hair flying, as she subsided into silent spasms of mirth.

Javin felt abashed for a moment, but soon, he saw the reason for laughter as well and sleepily nodded his appreciation of the stupidity of the question. The energy subsided between them and he caught Della looking at him seriously. She reached out her cool hand to place it on his forehead. "The answer's in there, Javin. But I can see that the thought of finding the memories is...scary?" Javin nodded, suddenly feeling very tired again. "If they are there, if your early life is there, just think back. I suppose that's how it works. If it's not there, it's not there. And we'll worry about what to do about that, or not, later. Right now, you can sleep. Shall I give you something to help you?"

Javin thought for a moment but shook his head, still careful not to move too quickly. "I think I want to find out about myself." He smiled weakly up at her. "Let me think, for just a moment." Della nodded and stayed still, looking down at him, her eyes narrowing as she frowned her concern. Javin let himself push back as far as he could. The same memories he had with Tarla. But there was something else beyond those now. No longer a wall, but something else. A view? Faces? Feelings? There were snatches of things he possibly had known before, but he couldn't put them into place, connect them to anything he knew now. He shook his head again slowly. "I can almost sense something that I haven't known about before. But it's all vague."

She sat back, eyes narrowed, and nodded, whether in frustration or relief, he couldn't tell. "Don't worry, Javin. It's a start."

"But what if it never comes back?"

"What if it does, though? That's the question you should be asking." She bent to collect the tray, bringing her face closer to look directly at him. "It might take time. But it will come back. Don't ask me how I know. It will. And that's what you have to be prepared for."

With his mind feeling clearer, Javin's body also seemed to make quicker progress. He was soon able to move from the bed to the chair, and from the chair to the table in the other room where he watched and helped Della as she worked. All the while, fragments of memories, fractured pictures with no reference at first, appeared in his mind. Names of places and people arrived without warning, but also without any way of knowing how old they were, or where they came from. They were just isolated moments out of sequence. Occasionally, there was a memory which ended abruptly or switched to something else without warning.

Over time and with repetition, he came to understand and then to actually know which faces were of his father and mother. As yet, that's all they were. There was little emotion attached to the pictures, because he hadn't yet formed connections from them to anything else.

And all the time he was forming the fragments and rearranging them, he was able to do more and more. He learned, very quickly, that being a healer meant being constantly active. There were all sorts of tasks needing to be done, many of which could be carried out sitting down and taking little effort. So it was that in the days following his newfound clarity and returning memories, he sorted, swept, tidied, counted, moved, removed, soaked, boiled, dried, crushed, baked, shredded, picked, pickled, smelt, tasted, rubbed in, scrubbed off, washed out and crumbled all sorts of plants, roots, seeds, insects, rocks, clays and even crystals. Sometimes he just watched as Della worked with the array of herbs, plants, roots and insects in her home. It was, he realized, like the farm: there was always something to do, something needing to be looked after from first light to falling into bed.

He started out weak and tired but, in the careful, continual work, he slowly gained strength and endurance again. His frame began to fill out. His mind took in everything. He became immersed in everything Della introduced him to. It was as if he needed something outside of himself, something he could lose himself in, to allow the internal healing to take place. But still the urge to leave was in him and every now and then Della stopped him with a gentle touch and said, "I promise I will let you leave when you are strong enough. But that is not yet, and I have not forgotten my promise to you." And that would have to suffice, because, despite his eagerness, he heard the truth in her voice, echoed as it was in the slow recovery of his body. The swelling had long gone, the bruising was just a memory, but there were lumps on his head and face where there had been none, and the weakness of his limbs showed in the trembling he could not control when he was tired. He knew he was not fit for a long trek. But that did not stop him yearning to begin it.

The two of them, the healer and her reluctant patient, shared slices of their lives with each other; snippets of their past, told and lingered over again as they worked. She spoke of her childhood and some of her patients as well as her hopes for the future. Javin told her the things he could recall and how they might be related to each other. He spoke of Torrint and Blackeye and Hanlar and the farm, but little about Meldren beyond the fact that he wanted to get back to her, that she was something special to him.

Javin was at the sink one damp, cold day, the wind sliding under the door and finding cracks to discomfort them no matter where they were or what they were doing. He was rinsing some crackbane and his sleeves had fallen down again. He rolled them up, cold and clammy on his skin. These were clothes Della had found or acquired in some fashion, but they were too big for him. He had lost a lot of weight and any clothes simply hung from him. Wrinkling his nose at the unpleasant coldness on his arms, he looked at Della who was concentrating on making a paste or poultice (Javin was never clear on the difference), judging carefully the consistency by dipping a finger into it every now and then before adding more water.

"Did I tell you Harmony came to me? To me and Meldren? At the canyon."

Della stopped stirring and wiped her hands on her skirts, adding to the interesting variety of stains there. She stared at him, eyebrows raised in surprise. "No, Javin. I can honestly say that you have never told me any such thing. Any reason for either not telling me before or for telling me now? It seems a rather large thing to have overlooked, don't you think?"

Javin hid his discomfort at the question by trying to squeeze some water from his sleeves, without success. "I don't really know, Della." He gave up and let them dangle. "I didn't mean not to tell you. It's why I have to go to Meldren. We shared that, together. It was... well, it was a

strange thing and I'm not really sure what happened or what it meant."
He shrugged a little.

Della took a deep breath and opened her eyes wide as if she didn't
know where to start answering him. When she spoke, her voice was
calm, but it did not hide the fact that she was trying to be calm.
"Harmony? She came to you? To you and Meldren? And you say that
you have no idea about it, about what it means?" Javin gave another,
smaller shrug, to which Della added a nod or two. "I've heard of such
things, of course. I mean, everyone has. But hearing about it and having
it happen to someone, to you, that's something else entirely."

"So, if it's so special, you must know what it means, then"

Della's gaze was long enough to make him feel uncomfortable. "What
you're really asking is for me to tell you exactly what to expect, exactly
what it means for you in precise detail." A slight shake of the head. "I can't
do that. What I can do, instead, is tell you something you need to hear. And
that is, that if Harmony has come to you, in whatever form, however it
happened, it means one thing and one thing only. It means that you, and
this girl of yours, Meldren, have been chosen by Harmony. And before you
ask what that means, I can tell you that it means that you two are special to
Her. And I have no idea what that means, only that She has singled you
both out for something important. Important to Her, that is. And don't
even think of asking what that might mean. After all, can you really begin
to understand how a whole planet thinks?" She shook her head again at the
enormity of that thought. Her voice now really was calm. "There's nothing
specific I can tell you, except one thing. And you need to keep this in mind.
If Harmony has chosen both of you, it means that She will look after you."

"And that would include making me unconscious and bed-ridden for
days and days, would it?"

"You were coming to see me about your loss of memories, weren't
you? Instead, you hit your head. Do you think it's possible that I could
have helped you if you had just turned up? Probably not. Hitting your
head gave me the opportunity to try something I never would have
done. Before, I would have just given you some herbs and all the stuff I'd
been taught or heard of. And I can't help but think that the blow to the
head might have been a necessary part of the process in some fashion. I

don't know what goes on in the brain, or how it works, but, if Harmony needs you, She's going to be looking out for you."

"But I still don't understand why, if that's the case, I have to wait so long to get back with Meldren?"

Della smiled. "It's no time at all to a planet, is it? Perhaps, to Her, one of our years is only a day. If She wants you two together, you can be very sure it will happen. And, if you two had that experience, then it sounds like She wants exactly that." She crossed her arms, nodding at her own sagacity. "Besides, for all I know, there's a very good reason for you being here, apart from the memory." She smiled again, a broad, bright smile. "Whatever it is, I'm glad you're here. I'm glad I got to know you, and glad I could help you and so help Harmony."

"That's pretty much what Torrint said." Javin looked down at himself, his old clothes and damp arms. "I can't really say I feel special. I feel more like, well... just me."

"And who would that be?" Della's eyes still carried the smile.

And then the strangest thing happened. As Javin thought about how to answer, he was aware that the music which had been in and out of his head, now was stronger, at the same time as the bits and pieces of his memory began to slide together, creating a bigger picture, showing him his life, his whole life.

He stood transfixed, watching his life unfold. Names, places, smells, tastes, the whole of his life unrolled in a complex tapestry of detail, each piece linking to another and another and another. He not only knew his past, he understood it, he felt it.

His eyes were open but unfocused, his jaw agape, his arms hung loose by his side. Della rose and moved to him, but there was something about him, around him or emanating from him, which acted to caution her, to hold her as witness only. Finally, Javin closed his mouth, gulped once and saw her before him. That's when she moved to support him, reach for a drink, a chair, anything to help him.

He appeared dazed. For a long time, there was only a deep silence between them; Della feeling that simply being there was the best medicine she could provide, and Javin trying to bring his past and the present together in his mind.

Della resisted as long as she could but finally gave in to her impatience. "What happened, Javin? Are you all right?"

He turned his head slowly towards her, as if it was unbearably heavy. He spoke slowly, almost as if he couldn't believe his own words. "I know who I am. It's all come back."

"That's wonderful!" Her professionalism kicked in. "Do you have any aches or pains, or anything else like that?"

Javin gave another very slow shake of his head, still with a stunned look on his face. "Nothing. It just rushed in. It came in with the music. The same music I heard before... with Meldren." He let out a slow breath, closing his eyes.

Della's eyes widened. "That must be Harmony! You heard Harmony!" A look of yearning, of envy, filled her face. "Oh, Javin! Harmony spoke to you. She spoke to you here," she indicated the cottage, "in this place. She spoke to you in this place!"

Javin put a hand to his forehead. "All I know for sure is I feel tired now, exhausted, after that. Suddenly, really tired. I need to sleep, Della. Really need to sleep." She went to help him to the bed but he waved her away. "No. The couch will do fine. It's your bed now. I've had it too long. I'll be fine. Really."

He fell onto it and was instantly asleep.

21

There had been, not arguments as such, but gentle disagreements, about his leaving. Della was adamant that he did not have enough strength to walk to the edge of the village. Javin was quite positive that he was able to. "After all," as he had said, "you told me that Harmony would be looking after me. So I'll be fine, won't I?"

It was hard for Della to argue against her own advice, so she reluctantly gathered some food for the journey. As she did so, Javin shared his new memories with her; of his father, the president of Haven, of the coup where his parents died and he was taken and had his memories wiped, of his living in a ghetto, struggling to survive by stealing and lying, and of being captured again and sent to Harmony. All of it was there now.

As Javin told her, he was surprised at how little he was upset to learn of how he and his parents had been treated. It was, as he said, "...just something that happened to me, but it doesn't feel like it was me. I can remember it all. The sounds, shooting, everything. But, the strange part is that it's almost like I don't really mind. I'm not angry. I don't really feel sad, either. It's a bit like thinking back to working with Hanlar and Paysa. Yes, I know it happened, but beyond that, it's like it's not so important anymore. Is that normal?"

"Normal?" Della snorted as she stood at the table, packing a weather-beaten leather satchel for him. "Harmony speaks to you, more than once, you regain all your memories and as a result, you realize that you're the son of the leader of another planet, and you're asking me what's normal? How should I know? I'd say that if it feels that it's the right way to feel then it probably is the right way to feel. And I still don't think you're well enough to be doing this." She leaned over the table where Javin was finishing his meal. "Are you?"

He had to admit to feeling less than certain, but the thought of Meldren thinking he had abandoned her was enough to drive him on. Besides, if Torrint and Della, both people he trusted, thought the same about him and Harmony, it was probably about time he put some trust in it himself. "I'll be fine. And, if I'm not, then I'll make sure I collapse very close to here so you can pick me up and tell me how stupid I was." He smiled reassuringly, but Della just narrowed her eyes and shook her head.

Javin changed the subject. "I should pay you for everything you've done for me. Food and clothes and all your time. But how do I do that, Della?"

She snorted at him. "Pay? What with? You have nothing, do you?" Here she grinned. "Except one thing. Well, maybe two. First, you told me many new stories and brought Harmony into here. Secondly, I did some real healing." Her face softened a little as she regarded him. "I think we've traded well. You have given me much, and I think I have given in return. Now, if you really think you are capable of going anywhere; I could still change my mind about that," she teased gently.

Saying goodbye was harder than he thought it would be. Della was clearly still worried that he would fall over and die somewhere where he wouldn't be found, despite Harmony's attentions. She handed him the satchel and a tightly bound blanket roll, the cord of which he looped over his shoulder opposite to the satchel to balance it. She said, "I can't help feeling I'm being irresponsible, letting you go off like this. What if--?"

He cut her off. "You're not responsible, Della. I am. If I cannot pay you, then I cannot, will not, forget how you have helped me. But it is time I moved on. I have to find her and, if you are right, then Harmony will help and, maybe, there's something else She has in mind for me. For me and Meldren. Or maybe, She's just playing with us. Either way, I can go back to Meldren now, knowing who I am, knowing my history, and not being ashamed of it." He touched her cheek briefly. She let him. "You gave me my memories back. That's something I cannot repay. Thank you." He adjusted the set of the blanket. "And, thank you for this! Despite what you say, I do not think I can ever repay you," he repeated. She gave a wan smile and waved him away.

As he walked away, she called out, "Hey! That's the wrong way, you idiot!"

He turned, a broad smile on his face. "I haven't lost my memory again. There's something I want to do first."

He walked up to the hut he and Banith and Torrint had come to from Blackeye. During his recovery, he had recalled how Lisick, back at Landing, had said that one day he would hear Harmony. He doubted that she meant it in the way he had experienced it, but he wanted to let her know her prediction had come true.

Arriving there, he found the same boy as earlier, wrapped up against the cold. His early memories might have returned, but, for the life of him, he couldn't recall this boy's name. "Erm... I'm sorry, I've forgotten your name?"

"Lannis. You're the one who fell over, aren't you?" The boy looked chilled.

Javin smiled at how he was recognized. "Yes, I am the one who fell over. And right now, Lannis, I'd like to send a message to Landing."

"I'll get the Speaker, sir. He's just having some lunch in there." There was a note of wistful longing in the boy's voice as he pointed out the place where he and the traders had eaten before.

"How does this work, then Lannis?"

"I go and call up villagers if there's a message to be sent, and Bendiss, the Speaker, he actually sends it. I don't know how it works, but it always has."

"What about receiving a message?"

"There's a sound which comes out of them and I go and get Bendiss and he listens to it; the message, not the sound."

"And you're the only one here?"

Lannis nodded. "There's usually two or three of us, but I haven't seen either of the others. I think they're hiding somewhere warm."

"Can't say I blame them." Javin felt the breeze, carrying the touch of autumn and the promise of later cold, knowing that sitting and doing nothing made it more acute. He felt sorry for Lannis. "Tell you what, Lannis, I'd like to give this a try by myself."

"What? Send a message on your own?" The boy was frankly amazed at the temerity of the suggestion. "Can't be done," he maintained flatly. "You need people. Lots of people."

Javin was persistent, however. "Ever tried or seen it tried? No. Well, after today you'll be in a better position to give an opinion won't you?" He tempered his words with a grin.

Javin turned and leaned against the central pole, the disks directly above him. He appeared to think for a moment, head lowered, eyes closed. In reality, he was rehearsing what he would say. He rehearsed a few times, with Lannis looking at him in a way which was somewhere between a challenge and wonderment, and then suddenly straightened up and nodded to himself. His eyes were twinkling with anticipation.

"Lannis! I'm going to try this for myself and see if anything happens. If it doesn't, then only you will know I've made a fool of myself. If it does, then you'll be the only witness to it." Then he frowned. "I don't suppose you know how Bendiss does it, do you?"

Lannis just shook his head. Whatever was going to happen, he was determined not to miss it. Either way, it was a great story and would make up for the boring days he spent, mostly alone, watching other boys his age going past, laughing and chasing each other. His time of service was nearly up, thank goodness. He had a feeling that what was about to happen would make it all worthwhile.

"Never mind. Wish me luck!" And, with that, Javin closed his eyes, saw the buildings at Landing as clearly as he could, saw Gerant there just as clearly, Lisick beside him and Bellis in the background. There was music humming into background of his head as he imagined them at landing. Then he focused on his message to Lisick. "It's the boy! You were right, I did end up hearing Harmony. I thought you would like to know that, plus I have my memories back. Say hello to Bellis and to Gerant." Then he put the two together and imagined it all going through the disks above his head. He had no idea what to do beyond that or how long he should try.

He kept the two ideas; the image and the message together until he heard a howl of anguish and opened his eyes, letting them both fade. He looked up to see Bendiss staggering towards him with his hands clamped to his head, tears streaking his flabby features, his eyes wide with pain.

"What are you doing? What have you done?" The words squeezed out between sobs as Bendiss sought to catch his breath. He sagged at the knees and reached blindly behind to find the low wall to sit on, his head bowed, eyes still squeezed shut against the pain.

"What do you mean?" asked Javin, mystified.

Bendiss, still clutching at his temples, managed to look up at Javin, his eyes narrowed, tears leaking from the edges still. "What did you do?" His voice was more of a squeak.

Javin still couldn't think that anything he'd done could be responsible for Bendiss' distress. He waved vaguely at the disks perched upon the pole behind him. "I thought I'd try to contact Landing. I wanted to speak to Lisick there and tell her some good news," he said hurriedly, trying to explain everything as fast as possible to exonerate himself from blame.

"Lannis here had nothing to do with it. It was my idea. That was all I did. A simple message to Lisick. Nothing more," he ended lamely. His explanation had given Bendiss time to recover a little.

Bendiss grunted, "What you did... what's your name?" he asked peevishly, not wanting to stop his anger for this but wanting to direct it better.

"Javin."

"...What you did, Javin was to scream into my head so loudly I thought my brains would run out of my ears. What you did, Javin," using his name now as a weapon, "was to hurt people. Badly. You, Javin," another stab, "had no right to do what you did. No right, no authority, no intelligence, no manners, nothing! Nothing can excuse what you just did." He stopped for a moment to rub at his temples again.

"You have no right to do this. No right at all. It is my authority here. My talent which uses this. Not you. Not some ignorant idiot. You could have killed me, would have killed me if it had gone for longer. You have given half of Sweetwater headaches and none of them, I am guessing, know why. But I do, because it is my talent to hear, to talk, not yours. Not your talent to scream at me, to blind me with pain." He was able to stand now, but the pain still made him move gently. Nevertheless, he glared at Javin, breathing heavily with righteous indignation and barely suppressed rage.

"I shall not tolerate this invasion, this intrusion. I shall make sure that you are held responsible, are punished for this outrage. You do not have the right to do this. You could have killed me, killed many others. You will not get away with this. I shall make sure that you are hunted down, Javin. Hunted and punished. Do you hear me, boy?"

Throughout all of this, Javin had tried to understand and come to terms with the fact that his contact with Landing had actually injured Bendiss in some fashion. He was still trying to accept that when Bendiss announced his intentions. All Javin had wanted to do was send a simple message to Lisick, and here he was being threatened by a fat man who let his young helper sit out in the cold while he was safe and warm, feeding his face.

"Don't you threaten me!" he said, feeling his anger building. "You talk about your talent as if nobody else is allowed one near you. You think you know Harmony? Really? You have no idea what Harmony is like. You have no idea about how Harmony feels. You are so concerned for yourselves, for your talents, that you never see beyond them." The force of his words, of his presence, had made Bendiss sit back down on the wall. Javin loomed over him. "You'd do best if you tried listening to Her properly!" He stared down at Bendiss who sat glaring up at him. "One more thing and then I will be gone. You do not have the right to any one talent, any one thing. Stop guarding it as if it was just yours and yours alone. I am sorry, truly sorry, to have hurt you. It was not my intention. I sought only to call to Landing. Now I know what not to do. I am sorry." He bowed stiffly and made to march away. One last thought came to mind. "And one other thing. You have no right to keep one young boy out here, freezing cold and with no food and nobody else to share the duty. That is not right, either." He turned to Lannis, but the boy had already begun to run. It was going to be the best story of his young life. And he'd tell it, just as soon as this awful headache had vanished.

22

Gerant stumbled into the kitchen, holding his head, eyes tight shut, grimacing with pain and bumping into the table. Bellis had mild nausea herself but was not suffering as much as Gerant was. All she could do for him was to make him sit down and lean back as she put a wet rag on his head. She stumbled around the kitchen pulling some herbs down and crushing them before adding them to water. Refreshing the compress, they served to dull the pain a little, and Gerant nodded his thanks. She turned back to the sink, trying to contain the nausea.

After focusing on swallowing and controlling her breath, she was able to speak. "What happened? I was tidying some clothing away and then... this huge sharp pain."

"Don't know," mumbled Gerant. "Where's Lisick?"

"I'll go and find out." Bellis moved carefully, one hand on her stomach as she did so, taking slow, deep breaths. She found Lisick unconscious on the floor outside the main communication room. Careful not to bend over too far, she tried to make her comfortable before going back to get some herbs and a pillow for her head.

Gerant was sitting up rubbing gently at his temples, his face pale. "How is she?" he asked. Bellis simply beckoned for him to follow her. Lisick was barely conscious as they tended her. After a couple of failed attempts, they managed to get her to a couch in the next room. From there, it was a short walk to the kitchen and Bellis brought back some juice and a wooden bowl of water into which she had thrown some more crushed herbs, "...good for headaches" and some rags to apply as compresses.

It was some time before anyone was ready to talk. Eventually, it was Lisick who broke the silence.

"I was in the room, listening, sending, all the usual things. Nothing strange. And then, this huge blast! It was like... well, you know what it was like." She winced.

"Do you have any idea what happened?" Gerant squinted at Lisick.

"I wish I did. Truly. All I got was a glimpse, a sudden flash of something as it happened." She winced again. "Let me try and get it back." She closed her eyes as she recalled what had happened. "I'm not certain. But I don't think this came from any village. It was simply too powerful. Nobody could be doing that. It would take hundreds of people." She opened her eyes and Bellis replaced the compress after a questioning look. "Ah! Thank you! That's most definitely helping." Lisick relaxed a little. "I clearly heard a voice. Not so much just a picture, like normal. A voice. And it said, as far as I can recall, 'It's the boy'. I have no idea who that was. But, yes, it was definitely that: 'It's the boy'. And then, after that, I got a picture. A straggly youth. Thin-faced. Looked half-starved. And then it was the knife to the brain."

"The boy? Who's the boy? And if it wasn't a village, then who, or what was it? Oh!" Gerant's jaw dropped as he the implication struck him. "Lisick, could it possibly have been Harmony? Could it have been, do you think? I mean, I can't think of anyone capable of such power, can you? I know it's a reach, but... could it be, do you think?"

"Well, it was certainly powerful enough. But why? Why now? What for? After all these years, all of the people who have been here at Landing? It seems, well, difficult to accept, doesn't it? And it still doesn't explain anything about the boy, does it? I mean, Harmony has always been 'She' not 'He'. Unless we're really wrong about that, as well."

"I think I know who the boy is," Bellis said as she sat down. The other two looked at her. "I think it was that one who was dumped here. The kidnapped one? You were always calling him 'the boy', Lisick, even though he wasn't. I can't think of anyone else that fits. I mean, it can't be Pasker, can it? He's here somewhere still. Which reminds me, he's probably suffering just as badly." She got up gingerly. "I'd better go find him now. I hope he's not been as badly affected as us." She left the room.

"Could it have been him that was meant?" Gerant asked. "What about this picture you got? Did it look like him?"

"I don't know," Lisick sighed, still holding the compress to her head. "Maybe. I suppose it's possible. But only if he was ill or something. He looked half-starved."

"Well, maybe he was, or is, rather."

"I'll be better able to think when I lose this headache. Right now, I can't touch anything. How about you?"

"No. Too much pain. I can't even feel you."

They sat in silence, nursing their pain and their fears until Lisick spoke. "I can't stand being like this, unable to feel anything. The first time in my life. It's not a good thing. Not at all." Gerant grunted his agreement.

Bellis arrived back and set about filling some mugs from a bowl into which she crushed some different herbs. "Pasker will be fine, I think. It was nowhere near as bad for him. I gave him something to help him sleep, and I think you two could do with it as well." She held out the mugs. Gerant took his and sniffed at it before taking a cautious sip. "Oh, for goodness' sake, Gerant, you're worse than the lad! Here," she moved to support Lisick and help her drink. "It will help dull the pain a little and you'll be able to sleep. Hopefully, it should be long enough for the pain to ease off."

After Lisick had finished the mug, she looked up at Bellis. "What on Harmony would we do without you, Bellis?"

"Probably you'd still be on the floor and Gerant would still be in the kitchen, Pasker would be eating all the leftovers and neither of you would be able to make any food or drink," Bellis grinned. "So, yes, I think I am absolutely indispensable and you'd be hopeless without me. Now. Sleep!"

"No." Gerant put his mug down. "One of us needs to be available. That's why we're here. Lisick, you're worse off than me. When you wake, you come and get me." He got up slowly and stiffly. "No arguments.

Pasker needs time as well, so, you know where to find me, Bellis, if you need me," and he left the two alone.

It was later in the day, as Lisick was just coming out of sleep, when Gerant reappeared, his face serious. He touched Lisick on the shoulder. "Are you recovered yet? Because there's something you need to know."

Lisick blinked away the sleep from her eyes and moved her head gingerly, testing her reaction. She nodded for him to go ahead as she elbowed herself up. "What is it?"

"We can't contact anywhere."

She was puzzled. "What do you mean?"

"There is no contact with any place on Harmony. We cannot send any message. We cannot hear anything."

"Wait! What are you saying?"

"The deecees don't work anymore, Lisick. We can't transmit after that... that event, and I don't think we can receive either!"

"Are you sure? Could whatever happened still be messing with your head, making you think that?"

"I'm sure, Lisick. I have been able to sense you, and Bellis. It's been coming back gradually. I spent some time trying to send to anywhere and get any information back. Nothing. Everything is dead. I can't get any response at all. Nothing works, Lisick! The deecees are all dead. We can't contact anyone, and they can't contact us!"

"But can we still contact Harmony? Can you still feel Her?"

"That's more you than me," said Gerant. "I get the waves of emotions, the overall feelings, but you, you're more detailed than me. You know that. I can get something, yes, certainly. But what do you get? That's what I'd like to know."

Lisick closed her eyes and tilted her head back a little. She was still, and Gerant, despite wanting an immediate answer, kept quiet as well, allowing her to do what was needed.

Finally, Lisick opened her eyes and looked at him. "Yes, I can still feel Her in the background as always. It's not quite as clear as normal, but that might be just my head recovering still. She's there. But... ," she shook her head slowly, "there's something different. Don't ask me what. She feels, well, different. A little more distant? Weaker? I don't know what it is. But it's different somehow."

"But it could just be your head recovering, couldn't it?" urged Gerant. "I know I'm not back properly."

"It could be part of it, sure. But there's a different quality to it." She sighed helplessly and spread her arms wide. "Truth is, I can't tell you why I feel that way, but I do."

"So what do we do now?"

"Maybe it was Harmony who hit us hard. Maybe She doesn't know how to speak to us quietly. If it was, and so far it does make some sort of sense, then there's a message about a boy." Another frustrated sigh.

"Not much for us to go on, is it?" The tension in his hunched shoulders showed how much Gerant wanted to be able to do something.

"Let's say then that it was that boy, the youth, who was kidnapped. What was his name again?"

"Javin, I think."

"So. Javin. I heard the words, 'It's the boy'. If it was Harmony who was speaking to us, then is it possible that She was warning us about him in some fashion? But that She was too strong and we lost the rest of the message? And then there was that picture. I suppose it could have been him."

"But what good does that do us, even if you're right? What does it mean?"

"I wish I knew. But, what I do know is that there was that village where all the people died; Blackwater, Blackeye, was it?, and then I had problems really sensing Harmony? I mean, She's always there, at the back of everything. But I can't bring Her forward enough to really hear what I need to hear from Her. Then you were looking through those old records and found nothing." She looked up at him. "You have to admit, this has only happened since that boy, Javin, came here. I don't like coincidences. Not like that."

Gerant considered this. "That would mean that Harmony sees the boy as some sort of threat, then?" There was disbelief in his voice. "But how can one person, someone not even born here, be a threat to Harmony? It's just not possible."

"I agree it sounds strange, impossible even. But what else can we think about what happened? If you've got a better explanation, believe me, I'm willing to hear it."

"Let's say you're right. What does that mean for us? What do we do?"

"I think it means we have to help Her. Have to warn as many as we can to look out for Javin. Have him captured. Keep him in one place until we know what to do." She shrugged. "I can't think of anything else we can do. Maybe Harmony will let us know, but more gently next time."

"And if we can't warn anyone? If the deecees never work again? Then what?"

"If that does happen, Gerant, I think it means that Harmony doesn't need us anymore. I think it means we're no longer of any use." Her eyes filled with tears. "Oh, Gerant, that scares me more than anything else."

Gerant, for all his empathic ability, was unsure how to comfort or reassure his friend. It was one thing to feel emotions on the far side of the planet, but another to deal with them in someone directly in front of him. He decided, instead, to try to take her mind off herself and her fears. "You mentioned Blackeye. That village where everyone died. We never did understand that. I can't help but feel that maybe, just perhaps, there is something we've been missing there. For instance, there had to be a reason for it, but neither of us wanted to think that Harmony was responsible. Sure, they went deaf, but isn't that more likely because they had done something to upset Harmony?" He cocked his head at Lisick, silently urging her to join in.

"Maybe," was all she said, without looking at him. But it was enough to encourage him to continue.

"But neither of us sensed anything wrong there. The land was fine. Crops were fine. No disease. No sudden rise in predators." He rubbed his forehead, trying to think this through, trying to distract Lisick. "That means that there was nothing wrong in the way the villagers were living with Harmony."

That caught her attention. "Of course, there had to be something wrong! Otherwise, why did they die? Why did Harmony make them deaf?"

"But," Gerant continued gently, "if there was no trace of anything wrong with the balance of the land, then they had to have done something else instead, yes? What could that have been?"

His argument had penetrated. Lisick put the compress, which she had been holding in her lap, on the table. "Perhaps we were too quick when we were told. Perhaps we should have been more careful."

Gerant nodded. "But what could possibly have caused Harmony to have taken that action? That's the question we need an answer to. We just sent what we thought was the best way of dealing with the result, but didn't bother looking at much beyond that. Didn't look too hard to find the cause."

"Well," said Lisick, "if the land was fine, then it was something not from that area which was the reason. But everything around the place was in balance, as I recall. Did you find anything else there?"

"No. Nothing." Gerant, having started by wanting to distract Lisick by chatting aimlessly about an old issue, had been so successful that he was now fully engaged with the problem himself. "If it was nothing that the people did to the land, then it had to be some other type of...threat, maybe?"

Lisick was now also fully engrossed in this. If they could not connect with any people using the deecees, then at least they could try to resolve the problem of Blackeye. "A threat? Maybe. But what sort of threat? What would Harmony see as a threat and why would she punish the people if they didn't make it?"

"Perhaps She thought they should have seen it as a threat?"

"Yes, but what would threaten Harmony if they didn't do it?"

Both sat in silence, trying to solve this puzzle.

"I think I might have an idea," said Gerant slowly. "I know the sort of threat that Harmony would react to. Do you recall when that boy arrived, the one we think caused the problems just now? Think back to what was threatened by the people who brought him. Do you remember it?"

Lisick nodded, eyes widening at the thought. "You could be right, Gerant! They threatened to poison Harmony."

"Yes," Gerant continued. "But what if they, or another of those metal crafts, what if they landed at Blackeye? What if they wanted something and threatened Harmony again? We wouldn't know about such a landing, would we? They could land anywhere, might have landed anywhere any number of times, and we wouldn't know. Not unless they did something like poison the land."

Lisick waved a cautionary finger. "But there was no poison, so that wouldn't explain the deaths, would it?"

"Not poison, no. But it might explain things. If there was a ship landed and the villagers could have done something and didn't. Or...," Gerant's eyes narrowed as he followed his thoughts in detail. "Or, they gave something Harmony valued to them. Or had something given which they shouldn't have had." His eyes widened. "I think that's it! That's what happened. I think that the people in Blackeye did something they should not have done and Harmony punished them for it."

Lisick pulled at her lower lip as she thought about this explanation. "I don't like it. But it feels right. It has that feel to it when something is tugging at you to look at it but you don't want to because you won't like what you see. It feels that kind of right. I don't want it to be right, but I think it is. I think, if you're right, Harmony took the only action she could. It's not a good thought. But I can, in a way, understand Her doing it." She looked up suddenly. "But why not do the same thing here? After all, they landed here. They made a threat here. Why not make us deaf as well?"

"They took some plants, made a threat, left the boy." Gerant's face showed how bereft of ideas he was. But then, "The boy. Again, the boy. Maybe it was because of the boy that Harmony did nothing. Could the boy be special to Her in some way?"

"Possibly," Lisick conceded. "But we didn't take anything from them." She thought some more. "They didn't offer us anything. It was a job, a task, leaving the boy here. There were only those few plants. I can't see that as being a threat. If they did land at Blackeye, it's possible they did something else instead there. Whatever it was, I'll bet that was what Harmony saw as a threat."

After a silence, Gerant repeated his earlier point. "Those people could land anywhere on Harmony and we'd never know. It could have happened many times over."

Lisick had a somber look. "If you're right about this, and I think you are there or thereabouts in explaining it, then the question really is how many times has this happened before? And, more importantly, how many people have died because of it? Places too small for deecees?"

Gerant was grave. "I don't think we'll ever know. This could have been going on a very long time. It makes me feel so helpless."

"Speaking of helpless," Lisick replied, "we don't have any deecees."

Both of them felt very much useless at that point.

The next day started out somber and silent. Bellis, as always, was working in the kitchen. Pasker wandered about, getting in her way, but keeping out of the way of Gerant and Lisick, who both hated the enforced idleness and the bigger implications of it. Both also had short tempers and could not sit still for any length of time. They kept going over the same ground repeatedly. Blackeye and the boy, Javin. Haven's ships and dead people. They're sure that there was a connection. But they could not find one. Their hopes rested on having the deecees working again.

The day passed slowly. Gerant and Lisick ate together, being left alone by Bellis and Pasker. After eating, they still felt restless and found that they had both decided to take a walk outside, to help clear the lingering effects of the day before. There was nothing left to discuss. They just wanted to be able to do something.

Finally, feeling the chill, they made their way back, together but silent, to resume their pacing. As they got to the main door, Pasker was waiting for them, looking both scared and excited at the same time.

"Well?" Gerant's booming voice filled the one word with enough energy to force the boy back against the door, as though he had been struck. Gerant covered his eyes and took one, slow, deep breath. He forced himself to be calmer. "Are the deecees working?"

Pasker pushed himself upright and took one stride forward. He was determined not to show how afraid he was of the bulky man before him, even though a part of his brain kept yelling that the bulky man knew exactly how afraid he was.

"Sir, I wanted to let you know there's a message." He waited a moment but could not contain his excitement. "The deecees, sir. Yes. They're working again!"

Actually, it became clear that Pasker's statement was optimistic. The truth was that only a couple were found to be working at first. But, over the following days, others regained their function. As nobody knew anything of their construction, their operating principles, they were simply grateful and hoped that all would return to service quickly. However, the recovery was patchy and some areas were still not reachable many days later.

As it became clear that the previous level of communication was unlikely to be restored quickly or easily, it gnawed at both Gerant and Lisick. But it also affected Bellis as well, as she was frequently in their company, cooking, or clearing. As for Pasker, he attempted to do his duties with the absolute minimal contact with either Lisick or Gerant and, as a consequence, became a more or less permanent fixture in the kitchen.

It was the beginning of a tiring new regime. Communication remained irregular and sometimes several attempts were necessary to send longer messages, but some semblance of the old communication network was in place. They took turns dealing with such messages as made it through to them and sending out what helpful information they could. Sometimes that meant eating in the message room, sleeping on a couch outside it.

It was strange. Normally, they would have been more leisurely, taking time off to travel or relax whenever they sensed Harmony was quiet. But now, they didn't have that connection anymore. Although they were used to the duty, they wanted to be there. But to have so few messages to deal with, that was disturbing, unsettling. One or two places did ask what had happened to the deecees, and were told that they had been harmed by someone and then they passed on the warning about Javin. To those places which hadn't realized anything was amiss, they kept on repeating that Javin should be held captive. If there had been widespread headaches or other effects, they weren't told because nobody would think to tell them.

The weight of the duty, of the ritual of it, kept them anchored there but took away their interest in it. They were committed to it more through habit than intent. In truth, there was little they could send that was of help. They kept on trying to contact every deecee. Some villages might no longer have a Speaker available. Perhaps he or she was ill when they tried to send. Or, perhaps, that deecee was simply not working again. So much was unknown.

Where once there had been bustle and purpose, now there were long periods of enforced idleness, when no messages came in and none went out. The inactivity gradually slipped into laziness and there was less effort made to keep the place clean or neat. Meals were eaten and plates not cleared away because Bellis needed time to sleep and Pasker had finally, and gratefully, left for his home when it became clear he could no longer serve any useful purpose.

A feeling of worthlessness crept in to underlay all of their days, making it harder and harder to believe that they were actually doing anything useful at all. Little now was asked of them; a message here, a request passed on there. Disinterest and apathy lay behind their actions.

The final act was carried out in the kitchen one day. Bellis was putting food on plates and Lisick was sitting at the table, staring off into the distance, unable to sleep. Gerant was in the communication room, taking his turn.

"I hate not feeling my old connection with Harmony." Lisick's voice was small and full of sadness. It was as though she were talking to herself, letting her thoughts drift out into the room. "I had such a feeling, such a wonderful feeling. She is so wonderful when you get to be with Her. And now..."

"I'm sorry for you." Bellis sat and pushed the plate toward Lisick. She had decided she would eat first and then take food to Gerant. She felt Lisick needed the company.

"I hate what's happening. It's like for the very first time in my life, I have no idea what to do. Ever since I can remember, I knew what it felt like to have a connection, be really connected to Harmony. It's always been there. And now? There's only the same connection that everyone has. But that's not what I had. I always had something stronger, something more than just a background noise. I had a real connection." She gestured at her plate. "The difference between looking at food and eating it. Now I feel empty. I have nothing left inside. No purpose, no use." She poked disinterestedly at the plate. "I can't tell people the truth because I don't know what it is. I can tell them to look out for a man, but I could be wrong about that. I try to listen for Harmony, but, She's left me alone."

Bellis was at a loss as to how to comfort her. She ate without tasting anything, watching as Lisick pushed food around, lost in her thoughts.

"Then perhaps it's time we left here." Gerant's words startled them both. He was leaning against the door. He had lost much of his bulk in the days since the blast in their heads. There was a new slackness at the jawline together with shadows beneath the eyes, and his clothes were looser. He looked tired and empty. "There's no point in staying any longer. We've done all we can. Why shouldn't we just leave now?"

"And go where and do what?" Lisick's soft voice asked, her head still bowed over her plate, as if too tired to even look at Gerant.

He spread his arms helplessly. "I don't know. But anything which has some purpose to it. And that's not here. Not anymore. I'm too tired, too old, too whatever, to keep doing this. It's useless, Lisick. And you know it is. Neither of us have our old connection back. I can barely feel anything anywhere anymore. Neither of us is capable of doing what we came here to do, so long ago."

"You may be right. Maybe." Lisick sighed as she sat up straighter. "But, sadly, Gerant, my old friend, I can't think of anything else, of being anywhere else. And that means I don't think I'm going anywhere else, either."

"You mean you'll stay because you can't think of anything better? That's not a good reason."

"True. So, the only reason I'm going to give you is that I'm staying because that's what I promised I would do. I'm staying because it's the right thing for me to do. You? You have to decide that for yourself. I know you've been drawn to the land, to farming it, living on it, not listening to it, and perhaps that's where you should end up." She rubbed her eyes tiredly and gave a small smile of self-regret. "Me? I'm just going to sit here, ready and waiting if ever Harmony wants to let me in again." She gave the smallest of shrugs. "I can't do anything else." She reached over to pat Bellis on the arm. "I would be absolutely delighted if you would stay and help. You know cooking is something I just never got round to. If not, I'll understand. Just leave me some stuff that's easy to eat and won't rot too quickly, because I have a feeling that whatever is going to happen isn't too far away, and I won't have too long to wait. Whatever you choose is good. You could have had a family, been a proper mother, instead of tending to us here. I think it's time you lived your life as well." She waved her hand dismissively to show she meant it and slowly stood up. She took her plate and added a chunk of bread to it. "I think I'll go now." She nodded gravely to each and walked dejectedly away.

Gerant had tears in his eyes. "I don't know what to do. I feel I am betraying everything I promised to do when I came here. But there's nothing left for me to do."

"I think you should go," said Bellis. "I'm going too. I don't have the talents you two have, but I can feel things have ended here. I'll get some food ready for her when she's hungry, then I'm going to pack my things." One hand on her hip, the other at her mouth, as if surprised at her own words. "Do you realize, Gerant, how long I've known you? I don't know anyone else outside of here." Her voice caught. "I'm scared, Gerant. Can I go with you? Please? I can't do this on my own."

He didn't need his talent to see the feelings running through her, as he reached to hold her. He was grateful to have her distraction, to block him thinking, just temporarily, of what he was doing. She sobbed against him. "Of course you can come with me," he murmured. "It will be perfect that way. Of course you can come."

23

As he left Sweetwater behind, Javin hoped that Della had not been affected like the Speaker, Bendiss, had been. It would have been a poor way of saying goodbye.

All he knew was that he would follow the tracks to Luck and keep asking. After all, as she had said, there would not be many girls with red hair and blue eyes, driving a herd of gorries with two dogs. He simply needed to keep going. And to do that, he needed strength. Strength and endurance.

He sat down on a rock and made an accounting of his possessions. Della had been more than generous with provisions. There was a whole loaf as long as his forearm, several fruits, some fresh and some dried, a handful of berries in a cloth twist, which he ate one at a time as he continued taking stock. He laid out fistfuls of dried meats, something round and yellowish which smelt and looked like the cheese he had seen at Hanlar's as well as some herbs he thought might be for cuts or bruises. There was even a small wooden mug and, wonders of wonders, a spare tunic as well as a blade and the tools for touching it up.

He finished the berries, repacked everything and silently thanked Della once more. If he was very careful, he thought he probably had four days of food. Water he would have to find on his own, but that was a small problem, given the number of rills and ponds he had seen in this area previously. His only concern was if he was well enough to walk for one whole day, never mind four. He was aware that he was only partially recovered and that Della was right to have been concerned for him. But the thought of spending more time there with her while the need to be with Meldren gnawed at him was anathema.

He stood slowly, adjusted the satchel and blanket on his shoulders again, straightened up and set off.

By the time dusk was covering the land, he was tired. Very tired. He was sweating profusely and his legs were trembling. He found a small stream nearby and slaked his thirst before chewing on some bread and dried meat. He was careful to eat slowly. He cut some fronds from a bush and managed to make a bed which was not too uncomfortable. The chill he had noticed in the town was just as sharp now. He put on the extra tunic before he wrapped the blanket around himself and piled extra fronds on top. Quickly, he fell into a deep sleep. His last thought was whether cats were in the area and how he could protect himself from them.

When he awoke, he could tell that a large part of the morning had slid by, but he did feel better than he thought he would. A splash of water on his face, a piece of fruit and he was on his way again, although he had to walk the stiffness out of his legs.

He stopped once at midday, again in the afternoon and ate and drank sparingly both times. Each stop was short enough to prevent his muscles from becoming a problem, and he made sure to massage the tiredness from his legs at night and again in the morning.

This routine helped him travel further and more quickly than he had thought possible when he had first left Della. By the third day, he realized that he was feeling much stronger, able to walk faster. The weather remained cool, and there was a light mist which chilled him, but also hurried him to keep warm.

On the fourth day, he arrived at Luck, his food virtually gone. It was as small as Meldren had intimated, no more than a handful of houses scattered around a central large tree growing beside a pond of clear, cool water. The usual jumble of fields seemingly appearing out of the land, and the faint smell of cooking fires were the signs he was nearing it.

Arriving at the tree, he rested and looked around. It was so quiet that any herd of gorries would have been obvious. Meldren was not there. He had expected that, but still, it was saddening. However, he realized that he had been traveling much more quickly than she would have done and had covered the same ground in a day less than she had said it would take. The gorries would have slowed her down. The thought gave him hope.

His first concern was food. He doubted that Luck boasted a place for travelers to eat and rest. He had no money anyway. He looked around him and chose a place at random and decided he would see if he could barter for a meal. After all, as Torrint had once told him, he had a story to tell. Also, he could wash dishes if nothing else. And it was likely that in a place this small everyone would have known of Meldren and could help him find her.

Feeling unsure of what to say or how to say it, he approached the house. Like the others, it had weather-stained walls, a battered-looking door and a couple of small windows. Some plants were using the wall by the door to support their efforts to reach the roof which leaned down to provide some shelter. The mix of fronds, branches and plants from which it was constructed made it look alive. He knocked and called out, "Hello?".

The door opened and a woman with a weather-beaten face peered at him, and then smiled broadly. "Come in, come in!" She beckoned him inside. "I've been waiting for you to come. Thought you might have been a bit earlier than this. But you're here now."

Javin felt obscurely guilty at keeping this woman waiting and wanted to explain to her why he was so late. Catching himself, he realized that he had not been surprised when she had said she was expecting him. That was stranger than the guilt. He ducked through the narrow doorway. She gestured him to the table and the stools there. "Sit down. Please. You're probably tired and hungry? Thought so. Let me get you something." And she bustled around gathering bread and plates and fruits and smoked meat, dipping a mug of water from the barrel under the window.

Placing them before him, she sat herself opposite Javin and smiled broadly at his confusion, her browned face full of wrinkles.

"She said you might be in need of some help. She asked us to keep a look out for you. Meldren, that is. The girl with the gorries, yes?"

Javin nodded. "Meldren. Yes. I'm looking for her. But..."

"Oh! I'm sorry!" She stood and touched her forehead in the salutation Javin was becoming familiar with. "Narlaveena Sallantay. Greetings and welcome."

Javin nodded in his turn and stood to introduce himself. He was becoming less self-conscious with the formality. "Javin Sarnum. Thank you for your hospitality."

Narlaveena beamed at him. "Most call me Narla." She nodded at the food. "Now eat! Then we can talk, hmmm?"

So Javin ate, after first offering some to his hostess. She declined, seemingly just content to watch him, her eyes twinkling. Very quickly, the food disappeared. When the last crumbs had vanished, Narla said, "I suppose you want to know where she went?"

"And how long she's been gone. I -- I had an accident. In Sweetwater. My head. I was in bed for a long time and the healer, Della, looked after me. That's why I could not come before this. I really wanted to come, but it was not possible. In fact, Della did not want me to come. She said I was too weak. But I made it!" He smiled a little. "And I'm sorry if you were worried about me."

Narla dismissed that with a careless waft of her hand. "I knew you would come. Not that I can 'see'. I can't. It's more like a feeling of the future. When I thought about you, I got a good feeling. So I knew you would be here sometime. And, as today got closer, so the feeling got stronger. Then you turned up and," she shrugged, "and, well, that was it."

"Have you known Meldren long?"

"Can't say I know her at all, really. She comes through here maybe once a year, or every two years, stays about a day or so and then moves on. Takes longer than that to know somebody. No, I just know of her."

"But why...?"

Narla grinned again. It seemed a semi-permanent state of her face by the way the wrinkles flexed. "Why look out for you? Why help her? Why not? Plus she left some trade to pay for your food. Not that I'm keeping it." Here she turned to take a small pot from the window ledge and gave it to Javin. "It's all there. You can tell her when you give it to her. It was sweet of her, but not necessary. She was worried about you. So she asked for help. We are giving it. That's all there is." It was obviously that simple to her.

"So I could have knocked on any door at all and everyone would have known who I was?"

Narla rubbed her neck as she thought. "Well, maybe not Venchi, because he's a bit slower now and might not remember. But apart from him? Yes."

"And she gave everyone something for trading?"

"Goodness, no! She gave it to Hennick and Magalena just over the way. But everyone knew you'd be coming here, so Hennick, he gave it over to me to keep for you."

Javin was about to ask how everyone knew, but stopped himself because it would just be another example of the way people were here. He was beginning to accept it even if he couldn't understand it, so he just nodded, hoping it would look like something wise and insightful.

And so Javin found a warm welcome in this smallest of places. That day, one person after another arrived to meet him. Everyone had heard of how he and Meldren had been chosen by Harmony and they each wanted to hear all about it. He had experienced something that they all had only heard or dreamed of. He was, he realized, a celebrity. They saw Javin as their personal representative, the embodiment of their connection with Harmony. Prior to Meldren and him, there were only stories, only hints of what Harmony was. And now, here was someone they could talk with, who could tell them about Harmony in a way they would never experience themselves. He was their intermediary, their priest almost. And, as such, he was precious, and the time with him was precious also.

He told them what he could, trying to find words for it, some way that he could help them gain a new understanding. Each time he told it he felt he had failed. But the looks on their faces, some almost of rapture, made him think he had done better than he thought. They compared his story, their hearing of it, amongst themselves. They weighed it against what Meldren had told them. It fed them. In such a small place, there was only a narrow range of talents, but they were used to seeing deeper into what had happened, what was happening and what would happen. Some just had a feeling, like Narla, stronger or weaker, according to the person. Others had visions, imperfect and not always under any obvious control. Still others wanted just to touch his satchel to get information that way but became confused with pictures of Della and Sweetwater. It made Javin think that perhaps the size of Luck mitigated against stronger talents. Everyone's needs were met and everyone was a neighbor. What need for talents here? But that did not stop the natural human need for inquiry, for novelty, for change to act as an excuse for exercising those talents. Above all, Harmony had been with him. How could that not fire their minds?

After everyone had heard Javin's side of the story, even old Venchi who needed details filled in again that had swiftly fallen through the gaps in his memory, Javin was given space and time as the villagers hugged the story to themselves. The first full day he was politely and tiredly telling and re-telling his tale, the next day he was silent and the atmosphere of this tiny place was lighter and filled with laughter and wonder.

The day after that, Javin prepared to leave.

"You can't really get lost," Narla told him as he sat at the table in the sunlight from the window, enjoying a hot, sweet stew she had made. "There's only the one path. You follow it a way until you meet a river. The Green River. It's wide. You can't cross it there. You'll see. Follow it along downstream. Not upstream. Downstream. Follow it far enough and you'll come across Meldren or, if she's gone on, you'll come across a town. Big place. Much bigger than this. Called Arlen." She paused, eyes screwed up as she silently probed the world around her. "I get the feeling that Meldren might be waiting before that." She looked at Javin. "I can get others to see if they can be clearer for you?" She cocked her head, waiting.

Javin dismissed the idea with a smile. "Thank you, but no. I'm sure it will be easy to find her. I guess if I don't find her, then I ask again in this town. Arlen is it?"

Narla nodded, a more serious look on her face. "Problem is, Arlen's a big place."

"How big?"

This time, she scratched under her chin as she thought, her face screwed in concentration again. She took a small jar of seeds down from a shelf and carefully poured some in her hand. She counted out some on the table, muttering the names of her neighbors as she did so. "There," she said, pointing at the cluster of seeds with her stubby, work-roughened fingers, "That's us. Luck. And Arlen is...," and here she poured more seeds out, comparing them with the first pile. "That's Arlen." The pile she was pointing to was about three times the size of the original one. Javin studied them carefully, judging that Arlen was about half the size of Sweetwater.

"Have you been to Sweetwater?" he asked.

Narla shook her head. "Don't think anyone here has."

"And when was the last time you were in Arlen?"

"Maybe once? I was small and my father wanted to see a boat. Don't know why. He was like that. Taken with ideas. So we went. And we saw it was a big place. He saw his boat and came back and never bothered again." She smiled fondly at the memory and scooped the seeds back into the jar. "No need, you see? Everything we want is right here. I know it's small, but everything we need is either here or it turns up here. Look at you, for instance. Just us few neighbors and friends living here and yet the two people on this whole planet, on our Mother, the only two who have spoken with Her, whom She chose to speak with, the two of you came here." She replaced the jar and turned, beaming, back to Javin. "Now, tell me. If that can happen to us, why would we need to go anywhere else?"

Javin had to admit it was strange. "But doesn't Torrint, the trader, doesn't he come here?"

"Some years he does. Some years he doesn't."

That gave Javin an idea. He took out the small leather case into which he placed the trade items Meldren had left and put it on the table. "In that case, when he comes next, I want you, this whole village, to use this to buy and trade with Torrint. And it's my gift to you and to Torrint himself. He knows about me, but not the whole story. Not what I've told you all. Not what Meldren told you. He only knows that Harmony came to me in a dream. So this," patting the leather, "this is my repaying him for what he did for me." He looked up at Narla. "Will you do this, please?

Accept this gift and buy something fancy. Something you don't need. Something that will remind you of this time, of Meldren and me?"

Narla's face broke into another huge smile. "Nobody here needs reminding of this." She tapped her head and then her chest. "It's inside us. Always will be. Can't not have it with us now. But, yes, I will take it and keep it for us all here. I will tell them and we will decide what to buy." She opened the leather case and placed the items on the table, stirring them with one finger. There were, Javin noticed, a couple of small blue credits. There were some beautiful small shells of a brilliant orange as well as several tiny pieces of gold in amongst the other items, such as odd-shaped seeds and small, carved stones. "I have no idea what this amounts to, but it is more than we have now." She bobbed her head quickly. "So I thank you. You and Meldren."

Javin felt glad to have done it. "I'm going to leave tomorrow. Do you know how far it is to the river?"

"Green river is, oooh, maybe three days?" She frowned. "Actually more like," and she started counting on her fingers. "I forgot about the hills. And then there's the long path..." she muttered to herself. She looked at her hands and held up both to Javin, fingers spread and flashed them once. "Probably more than this. It's been a long time. But you can't get lost."

Javin found himself smiling at her certainty combined with her vagueness. Then he recalled what Meldren had said, the day they parted. "One thing, though, before I leave. Why is this place called Luck?"

Narla laughed softly, her eyes twinkling. "After what's happened here, to us, can you think of a better name?"

24

The following day, Javin said his farewells to each of the people there who wanted to wish him well one last time and also to pass on their thanks for the gift.

Hitching his satchel, now filled with offerings of bread, nuts, seeds and fruits as well as spare clothes, a sewing kit and any other small useful items they thought would be of use, he left Luck behind him as the sun rose in the clear sky and the cool night breeze eased and the air became still.

Although the path was little used, it was plain to see; a depression following the simplest route. Easing around rocks, following the downhill slopes, skirting small groves, avoiding the boggiest ground; it was an easy walk for him now.

As before, water was plentiful in ponds and rivulets. The satchel weighed more now than when he had left Della and he needed to switch shoulders with his blanket every so often.

At what he judged to be midday he stopped to have a bite to eat and to take a fresh inventory. After doing so, mindful of Narla's estimate, he was doubtful of reaching Arlen before needing to resupply himself. Therefore, he determined to keep his eyes open for fresh foods he could use to eke out the generous provisions he had received.

As he continued to walk, his legs beginning to feel like they could stretch longer, move more easily after their rest, so he found the music sliding into his head again. It was similar to the music he had heard with Meldren. Similar, but not the same. He thought, perhaps, that it was his mind making up for the peace of the countryside and filling it with something familiar. So he hummed along with some of it, whistled snatches of it here and there, even sung to it, making up sounds as he went. It was an activity which passed the time and which made him feel surprisingly good. Doing it made him forget to keep an eye out for food, however.

By the time evening came and he was searching for somewhere sheltered and near water, he was annoyed at his failure to be more alert. But, looking at the horizon and the silhouette of the hills ahead of him, he was surprised at how far he had traveled. What had been a low smudge of purplish ridges in the morning had become clearer, sharper mounds with trees and bushes clearly outlined against the sky. And he didn't feel as tired as he thought he should have.

That night he dreamed of Meldren again, seeing her clear blue eyes and enjoying her smiling at him. The music filtered into and out of the dream, acting almost as a backdrop to it. He woke feeling refreshed and eager to get going. The surroundings caught his eye. They didn't look quite the same as when he had arrived. He thought that the hills had been more distant. But here the trees were close enough to see individual branches, and the slope of the hill started only a few paces away. He put the confusion down to the previous night; his tiredness and the darkness which had presented him seeing such details. He splashed some cold water on his face, chewed on some bread, which still tasted surprisingly fresh, shrugged the carrying straps into a comfortable position and made a promise to himself to be more alert today and harvest some food as he traveled along.

By the time he stopped for a midday break he realized that he had, once again, failed to keep his promise. The music he had sung and whistled and hummed had kept all his attention all morning. So it was that he chose to leave the path and make for a nearby grove or thicket of some kind of bushes, in the hope that he would find something edible there and assuage the guilty feeling he had.

He tramped up the hill, keeping his eyes open for anything which looked even slightly edible. Soon, he was in the grove, peering up amongst the jagged fronds with their irregular bursts of flowers, or were they fruits, but without any luck. He sat down and decided to eat his meal there and find water later. As he was chewing on some nuts, he felt as though he was being watched. He glanced around surreptitiously but could find nothing to explain the feeling. It didn't feel like a threat, but he wanted to find out what it was, nevertheless.

Standing up and hitching his load into place once more, he made a more thorough investigation. He could see clearly between the trunks which were themselves too spindly for anyone to hide behind. He turned his attention to the canopy above, wondering at one point about those cats Torrint had referred to, and whether they lived in trees. But he didn't feel like he was being hunted. Not that he could have explained to anyone why that was so.

About to give up and turn downhill again to the path, his eye caught a brief sparkle from a frond. It had not rained, so he was sure it was not moisture catching the sun. Nearing it, he noticed that the leaves where he thought the sparkle had originated from were subtly different. Not quite the same color. Not quite the same shape. But almost like them. Similar enough that a casual glance would not have marked them as different. By following the shades of color of the 'wrong' leaves, he discovered a camouflaged creature. What it was he could not tell. But, now he could see it, he saw that it had a long, slim body and that it was wrapped around the branch, and the sparkle had been its eye catching the light.

Javin was delighted by it. Something so carefully camouflaged, he wanted to see it more clearly. He slowly reached up to it, hoping somehow to coax it to where he could examine it more easily. The small head turned from side to side as if examining him, watching his hand. Once in a while, it opened its mouth, but he could see no teeth. And he felt no fear in reaching for it.

Making cooing noises, he was a handspan from touching it when it uncoiled from the tail-end and launched, or slid or glided or swam (Javin never could clearly recall how it moved) and coiled itself around his upper arm in such a way that the head and its bright eyes were at his shoulder, inspecting his face.

The speed of it took him by surprise as did the warmth of its body through his tunic. He stood still, his arm held out stiffly, uncertain what to do next. He was concerned that he might injure it if he brought his arm back down to his side. As if reading his mind, the creature moved in its fluid way to encircle his neck, but this time, it left enough of its body suspended in air so that the head could regard Javin. He was surprised at his lack of fear and, oddly, felt rather comforted by the warmth of the creature around his neck. It was only wrapped tightly enough to prevent it falling off. There was no pressure there, just contact.

Squinting at it, Javin fumbled in his satchel to find something to offer it to eat. He offered scraps of cheese, which were rejected, some jerky, which was accepted, and some pok berries, which were also accepted. The creature ate by extending its mouth outwards, again, fluidly, swiftly, and enfolding the food, drawing it back in again. Not so much biting as enfolding. That which it did not like was rejected simply by opening its mouth again. That which it accepted, seemed to disappear into the length of the body.

Having eaten, the little creature finished coiling itself around him, the head ending up nestled in the soft curve under his jaw, for all the world as if it had been trained to do exactly that; maximum contact with minimum discomfort to him. It was, without doubt, a strangeness to have happened. But Javin trusted his feelings and smiled to himself. He decided that, as long as the creature did nothing to threaten him, he would be content to let it reside where it was. If nothing else, it would be an uncritical audience for his singing!

The rest of the day, Javin walked and hummed and whistled his way to Meldren, occasionally reaching up to reassure himself that the creature was still there and to stroke it gently. Over the next two days, the landscape seemed to be changing around him, morning and night. Nothing he could identify, just subtle differences. What he thought he recalled at night was never quite as it looked in the morning.

It was on the fourth day after leaving Luck that he began to wonder how far ahead of him Meldren was by now. There had been the odd sign of her passage; a crumpled stub of a feather, the outline of a large paw print at the edge of a pond. But he was not a good enough tracker to know how old such things were. All he knew was that he was traveling faster than she could have managed, but that there were many, many days to make up.

It was a great surprise, therefore, when, at the end of that day, tired but wishing he could have made even better progress, he found a place to rest and saw definite signs of recent use. Some cold ashes, a few wisps of fur, the distinct markings of gorries' feet, and even a broken wooden bowl; all spoke, even to his slight knowledge, of fairly recent use. His heart leapt at the thought of seeing Meldren soon, but he had no idea how that could even be possible. He had resigned himself to asking after her in Arlen, sure that she would have passed through there long before. But now? Everything was changed by these signs. He was almost too excited to eat, but did so in what was becoming a familiar routine. First, he took off the satchel with a thankful sigh, took out the blade and found and cut some branches for a bed. Then he picked through the remaining food to find which was most in need of being eaten before it went bad. As he did so, the creature unwound from his neck so that he could easily feed it small pieces. They both ate together. Then he took a drink from the water nearby, put on his spare clothes against the night chill and draped some more cut fronds over him. The creature appeared not to be bothered by his lying down, merely shifting enough so that it was not pinched or pressured by Javin's body.

But this night, he could not sleep, and the creature was not responsible for keeping him awake. He was too excited at the evident and unexplainable proximity to Meldren. He lay on his back, gazing at the stars, humming the tunes he had heard all day, wide awake and happy to be so. Finally, in the early part of the morning, or the late part of the night, he decided to start walking. He couldn't wait any longer. His eyes were well-adjusted, and he judged the reward was more than worth any possible risk of stubbed toes or twisted ankle.

He began cautiously but his eagerness to complete his journey soon encouraged him to make haste. The music was louder in his head and he found himself bubbling over with a feeling of joy and anticipation such that he ended up singing out loudly as he went along, with sounds that came to him, syllables that made no sense when strung together, except that, with the music inside him, they did have meaning. But it was a meaning he could only feel, not explain; a feeling that the world and everything in it made sense to him.

He stopped once to eat quickly and to share with the creature before hurrying on. It was late in the afternoon that he breasted a rise and saw before him the broad stretch of the river, and along the recognizable path leading to it was the unmistakable shapes making up Meldren's camp. There were the gorries in a straggly bunch, too loose to be called a herd. There was the wagon and nearby was the mandria. He could just make out the dogs and thought he could almost see her sitting down, but not clearly enough to be sure.

His singing stopped and he began to stumble into a run, trying to lessen the bouncing of his satchel and blanket at the same time as waving and calling. The two dogs, Skort and Fallack as he recalled, had gone on the alert, facing him, tails straight and unmoving, quietly assessing him as a threat.

As he neared the camp, so he slowed. Partly due to being out of breath and partly because he was reminded of what Meldren had said about the dogs. One of them had, sort of, accepted him, but the other one hadn't, she'd said. They were very large. Perhaps prudence was called for...

He still could not make out Meldren there and the dogs were strangely quiet. It all added to the air of unreality. Finding her so quickly, and now this silence. He halted and strained to see her, but could not. She was sleeping, perhaps? Off somewhere else? At Arlen, maybe? He could not guess and did not want to challenge the dogs directly. He called out again. "Meldren? It's me! Javin! I'm here! Is there anything wrong?" He waited anxiously.

He was about to call out again when she appeared from behind the wagon. Walking slowly, with the hood of her cape brought forward so that her face was in shadows, she beckoned him into the camp. He assumed her hood was shielding her from what breeze there was, but was not in the mood to think clearly about it. He was here! She was there! His aching legs were irrelevant as were his sore shoulders.

With a surge of relief, he made his way quickly to her, the dogs merely swiveling their heads as he passed them. She remained standing at the rear of the wagon. His heart was pounding and he knew there was the biggest and silliest grin on his face.

"Meldren! It's so good to see you again. I am so sorry I took so long, but I had an accident. Then I met the people in Luck and they told me about you and I hurried on, and it should have taken so much longer than it did, and I found this little creature." He realized he was babbling at her. And she stopped him with a brief gesture.

"I see you have found one of them." She pointed at his throat where the lithe being had unwound itself, as if waiting for food. She threw back her hood and smiled at him, dreamily almost. "I have one as well." She drew his attention to her throat where the twin of his was nestling.

Something was different about Meldren. Javin knew it, but could not define it. She was there, in front of him, yet seemed remote, distant in some fashion. "I think we need to meet again." The words she spoke were strange and out of place. And then, two things happened in quick succession. First, Javin realized that Meldren's eyes should have been blue, but they were dark, almost black. And, as he was about to point that out to her, so the creature around his neck lunged and bit him on the neck. It was too quick for him to do anything other than register the sharp pain and his own shock before he crumpled into unconsciousness; ankles, knees, hips, shoulders and neck folded him down onto the ground.

25

He was in a place between consciousness and unconsciousness: able to see, but with more than just his eyes, which could not focus. He knew that Meldren was beside him, even though some very tiny and persistent part of him knew it wasn't Meldren. He was on his back. She was next to him. She rolled her head to look at him and he tried to look at her. And suddenly, he knew she was not his Meldren at all. He shut his eyes again.

She was, somehow, Harmony Herself. Here, with him, with them both. It was impossible and ridiculous but it was true and real. And he was not frightened. He did not worry. He had already had a taste of this wonder back at the cave.

This time, the music entered more swiftly, engulfing him more completely, if that were possible. The same boundless vision of the planet was there with its breathtaking intricacy. But, this time, it did not end there. Javin, or his perception of himself, or Harmony's perception of him, moved swiftly upwards, leaving the planet dwindling behind. He was moving outward, into the space beyond Harmony. No longer within the world, he was moving beyond it.

As he did so, he felt or heard or touched another level of music. This was not like anything he had so far sensed. If what he had seen first of

Harmony was one small aspect, then this was another, grander view, like changing from studying a pebble to seeing the mountain it was part of. It grew from within the existing sound of Harmony. And, as it grew, so it lifted him further, to the source of this majestic, intricate and consuming sound. As he was moving, so he realized that what he had been aware of, the harmony of the planet in all Her glory, was no more than a sub-theme of this grandeur he was approaching.

Around him was nothing, or everything. A vastness whose distance made vision useless. but it was filled, filled with so much emotion, so much energy. Behind him, if that made any sense, was Harmony, singing Her song, tying Javin to Her with the notes and choruses he had been listening to. Ahead, or in a place he had not yet seen, the source of all sound was drawing him. Pure awareness alone made up Javin's existence and that awareness doubled and re-doubled until he was filled and stretched and a million miles tall and squeezed to a point all at the same time. He could take no more. It was too much. And still he was being drawn on and on. He felt he could die, would die here and it was fine, it was right. His death would just add one more note, one more tiny, minute sound to everything. But that note, made up itself of smaller notes, rhythms, echoes and sounds, would be his. Death was not to be feared, for it would add to the grandeur of everything.

Just as he was about to surrender himself to the music and become a formless sound, so the source, the origin of it all, made itself known. Blinding brightness reached to engulf him, accept him. He opened his mouth to sing the simple song of his life, offer it to the composer and conductor, giving it as the only thing truly his to give, back to the place of his birth. And, with that moment of intended surrender, everything became black and still and, worse, silent. Then there was nothing at all; the nothing of his own emptiness once more.

In that intense loneliness, Javin moved, became aware of his body again. Time was not part of that awareness.

He cried out, both at the pain of being left here and at the physical agony which followed that awareness. His head felt on fire from the inside. Scrunching his eyes against the light, he sought to turn his head but could not stifle the whimper it caused. Everything hurt beyond belief. He retched and felt moisture on his chin but could not move to wipe it away. The taste of bile in his mouth did not diminish. He wanted to fall into the blackness again, become unconscious, leave the pain behind, but he couldn't. Breathing in shallow gasps, he wanted to die, or at least to fall again into that blissful unconsciousness.

How long he lay there, he had no idea. At some time, with no way of knowing when, he was able to realize that he could feel something beyond him, beyond the agony. There were drops of coolness on his skin which did not burn or lacerate him. Raindrops. Rain fell upon him, some drops finding his mouth, moistening his lips, from where he licked it, took it within. Slowly, he was bathed from head to foot in cool, soothing water from the skies, washing away, dulling the pain until he finally could move without retching, breathe without flinching.

At some point, he was able to roll over and bring his knees up, his back now being washed. He saw Meldren nearby. She was sleeping, but under the wagon. He managed to crawl toward her and flopped down. Now he wanted to sleep because he was tired, not because he wanted to escape the pain.

26

Recovery was slow and was a head full of pulsing needles of pain the next morning, for both of them. The clouds remained, but the rain had stopped and there was now a gentle breeze, almost refreshing, but it whispered of rain in the future. They sat in silence, acknowledging the need for it with squinted eyes and deep breaths. Gradually, it became thinkable to speak.

Javin pointed at his neck. "Where did you get yours?"

Meldren half turned and fumbled around in the wagon. "I don't know. I woke up with it. And, the strange thing is, it doesn't feel surprising. Which, in itself, is a surprise." She turned back with a cloth in her hand. "What are they?" She wrinkled her brow. "Shouldn't we at least be a little more curious about them? A little more surprised? I've never heard of such creatures. I've never seen one before, let alone two. And here they are wrapped around our necks. For all we know, they could strangle us now and we couldn't stop them."

"Mine bit me. Knocked me unconscious." He explored the tender area of the bite with his fingertips. "Does yours bite?"

"Who knows?" She poured some water out into a bowl, and then paused as she thought about it more. "What worries me more is that I'm not worried about it. Should I be?"

Javin shrugged. "I found mine in a tree. But, generally speaking, in terms of strangeness, compared to what happened to us last night, no, not strange enough to worry about." He shifted his position slightly. "I really don't think I like this." He rubbed his temples gingerly. "Really. Everyone who knows about us has said what a wonderful honor it is. They have no idea!"

Meldren had dipped a cloth in the bowl beside her and was holding it over her eyes. "It wasn't like this before."

"No. It wasn't. This time, there was more to it. More going on."

She removed the cloth to glare. "What do you mean? That's not how it was for me! Just like last time, I don't remember anything. Not a thing! And you talk about not liking it! I meant that this is just more painful. What happened to you, then?"

Javin gestured helplessly. "I wasn't that good at explaining things the first time. And this? Well, it's just as difficult to explain. I'm not trying to be awkward, but I really don't know how to say it." He was silent for a moment, trying to marshal his thoughts. "Put it like this. If the first time was about how everything on Harmony is connected and it's all made up of songs, then, this time, it was about how Harmony is only part of something much bigger which is also made up of songs." He smiled apologetically. "It's all about songs. Everything. It's all songs." He sighed. "Which sounds really simple and stupid when I say it out loud. And it doesn't make much sense if I said that even the sky was a song, or part of one. Which it is. Or that that river is a song. Which it is. The water and the stuff growing in it? Songs. The water is just the way we see the song, that's all. Sorry, I can't tell you better than that."

Acknowledging the inadequacy of his own words, he tried again. "It's like the difference between singing a song and hearing one. If I hear a song, it can change my mood. Make me happy or sad or something else. But, if I sing it myself, then I'm making those emotions happen to others, assuming I can sing in a way which doesn't upset people. Well, that's the sort of thing about Harmony's songs. She sings songs which make things happen. We hear them and we are changed by them, see things, experience things, all because of Her songs."

Meldren wrinkled her nose at him, soaking the cloth again. "At least you got to remember. I never did have anything to remember."

There was something about remembering that nagged at Javin. Something he was going to say. He closed his eyes in an effort to recall what it was.

Meldren applied the cloth again, but this time to the back of her neck, gently twisting and turning her head to loosen the muscles as she did so. "All that happened to me was that, one moment there I was, settling down for the night and the next I was waking up in a different place under this wagon. In between? Pfffft!"

The 'something' was wriggling nearer the surface in Javin's mind. "So you don't remember meeting me last night?"

Meldren stopped and looked at him, sadly shaking her head. And that's when he remembered. "You have blue eyes! That's what it was. You have blue eyes!"

"Yes, and what of it?"

"But last night, they weren't blue! They were dark. Almost black? Maybe a really, really dark brown? But most definitely not blue." He grinned. "That's how I'll be able to tell. When you're you, you're blue. When you're Her, you're dark! Can't be any other explanation."

"My eyes changed color? Are you serious?"

"Oh, read my colors, girl! Am I lying? No! Think about it! Well, except you can't because.... Anyway, last night, I couldn't see your eyes because your hood was over your face, right until the end, when my little beast bit me. And the first time? Back at the cave? It was dark. Nighttime. I couldn't see your eyes if I wanted to. But if I had, I'm sure they would have been dark. Don't you see? It's an easy way of telling if I'm talking to Harmony or to you?"

Meldren was thinking about something else. "Last night?" She shook her head. "Can't have been. Last night I was in a different campsite, back along the track. I was going to wait there a few days. Close to the river, but not very close. Not as close as this." She looked around, puzzled. "But I'm here. How? And why didn't I notice it first thing?" She sat back, a baffled look on her face. "Something very strange is going on. Very."

"How long did it take you to get to the previous campsite?"

Meldren thought back. "Maybe fifteen days after leaving Luck. Can't have been much more. I was moving really slowly for you to catch up.

Staying in one camp long enough for the gorries to stink the place out before moving on."

"And you took how long to get to Luck in the first place?"

Meldren frowned in recollection. "Maybe five days? Maybe a little more? And then some days in Luck itself. Three, maybe?"

Javin did some brief figuring in his head. "That can't be right. That makes about twenty-five days. Call it thirty to be on the safe side. I left Luck about four days ago. Before that, I came from Sweetwater, and before that, I was ill and useless for anything for at least thirty days."

"Thirty?"

"Nearer forty, if you count the time I spent traveling to and from Sweetwater to the place we split. So how could I catch up with you if you took the same time, even counting from where we parted, to get here? It doesn't make sense. There are some days missing."

Meldren rubbed her eyes tiredly. "Don't you think that things not being explainable is actually the only thing which makes sense, in a sort of strange way?" She stopped rubbing and sat back. "You and I, we have creatures round our necks, can't understand how we got here, I can't remember what happened and you can't tell me much. Other than that, everything is normal." She let out a small sigh of exasperation. "But it still comes down to the same question. Why us? Are we just somebody for Harmony to play with? What is the point of it all?" She had a grumpy look on her face. "I'm with you. I don't like it either."

They sat in silence for a while, feeling sorry for themselves.

Meldren couldn't maintain it for long, however, and tried to change the mood. "Well, at least you have your memories back, which is a good thing. It must be a relief to know who you are at long last. Do you think it was the crack on your head which did it, or was it Della's doing?"

Javin ran through the morning again in his head. "I don't recall telling you anything about Sweetwater. How did you know?" He peered more closely at her. "Let me have a look at your eyes." Meldren made a face at him, eyes wide. "Blue. So it is still you. But I didn't tell you. I'm sure of it."

Meldren threw her hands up in a show of ignorance. "I don't know. I don't know how I know. I just know that that's what happened to you. Are you sure you didn't mention it?" Ignoring Javin's head shake, she continued, listing the points on her fingers. "You hit your head on a stool and then the floor and you were unconscious and Della helped you. You were sick and she gave you medicine and one day you just realized who you were. How could I know that to be true if you didn't tell me? And I know it's true. Know it," she emphasized by tapping her chest.

Javin had no answer to it. He felt frustrated at not understanding what had happened. "Let's agree on something together, shall we?"

Meldren cocked her head inquiringly.

"Let's agree that we are not going to get any answers to the questions we have. All we can do is compare how things are for each other and leave it at that. Not my favorite solution, but it might be the only one which has any chance of being right. What do you think?"

Meldren, clearly irked, picked at one of her fingernails as she thought about it. "It does seem that the more we ask questions, the more confusing it becomes. And we haven't got any decent answers yet, have we?" She looked up and shrugged. "So, why not? Let's just share what we know and see what happens. The thing which annoys me most is that, well...I was looking forward to us being together and, this...mess, it's got in the way. I wanted to be happy and instead I've got a headache, questions I can't answer and no idea about anything anymore. It's not fair!"

Javin made a 'me too' face. "Can't help but agree with you. I think it all comes back to what we said before. It's all about us making choices. Yes, things might still happen to us, but we can at least choose what to do in the meantime, can't we? Choose where to go, where to stay." A more serious tone entered his voice. "Like I said before, I know that I've had very few choices so far. But I'm going to change that. And, for all we know, Harmony could be playing with hundreds of other people like us, making life as difficult or strange for them as it is for us. People tell us we're special, but how do they know? For all we can tell, there might be other couples, or whole families having the same problems we are. Come to that, why not whole villages?" He frowned in thought. "That could explain what happened in Blackeye. They all died. Perhaps Harmony was trying to speak with them and killed them?" He shook his head. "That can't be right, because Banith found that metal there." He caught the question in Meldren's eye. He shaped it with his hands. "About so big. It was not from Harmony. Banith could tell that. I suppose they died because of that, of not wanting to hear Harmony any more, of taking something which was not Hers. She just did it on a whim, perhaps." He sucked in a breath at the implication of what he had just said.

"I mean, we all of us think that Harmony is looking after us. But what if we're wrong? What if She's actually just using us for Her amusement in some way. Showing me what's going on and locking you away from it. How do I know that what I was shown was even the truth? I don't think we should trust Her or rely on Her. I think that it's more important that we choose to live our lives as we want. On our own terms, as far as possible. And if Harmony wants to push Her nose into our lives, well, there's not a great deal we can do to stop Her. But, in the meantime, why not live as we want to?"

Meldren had been watching him carefully, judging his words by the colors around him. When he had finished and was looking expectantly at her, she nodded once to show she believed him. "Why not? The question then is, what do we do now?"

"Ah! That's easy!" Javin smiled. "First, we eat. I'm starving!"

"I'll see what we've got." She turned back to the wagon and shivered. "Didn't realize I was chilly until I moved. Where's my other shawl?"

Javin found his satchel and delved into it to help with the food. He found that there was a lot more left than he recalled and it was all fresh looking. It was another strangeness to add to the list. All he could do was be grateful. Meldren's eyes widened as he offered her the food, but she refrained from asking questions, seemingly having the same thoughts about it all as Javin. They ate their meal quickly.

"What do we do now?" Meldren repeated her question, voicing what they had both been thinking. "I mean, it's all very well saying that we should live as we want, but the thing is, now I'm being asked to do just that, it's not as easy as I thought it would be. I've gone where I wanted to, done what I wanted, but I did it without much thought. Is that what you're saying? That we have to plan it all out now? And what about the gorries, which, I might remind you, could all be dead for all I know about it. The gorries and Skort and Fallack and Sarlin and the wagon... What happens to them? Where do they fit in? What about us?"

Javin wiped his mouth clean and stood up. "First, let's go find the gorries and make sure they are all alive. Then we can think about what to do. What do you say?" He held out his hand to help Meldren to her feet. He peered at the sky. "I don't like the look of those clouds. Let me grab my spare tunic and then we'll get going."

The first thing they did was to check on Sarlin. He rumbled at them as they felt his legs for tender spots. Javin noticed that his coat was thick and only a few strands of it came loose as he ran his hand over him. He recalled Torrint telling him that it was a sure sign of the end of summer.

Once they had satisfied themselves that the mandria was healthy, they set off to check the gorries. It did not take very long to find the herd, mainly because the two dogs led them there directly, walking ahead and turning to check they were being followed. The gorries were spread out over a wide area. Some were paddling in the edges of the river while others were scattered amongst the shrubs; sleeping or feeding. Gorries being gorries, it took a while to muster them into one place. Meldren took a head count and nodded in satisfaction.

"They're all here."

"Somehow, I'm not surprised," Javin replied with a wry smile. "In fact, I think it's going to be hard to make me, us, feel surprised about anything anymore. All the gorries are here, we've got plenty of food, we're together again and life is wonderful. Except that we have no idea what's happening to us or what's going to happen. Which means," he said putting his arm around Meldren, "that it's time to think about our future."

She leaned into him. "I agree. And the reason I'm snuggling is because you are nice and warm."

"And...?"

"And it's chilly."

"And...?"

She pulled back just far enough to look up at him, an innocent expression on her face. "And if you have to be told everything, then obviously you have no imagination. I think there should be some mystery in our relationship, don't you?" She graciously allowed him to kiss her on the forehead before resuming her snuggling.

"Oh, there is plenty of mystery right now."

On the slow return to the campsite, they talked over the idea of choosing what to do next.

"It's easier for me," said Javin, holding hands with Meldren. "After all, I have no home here, no birthplace, nothing to keep me in one place." He waggled a remonstrative finger at Meldren's pretend shocked expression. "You know exactly what I mean. But it is easier for me. You are the one with possessions, things, plans." He looked at her. "Do you want to keep doing what you have always done? I can share it with you. We can go where you always go. I don't mind. It will all be new to me. If we're thinking about living our lives, then it's only fair that you should have the biggest say in that because you have the most to consider."

They walked on in silence for a few more slow paces.

"You don't have to decide now," he added.

Meldren studied the ground, thinking. "It seems to me that, since meeting you, my life has not been the same." She smiled at him and held her thumb and finger of her free hand close together. "That's about how much I feel is left of how I used to be, how I used to think and live. And now? Now everything is possible. And 'everything' is a big word. It's too big. If I have everything to choose from, I can't choose anything. But, if I can choose only from some things, that is easier. So, if it's all the same to you, I'd like to choose being with you. The rest of it, I don't know about." She leaned into him. "But I'll choose you and whatever comes with that choice." She gave a little jump and a gasp, her hand going to her throat and the creature there. "Oh! It sort of pulsed when I said that," and she made a grasping movement to illustrate.

"Ow! Mine did, too! But not painful. Just a sort of throbbing." He regarded Meldren at arms length, peering at the creature around her neck. "And, no, I have no idea what that meant. Another strangeness."

"Well, I'm going to think it was agreeing with me, that it was happy for us."

Javin smiled back. "Sounds good to me. And I like the choice you made. Thank you." He kissed her. "It fits very neatly with the choice I wanted to make as well."

She dimpled at him. "We're geniuses, then. But it still doesn't help us much. What, exactly, are we going to do?"

Up ahead, the campsite was visible. "Can we let the dogs look after the gorries now?" Javin asked. "I have some ideas about our future, but I'd like to sit and maybe get a fire going and get a bit warmer. Sound good?"

The fire would not catch. The wood was damp and there was none dry after the earlier rain. Meldren was philosophical. "It happens sometimes. I should have kept the kindling in the wagon."

"Hardly your fault, was it? I mean, if anyone's to blame, then it should be Harmony. She was the one who should have taken care of it." Javin stopped suddenly as a thought struck him. He pointed at Meldren. "If you are not to blame and Harmony is, and I was shown that everything that happens is nothing more than a song, then..." He tailed off as he thought more about what he was about to say.

"You can't just stop there," Meldren urged.

"Give me a minute. I need to listen. I need to see if I can hear it."

"Hear what?" Meldren asked impatiently.

"Everything." His gesture prevented her from asking more questions. He shut his eyes, took a deep breath and slowed his breathing, a look of concentration on his face. At one point, he bent his head to one side, as if hearing something beyond Meldren's capabilities, a frown followed by a nod. Then, with his eyes still closed, he sat up straight and stroked the creature around his neck before beginning to make a small, crooning noise, punctuated by an odd low whistling sound, all the while keeping an unheard beat with the nodding of his head. The creature around his neck also bobbed to an unheard beat. After a few moments, ending with a nasal sort of humming, he opened his eyes and looked at Meldren, who had been fascinated and confused in equal portions. At one point, she had reached up to her neck in surprise as her creature's head also bobbed to and fro to the unheard music.

"That should do it," he said.

"I hate to ask this," she said, "but do what exactly? What did you just do? It's like nothing I've ever heard before, although I have to admit that it sounded vaguely like something I've heard, if that makes any sense."

"Try the fire again. The wood should catch now."

Shaking her head at this new strangeness, Meldren rearranged the wood. As she touched it, her eyebrows shot up. "It's dry! I can feel it is really dry!" She looked from the wood to Javin. "Are you saying that you did that? With those strange sounds?"

"I think so. At least, I tried to. That's what I meant earlier. Everything is a song. It really is. A song. I thought that if Harmony had been in my head, showed me what She did, the songs of everything, then I had a chance of hearing it for myself. And if I could do that, then I could, maybe, sing a song myself. Just a small one. A tiny one about dry wood."

The fire caught quickly as he was speaking, and Meldren had to hurry to pile more wood on before the first was consumed. "I might need to make that a bit less dry, next time," Javin said, warming his hands, making an 'I haven't a clue' face.

Neither knew what to say. Both sat in silence, puzzling over the fact that wood, which had been too damp to catch, was now bone-dry and blazing merrily in front of them despite the fact that it had been in the open all the time.

"How much stranger can things get, Javin? Singing wood dry. Now that's new. I was watching your colors and they were blazing and then they went very strange. Sort of spikey. Instead of some colors being stronger and showing up brighter, they all seemed to stand out from you. Much further away than usual. I mean, way out." She opened her arms as wide as possible. "And they were like beams of light shooting out. I have no idea what that was all about." She gave a sigh. "But, then, I have no idea what the whole day has been about either."

"All I know is that I tried to listen to what I needed to hear. I thought, if everything is a song, then there are songs going on all around us all the time. Around us and in us. So, if I could hear that, the song about wood, then I supposed that I could at least try to sing something like it. But it was very much trial and error."

Meldren pointed at the fire. "If that was trial and error, I'd hate to see you when you get it right!" She gave a small breathy laugh. "Is this how we're going to live? Singing fires when we need them? I assume you can sing food so we won't starve? Is that it? Is that our lives from now on? Singing whatever we want. Well, you singing whatever we want."

"I don't see why you can't do it as well. After all, Harmony has been in you, too. She's been part of you in an entirely different way. So why couldn't you sing things as well? Perhaps we'll try it later on." Javin looked over the flames at Meldren. "But what you said is true enough. What are we going to do with our lives?" He gestured at the fire. "Before this happened, I was going to share some ideas I had." Meldren motioned him to go on.

"I was thinking that, if we can go anywhere, and you and I want to be together, which we do," he added with a bright smile, "then would you feel really bad about leaving your gorries behind?"

She shook her head. "Of course not. As long as they were with people who would look after them."

"Of course. Of course. But what about Sarlin or Skort and Fallack? How would you feel about leaving them behind as well? We have absolutely no idea how all this is affecting them. And we also have no idea what else will happen." He waited anxiously.

Meldren was slower this time. "They've been with me for so long. They're like my family." She was still, her eyes half-closed, thinking. "Sarlin, he's less of an issue. After all, he's happiest when grazing. But the dogs? Not so easy. They protect me, look out for me. I've had them since they were puppies." She looked at Javin. "I don't know. Not for sure."

"That's fair. You are right. They deserve to be looked after well." A pause. "But, I was thinking..."

"You've started, so you might as well get to the end."

"We don't know what's going to happen, but whatever it is, it seems like we have no control over when it happens. Harmony arrives and...things happen. Today, for instance, the gorries were all over the place. Sarlin was lucky in that he was hobbled but still able to fend for himself. And the dogs? We don't know what happened to them. Yes, they're big and can probably look after themselves. But this last time with Harmony was bad. Painful. Scary, in a way. What if, when Harmony comes the next time, we scare the dogs and they attack us?" He saw Meldren's reaction. "I know. I know. They have always looked after you. And they seem to be fine with me. But, the point is, when Harmony is... doing whatever it is She does to us, then we aren't ourselves anymore. And who knows how long it will be before we are awake and capable of looking after them the next time it happens?" He put a hand out to her, trying to reassure her. "I'm not saying that they are unreliable or that they could attack us or have problems when we were incapable of doing anything for them. But, what I am saying is that we don't know. The next time could be worse for us. And that might mean it's worse for them. They are not mine. I haven't raised them from pups. Your relationship with them is entirely different. I appreciate that. And, maybe, sometime in the future, we could come back for them, be with them again. I just don't know. I'm just trying to think of all the possibilities. I was going to suggest that we leave all the animals with people in Arlen. But, since the fire here, I've had another thought." He took a deep breath, picking his words carefully. "And the thought was, if I can dry wood with a song, would it be possible to, for example, perhaps sing a song for the dogs so that they won't miss you and you won't miss them?"

Meldren's face showed astonishment and skepticism in quick succession. "That's a lot to think about. I agree that what Harmony wants She is going to get, whether we want it or not. And, hard though it is, I can see that there's something in what you say. But, do you really think you can do that, sing songs like that?"

"I don't know. That's the truth. But what I do know is that we, you and I together, we have the knowledge of it. And, I think that it can be done. We'd be careful, of course. But, despite everything I've said about Her, I also think that Harmony really will take care of us. I truly believe that if we were doing something which would turn out harmful, She would stop us." He winced. "We might not like how She did that, of course."

"And if I don't want to forget them, my beautiful dogs?" Meldren held back tears. "I don't want to not have them with me in my head. I can't just abandon them like that."

Javin rose and came round the fire to sit beside her, and put his arm round her shoulder. "You are, again, right. I should have been more thoughtful." She rested her head on him. "But we could help only them to forget. Or, maybe just leave them with a happy feeling? It sounds stupid, but I know that everything is a song. And you've seen it happen. Why can't we help Skort and Fallack live happily without us? And, as I said, maybe we can come back for them, when we are more certain of what's happening with us."

He felt her give a big sigh. "You keep saying 'we', as if I know anything about it. But I don't!"

"Then let us try something. Shall we?" There was a brief nod. He pushed against her gently. "You need to sit up for this. At least, to begin with. Ready?" He kept hold of her hand. "Close your eyes. Take a few slow, deep breaths. Good. Now, you know very well that the fire is in front of you, don't you? I want you to listen to it. I don't mean hear the crackling and the other small sounds. Ignore them. Listen to what's behind those sounds." He watched her face carefully. He spoke gently, quietly. "If it's not clear, then think back to when Harmony came to you. You lost touch with the world. But not really, because Harmony, the whole world, was there, somehow. There, in you. Think back to that, the moment when you had Harmony arrive and then...listen to the fire again. Listen to how Harmony hears the fire." Again he searched her face for a clue as to how this was going. He was about to tell her to give up and open her eyes when suddenly she broke into a huge smile. With her eyes still closed, she turned to him.

"I can hear it! It's a song! It's wonderful!" Her mouth opened in astonishment. "I can hear you! You're there." Her hand reached out to him. "Right there! A beautiful song!" She swung her head again, eyes still closed. "And that must be my beautiful Skort. Or is it Fallack?" Her eyes popped open. Her face was full of wonder. "You were right, Javin! You were right! I can hear the songs. Oh! It's...I...there's no words." She laughed in delight at the experience. "It's when you said about Harmony coming to me, it suddenly made sense. I could feel Her and then it all just happened! Suddenly! And this is what happened to you?"

"Sort of. But Harmony more or less emptied everything into my head at once. I didn't get any choice about it."

She could not stop grinning. Every now and then, she shut her eyes to listen again then opened them, still beaming.

"It's unbelievable. Truly unbelievable. Except..." and she looked at Javin. "How do we know we can sing what we want? I can hear things, but singing them? That's harder. And something as delicate as memories?" She raised her eyebrows at the thought.

"I agree. Totally and completely." He became more serious, staring into the fire. "But I still think that we can do it and that Harmony will look after us. If She lets us hear Her, hear the songs She sings, then surely She will make sure we are safe, that those we care about are safe?" He looked to Meldren for support.

Meldren ran her fingers through her hair, combing it absentmindedly. "I keep thinking that the dogs could be safe with us. But, like you said, we don't know enough." She gave a big sigh of frustration and resignation combined. "I want them to be with us, because I'm used to them. But I also know that we can't be sure. Not yet, anyway. And, maybe, perhaps, we could come back for them when we do know for sure." For a brief moment, there was a distant, almost lost look in her face, before she turned to Javin with her decision. "I think you could be right. But I still want my memories. I don't want to lose them." She grinned suddenly. "But I do love being able to do this." She shut her eyes and turned her head this way and that for a moment in silence. "It has to be the best thing ever!" Her eyes were bright with excitement and happiness when she opened them again.

"So shall we go to Arlen and find people who will look after the animals for us?"

"Yes." And then more definitely. "Yes! And then...What happens then?"

"Ah! If Harmony is all about songs, then we are all about choices right now. We get to make choices. Choices about where to go. What to do. When to do it. Like I said, everywhere is new to me. But what about you? Where would you like to go? What would you like to see?"

Meldren returned to running her fingers through her hair, chewing at her lip and narrowing her eyes as she thought. "I have always wanted to see the ocean. I hear it's very big. A lot of water. I'd like to see that, I think. And there's a tree I heard of once. Apparently it has fruit which explodes with a loud bang. That would be fun to see as well. From a distance, that is. Plus, I always wanted to be able to cook. Learn it well. Sure, I can feed myself, but I want to do more than that." She closed her eyes in recollection as she spoke. "I want to be able to cook really well. My mother, she was such a wonderful cook. I'd like to be able to be as good as she was." She looked at Javin. "But, herding gorries is not a very good way of learning to cook. You have to have a kitchen, an oven, not a campfire." She puffed out her cheeks in disappointment but then looked to Javin. "That's me and what I want. What about you? Is there nothing you want to see or do?"

Javin thought for a moment. "Torrint mentioned the ocean once as something special to see. For me...? Actually, there is something. Banith mentioned that once he had seen a volcano from a distance."

"Volcano?"

"Like a mountain, but there's smoke and fire coming out of it."

"Oooh! Any idea where that is?"

"Not a clue."

"Good! Then we can take our time getting there."

"At times, my lovely Meldren, you are completely silly."

"Thank you. And you are completely..."

"What?"

"I'll let you know when I think of the word."

"What about these...creatures? We can't keep calling them 'creatures'. We'll have to give them a name."

"Later."

"But what if they...you know...get in the way?"

A giggle. "Ooooh! So that's that question answered. Do you think they're watching us from up there?"

"I'm sure Harmony is."

"But that's different. At least, I think it is. Isn't it?"

"Shhhh! Come here."

"I thought you'd never ask!"

Some time later. "Your colors are so bright. You should see them!"

"And your music, your song! It's perfect."

27

The next morning, they were later starting out than they had originally planned. Breakfast was extended and packing was sluggish, as was checking in on all the animals. But everything was done with smiles and 'accidental' bumping into each other; gentle brushes of hands and hips and a certain languid enjoyment in each one.

Arlen was, Meldren thought, two easy days away, around the bend in the river. They moved off in amiable silence, grins seemingly permanently attached to their faces, indifferent to the overcast skies and accompanying breeze.

After they had been walking long enough to settle into a rhythm, and for the smiles to be gentler, Meldren asked, "Do you think it is the right thing to do, still? Help Fallack and Skort forget us, forget me? Do we have the right to do that to them? Assuming we can, I mean."

"I don't know if it's right, but I do know we are trying to help them, stop any distress. I'm not sure if it's 'right' or not." Javin paused for a moment, collecting his thoughts. "No, it might not be right. But, we're guessing that if Harmony comes to us again, things might not be easy for them. And that might be a bad guess. After all, Harmony looks after us." He smiled wryly. "Admittedly, it doesn't feel like it at times, but we are still alive. And, if She looks after us, I suppose we could guess She'd look after the dogs as well. But," he shrugged, "that's not certain either. For all we know, She has already altered what's in their heads." He reached for her hand and squeezed it gently. "So, honestly? No. I don't know if it's right for us to even try. But I do think that we are doing it for the right reasons, if that's any help."

Meldren was silent for a few paces, looking sadly at the dogs as they shadowed the herd away to her left. "At least, that's the truth. We don't know, do we? And I do love them. I want to do the best I can for them, and, perhaps, you're right. After all, we don't even know if it can be done. Which leads to the next question. Which is, if it can be done, when do we do it? We can't do it now, I think. We still need them to keep an eye on the herd. And walking away from them, I'd be too upset to even try. So that leaves...?"

Javin's face showed he hadn't thought of that. "I'm not sure. I suppose we could do it just before leaving them? When they're with someone else? Or do we do it much later, say the next day? That way it gives us a little time to get over it, and it would mean only a relatively short time for them to be concerned about us?"

Meldren gazed at her dogs without answering, as if trying to imprint their every hair into her memory. Finally, she broke away and looked at the ground in front of her and gripped Javin's hand as tightly as she could. She nodded. "I think that would be best. Somewhere where we can concentrate. Only," and she looked up at Javin with tears brimming, "I'd want to know it worked. I don't want to have to guess, to hope. I'd want to know they were well."

"We can do that. We can certainly do that."

They walked on. The rumble of the wagon, the creaking of the harness and Sarlin's occasional low grumbling reverberation just a few paces behind them kept them company.

That night, they were both quiet. The breeze, which had stiffened somewhat throughout the day, made them huddle inside their blankets. Meldren was obviously taken with what would happen tomorrow, and Javin with trying to understand what was happening to them, to their lives. The exhilaration of being together again had evaporated slowly as they realized that the only certain thing was that momentous change was in the offing, whether or not they could help the dogs. They both sensed it, both felt it approaching. It made for a somber atmosphere. The only thing they spoke of was what name they would give to their creatures which had, all day long, been wound around their necks again.

In the end, they agreed on the word 'sprites', mainly because Javin had once heard it and thought it had something to do with nature, although he could not recall what that was exactly. Meldren had liked the sound of it, no matter what it meant. So it was agreed: they now had sprites at their necks. Then they slept as best they could.

The following day, they gathered everything together for what was to be the last time. It felt strange to think that by tomorrow everything would be different for both themselves and the animals. The thought made them quiet and contemplative. The wind had dropped back to a gentle breeze and the sun poked through the ragged clouds every now and then. They walked slowly and around mid-morning Arlen was visible, an easy half day's journey ahead. They stopped, taking a last rest. Meldren said, "Don't you think we should at least try to see if we can actually do what we planned on?"

"What do you suggest?"

"I wish I knew!" She looked around for inspiration. "Why not try influencing a gorry?" she said, pointing at the herd as it milled around in its usual haphazard fashion.

"To do what, though?"

"How about helping just one of them to set off directly for Arlen and be happy to get there. No distractions, just determination. What do you think?"

Javin considered this for a moment. "I agree we ought to try and having just one gorry go in a straight line would be something to see."

Meldren gave him a small, encouraging smile. "Well? Shall we?"

Together, they sat in silence, easing into the place in their heads where they could hear the songs around them. From them all, the herd of gorries stood out. And in that chorus, one was chosen. And that one was sung a new sound. A subtle change, minor keys, inflections and pauses here and there. The new song was something which both Javin and Meldren knew automatically. It followed them from where they had first listened to the herd and filled them so that they could hear the new sounds, sing the new, small song. First Javin formed the sounds and then

Meldren joined him, adding her flavor to it. It was gentle and calm and peaceful. The sprites added their cooing and bobbing to it. And then it was done.

They both opened their eyes and scanned the creatures. And there, striding out, head high, burbling quietly to itself, one lone gorry headed off towards Arlen. They exchanged smiles, gave each other a brief hug and then hurried to set off after their new leader. The dogs both eyed it suspiciously, sniffing after it as if they could not believe what they were seeing.

"I think we can do this. I think we can help Skort and Fallack, don't you?" Javin looked to see how Meldren felt about it.

She looked up at him but did not smile. "Yes. I think we can. I'm still going to miss them, though."

He drew her to him and hugged her close as they walked, hip to hip. "I know you will. I know. And that's just another reason why I want to be with you. Because you will miss them and not spare yourself the pain, the memories." He planted a kiss on her head. They continued in silence, before Javin asked, "Are you going to be fine in Arlen, with all those people there? After all, you thought Sweetwater was too big, too much of a problem for you. I know this place is smaller, but still..."

This time, she did smile at him. "We aren't planning on being here for long, and, as you say, it is smaller than Sweetwater. I think I'll be fine. But the sooner we can leave, the better."

They arrived in Arlen with much daylight to spare. It had become warmer as the day had developed so that they were comfortable in light clothing again; a brief reminder of the hot summer days that were now past.

It did not take very long to find someone who was interested in having their animals. Meldren only needed to watch the colors of the man as he spoke to know he was telling the truth about how well-looked after they would be. After agreeing on a price, they led the herd of gorries to a nearby field. Javin noted that there was a deecee here as well, and an idea occurred which he put to one side for the time being.

The price was paid in food, clothing, a large leather satchel, two fine blades, some jewelry made out of leather and pierced stones, two fine silkie hides and some small, rounded nuggets of gold. Javin felt completely out of his depth in all of this and was happy to let Meldren take it over. The haggling over the payment took the longest, with the buyer showing particular interest in the sprites. It was made very clear that the sprites were not ever going to be a part of the negotiations, and, eventually, both sides were satisfied and Meldren and Javin gathered all their possessions, distributed them between their two satchels and set off to find a place to rest for the night. Meldren's eyes brimmed as she walked away, having told Skort and Fallack to stay one last time. Javin scanned the area for a place where they could not be seen, and guided her toward a small copse of tall, thick-leaved bushes. Pushing the fronds aside, he said, "Let's do this now. Waiting will be hard, for everyone. Are you willing?" She turned to him and wrapped her arms around him in answer. And he, in turn, held her tightly until she was able to concentrate.

Together, they heard the song they wanted and they sang it quietly. "Let's go see if it worked, then?"

She nodded. "I don't know which I'm more afraid of; that it worked or that it didn't. Whichever it is, I know it's going to work out fine. In the end." She wiped her nose with the back of her hand and squared her shoulders. "Here we go!" Her voice had a brittle brightness in it.

Returning to the field where they had left the dogs looking after the gorries, Meldren held her breath. The dogs were still sitting there, gazing amiably around them, occasionally poking a muzzle at a too inquisitive gorry. She stood where they could clearly see her and called out, "Come on, then," as she normally would have done. Two large heads swiveled to stare blankly at her, assessing her for a threat and deciding she was none, turned back to the herd.

Meldren stayed looking at them for a long time, Javin waiting quietly beside her. Finally, she turned to him and gave a thin, watery smile. "Well, that's that part of my life over with. I hope the next part will be just as good."

Javin held both her hands in his. "Me, too." He did not want to press her, but, eventually, he asked, "Are you ready to go?" When she gave the smallest of nods, he continued, "Then let's find somewhere to stay tonight, have a meal cooked for us. After all, we can pay for that now. But first, I want to do something. It will be quick and then we'll find a place. I want to tell Landing something." He made a question of his face.

"Of course. That's fine. But what are you going to tell Landing and there's no speaker about. We'd have to go find him."

"No need. I think I can use these things by myself. Only, last time, I gave everyone a headache." He gave a guilty grin. "This time, I won't. I hope. I want to let Lisick know for certain that she was right after all. She believed I'd hear Harmony one day. She had faith in me, faith for me. She so wanted to be around when I did." He shrugged a little. "I thought it would be good to let her know she was right, that's all. I tried before, in Sweetwater, but I'm sure I messed it up because I tried thinking about other things, other people there. All I did was give people headaches. But this time, I'm pretty sure I'm better at it and I'll make sure I only speak directly to Lisick. I'd really like to see her face when she hears, though."

"I think it's a sweet idea. Can I come?"

"Of course! We're together, remember? Come on."

The arrangement was very similar to Sweetwater's. A knee high wall with a roof held up by pillars, stone in this case, and the central pole with the two discs. There was no boy in sight to persuade him it couldn't be done. "I won't be long. I am not even sure whether I need to use these now, after Harmony got so friendly with us. But I know they work, so I'll use them. Ready?"

He didn't bother to sit this time, but simply bowed his head and thought, as carefully and directly as he could, about Lisick and about Harmony and about Meldren. No song this time, just a clear and steady focus, which he found was much easier to do than previously.

After a moment, he looked up and smiled at Meldren. "There. I think I've done it. How do you feel? Any headache?"

"No. I was watching your colors as you did it. They fascinate me. There was a sort of tickle at the back of my head, almost like a song, but it wasn't."

Just then, one of the villagers, on his way somewhere, stopped and said, "You do know that it doesn't work anymore, don't you? It stopped some time ago. Haven't heard or sent for many days now. Hope it wasn't important. " And continued on his way.

"Well, that would explain why there was nobody here on duty," said Javin. "But I'm sure I managed to do something, anyway."

Malden agreed. "Those colors showed me something was definitely happening." She thought a moment more. "Do you realize that I have had no problems with the people here and their colors? At least, not yet. I thought I would get some sort of reaction, but maybe I can filter things out now. Doesn't mean I want to live in a big place, lots of people, animals and so on. I don't plan on staying here long enough to see if people affect me anymore. But I think perhaps I could, without feeling terrible." She gazed off into the distance. "Life is very strange right now. Very strange indeed."

"Really? I hadn't noticed, what with the sprites, Harmony, songs and so on." He swayed away from her playful attempt to punch his arm and swayed back in to hug her tightly. "Let's find ourselves somewhere to sleep and eat. We can afford to. Probably," he added, "we could stay anywhere for as long as we wanted using only our stories as payment. They're so unbelievable."

28

Bellis had carefully scraped the silkie's hide clean and placed it in a large pot of water, after measuring and throwing in the herbs and earths to dissolve the hair. She planned on taking it with her and working it after she had prepared the silkie's meat for Lisick. She went back out to check on the drying racks and to make sure that the green fronds in the smoke hut were not burning too hot.

Both she and Gerant had been unable to turn their backs on both Lisick and Landing. They felt that they had to do something to mark the last Group, but didn't really know what to do.

Bellis had decided that, as Lisick was completely useless in the kitchen, she had to at least provide easy and nourishing food for her to eat. That meant preserves and smoked and dried meats as well as some dried fruits. Bread would be useless in the long term but there would be water to drink.

"I can't just walk away from here, knowing that Lisick will run out of food in just a few days."

"But you also can't know how much to make for her," Gerant had replied. Implicit in what he said was the death of Lisick in the not too distant future. They had both watched her become more and more despondent, more and more lethargic. Even the slightest hint of her being asked to leave with them was met with stony silence and a long, uncomfortable stare. She had nothing left in her life except her duty to Harmony and that was denied to her by her inability to be close to the One she had willingly served for so long. Being held apart from Harmony, only hearing what anyone else could hear, was draining Lisick of all vitality and hope, gently wiping out any future she might have conceived for herself.

"I can make enough for her to eat well for a long time. I can do that for her." Bellis had tiredly brushed a strand of hair from her face. "All I know is that I cannot walk away and leave her to starve. She is my responsibility still."

Gerant had nodded gloomily. "You are right, of course. But me? What do I do? I have nothing left to do here, nothing to hold me. Except you, of course." He had reached for her hand. "You have a goal to complete. Lisick has dreams she cannot fulfill, and I... I have nothing left to give." He shivered. "This place now, it feels cold and empty of everything, even of the past. And there is no future here." He looked around. "To think that here, this very place, was where our ancestors first lived, first came into contact with Harmony. All those years ago. Many, many years ago. And we're the last. The very last. It will soon be swallowed by Harmony and nothing will be left for anyone to see."

Bellis had placed her hand on his and gave a tired smile. "Maybe so. But, that is not now." She patted him. "I have an idea. Listen. This old place has seen many people. It has lots of secrets it will never give up. But it is the first place on this wonderful, frustrating planet. And you are the last of the people using it. All the initials on the walls? They are the memories of this place. My idea is that you help honor it. Lisick is doing it in her way. I am doing it in my way in this ancient kitchen. And you? You can make it like it used to be."

She had smiled at his puzzlement. "Repair it, Gerant! Bring it back to how it was. Polish it, patch it, look after it. That's one thing you can do. That's your goal. Put your touch, your heart in it."

In the five days since then, Gerant had worked with a newfound energy. He had seen the truth in Bellis's suggestion. Now he was methodically working through each of the many rooms. Doors needed re-hanging. Furniture needed new legs and armrests. Tables needed polishing, beds needed making, linen needed folding and floors needed sweeping. When he ate with Bellis (Lisick refused their company) he was more fulfilled than he thought could have been possible. He found pride in the results and sometimes came and dragged Bellis with him to see his latest accomplishment.

And now, Bellis was preparing the last of the food that was available. She had added some sprinkles of water to hold back the fronds from burning and turned all the strips of meat, checking them for mold or insect infestation.

She paused to take a mug and sip at some water. This kitchen had served everyone at Landing since it was first built. It was huge. Too big now. Briefly she wondered what it must have been like, filled with people. All the steam and the smoke and the smells. And so much food being prepared! Ever since she had first started here, she had kept to one corner, one end of the kitchen, almost intimidated by the size of it and the history it contained. Three-quarters of it she had never used except for some occasional storage. She saw, in her mind's eye, all her ancestors working here. And now, it was an empty shell. It left a lot of cleaning to do. She had decided that this one end, nearest the corridor, the end where she and Lisick had shared occasional meals, was where everything would be left. She took a deep breath as she surveyed the work still remaining. She would not let her special empire, small though it was in comparison with the building, let her down by being untidy, unkempt, poorly cared for. She put down the mug, picked up a rag and set about making it something she could be proud of.

Several days later, Gerant had done all he could. Those things he could not repair or make look better he had stored outside; an offering of human history to Harmony, where She would more easily embrace them with Her weather and soil and plants.

Bellis had lined up pots full of preserved fruits and vegetables on one wall. On the bench before them, wrapped in cloth, the smoked and dried meats. The last of the nuts she could find were in open dishes and a clean-scrubbed mug sat ready on the table by the door next to a plate.

She and Gerant stood, hand in hand, in silence. These were their final moments here and there was too much pressing in on them for words. They turned their heads as if trying to memorize every single item, see the past and burn it all into their heads, where it would live a little longer. At last, a gentle squeeze from Gerant, and they turned away. He grabbed his bundle from the floor. Bellis opened and re-rolled and tied the skin as tightly as she could, slung it over her shoulder and balanced her small bundle of belongings on her hip. A brief, fleeting smile passed between them and they turned their backs and stepped away from this, the home that had meant the most to them.

Lisick knew they had left. She felt it at some level; felt the emptiness become more empty still. She had been grateful for Gerant's work, although she did not think she could have told him. It would have been too painful to speak. In the same way, she missed Bellis and all that she had done to feed her. She wandered down the corridor to the kitchen and took in everything that had been done for her. She was not sure, but she thought she could still glimpse them in the far distance. She raised a hand in farewell and then sat down.

She was numb. She had been numb for too long. She was empty, like the building. Her home was empty even with her in it, because she was empty herself. Harmony had always filled her, always been part of her life. And without Her, Lisick was a husk. She would have done anything to re-connect and had tried everything she could think of, and still there was only the background noise in her head, worse than silence, and an emptiness in her heart and soul.

She looked once more at the food and half-heartedly began to calculate how long it would last. She did not know. Did not really want to know. She had nothing to do. She could go anywhere she wanted and nothing waited for her anymore. A life without purpose, without hope.

She was turning the mug over and over in her hands, a blank look on her face, when she suddenly felt something. It was a familiar feeling. One which she thought never to have again.

It was Harmony! Harmony distant and dim, but Harmony nevertheless! Normally, she would have been in the communication room, amongst the strange relics of the past which still, somehow, functioned. It had always been like that. But, now? Now she was connecting again. Harmony was strong in her head again. And without anything to help her!

Slowly, the connection grew in strength. And, as it did so, so it

273

became richer and more nuanced, more detailed than anything she had ever known. Instead of sitting and listening with one part of her while the other sifted the information and decided what to do, how to act, what to say, this was too full, too loud, too immersive for that.

She was transfixed with delight. Her old reactions were suppressed by the strength of the flow. At first, she thought she caught a glimpse of that boy, Javin. She thought there was something about him in there. Before she could wonder what that might mean, she was engulfed by something much greater. All the time she had bemoaned the loss of hearing Harmony was made up now in this one contact. Harmony was fully with her now. Lisick heard Her in a way she had not thought possible. Instead of a gentle, rolling noise, the constant background to her life before, now there was a symphony of sounds. But more than that, she now knew her value, her worth to Harmony. And then she was subsumed within it all, immersed in a roiling overwhelm of words, sounds, scenes, images, people; a cacophony of sensations which bowled her over, tumbled her around inside her head.

She saw, or, rather, heard Harmony fully at last. The animals, the planet, the rocks, the people, everything. She knew she was in there somewhere because she felt her place there, heard it in the music. And that was beauty enough for her. She couldn't comprehend the message, the contact, in its entirety, but she understood enough to know that Harmony was safe and well. But the biggest, the best, the most euphoric aspect was that, finally, Lisick was in full and total contact with the planet she had served for so much of her life. And Harmony knew her and recognized her and saw her as she was.

Her faith in Harmony, her love for it, they were both there. Harmony knew of her, and loved her! Tears brimmed and flowed unchecked. She did not care what else might be in the message. Harmony had spoken with her and loved her and knew her and let her know that she had lived her life well. She had lived it for Harmony, not for herself and now, this moment, this everlasting moment, she knew herself to have lived properly, lived a life to be proud of. Lisick, the scraggy little girl with no friends and too much energy, had lived a life few would have chosen. And she had lived it fully. Devotion, love, constancy and truth were her hallmarks. And now Harmony called to her, to her directly and, for the first time ever, she felt truly at peace, fulfilled, welcomed. And that was all she had ever wanted: completion. She smiled as the tears flowed and she gave herself completely to her one love who had finally embraced her totally in return.

She did not see, could not see, that Gerant and Bellis, hearing the same call, had rushed back. They both knew that something vital, something final, was happening and they wanted to be there. Unlike Lisick, they were not given the same volume or intensity. They, in comparison, heard only that Harmony was thanking them: a feeling of gratitude, which Bellis later described as what true love feels like. It flowed into them, around them and it uplifted them. As they arrived at the door, they were just in time to see Lisick slowly, with more grace than had ever been given to her before, fold forward gently onto the table. And her hair, seemingly aware at last of its responsibility, flowed around her head and face, veiling her in her final ecstasy.

And so, the last Group came to an end.

29

J avin and Meldren had headed south, fording the river further
downstream, following their feet rather than any plan. It had taken
some time for both of them to begin to admit that they were
together and alone and without anyone or anything else to consider but
themselves. Meldren's sadness at leaving her beautiful dogs behind had
softened into a gentle tenderness where before it had been raw. They
were adjusting to this new life, but all the time they were aware that,
lurking in the future, Harmony was waiting with all the attendant
uncertainty that created. It cast a shadow over their delight in each other
and the freedom they had created for themselves.

The weather had changed completely. Each day was warmer than the
one before. It seemed that they were back into summer again. Cloudless
skies and a little breeze made for hot hiking and they were grateful for
the cool of the evenings.

On the fifth day out from Arlen, they labored up a hill and saw,
spread out before them, a vast plain. Away to their right, they could
make out tall cliffs rising sheer from the plain, sparkling white and red in
the sun. Ahead of them, the view faded into the smoky blue of distance
without any major landmark to break the monotony. A vague trackway
led down into the plain where they thought they could see herds of some

kinds of animals and smaller clumps of trees scattered about in a haphazard fashion. The glint of sun on water in the middle distance picked out a river, curving and twisting lazily.

"Perhaps there will be some sheltered places down there. I don't really want to sleep out in such open country." Javin had stopped to readjust his satchel, changing shoulders to ease the strain.

Meldren put hers down and rummaged around in it, eventually finding a leather tie for her hair. Bunching her hair, she wrapped the tie around it and secured it, all the time taking in the scenery before them. "I have to admit, this is not what I was thinking of. Not how I thought it would be. How long do you think it will take to cross it?"

Javin scratched his nose as he estimated distances. "It's not so much how many days it will take as how much food we have left. I can't see any evidence of people down there. Let me see if I can hear anything that could help." He shut his eyes and bowed his head, turning it first one way, then the other. Opening them again, he said, "No. Nothing that I can hear anyway."

Meldren was sitting down, leaning back on her arms, face lifted to the sun, eyes closed, her sprite coiled loosely around her neck. "Maybe," she said, without opening her eyes, "we could sing whatever we needed."

"I suppose..." The doubt was evident in his voice. "Can we really eat and drink a song?" He shook his head. "Yes, I know that we know it's all a song. But it's not us singing it, is it? Does it seem right to sing something and then eat it? Why not just sing us with full stomachs?"

"Why not indeed?" Meldren opened her eyes and shaded them with one hand as she looked at him. "Me? I'd love to actually cook something for a change. Something hot. But that singing? It's worth a try, isn't it?"

Javin made a 'who knows?' face. "Well, we don't need to find that out for a few days at least." He sat down beside her and poked at the ground with a finger. "The thing is, I think I'm not really very trusting of Harmony. At least, I change between being willing to trust Her, to actually trusting Her and then to not trusting Her. Right now, I'm in the middle of a 'not fully trusting Her' period. Yes, I know She's meant to look after us and all that. But, the truth of it is that we don't know that for sure and, if She was going to look after us, then it would be because we were useful to Her. But, how do we even know that? Like I said, we could be just one couple out of hundreds She's been speaking to. It could be that there's another pair out there somewhere who are better in some way. More able to do whatever it is She wants." He nodded at the plains before them. "Once we start across that, we will run out of food. And the water? That's unlikely to be good to drink with all those animals there. It's not fast flowing." He rubbed his eyes as if tired. "I really thought that being with you, everything would work out easily. And it is. Being with you is wonderful. It's just that...." His voice tailed off.

"I know. I feel the same way too." She sat up and hugged her knees to her chest. "We don't even know why Harmony came to us, what She wants, or anything. I do know one thing for certain, though. And that is, whatever the reason, it brought us two together. And that has to be important." She screwed her face up against the sun as she turned to look at Javin. "I've never come this way before. I've always followed the river, not crossed it. And I've not heard anyone speak about that out there ahead of us. It looks huge. And, perhaps, it's meant to. Perhaps it's meant to challenge us, make us trust Her or turn back. Maybe, if we turn back and find a safer, easier route, we'll have lost somehow." She paused. "Why do you think we're together?"

"I don't know. Beyond the obvious, anyway."

She smiled at him. "Neither do I. But what I do know is that Harmony was responsible for it. Which means, I think, that we have not much choice left but to trust Her. Which means, I think, that we have to keep going. At least, that's how I see it."

Javin returned her smile, his eyes gentle and relaxed. "I really do think you are much better than me at making decisions. Oh, yes, I can talk about wanting to have a choice, but when it comes to it, you're the one who decides." He leaned towards her and whispered conspiratorially, "And, that's fine by me." He stood up and held a hand out. Meldren grabbed it and stood up, easing into his embrace.

"Just as long as you know I'm in charge, then."

"Whatever gave you the idea that I ever doubted that?" He kissed her and then helped her adjust her load and off they set, downhill, to whatever awaited them.

Two days out in the plain, they still could not see an end to it. The soaring cliffs, far away to their right, looked like a solid wall, marching along with them, only gradually diminishing in height. Other than that, the plain was as empty as it had looked from the hilltop. They had slept in the open; a feeling which, the first night, had unnerved both of them. They were used to some shelter. A wagon, a handful of trees, a boulder or two. There had always been something against which they could rest their backs. But not here. As a result, they slept poorly, aware that they were easy prey to any determined hunter. Not that they knew if there were any such creatures. And that uncertainty itself added to their discomfort. They couldn't sing songs in their sleep.

As the sun rose and warmed their backs again on the third day, they trudged on wearily. Javin nudged Meldren with an elbow and indicated a clump of what he called trees far off to their left. There were enough of them to make for a shelter. The sun was high when they arrived. They both watched and listened for the songs of predators. Satisfied, they entered and put aside their loads and sat, groaning gratefully, in the shade.

"I'm thirsty," Javin complained. "And this little sprite round my neck is just making me more aware of my dry throat."

"Same here. I'm sure it's getting hotter day by day. I think it's time we tried singing. There's no fruit left, nothing with any moisture in it." Meldren wiped her forehead and left a little smear of dirt across it.

"What shall we try first? Water? Fresh water?"

Meldren closed her eyes in ecstasy at the thought. "Oh, yes, please! Lots of it, bubbling out of the ground right here," pointing to a spot just in front of her outstretched feet.

"Do you know what it sounds like?"

She shook her head. "No, but I'm willing to listen really, really hard." She sat up straighter and looked at Javin, tired eyes smiling at him. "Ready when you are."

He nodded and then closed his eyes and began to listen to the songs around them. Somewhere, in amongst all these wonderful sounds, there should be the sound of water, underground, moving, flowing, sliding along. Both brows furrowed as they concentrated; the two minds acting easily as one. And, as they listened, so they both heard it. A deep song, a lilting song, a smooth and glistening song. A song they could carry and lift and bring to them here. Catching the sounds and the harmonies, each began to sing their own part of it; one the direction, the other, the freshness. Together they began to reel it into them, sing it up to the surface. Closer and closer.

Just as it was about to burst through the ground and bathe their feet in its cool flow, the song changed. Instead of both of them singing it, they became part of another song; a louder, more insistent one which poured into them.

Suddenly, from watching the song of the water rise to them, they were the ones rising, being swept away. Higher and higher they rose. The melodies held them relaxed and wondering at all they saw spread out beneath them. The horizon began to curve into an arc as they floated relentlessly onward, upward. Stars flicked on in greater numbers until they could only see broad swathes of land and sea beneath. They saw the moon, coming up at them from behind the horizon's curve, larger and larger. And, at that moment, their vision was turned away from the globe beneath them as they seemed to rotate and place it at their backs, the better to immerse themselves in the space beyond.

The sun, they both knew, was away to their right. They also both knew that they could not look at it directly. Nor could they hear it as it truly was. Its songs were not for them. Although far away and, to their eyes at least, invisible, it was the dominant presence. The universe drifted before them. They had no reference and could not tell if they were moving through the universe or the universe was moving towards them. All they knew was they were seeing what no-one else had ever seen; how their sun fitted into everything they were experiencing.

Their sun was but one of many suns, all singing in the blackness, spinning worlds and life from the darkness, binding together across the vastness; spanning space in their limitless families. For they could hear in their minds, in the faintest of fashions, the symphonies which pulled their galaxy into existence and which drove it and gave it order and pattern and governed the motions of every part; from the formation of planets to the movements of clouds, the dance of insects. And they heard and felt how this system, their sun's, was also singing other large systems into consciousness. The deeps were full of lyricism, of the sounds of existence and awareness. These were no sounds they could sing or even share with one another upon waking. Such sounds could only be felt. They were bathed in them; they were the sounds as they thrummed through them. They could only know of it, be aware of it, deep within themselves, just as in any dream when knowing something is so obvious yet becomes so elusive when awake.

Now, just as when floating and flying above the planet, one part of the whole came closer to them, or them to it. Their awareness came back to their sun, their solar system. They, or the songs of which they were composed, flew by each of the six planets, hovering near enough to see the arc of the horizon against the blackened sky, star-frosted and eternal. Sometimes bigger than Harmony, sometimes much smaller in span, they were each unique. Each one a fresh song of their sun, a chorus in the greater symphony. After hovering at each planet, admiring it, reveling in the beauty, hearing the purity of it, they returned, again, to the planet nearest to the orchestral sun. The planet called Haven.

The song here began to sound off-key, as if parts were missing or too quiet. It lacked the resonant euphony, the breadth of the other planets' songs. The sounds brought them swooping down closer to the surface. Close enough to see whole cities. Straight roads ignored the shape of the land. As the planet whirled beneath them, the night side of it was full of sparkles of light, splashes of brightness. The planet's music never faltered, but it had some shrill notes, jarring and unpleasing. It was chaotic more than harmonic. It was more a competition to be heard than something to be enjoyed for its own sake; too many sounds trying to overwhelm each other. There was an underlying score, but it was struggling to coordinate so many individual notes.

Then away again, swirling away, back out towards the orbit of Harmony again. Back to Harmony and the moon. Looking now with fresh eyes, Harmony hung beneath them; green and blue and white and yellow; pure colors. A sense of peace accompanied the vision and was hinted at in the blending chords they heard. The difference in the songs of Harmony and Haven were clear. Harmony's song was pure, with just the slightest of dips in rhythm and the rare, brief, muted flat note here and there, to short to disturb the underlying rhythm and cadence of it all.

And then, a pause, a hesitation, a purposeful wait as the main theme song held them. There was no depth, no sense of near nor far against such a backdrop. And then suddenly, a movement. A star occluded. A light moving. A group of lights. The two tried to adjust their eyes in the dream, to focus on the movement. As when an optical illusion is resolved, there was nothing and then there was a new vision. A fleet of ships. Sparkling and small in the immensity. Ships moving out from the sun, away from Haven. Towards Harmony. The dreamers drifted along with them for a time, noting them, hearing the sun sing, hearing Harmony's chorus within that song.

Nearing the ship, there was again a sensation, this time of something raucous and atonal, a tiny echo of the unbalanced songs and edginess of Haven. Not frightening. Not fearful. Around that, holding it within it, another was being woven. It contained notes of sadness and determination.

And this feeling, this resolve remained as the dreamers were floated away again, before spiraling back, faster and faster, through Harmony's clouds and air. A long, last look at the aching beauty of Harmony before it faded gently into nothing more than shadows on the eyelids, and movements of branches in a gentle breeze.

The elusive music, at once so simple as to be entirely obvious, and yet at the same time with a complexity beyond words, beyond understanding, remained with them after they had woken. It circled within them, conjuring up the visions given them, allowing them to see the dream again and again. The scale of it, the reality of it, had them amazed, stupefied almost. They each knew that they had shared the same experiences, seen the same things and had been left with the same questions.

Each reached for their throat as the sprites keened and swayed, extending out and holding their small heads up, as if staring at the sky. Automatically, each tried to soothe them by stroking and murmuring gently at them. The sprites subsided and re-coiled again as suddenly as they had extended.

Before either Javin or Meldren were ready to speak, the earth between them gave a small shudder and a bubbling stream of water, fresh and cool, eased its way from a small fissure and ran over the ground, gathering in a small hollow within arm's reach.

Javin looked around, as if to reassure himself that, now, he was awake and that he was in the same place. He also checked Meldren, to see what color her eyes were. Realizing what he was doing, she opened her eyes wide at him before turning to the water. Reassured, he peered through the trunks of the trees and saw that the sun was now much lower in the sky.

"That took a long time. But I don't feel ill, for a change. How about you?"

Meldren had drunk from the new pool and was scooping water over her arms and face, dabbing at the back of her neck, reveling in the cool, clean feeling. She shook her head and brushed some wet hair from her face. "No. I feel fine. Confused. But fine." She scooted over a little to give Javin room to drink. "What was that about? Why were we shown that? And what exactly was the 'that' we were shown? Did you recognize the other planet, Haven?" She shut her eyes briefly to see the vision more clearly again.

Wiping his mouth with the back of his hand, Javin had the same look of confusion. "I've never seen Haven from space, but I guess that's how it would look. I thought I recognized some of the coastline from maps. But what were those ships we saw? And why show us?" He made himself more comfortable, leaning against a trunk, still puzzling over the experience. "I still don't understand why us? What are we meant to do about that? What's the point of showing us that stuff if there was no reason? There has to be a reason, but I can't begin to think what it is." He gave an exasperated sigh.

"Well, at least, like you said, we're not ill this time." Meldren brought out some dried meat from her satchel and offered some to Javin. She chewed a while in silence, occasionally picking off a tiny piece to offer to her sprite. "When I think back to being shown those ships, the song I heard wasn't right somehow. There was something wrong about it. I suppose they were headed here. Or," and she sat up straighter as the realization dawned. "Or, that is actually happening, right now. There really are ships coming here. And if I heard that song correctly, it means they aren't really coming for good reasons. Their songs weren't right." She turned to Javin, an urgent look on her face. "What if we were shown those ships because they are real and they are coming here and we've got to do something about it?"

"But what, for goodness' sake? Fly into space and push them back by ourselves? If what we saw and heard was real, then, again, why bother? Because if everything's a song, then a new song would make them disappear or something. It comes back to the same thing every time. Why show us?"

Meldren chewed some more as she thought about it. "If we are being shown this for some reason, then the only thing I can think of, and it's not an answer I like, is that we, the two of us, really are special and we have to do something about it." She hurried on to prevent Javin interrupting. "Yes, I know what you're going to say. I agree. How can we do anything?" She suddenly chuckled and shook her head in disbelief. "Listen to me. To us! Here we are talking about ships in space, how the sun sings everything and how we can hear Harmony and Her songs, and it's like the most natural thing in the world! I mean, we even sang this water to us! And we're trying to make sense of it all? It makes no sense. Nothing does! Do you realize? In the spring, I never knew you, you never knew me, we were normal people, doing normal things. And now? Nothing is normal and that is the new normal for us. How can we ever think we are going to do anything normal again? Normal now is songs and singing and stars and the sun taking us on a tour of all the planets. That's normal now. Which means, that nothing we can think of doing is stupid or wrong or impossible. We're living impossibly, every day."

She stared straight up at the sky between the fronds. "Is there a reason behind all this? Yes. Do we have to do something about it? Probably. Do we know what that is? No. Are we going to get some help? Probably." She looked now at Javin. There was tiredness in her eyes again. "My guess? I don't think we're going to have to wait very long before we find out the answers."

Javin had been watching her as she spoke, finishing his food. Now he nodded in agreement. "I think you're right. And I also think we're not going anywhere else today. It's too late to get started. Besides, we've got water and food and some shelter. Why leave? We may not be ill because of it, but I know I am tired, more tired than I should be from just sitting here."

"Me, too," said Meldren, yawning.

"Then let's see if we can get some undisturbed sleep and be ready for whatever abnormally normal thing happens next."

"Abnormally normal. I like that."

"It was your idea. And I like your ideas."

"Is that all you like?"

"I'm not sure. I need to take a closer look."

"I thought you were tired."

"Parts of me are."

"Ah. Good to know."

"Shhh."

30

Waking the next morning, Javin again reassured himself that he was still in the same place and that the water was still bubbling into the new pond before trickling away to soak into the ground beyond the tiny grove. He bathed his face clear of sleep and watched Meldren still sleeping, a tender smile on his face, quite content to wait.

Shortly thereafter, she woke up, blinking at him sitting beside her as her eyes adjusted to the brightness. She yawned and sat up, and searched for the tie for her hair which had come loose again in the night.

"The good news is that we are still where we thought we were and I had no visions."

"Neither did I," said Meldren. "Although I was rather expecting something to happen." She splashed some water on her face, took a few quick sips of it and rubbed her eyes free of any remaining sleep. "I'm hungry! What do we have left?"

Javin spread out their remaining food on their blanket. It was hardly tempting anymore. They had been eating the same food since leaving Arlen. What there was was either dried or stale by now. They picked it over and ate without much enthusiasm.

"What do you suggest we do now?" asked Meldren after cleaning her hands in the water which bubbled up between them and drying them off on her skirt. "Wait for something to happen or move on?"

"I didn't dream about anything. I thought I would have dreamt about the ships or something. But, no. Nothing." Javin was staring off into the distance. "I thought I might have an answer when I woke up. Something, some plan would have come to me." He brought his gaze back to Meldren. "I think I was hoping that would be the plan for today." He sighed a small sigh. "Oh, well. I suppose we'll have to do something ourselves." He pointed at the food. "We could sing some more food. But I was wondering why we have to walk all this way with nothing to help us? Why not sing ourselves somewhere else? Like those cliffs in the distance?"

Meldren had a doubtful look on her face. "Do you think we should? After all, shouldn't we be doing something about those ships we saw? Plus there's the problem of how to sing us there. Singing water up; that's one thing. Singing ourselves to another place..." She shook her head. "What happens if we miss by just a little and we fall from the height of the cliffs? Or, worse, what if we sing ourselves inside the rock?" She shuddered at the thought. "I'm not against the idea in theory. But I do really think we should be focusing more on what we were shown."

"And we do that, how?"

"I don't know. But, why not think of something? Anything. Remember, we know we're definitely not normal, so let's just say some ideas out loud and see if that helps. We don't have to know how it would work. Just ideas."

Javin thought for a moment. "Sing a song to turn them back?"

"Or, could we stop them leaving in the first place?"

"How about we make them nice people so they decide to go home on their own?"

Meldren grinned. "Let's make them grumpy with each other so they fight amongst themselves and never get anywhere."

Javin smile reflected her happiness. "And still the problem with all of them is the same: how do we sing any song like that so that it has an effect. We're good at songs here, on Harmony. But I can't think of being powerful enough to affect things out there, in space. Can you?"

"No. I can't," said Meldren, her good humor gone.

"Well, in that case, why don't we at least have a practice at singing ourselves somewhere? Nothing big," he added hastily. "I was just thinking that we could try moving to outside this grove onto the ground outside, just past where the water has soaked back in again. What do you think?"

Meldren judged the distance and then nodded. "Why not? It's better than just sitting here all day. Besides, if we take our mind off it, we might get an idea." She made herself more comfortable, bowed her head and took a deep relaxing breath.

"I have no clue what we're doing, by the way," Javin said. "But if we both feel it's right, then I suppose we sing it." He, too, relaxed and let his chin drop until it touched his chest.

Just as they were about to listen, Meldren thought of something. She was about to say that yesterday, when they had tried singing, they had been taken over again. But she was too late, because it happened again.

At first, there was no sound at all. No songs, just an inability to move. Not frightening, but they were held still. The sprites unwound from their throats and moved in that liquid way of theirs to coil around their heads above their eyes.

With the sprites in their new resting place, a voice entered them. It was as though it was made of music, not merely musical. Chiming, flowing sounds formed words in their heads and the voice was surely that of a woman.

"This is now possible. My small creatures have helped me understand you. They have... ," the voice paused as if searching for the right words, the right cadenced and lyrical sounds, to use. "They have seen into you, touched you, so that you may hear me. They link us. This is better than before. Safer. Easier. Clearer." Even the pauses were filled with a gentle, melodious echoing murmur.

"I have need of you both. Together. You are the two I need now. One is female and one is male. One was birthed and sung here. One was birthed and sung on my sister. The two of you both are now as one. More than that, you can both hear what is real and begin to make realness yourselves."

They were facing each other and Javin registered with some part of himself that Meldren's eyes had changed color, from blue to black. Even though they were held, they were both able to register surprise on their faces and they both formed thoughts.

"I can hear you, the small sounds inside you." The sweetly mellifluous voice sounded to them as though it were smiling. "Singing. Yes. You can sing. You are alone. No others are like you." A pause. "Unique. Thank you for that. You are unique." Another pause, filled with polyphonic sounds; perhaps the sound of Harmony thinking.

"Father sings this has never happened before. You and me. Us. A new song. I am learning it. It is a new realness. He sings that it can become a powerful song." Another musical pause. "I can ask you this now for you have watched realness. Understand it?" The way the musical inflection rose made it a question. "You have seen. Coming here. They come here... Thank you. Ships. They are in ships and they come here. My sister's realness is...wrong. Not pure song. Not like mine. Not like Father's. In the ships are those who carry that impure song." A longer space this time, as though not wanting to say what has to be said. When Her voice came back to them, there was a small discordance in it; a blemish on the pure music. A sign of stress?

"Are they to make my realness the same as my sister? Will they break up my songs? I must know. This is new. Unknown. I wish to know. I wish to be...true. To be...wisdom. You must help. You must...sing? Communicate...? With each other. This can be done. Listen."

Suddenly, they were able to move freely. Javin saw that Meldren's eyes were back to being blue again.

Meldren show her head in disbelief. "You heard that as well?Is She asking what I think She is asking? About the people on the ships?"

Javin nodded. "About whether they are going to..." he gestured vaguely, trying to find the right words.

"Hurt Her! That's what She is asking." She looked hard at him. "Well? Will they? I know what I think. But, you came from there."

Javin's face showed a distress Meldren had not seen before. A face of regret and sorrow. "I am sure they will." His voice was low and he spoke with reluctance. "Oh, they could come to love it as I do, but they will not give themselves the time. The ones in those ships?" He shook his head at the thought. "They're not like me. They are coming because they can. Isn't that enough of a reason?"

Meldren reached up and stroked the sprite, a sadness upon her. "She is probably hearing this anyway. But, if that's the case, what is to be done? What can be done?"

"Before we do anything, suggest anything, I want to be quite clear about what's going on here." Javin's face was drawn. He looked both tired and determined. There was sadness there as well. "I have had strange things happen to me, to my mind. I want to make really sure that we both heard the same thing and that this is not some sort of dream, or some leftover from when they messed with my head. I need to know this. I need to know that I am really not going mad and that a whole planet, this whole planet has been talking to me, to us. I want to know, first, if who I'm looking at right now really is you, Meldren. And then I want to know what it was you heard." There was now a defiance in his look, a challenge asking to be proved wrong.

Meldren moved to be closer to him and gently turned his head so that she could look directly into his eyes. "Feel my hand on your face. Then look into my eyes and tell me what color they are."

"Blue. They're blue."

She nodded but did not let go of his face. "And yours are now dark brown again."

"What do you mean 'again'?"

"Yours changed color as well. They were very, very pale. Not sure what color they were, but very pale. And now they're back to being dark brown again." Her quick, reassuring smile dimpled her cheeks. "So we both could see each other and the change that happened." She let go of his face, but remained close. "And I heard Harmony's voice." She closed her eyes to refresh her memory of it. "It is like listening to a river and the wind together playing with a mountain and the most beautiful song there has ever been sung, all wrapped into one voice." She breathed deeply, basking in the recollection. She opened her eyes to look once more directly at Javin. "Does that sound like your memory? I really am me and you really are you. But only if you agree. I mean, you could still be someone else if you wanted to." She cocked her head and raised her eyebrows as she teased him.

Javin could not but help to smile at her. Grabbing her hand, he nodded as he looked around. "I just wanted to be sure. In case there was a chance that this wasn't happening."

"I know. Me, too."

The sprites both began to sway from side to side and utter a surprisingly low-pitched hum.

Javin and Meldren looked at each other warningly. "Sounds like She's here again." Javin gave Meldren's hand a firm squeeze. "Ready?" And, as Meldren was nodding, so Harmony came to them again.

"You are... safe?" The immaculate voice poured like liquid sunshine into them; warming, friendly, caring. "Good. Now you have seen each real you, what is your answer? How to be?"

The silence that was not silence filled them as they each tried to answer, to think, to help. They formed their thoughts for Her.

"I cannot, will not, stop their songs. That is not my... realness? My... duty? That is for our father." Another listening silence. "Father is the loudest, clearest song of all. He sings that this is not the realness for him. This is for me, now. My sister. We must choose what songs to sing about this. Father sings us. We sing with Him. But this is a song between sisters."

Silence and thinking.

"Hide? Be unseen? Hide them? They will break my songs? Hide them? That would break their songs. That is not my... not as I am. It is not how I sing songs."

Silence, but with the same undercurrent of unseen movement and unheard sound.

"I hide? I am not seen?" The mellifluous voice purred into the beautiful not-quite-silence, as if thinking. "I am my father's song. I am singing with him. But, I can sing with him but a beat apart. And still be in his song, not break it. He will still hear me. I will still hear him. Hide? That is the name of this song? Be sung but not be seen? I can sing this. He can hear me. He will still hear me." There was a longer pause this time. Finally, the voice flowed again. "Father... smiles. This unseeing, hiding... a new realness. We must sing together to make the new realness. This is a good song, a new singing. My sister will listen and learn. Her choice of song will come."

Javin and Meldren both felt Her presence withdraw a little. Just before leaving them, She spoke one last time. "This is new. A new song. Here. This place. Father sung it so. I heard and sang also. You heard me. You are with me now. Tiny songs, but with me. I will always hear you. Always. And you will hear all my songs. Be safe with my small ones. They will be with you. I go to sing the new realness with father. Safe now. Safe." And then they were themselves again.

They shook themselves as if for reassurance that they again had control over their bodies. As they did so, both sprites slid from their foreheads and resumed their previous positions, around their necks, crooning gently as they did so.

Ignoring the creatures, they looked at each other in disbelief. Javin saw that the sun was again low in the sky. A whole day had passed. As Meldren looked up in response to his pointing this out, they both saw a flicker, a wave almost, cross the sky, as if it was a huge cloth being shaken. It hurtled away into the far distance. The merest echo of that movement was felt by them both in the smallest of tremors beneath them. If they had not seen the first movement above them, they would not have registered the second beneath them.

"Whooooo." Meldren breathed out the sound in one long note. "Now that was an entirely new type of strange."

"That's not even close to what it was. Not. Even. Close," said Javin, a bemused look on his face.

"And what was that about at the end? 'You will hear all my songs'?" She brushed at her sprite with her forefinger. "And are these the 'small ones' she meant? And when She said 'safe', did she mean She was safe or we are safe from now on because he have these around our necks?"

"Beats me," said Javin, and then, seeing her startled expression, hurried on to explain. "It's a saying from where I grew up. It means, I do not understand any of this."

"Beats me...," said Meldren, trying out the phrase quietly to herself before giving a grudging nod of acceptance and understanding. There was so much that was new to think about. Where to start? She made an attempt. "If we can hear all Her songs," she said, thinking it out as she spoke, "does that mean we can sing them as well? Which would mean that we would be able to do... anything at all!" Her surprise at what she had said she felt was evident on her face. "Whooooo," she breathed again.

Javin had a sudden thought. "Can you still see colors around everything?"

Meldren looked puzzled for a space and then turned her attention to the trees around them. She focused her eyes and tilted her head from side to side before nodding. "Yes. I can. Why ask?"

"Oh, I don't know. I think I was thinking that, if we could do all those things you said, then perhaps we had lost something else we could do. You know, sort of swap one thing for another. For you, maybe it was seeing the colors. For me... I don't know. Yes. That's true, I don't know. I have no idea what to think."

"I think," said Meldren decisively, "I think that we are not going to understand it all in one go. I think, we should decide what it is we want to do from now on." She gave an exasperated sigh at Javin's slowness. "Harmony is done with us. There's no reason at all She is going to come back again. She as good as told us that. And nobody was hurt by it. Nobody on those ships. Nobody here. She sang a new song, or something like it, and that was it. Over! Which means...," she said with emphasis, "we can live how we want. The other stuff, the songs and everything, that will become clear later. Or, maybe, it will never come clear." She shrugged. "So what? The point is, we have our lives back, Javin. We can choose what we want to do, where we want to go. Just like we said we wanted." She shook his leg, hoping to animate him a little, see what she could see. "You remember? We wanted to choose how to live? Well, we can. Don't you see that?"

He remained sitting slumped, his head bowed and arms folded. Meldren's face showed a spasm of fear at his inertia. But then, he lifted his head and looked at her, eyes bright with laughter. He planted a quick but thorough kiss on her lips. "Ah! Meldren, Meldren, Meldren! I love you because you are so sensible! You make everything clear and obvious. I would be still confused, lost, half out of my mind if it wasn't for you. You are amazing!"

"So, I'm amazing because I'm sensible? Is that what you're saying? I can't be amazing for any other reason? Just sensible?" Her disdain for the word was obvious. "I'll have you remember just exactly what it is that I

293

have done which is amazing and none of which was sensible. I went to meet you, a perfect stranger living in a cave and decided I liked you a lot." She pressed on against Javin's evident wish to explore that sentence a little more. "Then I waited and waited and waited for you, left money to help you, gave up my livelihood, sold everything I had, traveled with you when I had no idea where we were going and all you can say is that I'm amazing because I'm so sensible?" Her glare quelled any response Javin might have thought of making.

There was a tense silence for a moment, before Meldren poked Javin hard in the ribs and gave a short bark of a laugh. "Ha! Got you! Don't you ever make me wonder if you are suffering, about anything, ever again." Then, seeing the confusion and the dawning of understanding that he had, in turn, been duped, she gave way to her laughter completely and utterly.

He had no option but to smile and nod in appreciation.

When the laughter subsided, they felt a release from the tension of the earlier events. They were better able to think more clearly about their future.

"We have no idea where we are, do we?" Javin asked.

"As I said, I've not heard of this place, never been here or seen it before, and it seems to go on forever."

"Therefore, it would seem we have two options." He held up his fingers as he spoke. "One. We decide to keep traveling to see how far it and what is on the other side. Or, two. We decide to go somewhere else, by singing ourselves there." He looked from his fingers to Meldren. "Is there an option three that I've missed?"

"I don't think so." She gave it some thought. "Remember we said about going to those cliffs and I was worried about falling or ending up inside them? Well, I don't think that's going to be a problem anymore. Harmony said we were safe, At least, that's how I heard it. And she also said that we could hear her songs. So, why not pick a place to go and then hear the song for it? It should lead us there, shouldn't it?"

Javin reached to his sprite to stroke it's head. "Remember, as well, these little guys. I don't think we would come to harm if they were with us, would we?"

Meldren smiled at Javin's facial contortions as he squinted to try and see his sprite. "All that's left is to decide, to choose, where we are going."

Javin gave up trying to see the creature. Instead, he sat up straighter and hugged his knees to him. "Didn't we talk about this. About what we wanted to see, before going into Arlen? You said something about some strange trees."

"Mmmhmm. And you said something about, what was the word? Like a mountain, but it had fire?"

"Volcano. But I don't think that would be much fun, actually. Lots of smoke and fire and probably no shelter at all."

Meldren gazed off into the distance. "The one place I've always wanted to see is the ocean."

"I remember you saying that, now."

She turned with a pleading look on her face. "Could we? Could we go there? Really?"

"Of course we can. We can do anything! And it's got to be a whole lot better than a volcano."

Meldren clapped her hands in glee, a huge grin on her face. "So, how do we do it?"

"Beats me!" said Javin.

"Stop using strange languages on me. And, besides, you said that meant you didn't understand. But don't you mean that you don't know how?"

"It can mean that, too." He grinned.

"You're just making that up!" She lunged at him, but he ducked and fell on his back, still grinning. She made a 'You just wait' face at him, but ended up breaking into a warm smile.

"I know one thing, though," said Javin, still on his back and watching the bits of the sky that were visible. "I'm tired and I'm hungry and I think everything will seem a lot easier in the morning." As if to prove his point, he gave a jaw-cracking yawn and rubbed at his suddenly watering eyes. "Really tired. Aren't you?"

Meldren yawned. "I was fine until you yawned. Now I'm tired, too."

"Could this be Harmony playing with us again?"

"I doubt it. We've had a very strange day indeed and nothing to eat for hours." Meldren hauled her satchel toward her. "One day, I swear, I am going to cook and eat fresh food for a change. But right now, I'm too tired to do anything else except eat what we have left. How about you?"

"Whatever you've got is fine with me."

Munching their way through the remains of their food, they had no energy left for conversation. Finishing up with a drink from the still bubbling spring, they were swiftly asleep.

NOTES FROM HAVEN

The Results Of The Invasion

The following was discovered on the ship, The New Lander, in 1186, which had been built specifically to take an invasion force to Harmony. It was supplied only for that leg of the journey and for some minor provisioning once the invasion had occurred. The crew and all aboard were undoubtedly already dead by the time it returned to Haven. With failing life support systems and little or no food left, they must have succumbed within a relatively short time. Probably the autopilot program was responsible for the return to orbit around Haven.

The crewman who wrote this remains unknown and what follows is a series of extracts designed to give the reader an overview of this tragic event.

"...We had no idea what we were going to face. So many rumors going around. There were supermen who could control our minds. Some of them had super powers and could fight us without weapons. Some strange and some more believable. But in a ship full of people geared for a fight, anything was possible...

...We got close. That's all I know. I don't know how close. But we got close. We were being drilled twice a day before it happened. Emergency pressure drop drills. Casualty drills. Wearing full armor for a full shift. We were getting amped for it. Except it never happened...

...The stories about what happened, or hadn't happened! The officers, even they looked dazed. It was strange. That's the only word for it. Strange. There were some people saying that the planet had vanished. I mean, like that can happen! I have no idea what it was that actually happened. I just know we were turned around and heading back...

...I don't know how long we've got, but it doesn't take a brain to work out that we don't have enough of anything to last. I guess we're all going to die here. It's pretty much all over. Truth? I think most of us knew that in our hearts when whatever it was that happened happened. We were just busy trying to live. Yes, I'm going to die up here. Some people here, they cry a lot. Sometimes they fight. Most times we just wait to stop breathing. I'd like to go to sleep soon. But, before I do, I'd really, really like someone to tell me what did happen. I think we've gone through everything we can think of. One of them has to be right. The one which keeps coming up the most is that the planet disappeared. And it's the weirdest one of all. But more and more people are saying it. It's the not knowing which irritates the most, but I'm even getting OK with that as well. That's not who I was. Now, I'd like to know, but I know I can't know. It's getting muddled in my head. Must be low O2. I'm going to sleep when I put this down."

Excerpt from the conclusion of the deputy police commissioner's 1187 report on the events surrounding the arrival of the New Lander and the subsequent actions.

"We brought in over 500 more officers to deal with the threat to the security of the spaceport which seemed to be growing by the hour. The restrictions on broadcasting the arrivals and departures was in order to lessen the tension evident in the city as bodies were being carried out. On reflection, it would, perhaps, have been better if the bodies had been evacuated into space rather than have the lengthy spectacle of corpses arriving in a continuous stream. It merely served to heighten the protests against the invasion.

The fact of Harmony's disappearance added to the unrest. There were even many accusations that the planet had never been there in the first place and that the whole idea of an invasion was just a way for the military to harness all of Haven's resources for their own unspecified ends. There were more than 2,000 arrests over three days and it is my firm conviction that this episode was the beginning of the massive wave of civil unrest which developed in the following months.

My conclusion is that the failure of the invasion, for whatever reasons, the return of the New Lander with its cargo of bodies and the disappearance of Harmony (however that might be explained), were the perfect combination which, together with pre-existing organized groups antagonistic to the military government, created a new class of opposition to legitimate rule. This opposition can be seen in the present drift from the cities and the reluctance to use or interact with technology which is suspected of feeding information to the government."

The Disappearance

From the revised edition of the textbook, "An Introduction To Astronomy" 1215 edition.

"The initial confusion and alarm caused by the sudden disappearance of our sister planet slowly gave way to incredulity. This period was both the zenith and, in some ways, the nadir of interest in astronomy. Everyone at first, it seemed, had a telescope and scanned the skies each night in the hope of being the person to find the missing planet. But, when the planet failed to be discovered, there was a backlash against professional astronomers for being unable to either predict or explain what had happened. The lack of consensus amongst the members of this profession did little to help and acted as another minor impetus to add to the small, relatively new movement to eschew technology in general. (A side effect of this brief but intense interest was the discovery of several novas, a supernova, five new comets and a considerable amount of new data on the outer planets.)

In the months following the event, subsequent careful observations showed no unexpected perturbations caused by the disappearance of a large planetary body from the solar system. There has been no evidence of any kind that Harmony is still in the solar system. Neither is there any evidence to the contrary. It is as though the planet is still somewhere in the solar system, but is not able to be observed using any of the available technology. It is, in effect, a ghost in the system; it must exist in order for the remaining planets to remain stable in their orbits, but cannot be proven to exist by any means other than mathematical ones."

31

The next morning was clear to start with, but clouds began gathering and there was humidity in the air which had not been present before. A breeze began to blow through the grove they were in, strengthening swiftly and making the fronds at the tops of the trees snap in response to it.

"I'd say that this is as good a time as any to find out just what we can do," said Javin. "Are we still heading for the ocean?"

"Yes, yes, yes!" Meldren was still as excited as yesterday at the prospect.

"Fine. I think that sleep helped last night because I had an idea when I woke up. Here's what I think we should do. The ocean is big. That means it is bound to have a big song. That should be easy to hear. But, we want to find the bit of the song where the ocean meets the land. There has to be a difference between the two. Agreed?"

"Definitely. Plus, we want to be near somewhere where there are people, enough people so that there is some food we can buy. I'd love to have some hot, cooked food!" Meldren closed her eyes at the thought and gave a tiny shiver in ecstasy.

"Good idea! And, we can find out where we are then! Any ideas as to how to listen for that song?"

"Beat me," said Meldren, trying, unsuccessfully, to suppress a giggle.

"The phrase is 'beats me'," said Javin accenting the s. "If you're going to learn my language, then at least you can also learn to shake hands properly as well." He grinned at her. "And, to answer my own question, I would guess that we listen to this song," he patted the ground beside him, "because the river running through it will lead us to the sea. At least, I hope it will. Now, if you're quite ready...?" He gave a mock serious look and got one back in return.

They both settled themselves more comfortably, took two or three steadying, deep breaths and closed their eyes. Before, they had strained to hear the sounds around them, and now it was so much clearer. At first, they were taken aback by how easy it was to listen and to sort through the various songs winding and moving around and through them.

The land's song was a deep thrumming melody, repeating and repeating with occasional trills and runs of sound. They reached out to the river and heard its separate arpeggios chiming with the bass of the land. Blocking out the rest, they followed this in their heads, hearing the song speed up and slow down, swirl in small repeating pools, become slowly deeper, more sonorous and filled with other small melodies, widening and always moving. Finally, there it was. The river emptied its voice into a much larger, grander symphony. The ocean! Avoiding the stronger sounds, they sought out where the ocean's voice was weaker, muffled as it butted up against the land. They followed this strange sound of competing choirs for a long time before, in the distance, with the occasional hiccup in the rhythm and some sparkling high notes piping clearly above it all, they came upon the town.

They felt the resonance of the buildings and were fascinated by the weaving, wandering sounds, faint but persistent, of people moving around. Other songs swelled and sank, but each of those strands of sound, each tiny song and hesitant chorus, each of them was woven together somehow so that the songs of the land and of the sea carried the whole without loss of tempo or chord change. It was a miracle of composition. You could choose to hear the ocean or the land and allow the town to sink quietly into the background, or reverse it and listen to the town's song. Either way, it was beautiful, entrancing.

The two listeners, acting as one, bound together by their shared ability, aided by the sprites they wore, focused on the town and its placement between water and earth. They were able now to find the main chords, the distinctive sequences of notes underlying the many smaller songs; the ones which kept repeating and anchoring it to the planet. When they had memorized it and stored it in their minds with a newfound ability, they simultaneously withdrew from the concentration and felt again the building breeze and the growing humidity of their resting place.

"Everything is so much clearer!" Meldren's eyes were bright. "Harmony really did make it possible for us to hear her songs. It is amazing! Amazing!"

Javin shared her excitement. "And we get to hear it." Then, with a little more wonderment, "And to think that Harmony keeps all that going, knows every song and manages to make it work!"

"So now we...?"

"I'm not sure exactly, but my guess would be that we don't just listen to the song of that place, don't just hear it, I think we have to sing it. After all, the song is the place. If we sing it, we should be there, shouldn't we?" Javin asked.

"Either that, or we bring it here," said Meldren. "It doesn't feel quite right, though. I think we're missing something."

"I agree. But what?"

"Well," said Meldren carefully. "The one thing missing that I can think of is us. Our songs. Shouldn't we put ourselves into the town's song?"

"Of course!" said Javin, impressed. "Only, what do we sound like? What are our songs and how do we sing them ourselves?"

"That's easy. We sing each other. I sing you and you sing me."

Javin nodded as he thought. "I can't see why not." Then another concern. "But wouldn't that mean we arrive naked and without anything, any of these things in the satchels?" He screwed his face up at the image.

Meldren was confident, however. "No. Not at all. We'll each be holding whatever it is we want to take with us and, when I see your song, it will be the song of you as you are then. With everything, clothes and stuff included!"

Javin inclined his head in acknowledgement of the truth of her words.

They quickly sorted out what to leave and what to take and then sat opposite each other. They went through the same calming process and there, before them was the song they had to sing. Careful not to miss any note, any slight change in rhythm or tempo, determined to leave not one single, tiny note out of place, they each memorized the other. Then they brought out from their memory the song of their destination. Without thinking, they found the edges of the town, where it became fainter and the song of the land easily overrode it. There, just beyond the town, but within hearing distance of it, they inserted each others' songs. They sang them slowly and carefully, gradually building them into place. Their sprites added to it in their own slight voices, seemingly ensuring that everything meshed, harmonized and built up rather than tore down what was already there. As the two humans sang their songs, they were no longer listening to the land, but they were surrounded by its song, so subtly different from where they had started.

Together, as one, they stopped their singing. Cautiously opening their eyes, they first assured themselves that the other was there and looked healthy and in one piece. Then they looked around them and both broke into the broadest of triumphant grins.

They were sitting, facing each other, in a slight dimple of the land. Around them, moss covered rocks bulged out of the earth. The air had a wonderfully fresh smell unlike anything either had witnessed before. There was a heavy warmth to it, very different from the recent growingly oppressive nature of the atmosphere of the plains they had just left.

They first hugged each other excitedly before carefully peering over the biggest boulder to find out what lay beyond them.

At first, they felt a disappointment. There was little to see, beyond many tall plants of a kind they did not recognize. After looking around, Meldren pointed behind them.

"There's a hill there. Why don't we go up and see what we can see? I'd prefer to know at least something about where we are before we arrive there."

They walked up the hill to the top; not a huge rise, but high enough to see over the greenery that had surrounded them. And there, before them, sparkling in the warm, heavy sunlight, was the ocean. Neither of them had been this close to such a large body of water before. It took their breath away. The flickering of light and the constant shifting of the waves was as mesmerizing as the songs they had heard, and were just as intricate. They could just make out some small craft with their sails, leaving tiny trails on the water. On the horizon, they could barely discern a low blue smudge; an island just too far away to identify any details.

They stood, hand-in-hand, with fascinated smiles on their faces. It was real and they were really here. They had done it!

From their vantage point, they could just make out the tops of some buildings, with the inevitable small drifts of thinning smoke easing out over the water. There was too little to be seen for them to form any sort of opinion of what the place was like, but they knew that they would have to go down there sooner or later.

"Are you sure you will be able to cope with all the colors of people down there?" Javin asked.

"I think so. With everything else we've seen and done, that seems to be one very small thing to worry about, don't you think?"

"Not if it's going to make you ill, it isn't," he said gently.

Meldren gave him a swift kiss on the cheek. "Ah! But you forget! I have a wonderful healer I can turn to whenever I want. He'll sing me healthy anytime I need it." The smile she gave him was like that of a child who had all of its dreams come true at once; elation, contentment and love of the world in general all rolled into one simple expression.

Javin grinned back at her. "How can I possibly argue with that?" And, half turning to her, he swept his free arm toward the town as an invitation. "Shall we go and introduce ourselves, then?"

"I'm not even going to wonder what to tell anyone about us. Or our little sprites," Meldren said, stroking the creature at her throat. "I'm just going to enjoy being here."

Javin took a deep lungful of the fresh tasting air. "Me, too," he agreed. And off they set.

NOTES FROM HAVEN

The Return To The Land

From "The View From The Trees: A History Of Protest" published 1260.

The full manifesto of the 'Return To The Land' movement is tiresomely long and argumentative in tone; in short, a dreary read. However, sprinkled throughout the overblown prose and self-congratulatory phrasing, there are some few important paragraphs which are worth sharing here to highlight what can be seen, in retrospect, as the beginning of a movement which changed over time from an idealistic anti-government propaganda to a practical lifestyle which continues to attract more and more people with each year.

"...The failure of the militaristic government to fully comprehend exactly how those to whom it was supposedly responsible felt about its intrusion into their private lives was the chief reason for its own citizens to reject it wholeheartedly and resolve to leave the cities to the despotic overlords...

"...Severing the links to technology was by no means easy. However, the dedicated few who first trod this path were able to provide encouragement and a growing band of resources to which the government did not have access. Privately printed pamphlets distributed by hand to vetted individuals was just one of the ways this movement was able to grow.

"The advantage of leaving the city behind was that the people became a distributed network, all dedicated to the same ideal, but, because of the distances involved, the continuing number of converts and the idealism of all concerned, the government was unable to dispatch military and civil units in sufficient numbers to halt this tidal wave of anarchy. Some few families and villages were imprisoned and destroyed, the fields poisoned and crops burned, but for each fallen member, new ones came and built and planted."

Found in the notes for an undelivered lecture by the pre-eminent cultural historian, Prof. Esme Caldicott, probably in the year 1272:

"Whatever really happened to Harmony is unknown and is likely never to be known. And it is, strangely, that very lack of knowledge which formed the turning point for this, our home on Haven.

Prior to the launching of the invasion fleet - and there is, and never can be, any excuse for such an action - the spirit of this planet was aligned always with something beyond the atmosphere, beyond this solar system. We had come from a place in the galaxy, tumbling into this system. Our ancestors had supposed that they would be part of a lengthening chain of other settlements, other colonies, to always be in touch with ourselves, our history. To be left here, alone, was an unbearable punishment for no conceivable crime. It is difficult now to begin to understand the piercing awareness of isolation suffered by those first settlers.

Therefore, there had always existed in the psyche of the people an urge to explore and leave this remote island in the vast, impersonal galaxy and join with our fellow humans. As each generation passed, so this became more deeply embedded within us. The brilliance of General Mikkan's government was to tap into this deep, unspoken yearning for space. The creation of a huge fleet by harnessing the resources of the planet to a degree never before possible, served to give the deep and hitherto suppressed idealism a reality; visible, touchable, definite, and it brought the dream into the open where it could be both acknowledged and also be in danger of being destroyed. For one cannot destroy that which refuses to be acknowledged, for it does not admit to being real.

Nevertheless, when the New Lander returned, it effectively destroyed, at one stroke, all those centuries of unspoken dreams. And, as anyone knows who has had a broken dream of their own, the pain is real and the reaction is often unthinking.

The very lack of knowledge obviously gave room for wild speculation. But, more importantly for our purposes, it also allowed the government to be attacked, ridiculed and, eventually, largely ignored. For it was the government which had harnessed the dreams of the people into something tangible. When that failed to deliver, the people turned against the creator of those hopes, the deliverer of their now failed dreams.

And what do people do when their original dream is shown to be impotent? They create a new one. Therefore, from looking to the stars as the way to prove themselves, they turned downwards and inwards, to the earth and to themselves, for their deliverance."

32

They had been there some time. Javin could not tell how long. Meldren, however, was more certain and said they were now well into autumn. It had been another warm day and now even Javin could tell the days were shortening by the way the shadows moved along the walls. It was late in the day, or early evening, depending on how tired you felt.

Meldren held her head tenderly as she sat on the doorstep of their home.

"Is it painful still?" asked Javin as he wiped his hands dry and came to join her. Nobody else was out enjoying the last of the cooling day. But, to the two of them, it was still delightfully warm.

"Mmmmm," said Meldren, creasing her face against the pain. "It was a busy day again. I think I am able to be all right if I have some spare time to myself. But, when it's busy..." Her voice tailed off. She had found what she thought was the perfect way to pass her days here; cooking in a place near the water's edge for fishermen coming and going and the occasional townsfolk who wanted someone else to feed them. Both Javin and she had eaten there once and she had asked the owner, Orland; a gentle, thin man with a bald head and large hands, if he wanted some help. The trouble was, she found that her ability to see colors was still just as potent and just as liable to make her feel sick. The fact that Arlen hadn't affected her was, she had said, because they hadn't stayed long and she had had plenty of other things on her mind.

Javin thought that was the truth of it and sang her to health whenever she needed it. He sat beside her now and listened to the slight discordancies he heard in Meldren. Then, gently, he heard the notes needed to bring back her song, pure and clear, and fed them into her. As ever, his sprite on his neck moved in time and seemed to add some rhythm or harmonics to his song, although he could never tell for sure. He watched as she sat up straighter and took a deep breath.

She leaned into him and slipped a kiss onto his cheek. "Thank you, again. And again. What would I be like if not for you?" She gave a happy sigh. "Oh, I forgot to ask. What did you do today? Anything interesting?"

"No, just one sprained ankle. The rest of the time, I lazed around in the sun eating and waiting for you to come home and cook me something." He smiled at her. She was doing something she had always wanted to do and he was doing something he had never thought of doing; being a healer. Abalan, the only other healer in Littlehaven, was getting old and had welcomed Javin's idea that the two of them helped the town. Javin was nearer the hills and Abalan nearer the sea. People could choose between them now. Javin did not tell about his real talent and used songs to heal, although he held his hands on the people, or gave them herbs. He knew it was the songs he heard that were really doing the work.

"I really do think that you are pushing yourself too hard to be amongst people," Javin said. "I know that it can be healed, but the point is, should it always have to be healed?"

Meldren sighed a little. "You're right. But. It's not just the colors mingling in my head. It's the songs, the sounds that go with them. I don't know if you have noticed, but it's like there's no way to turn either of them off. And the combination is...what's a good way of saying it? It's tiring."

"Maybe you're right. I am listening for the songs, remember. So I'm not in the same position as you. What if it's not just having been with Harmony, though? What if it's to do with our sprites? After all, She did say they were Her way of contacting us."

"So we leave them off? Assuming they want to stay off, that is." Meldren stroked hers. It wriggled slightly, adjusting its position as if it was responding to the conversation in some way. "I'd have to leave mine off all day. I've never been that long without it. I'm not sure I really want to be, either. I'm used to it now. Besides, people come to see it. They expect it. And it's comfortable."

They sat in silence as the shadows lengthened around them, finally moving indoors. As they were about to step inside, Meldren turned to Javin and said, "This isn't exactly how I thought it would be." It was more thoughtful than angry or upset. "But, then again, maybe I didn't really know what I thought it would be."

"Do you regret leaving the dogs behind?"

Meldren thought for a moment before shaking her head. "Not really." She indicated their home. "They were never inside, didn't really stay in any one place very long. I don't think they would have liked being here, especially as they would not have had a job anymore. So, no. I think we did the right thing for them. And for us." A small sadness flickered across her face. "It was hard at the time."

"And now?" Javin asked.

"Now? Now this is a different type of hard."

The next few days were easier ones, for both of them. With fewer customers because of the storms out at sea bringing cooler, wetter weather, she had less to cope with and came home tired but happier. Javin saw only a very few patients and spent most of his time, when he wasn't worrying about Meldren, collecting plants and preparing herbal remedies. He took to listening in on her song and catching the dissonance before it built up. He told her about it one evening after she had walked home, carrying a leaf-wrapped parcel.

"I thought there was something going on, but I didn't really know what it was. It was...easier." She beamed at him. "Thank you for taking care of me."

"You don't mind my doing that; spying on you like that?" Javin was unsure of how he felt about it. On the one hand, he was helping her. On the other, he was prying inside her. He was relieved she accepted the help.

"I don't call it spying. I call it caring! And to show my thanks properly, I will cook you something I learned about today. It's a fish called...actually, I don't know what it's called, but it's long and thin and tastes wonderful. Or it will do by the time I've finished with it." She brandished the parcel. "It's in here."

She was as good as her word, and Javin was very appreciative, finally pushing away the remains with a huge sigh of thanks.

They sat in companionable silence in the afterglow of the food.

"Maybe," said Javin, tentatively, "maybe, we shouldn't be here. All these people..." He let the sentence dangle, unfinished.

Meldren was gazing off into the distance. "We did say that we could choose what we wanted to do. And then we chose this. Which," she said, reaching out to touch Javin, "I have not regretted at all. I did what I said I wanted to do. I learned to cook. I have my very own oven! And you? You became a healer. There's nothing in what we do which ties us to one place. There will always be food to cook, and there will always be healing needed." She shrugged.

"But...," added Javin, letting the word hang there. "Do you want always to be moving from one place to another?" He looked around him. "I like having a home. I like this place. And yet, here we are talking, thinking about what to do, where to go and how to live. It's like nothing's really changed, has it?"

Meldren cleared the table, poured some juice out for them both and then came and sat on Javin's lap.

"Well, the deecees don't work anymore, so that's a change. But I know what you mean. I know things have changed. A lot. But, you're right about one thing. I don't want to keep moving." She rested her chin on the top of his head. "But I also don't want to have so many people around all the time."

"I wonder what happened to Lisick and Gerant and Bellis," mused Javin. "If the deecees don't work, what do they do?" He shook his head clear of those thoughts to focus on the here and now. "I sometimes wonder about hearing these songs." Javin hugged Meldren closer to him. "Yes, it's wonderful. Yes, it's a privilege. But how does that really help us? You hear the songs of people and they're mixed up with the colors and it hurts you. Me? I hear the songs I need to heal people. But that's just like another talent, another way of healing." He kissed her neck. "I don't know what I was expecting, after Harmony. But I don't think I was expecting this."

Meldren snuggled down to bury her head against his neck. "I know what you mean. I thought our lives would be, I don't know, amazing? Strange? And, to others, they would probably look like that. But living them, being inside our lives, it's not what I thought it would be."

"So what do we do about it?" asked Javin, brushing stray strands of Meldren's hair from his face.

"Ah! Good question. What do we do about it?"

"I do seem to recall that Harmony said She would always hear us. Didn't She say that?"

Meldren agreed with a murmur.

"Wouldn't that mean that She's hearing us right now? We're adding this question, this problem into the song She hears because we're saying it out loud, together. So wouldn't that mean that She's going to help in some fashion?"

Meldren sat up a little, the better to look at Javin. "She might. But what if we're meant to solve this ourselves? We can't always have Her solve our problems, can we?"

"It's not really our problem, though, is it? The songs and the colors together, the difficulty of living with this many people...that wasn't our choice."

Meldren frowned as she looked more closely at Javin. "Are you saying that you have problems being amongst all these people? Why didn't you say so?"

Javin face said 'lets not make a big thing out of this'. But Meldren was not about to let it go. "How is it a problem for you? It's not fair to make this all about poor little me, you know."

"It's not so obvious as what happens to you." He paused, trying to find a way to describe it. "I spend a lot more time here on my own. And, it seems like I've become more sensitive to songs as a result. Not the songs of the plants and the house, what I call Harmony's natural sounds. They are clear and I love listening to them when I can. But, when someone comes here to see me, or I am asked to go to another home, it's like everything becomes louder and louder and I can't stop hearing it. I can't hear you in the middle of all that noise. It's painful. For a short time, it makes a sharp pain in my head. I can always bring it back to where I can cope with it. But," he nodded, "it does hurt."

"And it's been like that ever since we arrived?"

"Well, that's the thing. I think it's getting worse. It wasn't a problem to begin with. It's hard to say for sure, because I don't see as many people as you. I didn't want to say anything until I was sure. But, with you and your pain, well, that's why I said about going somewhere else."

Meldren got up from his lap and kissed him on his forehead. "If it's true that She hears us, understands what we're thinking, talking about, I suppose She will let us know, don't you? After all, what good would having these little sprites be otherwise?"

"Maybe you're right. Just saying it out loud does alter the song. I know that." He took a sip of his juice. "I hope that She doesn't bounce into our heads so hard that it hurts, that's all."

Later that night, Javin woke up and was immediately wide awake although he had no idea why. He couldn't sense anything around which might have caused him to wake up. The moonlight, still an enjoyable sight for him, was streaming in through the window, glowing high enough up on the wall opposite to indicate moonrise. He had a sudden urge to go outside and look at the moon.

Moving carefully to avoid waking Meldren, his bare feet made no noise as he reached the door. Grimacing against the slight creaking of the door, he opened it just enough to slip through. He realized, once outside, that, because the moon was low on the horizon, he would have to find a better vantage point. About to turn and go to the hill they had first climbed on their arrival, he realized that if Meldren woke up to find him gone, she might be concerned. She would be able to hear his song, no doubt, but he stopped and decided to go back and wake her. Together, they would watch the moon. That decision made him feel better.

A short while later, with Meldren still bleary from sleep, they walked hand in hand up the hill outside of the village. At the top, they both turned to take in the view.

"Why are we here?" whispered Meldren.

"I was awake and I wanted to see the moon and then I thought you would like to see it as well."

Giving a huge yawn, she said, "You do realize we can see the moon from our bed?"

Javin looked puzzled. "I know that. But, somehow, this was more important. It just felt...right."

The moon was still only slightly above the horizon and ascending slowly. The rippling of the waves way out from the shore was captivating. This was the first time either of them had witnessed the play of moonlight on the water and the way it created a twinkling path there. They sat, arms around each other's shoulders, Meldren's head resting on Javin, silently enjoying it all.

As they watched, so the moonlight's path shifted slowly and it seemed to lead directly in front of them to that distant island they had first seen as a blue haze. The moon's pale light made the island look darker against the sky and the glittering pinpoints on the water seemed to lead their eyes straight to it. The moon climbed higher, but the pathway did not move. It remained, leading to the island where now the tops of its distant hills seemed to catch the moonlight. The effect was as if the island had been painted with strokes of light on a dark canvas.

The two watchers gradually sat up straighter, their attention now given entirely to that distant island. Still the moon climbed and still the shining pathway never moved away from it and the highlights of the island became sharper and grew in number.

Javin leaned in towards Meldren and whispered, "Can you hear it? That new song?"

She nodded, still staring at the view. "It's drowning out everything else. But it sounds so...welcoming?"

Javin gave a gentle, quiet laugh. "Well, I suppose that answers the question about Harmony hearing us." He pointed. "I think that island out there, that's the answer."

"It's better than a dream and it's better than feeling like I've been hit by a rock." Meldren held her hand up to her sprite. "Thank you," she whispered to it, brushing its head gently with one finger. "Thank you."

Preparing to leave was easy. They had accumulated few possessions and those they did have fitted into their two satchels again. Javin went to see Abalan to tell him he was leaving and to give him the herbs he had collected. Abalan was philosophical about it, realizing that there was nothing he could do to hold Javin in Littlehaven.

In the meantime, they discovered that the island was called The Sleeper, because it had looked, to the first settlers there, as though some giant had lain down, and all they could see was a series of hills which they took to represent the side of the head, the shoulders and the hips. It was a two-day journey to reach it. Apparently, it also took four days to sail round it and a day to walk across it, but nobody they found had actually done those things. Nobody had bothered to settle there because Littlehaven had the better harbor. The Sleeper was a place nobody bothered with and was, therefore, perfect for their needs.

One day, not so very long after seeing the moonlight on The Sleeper from the top of the hill, Javin and Meldren stepped aboard a boat whose skipper had been persuaded to take them. They cast off, catching the light breeze which stiffened as they left the cover of the land. The day was bright but the wind was cold, making them shiver as they stood in the bow, facing their new home.

Meldren dug out a blanket from her satchel and threw it across her shoulders, holding one end out for Javin to duck under. She shivered a little. "This feels good to do. And I'm glad we're doing it."

Javin was quiet.

"Are you feeling all right?" Meldren asked, noting his pale face.

"I was wondering why we didn't sing ourselves to the island. This is the first time I've been on a boat. And this ocean is big and I wish the boat would stay still, that's all. I'm trying to hear something other than this huge song right now."

She smiled and hugged him closer. "Big, brave man! You'll be fine."

There was silence between them for a while as they watched the island ahead. Meldren pointed with her chin at their destination. "Do you think we'll be able to live the way we want to on it?"

"I hope so," was the quiet reply.

Another silence before Meldren spoke again. "And what about Harmony? Do you think She will come into our lives again and change them again?"

Javin didn't answer at first. When he did, it was slow and thoughtful. "As long as we're here, She will hear us. But whether She will leave us alone from now on, that I'm not so sure about. As long as we can hear Her, as long as that connection exists, I don't think we're ever going to have our lives entirely to ourselves."

Meldren considered that for a moment. Then she smiled at nothing in particular. "Good," was all she said.

The sun shone on them. They were not capable of hearing the song it hurled across the vastness of space to the other suns, the other galaxies. This sun, their sun, sang of a new note that had been added. A seed note. It sang of the new melody that tiny note was developing into. It sang that the melody was being added to the symphony of the universe. And the new melody, the new songs it would be creating, were songs of Harmony.

PREVIEW: SEEDS OF HARMONY

Chapter 1

Larrick was on his hands and knees in the long grass at the back of one of the pigsties trying to find the hole in the wall where the rats were coming in. He had volunteered to do it so that he could spend some time on his own generally out of sight and have the chance just to stop for a while and rest a bit: enjoy the day for a change instead of working, working, working. He must have dozed off, for the sun was much higher now. He had started up guiltily before hunkering down and scuttling crab-like back to the pigsties in case anyone saw him. He was now poking around, his head close to the ground, looking for any holes when he heard the sound. It wasn't one he recognized, being more like a short, loud pop than anything else. Puzzled, he peered around the corner and saw someone looking as if they had tripped and fallen. He shook his head at the clumsiness of someone -- was it Haller laying there? -- tripping on flat ground. He was about to go and help, because it was obvious Haller wasn't moving, when he heard the same sound again, only this time it was followed by a cry of pain. Then he saw a strange, helmeted figure sidle from the sty with his or her back to him He, or she, was wearing camouflage. It was so strange to see, so out of place. But whoever it was was also carrying something high up, tucked into the shoulder. Larrick put his hand to his mouth in shock and fear. A weapon!

There were more explosive sounds which he now recognized as shots. The one soldier he could see still facing away from Larrick, walked slowly away from the stye and past Haller as the gun swung back and forth. Pausing briefly by Haller, the soldier pointed the weapon down and shot Haller twice in the head, causing the large body to spasm in reaction, bouncing slightly with each shot. The number of shots further away increased and so did the shrieks of fear and pain. There was some shouting but it seemed mainly to be from the soldiers calling to each other. The pigs began to squeal, adding to the calls of cows and sheep: a swelling noise drumming at Larrick's ears.

From where he was crouched, Larrick could only see Haller's body, now missing part of his head. Too numb with fear to move, he was unaware of the tears streaming down his face or the way his whole body was shaking. His breathing was ragged and he slumped against the wall, turning away from Haller, his neighbor. With each shot, each cry of anguish, each half-heard pleading voice, he shook and closed his eyes only to open them and stare sightlessly ahead before the next one.

Gradually, the shots came further and further apart and the soldiers' calls took on a less urgent tone. He had no idea how long he had been there. By now he was hugging his knees to him, too frightened to do anything. Finally, he heard some soldiers closer than the rest entering the stables closest to the pigsty.

"How many do you think there were here?" asked one young-sounding voice.

"I don't know. Fifty maybe? More than the last place anyway." This second voice sounded older, rougher. "Beats me why anyone would even want to live like this. Look at it. Dirt and rags and nothing else. No luxuries. And if you want something, you have to make it yourself. Absolutely crazy people. They're insane."

"But why do they do it? Live like this, I mean?"

"Because they're not right in the head, are they? Take a look at their homes for starters. Why would anyone choose to live inside earth walls and under grass roofs when you've got a perfectly decent town nearby?

They have to be crazy. We did them a favor. They had to be dead inside to live like this. Dead inside but didn't know it."

There was a pause and the sounds of shuffling and cows protesting. "Are you any good at making these things move in the direction you want?" asked the young voice.

"Just give 'em a good slap on the rump to get 'em going, then prod 'em to keep 'em going. It's not hard." There was the sound of a slap and another cow protesting. "Ain't you ever seen a cow before?" There was incredulity in the voice.

"Not up close. Not like this."

"Well, let's get them loaded and then we'll come back and round up the pigs. They're the ones you have to watch out for."

"Why's that?"

"You'll find out soon enough. Now let's get going so's we can torch this place and finish with it."

The cattle made their feelings plain amidst the shouts and calls. Larrick listened to them until those sounds were lost amongst the general noise and confusion going on. He wanted to move, to do something, anything to prove to himself he was still alive, but he was locked in shock. He tried to say her name, to say 'Shelleer', but something in his throat caught and he could only gulp in spasms. All he could think of was the older voice talking about the pigs. They were coming back for the pigs and they would find him. And then they would kill him like they had killed all the others. But she wasn't here with him. She was dead. They had shot her and he hadn't even been able to recognize her voice.

Something inside of him at last let loose of his limbs and he found himself scrambling on hands and knees through the grass, heading for the bushes and, further, for the trees. There was no plan, only the urge to leave this behind and not be killed. Nothing else counted. He scrabbled on and on, his lungs screaming at him, every part of his body aching, bruised or cut. Only when he could no longer move, only then did he allow himself to think of her, of Shelleer, his wife, his beautiful, young wife. And the tears flowed as he thought of leaving her behind. The guilt of being alive crushed down on him and he hugged himself as he saw the smoke rising in the distance, knowing that his life was over. Nobody needed to shoot him. He was, as that soldier had said, dead inside. Dead. He knew it for certain.

He waited in misery until the soldiers had left and fire had died out and the smoke was only a few wisps before going back. He wanted to do... something. Say farewell? Apologize? Let them all know he would remember them?

The homes they had built had all been burned or pulled down. Fences had been torn out and the crops had been set on fire. But worst of all were the bodies. They lay where they had fallen. A few he recognized from their clothing, but the rats had also found them. They were still feasting when he arrived and he screamed and kicked at them. He wanted to find Shelleer, but also wanted not to. Then he recognized her hair: that long braid where ribbons twined in and out. She was facing away from him as he knelt, her limbs spread as if she was about to run, the ground around her dark from her blood. He stroked her hair and found he lacked the courage to see her face again. He tried to say something to her, to apologize for being alive without her, but his voice failed him. Looking around he felt useless and irrelevant; a helpless fool. He realized that there was nothing he could do or say here that would have any meaning at all, least of all to him. So he turned his back and left, empty of tears and of hope. If he was to die, it would be somewhere else; on his own and wrapped in his own guilt and shame.

He walked. The direction didn't matter. He kept walking away.

ABOUT THE AUTHOR

I was always drawn to history, as long as it was social history: about how people really lived. That was the most interesting part of the past for me. In addition, I was also strongly drawn to the things which were not easily explained or not well-understood. Here, things like fairy-tales and legends entered into my awareness. And poetry also, for me, was a way of seeking to explain the inexplicable. The phenomenon of the mind became deeper and more mysterious the more I discovered.

Essentially, I like the limits of what we think we 'know' and 'understand'. Those limits are, for me, where the most interesting things happen and where the most interesting things are waiting to be explored.

But, let's not overlook humor. I love humor and I love what can often be called 'zany' (ugly word) or 'surreal' (not a helpful word, either) humor where it takes off in unexpected directions. The same idea of limits as above, but arrived at differently.

I spent a whole lot of time teaching. It happened. Some of it was fun, much of it wasn't, but I was too dumb to strike out in a different direction for far too long.

But, here I am now. I also write nonfiction under my real name, Nigel Percy.

www.ingramcontent.com/pod-product-compliance
Lightning Source LLC
Chambersburg PA
CBHW070830280626
47161CB00015B/432